T0168721

THE OSAGE ROSE

THE OSAGE ROSE

Tom Holm

The University of Arizona Press
Tucson

In loving memory of my mother, Maebelle,
and my grandparents, Mr. and Mrs. Tom Blackwell

The University of Arizona Press
© 2008 by Tom Holm
All rights reserved

Library of Congress Cataloging-in-Publication data appear on
the last printed page of this book.

Publication of this book is made possible in part by the proceeds
of a permanent endowment created with the assistance of a Challenge Grant
from the National Endowment for the Humanities, a federal agency.

Manufactured in the United States of America on
acid-free, archival-quality paper.

13 12 11 10 09 08   6 5 4 3 2 1

Prologue

The touring car pulled off the road next to a ditch. The driver pushed in the clutch, put the gearbox in neutral, and set the hand brake. He let the automobile's motor idle. Even though it wasn't cold, he shivered. He laid his forehead against the steering wheel, sighed heavily, and turned his face to his right, all the while pressing his head against the solid warmth of the wooden wheel. He could see his passenger's narrowing eyes and sneer-like smile even in the closing darkness.

"Think this is good enough?" the driver asked in a low, breathy whisper.

"Hell, yeah," said the passenger darkly. "Let's carry it over there." He grunted disgustedly and threw open his door. Stepping out, he pointed with his chin in the direction of two large cottonwoods on the opposite side of the dirt road. The look of disdain he gave the driver could barely be seen, but it was unmistakably felt.

"Come on," he said with authority, "get out and take hold of him. Leave the motor runnin', this ain't gonna take long."

The driver got out of the car, opened the rear door, and put one foot on the running board. He stared down at the large, blanket-covered bundle on the car floor. He kept staring until he felt a hand squeeze his shoulder and then give it a quick, but far from reassuring, pat. His partner had circled the automobile and come up behind him without making a sound.

"Just grab him by the shoulders and heave," he said flatly. "Get him out of the door, and I'll take hold of his feet."

The driver bent over and pulled back the blanket. In the dusk, the dead man's shirtfront was stained black with crusty blood. Its metallic, coppery smell filled the driver's nostrils. He threw the blanket onto the back seat, took hold of the dead man's shirt collar and pulled.

The body slid out with relative ease. The driver moved slightly to his right, and the passenger grabbed the dead man's trouser leg. As he did that, the driver reached under the shoulders and grasped the dead man's armpits. The man's head lolled backward sickeningly as they lifted him. His throat had been severed through the connecting tissues, and the wound gaped open; the windpipe jutted outward. The vertebrae and spinal cord were still intact, but as they carried the body to the far side of the road, the neck tissues and skin stretched out, so that the dead man's head hung straight down and swung back and forth like a grisly pendulum. His newly barbered hair touched the ground.

Together they dropped the body between the trees. As it fell to the ground, the head turned almost completely around. The driver bent down and lifted the dead man's head face up. Scratching up some loose soil and last fall's leaf debris, the men tried to cover the corpse. "Somebody's gonna spot him easy from the road. There ain't enough dead leaves to cover him proper," the driver said with revulsion.

"Who cares," the passenger retorted. "We'll be long gone." He paused for a moment thinking, then he stroked his cheek and said with a slight grin, "Maybe I oughta skin his face, so's they can't tell who he is right off."

The driver looked at the ground. Seeing the man's throat get cut, the blood spurting all over the place, and then loading the body into the car had been enough. Skinning the dead man's face would be too much for him to stomach.

"Let's just get on outta here," he said quickly. "Even if somebody finds him, they won't know who he is. He's just another redskin dumped alongside the road."

"You got any whiskey in your poke?" asked the passenger.

"I got me some," he answered with suspicion.

"Go get it."

The driver went to the car, picked up a medium-sized leather bag from the back seat, reached in, and pulled out a silver flask that had seen better days. He took it back across the road and handed it over. His partner undid the stopper. Bending over, he brushed some of the debris away from the dead man's face. Then he poured the whiskey over the hair and rubbed some into the cheeks.

"I'll buy you more," he said, handing the flask back. "Now, even if they find him, they'll think he was drunk and got into a fight. Let's go."

1

The Chichester Operation

J.D. Daugherty was about as happy as J.D. could get. Despite his usual dour, tight-lipped, serious demeanor, he couldn't stop himself from leaning back in his chair, looking at his new straw boater dangling from the hat rack, and stretching his mouth into a wide, rather smug grin. His new business was finally paying off—paying off very well indeed.

Never a man to fritter away his time in frivolous activities, J.D. quickly returned to the society pages of the morning *Tulsa Daily World* for May 29, 1921. Above his thin lips and thick, multihued moustache, his forehead became a mass of taut, horizontal lines. He studied the society pages as closely as his devoutly religious mother had once studied the Bible.

J.D.'s business depended on what passed for high society in fast-growing Tulsa, Oklahoma, his adopted city. If not *the* first, he was certainly one of Tulsa's first independent private detectives. He had worried about starting the business in the boomtown atmosphere, because the people in Tulsa seemed to like handling everything themselves, personally, and more often than not with a gun, knife, blackjack, or crowbar. But J.D. had discovered in his long career that "the rich" were somehow different from everybody else, and they were always in some kind of jam that needed "fixing."

Apart from their personal embarrassments, the Tulsa "rich" were trying desperately to change the city's boomtown, frontier image and turn the old Creek Indian village into a cosmopolitan metropolis on the banks of the Arkansas River. J.D. was helping them to do so. He was a thorough, no-nonsense fixer, who had learned the trade in the biggest and oldest detective agency around. Most importantly, J.D. was discreet, and the Tulsa upper crust liked to keep their secrets to themselves.

J.D. knuckled his moustache and rolled his head to ease the strain on his neck. He looked pensively at the new boater on the hat rack. The case he just finished had netted him three hundred bucks just for asking a few questions, making a short trip to St. Louis, and bringing back a runaway wife. It was a good business in many ways.

Tulsa was rolling in wealth even though the rest of the country had fallen into a depression following the Great War. Whipping Kaiser Bill had been a hardship on America, but J.D. was certain that everything would return to normal now that Warren G. Harding had been sworn in as U.S. president that past March.

J.D. had opened his agency nine months before, in September 1920. Back in the '90s, when he was a young police officer in South Chicago, he had made the decision to hire on with Great Western Investigations, Inc. It was a hell of a lot more glamorous than walking a beat. He ran down crooks all over the country. Out west, J.D. helped bring in "Flatnose" Curry of the Hole-in-the-Wall Gang, and he witnessed the gruesome gallows decapitation of "Black Jack" Ketchum in Clayton, New Mexico. He had also tracked down the runaway daughter of one of the biggest investment bankers on Wall Street.

That decision to join Great Western had proven costly though. He had been constantly on the move, never settling in one place for more than a couple of years, and he'd forgone wife and family. During his entire time with Great Western, he'd purchased only four suits of clothes and a 1915 Ford flivver. Finally, he couldn't stomach busting the heads of Tulsa's poor oilfield workers, as he had to do once Attorney General A. Mitchell Palmer got everybody worked up about the Reds. So, he started in business for himself. Maybe his life would change for the better now. He'd been in Tulsa for three years. "Hell, it already has gotten better," he said out loud, eyeing the boater once again.

Besides, people were coming to their senses: the time for busting heads and spying on dirt-poor oil-rig workers was over. Even the notorious Industrial Workers of the World—the Wobblies—had seemingly outlived the reckless violence directed at them. They had even managed to establish the Oil Field Worker's Union on the edge of Tulsa's segregated black district, just a few blocks from police headquarters.

"Yes, indeed," he said philosophically to himself, "it's a lot easier tracking down a runaway wife than roughing up people for Great Western, Robert Dollar, and Uncle Sam."

J.D. charged $10 a day plus expenses—costly but easily affordable for his oil-rich clients, and they were wont to toss in fat bonuses once he'd "fixed" things. He had a small office in the Blackburn Building on Third and Boston. A lawyer named Sam Berg drew up contracts for him and sent customers his way. J.D. paid Sam a $25 retainer every month and considered it money well spent. Sam was a great lawyer, originally from New York, who, in addition to his work with Tulsa's upper crust, took on numerous cases involving union organizers and oilfield workers.

J.D. had met Sam during the trial of a union organizer, indicted on trumped up charges of assault and battery. It was during the time that J.D. was growing dissatisfied with his Great Western job, and he secretly told Sam about a witness who could provide his client with an alibi. The union organizer was ultimately acquitted.

J.D. liked Sam precisely because he took on the hard-luck cases, especially those of drifters, migrant laborers, and the local Indians. Indians were always taking a beating from the railroads, oil companies, land speculators, and the legal profession. Sam told J.D. that the government had forced the Indians to divide up their lands into individually held plots, called allotments, just prior to Oklahoma statehood in 1907. Oil was discovered under some of those allotments, and the lawyers jumped in to make a quick killing. They had been called upon to act as guardians for Indians who the Oklahoma courts had declared legally incompetent and, as lawyers will, they helped themselves to the newfound riches. As Sam put it, "They called in the foxes to look after the chicken coop." Some of the Indians, especially the Osages northwest of Tulsa, had fine houses, automobiles, and store-bought clothes, but the lion's share of their oil wealth found its way into the coffers of the oilmen and the lawyers.

Sam Berg had also taken on several cases involving the city's Negro population. The black people lived north of Archer Street. Many had worked as scabs when the white oilfield workers organized and went on strike. When a strike wore itself out, the blacks were always thrown out of work. They had attempted to organize, but for the most part, the white workers refused to accept them. Finally, the Wobblies offered them an organizational umbrella. But that only meant that Tulsa's white population associated Negro workers with the Reds. Some of the city's black population did domestic work or swept out the stores, collected the garbage, or shined shoes. Many were migrant farm and ranch workers. They picked cotton, harvested corn and sorghum, cut and hauled hay, and worked cattle during the roundup and branding season. A lucky few worked permanently for the railroads as stewards and cooks. A number of blacks and quite a few Indians worked for the railroads on repair crews, called road gangs.

In spite of their menial and often sporadic work, the city's black population had built their section of town—the whites called it "Little Africa"—into a prosperous and vibrant community. Black-owned grocery stores, restaurants, repair shops, hatters, and haberdashers flourished along Greenwood Avenue, which came to be called "The Black Wall Street." It boasted several seminary-trained and college-educated ministers, at least two doctors of medicine, four morticians, several trained nurses, six lawyers, and a number of fine teachers. Sam Berg often did business with a black lawyer who worked in his large, beautifully furnished office next door to Tulsa's most notorious and liveliest speakeasy. J.D. had worked on a case for this particular lawyer, tracking down another runaway daughter—no less than the daughter of the minister of the largest black Baptist church in town.

One of the reasons Sam was drawn to helping out the blacks, Indians, workers, and union organizers was the rise of the Ku Klux Klan. As Sam explained: "I'm a Jew, J.D., and those boys in the bed sheets would just as soon kill me as they would a Negro, an Indian, or a Roman Catholic like yourself." J.D. had not really thought of the KKK in that way. The newspaper depicted them as the saviors of the white race against the forces of evil, including Kaiser Bill, anarchists, and the

Bolsheviks. But then, last summer, the KKK had lynched two Tulsa boys, one black and one white. After that, J.D. saw the Kluxers for what they truly were: violent racists and corrupt know-nothings of the most contemptible sort. Most of the Kluxers worked in the oil fields; the biggest company, Shelby Oil, employed the local head "Kleegal," or whatever he was called, as an office manager. J.D. had discovered this fact while conducting an investigation for Great Western and Shelby Oil to find and root out infiltrating Bolsheviks; instead, J.D. found the Kluxers, who stayed on the job.

Ironically, the first lady of Tulsa, Mrs. William Frederick Dunn Shelby, wife of the head of Shelby Oil, had hired Sam to argue a land-claim case for a Creek Indian friend of hers. Sam won the case, and ever since, Mrs. Shelby had been throwing jobs his way. Sam, in turn, had recommended J.D. to handle several cases for Shelby acquaintances. The operation that J.D. had just wrapped up had, in fact, been one of those.

The thought of Mrs. Shelby prompted J.D. to return to his society page. Sure enough, there was an article about her and one of her hobbies. Mrs. Shelby's name was Rose, and she employed a battalion of gardeners to care for and breed roses on an industrial scale. The paper duly reported the introduction of a new flower, named the "Osage Rose." It had a blossom of a vermillion hue and exquisite bouquet. This perfectly shaped flower was generously proportioned and symmetrical, with large, velvet-like petals. Mrs. Shelby's American Beauty roses had already won prizes, and with this new breed, she combined her love of roses with another interest, that of recording and preserving American Indian history.

J.D. had little interest in roses, but he dutifully read the entire article for bits and pieces of information about the Shelbys. He was preparing himself for a meeting that morning with another Shelby acquaintance. Mr. E.L. Chichester of Pittsburgh, Pennsylvania, was due for his appointment with J.D. at nine o'clock.

Chichester was more closely connected to the Shelbys than any other of J.D.'s wealthy clients. J.D. had read everything he could find on both families, and what he found was a very long and intricate association of riches, oil, and high finance. E.L. and "Big Bill," as William Shelby was called behind his back, had an old partnership that began when their fathers had jointly struck it rich drilling oil in Pennsylvania. When Big Bill decided to cash in on the Oklahoma boom, Chichester invested in Shelby's new company. Big Bill eventually bought Chichester out and made both of them even more money. They had remained close friends, and the two families took trips abroad together and visited back and forth between Pittsburgh and Tulsa frequently. J.D. remembered that three weeks ago, the society page had announced the arrival of Chichester and his eligible young daughter for an extended visit with the Shelby family.

J.D. pressed the palms of his hands against his eyes in an effort to rub the fatigue from them. "I must be getting old," he thought. "Can't read that long."

He was wondering if he needed glasses when someone began to pound on his office door. J.D. jumped up from behind his desk, bumped his knee on a drawer handle, and stumbled toward the door in an effort to prevent the hard-fisted visitor from knocking again. He opened the door and found a large, scowling chauffeur dressed in livery. The man shouldered his way in and stated in a flat voice: "Mr. Chichester is here for his appointment."

The chauffeur stood aside smartly to allow a short, well-dressed, balding man to enter. Chichester was attired in a soft-gray suit. J.D. could tell that the watch chain draped across his vest was 24-carat gold and his stickpin was not cut glass. Chichester wore spats over his highly buffed black shoes and carried a charcoal Homburg hat of the finest felt. The effect of the man's entrance and dress was such that J.D. nearly bowed.

J.D. paused one beat and then said, "Good morning, Mr. Chichester. I'm at your service." He shook the man's hand, sat Chichester in the customer's chair, and quickly returned to his desk.

Chichester pulled his pink lips into a half-smile, breathed deeply, and began: "Mr. Daugherty, I come to you with a grave problem, the details of which I would prefer not to have commonly known. You have been highly recommended. I have been assured that you are efficient and discreet. Still, I wonder if I might inquire into your credentials?"

J.D. put on his most businesslike demeanor, leaned forward, and looked directly into Chichester's eyes. "Sir," J.D. began, "I started out as a Chicago police officer from '92 to '97. After helping one of their operatives with a case in Chicago, I was asked to work for the Great Western detective agency. A year ago, I decided I'd open my own detective service. I've grown to see Tulsa as my home. I'm bonded and can guarantee client confidentiality."

Chichester cocked his head and a grimace flashed across his face. J.D.'s voice still had a slight Chicago Irish accent to it. Chichester touched his chin, smiled thinly, and asked, "You're Irish, are you not?"

J.D. paused and ran a thumb along his moustache. "What is Chichester up to?" he thought.

"I am, sir," said J.D. flatly, "is that a concern?" J.D. purposely accented his language to make it sound as if he had only recently immigrated. "If I'm not mistaken the Chichester family name comes from Ireland as well."

"Indeed so, Mr. Daugherty," said Chichester, "but the Chichesters have been Americans for a very long time. You're Roman Catholic no doubt." Chichester paused and looked down at his cravat. "Be that as it may," he said, "I'm only inquiring to make sure that there is nothing standing in the way of doing a sound investigation. This is extremely important."

Chichester's mouth looked as if it had been drawn with a ruler and pencil. His lips were now bloodless. J.D. responded bluntly: "I've got an Irish feeling, Mr. Chichester, that you are worried that I either drink too much or that my religion might interfere with my efficiency as a detective. Well, I rarely have time to practice the faith, and I drink moderately. I abide by the Volstead Act as much as the next man. But believe me, I am first and foremost a businessman. Like yourself, I want to prosper. Now, if there is a problem, then I'll say good day to you, sir."

J.D. started to rise from behind the desk. Chichester put up his right hand, "Please, Mr. Daugherty . . . "

His voice trailed off. He shifted uneasily in his chair and fumbled with the seams of his trousers. The chauffeur stood as silently as before, but J.D. detected a secret glee in the man's face over Chichester's discomfort.

Finally, Chichester caught himself, stiffened his spine, and said as humbly as he could, "Mr. Daugherty, I need your help. My daughter has disappeared. She's my only child. She left no note, no explanation. I can't . . . "

His voice trailed off once again, and J.D. suspected that Chichester's diversionary questioning about J.D.'s nationality and faith was more of a negotiating tool than a genuine concern. J.D. guessed that Chichester was the type of person who would use charges of incompetence or instability to gain the upper hand in a business deal. Chichester had entered J.D.'s office with the notion that hiring a detective was no different than dealing with business adversaries or hiring a new manager for less money than would be expected. Instead, his love for his daughter had broken his combative composure.

J.D. relented. He leaned back in his chair and said without malice or a trace of accusation in his voice, "Why didn't you contact the police? Your daughter might have been kidnapped."

Chichester dropped his eyes to the floor and slowly shook his head.

"I doubt that is the case, Mr. Daugherty," he said. "I think she has . . . she has . . . eloped."

J.D. paused, but the rhythm of the negotiation and dialogue had been broken. If the daughter eloped and was of age, then J.D. could do very little. Chichester would have to work this case out on his own.

"How old is your daughter?"

"She's twenty-two."

"Well, Mr. Chichester, I don't think I can help you either. Eloping is your daughter's decision. She's old enough now to make those decisions."

J.D. twisted his moustache into his most understanding smile and tried to make a joke: "We've got suffrage now, Mr. Chichester, your daughter can even vote. I'm afraid that we older fellas can't tell the women what to do anymore," J.D. chuckled.

Chichester simply glowered at J.D.'s awkward attempt to make light of the situation. "Mr. Daugherty, I didn't come here to be laughed at. My daughter is still my concern."

J.D.'s face took a downward turn. This time he nervously knuckled his moustache, fingered his tie, and said, "You're right, Mr. Chichester, your daughter is the first priority. My apologies. Now, please tell me the whole story. I will do what I can to help."

2
The Plan

After showing Chichester out, J.D. sat behind his desk to contemplate the information he had been given and to plan the operation. He prided himself on being thorough; efficiency rested on organization and precise planning. But snippets of his conversation with the distraught father kept intruding on his effort to map out a strategy for this case. J.D. was too agitated by what he'd heard to sit still.

He rose and took off his coat. He wanted to loosen his tie and undo his collar but thought better of it. He hung the coat on the rack and went back to his desk. Instead of devising a plan, J.D. gave in to reassessing the parts of Chichester's statements that he remembered distinctly.

After Chichester had dismissed his driver, he began to talk freely and passionately about his dilemma. It was easy to see just how much he loved his daughter and just how little he thought of her judgment.

J.D. had begun the actual interrogation with the most obvious question: "Do you know who she eloped with?"

"I'm afraid so. He's a boy she met while with Mrs. Shelby collecting Indian artifacts. He's an Indian boy by the name of Tommy Ruffle. This mustn't get out. It could cause a scandal. You see, the boy's grandfather is extremely wealthy, but—how can I put it?"

J.D. finished Chichester's thought, "Not good enough, eh?"

Chichester flushed but recovered quickly. "Don't misunderstand me, Mr. Daugherty. I am sympathetic to the Indian's plight. The Shelbys are my closest friends. Rose Shelby has done much for the Indian, and I've never hesitated to contribute to her activities on the Indian's behalf.

"My daughter is my only child and will inherit my estate. This boy, this Tommy Ruffle, like all members of his unhappy race, has no sense of the value of money. He is neither civilized nor cultured, and I cannot have our family name linked to someone one step removed from savagery."

Chichester paused for effect, and then said, "I'm asking you to find my daughter and find a way of compelling her to talk to me. I wish to counsel her, to make her understand that it would actually do harm to this boy and to her if she takes him into a life that he has no business being part of."

J.D. didn't like Chichester's bias, but he thought that the man had made a point. The white girl and the Indian boy probably had nothing in common, save for a strong physical attraction. On the other hand, J.D. was enough of a romantic to admire a young woman who threw everything away for love. J.D.'s mother was the most intelligent person he had ever known, and so if a woman wanted to elope with an Indian, he believed that was her decision to make. Chichester's daughter surely knew all about the problems that could arise and had still run off with the Ruffle boy. Besides, J.D. knew several successful Indian-white marriages, the offspring of which were upstanding, bright, and beautiful people.

But Chichester undoubtedly believed that a white man marrying an Indian woman might be acceptable, but a white woman marrying an Indian man was something else again. Even J.D., like most men of his age and background, felt that darker men—like Italians and Latins—were far more lusty than whites, making it difficult for them to maintain a stable homelife. When J.D.'s sister had fallen in love with an Italian boy, his father had opposed the marriage based on that very reasoning. But J.D.'s mother, independent as always, favored the union because the Italian suitor knew the catechism.

These thoughts that J.D. was having were reminding him of Klan talk, and he disliked agreeing with anybody crazed enough to parade around in masks and sheets, burn crosses, and lynch innocent people. He brought himself back to carefully considering his new client.

Chichester was an educated man whose prejudices were based on something subtler. Marriage "beneath her station" would mean marriage to anyone whose race, wealth, or membership in the high church did not match his own. In Chichester's world, marriage "beneath her station" would be the same whether his daughter eloped with an Irish-Catholic like J.D., an Indian like the Ruffle kid, somebody from the wrong side of the tracks, or just some plain old working stiff. Chichester obviously divided the world into his "equals," like the Shelbys, and the "help"—everybody else.

J.D. didn't particularly care for Chichester or the emotions that the man stirred up in him, so he had decided to add to his client's discomfort: "Mr. Chichester, you may as well know that I employ several field operatives. My associates have to be told about all aspects of a case. My best investigator is a Cherokee Indian. He speaks his own language, is well educated, and reads and writes English. He served with the AEF in France and was wounded in battle. He is experienced, bonded, and knows how to go about operations in places outlying Tulsa."

Chichester had visibly squirmed in his chair at the thought of using an Indian to investigate a family member. He probably took the view that one Indian would balk at chasing down another Indian, particularly if the one being chased was eloping with a white woman. In Chichester's eyes, Indians and other dark-skinned men would "naturally" want a white woman and would "naturally" aid each other in that pursuit. "My fee isn't the only price he'll pay," thought J.D. "Chichester is going to have to deal with being a snob and a fool."

He had to make his initial move. "First things, first!" J.D. said aloud to himself, putting the Chichester interview on a back burner. J.D. picked up the earpiece on his telephone, and clicked the arm twice.

"Number please," said the operator.

"Gimme Boston Garage."

"Yes, sir," said the disembodied voice.

Hoolie Smith had just completed installing a new magneto in a Buick touring car and was wiping his hands on a shop towel, when Howard Sears, owner of the Boston Avenue Auto Repair Garage, called him to the telephone.

Hoolie picked up the earpiece and said a quick " 'Lo" into the transmitter.

"Hoolie, it's J.D. Can you come over to the office?"

Hoolie hadn't talked to J.D. for awhile. He liked the gruff private investigator and found the detective business more than interesting.

"*Osiyo*, Jimmy," said Hoolie, knowing full well that J.D. hated being called by the diminutive of his first name. Hoolie enjoyed throwing a bit of the Cherokee language around in his conversations with J.D., too. It exasperated the detective to no end, and Hoolie liked to tease.

Through a quick rumbling in his throat, J.D. growled his dislike for Hoolie's greeting. Hoolie grinned.

"Okay, Hoolie," J.D. said, "can you get over here? And ask Sears if you can take a few days off. I need the help."

Hoolie did engine repairs for Sears on a job-by-job basis. He had a pension from the Army and worked for both J.D. and Sears to keep himself busy. Hoolie preferred working for J.D. The work somehow satisfied his need to roam, talk to people, and learn new things. He had always been curious about how and why people acted the way they did.

Hoolie had met J.D. through Mr. Sears, who often had J.D.'s rattletrap Ford flivver in for repairs. One of J.D.'s cases had involved taking testimony from a Cherokee woman who lived 75 miles away in Tahlequah. When J.D. mentioned the case to Sears, the garage owner introduced J.D. to Hoolie. Hoolie knew the woman's family and ended up interpreting for J.D. during the investigation. J.D. began to call Hoolie one of his "operatives" or "associates," posted a bond for him, and called upon him to carry out inquiries among Indian people who didn't want to talk to a white man. Hoolie knew the lay of the land out in the Oklahoma countryside. As far as Hoolie knew, he was J.D.'s only operative and associate. The pay wasn't all that great; J.D. was something of a cheapskate.

Hoolie glanced around the shop and responded, "There's nothin' 'round here now. I might be able to help you out."

J.D.'s voice sounded excited. "Something pretty big came up, Hool. Get down here as soon as you can."

J.D. hung up before Hoolie could reply.

Hoolie went to Sears and told his grease-stained, part-time employer that the Buick was finished and that he had other work to do. Sears told Hoolie to come back in a few days for his pay.

"I think we got a new Ford roadster coming in," said Sears, "as soon as they can pull it out of a cattle pond."

Hoolie laughed with Sears about the Ford. Since Volstead, a lot of people were driving drunk, and because the roads weren't much different than driving across open fields anyway, cars had a way of winding up in ponds, mud banks, creeks, and thick underbrush. Folks could be pretty crazy, especially in automobiles.

In his mind, J.D. was already calling the case "the Chichester operation." The girl's name was Rose, and she had been named after Big Bill Shelby's wife. She had obviously been given that name to draw the two families together. Rose Chichester was 5' 3" tall, slightly built, and had reddish-brown hair. By the age of twenty-two, she had been engaged to be married four times. Chichester had reluctantly admitted to buying off her various fiancés and that doing so had made a dent in the family fortune. Each of the young men she had promised to marry was handsome, personable, well educated, and virtually penniless, or as Chichester would probably put it, "beneath her station." No wonder the girl ran off, J.D. thought, her father was always undermining her choices in men.

In a way, J.D. understood Chichester's overly protective actions. The girl's mother was dead. Apparently—and J.D. wasn't able to get an exact time period from Chichester—she died shortly after giving birth to Rose. Chichester was also vague as to the cause of his wife's death. Chichester mentioned fever, physical breakdown, internal problems, and strain as causes for her untimely demise. J.D. figured that Rose simply needed a mother and had rebelled at being cloistered away by an overbearing father. In J.D.'s experience these women were the most liable to run away or get involved in the "wild life" of the speakeasies and dance halls.

Chichester presumed that Rose had eloped with Tommy Ruffle for several reasons. Rose Shelby was helping to finance the recording of Indian tribal ways before they vanished. When Rose Chichester was in Tulsa, she would go up to Osage country with Mrs. Shelby and a professor from back east, Arlen Potter, who was inquiring into the ways of the tribe. Rose Shelby had become especially friendly with an elderly Osage chief, who was Tommy's grandfather. When Potter and Mrs. Shelby talked with the chief, Tommy would interpret as the elder recounted the myths and history of his people.

Chichester himself had never gone along on these visits. Mrs. Shelby had told him that Tommy was taken with Rose. He gave the girl gifts and listened to her problems. And after the most recent trip, both Chichester and Mrs. Shelby had noticed that the young woman had talked on and on about the trip to Hominy: how she and Tommy had walked along a beautiful stream, and how they'd sat together by a bonfire during the dances at the ceremonial grounds. This prattling had not been lost on her father. And so, when she went missing, Chichester immediately assumed that she had eloped with Tommy.

J.D. knew a good deal about the Ruffle family. The newspapers had been filled with stories about them for a few years now. The family's history, especially that of its patriarch, Chief Ruffle, made for good reading, even more so under the headline:

HEAP BIG WELL COMES IN
OLD CHIEF A MILLIONAIRE

Shelby Oil, of course, had taken out the leases and done the drilling on the chief's allotted land. Rose Shelby had been appointed, as was usual in Tulsa's important cultural activities, to head the planning board for a new museum that would feature Osage artifacts, including the things that she and Potter collected when visiting Tommy's grandfather. She was helping fund the museum and Potter's scientific work, another association that connected the Ruffle family with the Shelbys. That headline read:

OLD CHIEF "COCKEYE" HELPS
MRS. SHELBY WITH NATURAL
HISTORY MUSEUM

The Ruffle patriarch's status as a warrior from the old days when the army battled the Indians for control of the country made him an Oklahoma celebrity. Even before Chief Ruffle had become a millionaire, Teddy Roosevelt, during his many sojourns in the West, would often pay the chief a visit. T.R. had had an affinity for meeting with chiefs like Geronimo, Quanah Parker, and Ruffle. J.D. recalled a picture taken of Ruffle with the president a few years earlier: T.R. in pince-nez, Chief Ruffle in a high-standing otter turban. Now J.D. remembered that standing behind and to the left of the former president was Big Bill Shelby.

Unlike Geronimo and Quanah, the old chief had been a scout for the U.S. Army against the Kiowas, Cheyennes, and Comanches. In a battle with the Kiowas some fifty years before, Chief Ruffle had received a blow to the right side of his head that badly damaged the eye muscle. Ever after, the eye would wander uncontrollably. Without knowing, or particularly caring, what the old man's real name was, the soldiers in whose service he fought took to calling him "Cockeye." When the Indian Office began renaming Indians so that they would have surnames in the white man's way, the people in charge felt that "Cockeye" wasn't distinguished enough for the chief. His Osage name was unappealing to an English speaker's ears. In translation, it was "Eagle Ruffling His Feathers on a Cold Day," which was much too long in their opinion for a proper English name. Since "Eagle" had already been given to another family, the Indian Office finally chose "Ruffle" for the chief's surname.

As he walked the six city blocks to J.D.'s office, Hoolie grew excited about the prospect of getting involved in a "pretty big" case. For some reason, investigative work gave him a sense of satisfaction he had not known before. It wasn't just solving other peoples' problems that he liked, although Hoolie enjoyed helping people out. In his twenty-six years of life, Hoolie had been thoroughly schooled in Cherokee beliefs and principles. One of those beliefs was the notion that helping others was a reward in and of itself. It simply made you feel good.

But Hoolie's work as a detective required him to poke into other people's lives. That aspect of investigative work went contrary to Cherokee principles. It was confrontational and intrusive; it was thus exactly the opposite of the emphasis Cherokees placed on harmony and consensus within the clan and household, and among the people. Hoolie knew, on the other hand, that Cherokees could be great gossips and finding out bits and pieces of scandal here and there enlivened Cherokee communities. When the gossip got out of hand and created internal strife, the elders put it to a stop immediately.

Hoolie rationalized his work in another way. His people had medicine that aided them in bringing harmony back to individuals and communities. He had pretty much decided that his intrusive work could be reconciled with his Cherokee beliefs since he used his job to restore harmonious relationships when discord had upset the right way of things.

Sometimes Hoolie disagreed with the way J.D. handled people's problems. J.D. had told Hoolie about what he called the "Simmons Operation"—the oilman's runaway wife. J.D. had brought the woman back, but he didn't concern himself with making things right all the way around. In fact, J.D. told a gruesome story that showed how white husbands could react to their wives' leaving them for other men. J.D. had found a young runaway and returned her to her husband. The husband, in turn, beat her up. After the beating, the wife became docile, and finally, she started using laudanum to relieve her emotional and physical pain. She ended up being locked in an attic, like so many other "crazy ladies" whose rich husbands had wanted to hide them rather than send them off to asylums. Having an "unstable" wife in an asylum invited scandal. "I'd bet money," said J.D., "that Mrs. Simmons will be on dope in a few days, and she'll end up as crazy as a bedbug within a couple of years."

Hoolie thought that J.D. should have stayed on the Simmons case until everything was back in place once again. "You should have had a medicine man in. You have to fix things up again. That family is sick, 'specially the husband. We believe that there's just two roads to take. The Red Path is war and chaos. The White Path is peace and justice."

"That ain't my job," J.D. responded. "I just do what the client wants me to do. Nothing more and nothing less. Simmons wanted his wife back, and that's what he got. You can't go preachin' to people about what they should do with their lives."

Hoolie kept mulling over what he saw as a big contradiction. Maybe J.D. was right. Maybe he knew that you couldn't restore harmony to white people or even fine-tune them, like you could an automobile. They seemed to like disorder. They thought it was natural to live in a world of crime, runaway wives, insanity, poverty, and hatred. But Hoolie was getting used to it; he even liked living in a chaotic boomtown like Tulsa. Maybe bringing peace and stability to a place like Tulsa would be a long, hard fight. Maybe only Cherokees understood what the White Path of peace was all about and that sometimes it took walking the Red Path to reach it.

Hoolie tapped lightly on the glass pane in J.D.'s office door and opened it just enough to look in. J.D. sat with his head turned toward the dingy window, eyeing the sunshine and looking thoughtful. Hoolie put his head in, "You wanted to see me?"

With a start, J.D. looked at the door and waved Hoolie in. "Sit down," he began. "This is how we're gonna handle this case."

"Well, 'hello, how are yah' to you, too."

For a moment, J.D. didn't catch Hoolie's sarcasm. "All right, how are you? Sorry, but my mind's on the case. I should've made time for pleasantries."

"It's okay," said Hoolie. "I was in the army. You're like an old sergeant of mine. All the time thinkin' 'bout things he can't do nothin' 'bout."

Hoolie took a seat in the client's chair. J.D. handed him a picture of a pretty white girl with dark eyes and a graceful, long neck. He let

Hoolie look at the picture for quite awhile. He kept knuckling his mustache. Finally, J.D. pulled a package of Fatima cigarettes from his desk drawer, offered one to Hoolie, and lit one up himself. He leaned over to light Hoolie's cigarette and sat back. "That's Rose Chichester. Her father thinks she's run off with an Osage boy, name of Tommy Ruffle. You've heard of the family. Now, I don't think that Tommy's gonna put eloping with a rich white girl in the newspapers. For the time being, he'll want to keep it secret. What I need you to do is go up to Osage County, probably around Hominy, and find him. It ain't gonna be easy, but he's the lead in the case.

"While you're up there, I'm gonna nose around and make sure that her old man is on the right track about the Ruffle boy. This girl might've run off with somebody else from here. Maybe she got herself into trouble in some other way."

Hoolie nodded, "After I've had a look around Hominy, I'll send a wire about what I've found out."

"I got Chichester to set up a meeting with the Shelbys. Mrs. Shelby, her daughter, Elizabeth, and Rose were up in Hominy to see the Ruffles about a week ago. That's when Chichester thinks Tommy and his daughter worked out running off together.

"I want to talk to the Shelby kids, Little Bill and the daughter. Don't know much about them and what they know. I think all of them, Chichester's girl, too, are a bit wild."

J.D. ignored Hoolie's quick look of disapproval for assuming the worst about the Shelbys and the Chichester girl.

"Anyway," J.D. continued, "you need to get up there pretty fast."

"What have you heard about the Ruffles lately?"

"Nothing except what the old man just told me about Rose's trip to see the Ruffles last week. Mrs. Shelby always stays in a boarding house in Hominy. On this last trip, she and the two girls shared a room there. They visited the Ruffles with a college professor named Arlen Potter. Chichester said they were collecting Indian stuff, and that the Ruffle boy gave the girl a few gifts—some beadwork and a shawl or something.

"On the second night, Mrs. Shelby woke up, and Rose was not in her bed. Elizabeth told her mother that Rose had gone to the privy. They fell back asleep and didn't hear Rose return, but she was there at breakfast the next morning.

"All right, they stay there another couple of days before coming back to Tulsa. Three days later, Rose doesn't come down for breakfast. They go up to her room and find that she's taken some clothes and flown the coop. Didn't leave a note or anything. They questioned the help, but nobody saw anything. She's been gone now for four days. Chichester said that he got desperate and came to me."

"I still can't figure out how they made plans that quick," interjected Hoolie. "How'd they get away?"

"I don't know. Tommy's got a car. As far as making plans, young folks with goo-goo eyes for each other can do things real fast and not think about anything but themselves. Tommy probably told her that he'd come get her at a certain time, and she packed up, found some way out of the house, jumped in Tommy's automobile, and vanished. Young people have been known to do it before."

"Okay," Hoolie began, "I go to Hominy, find the Ruffles, and then what? I can't take the girl if she ain't willin' to go."

"You're right. Just locate her. Speak to Tommy. Tell them that her father just wants to talk to her. You know, it could be a passing thing between them. She might want to come home. Tommy might be tired of her. Take it slow and easy. Don't press them. Find 'em, get 'em to talk, and we'll find a way to get the girl to speak to daddy. You take my Ford."

"All right, Jimmy. I have to get some stuff from my place. Where's your car?"

"Down on Sixth. Pretty close to your rooming house. Now, take care of that automobile. It's the best car around. And don't call me 'Jimmy.'"

"All right, I won't call you Jimmy, but that heap of yours?" Hoolie laughed. "It ain't hardly worth keepin'. Just be happy that the best mechanic around these parts is drivin' her."

Hoolie caught a trolley and took a short ride to pick up J.D.'s automobile. As soon as he twisted the crank, Hoolie could tell that the flivver needed an adjustment. He drove to his rooming house and packed some things: his army duffel bag with a few changes of clothing, his new fedora, a burlap bag with some canned goods, and four army blankets. He looked at his cane in the corner. Hoolie had not been shot like J.D. always told clients; he had been hit in the right leg by a half-dozen bits of shrapnel from an exploding German artillery shell. He limped slightly but didn't need the cane except when the cold brought on the pain. He picked it up and hooked it over his arm; maybe he'd need it for something else. He carried everything down to the car and paused, thinking. He dumped everything in the back seat of J.D.'s automobile, quickly returned to his room, exchanged his work cap for his army campaign hat, which he usually wore hunting, and picked up his old 44.40 Winchester rifle. He held it for a short time, giving some extra thought to whether or not to bring it along. Finally, he slung it over his shoulder, picked up a box of cartridges, and went out the door.

In the hallway, Hoolie bumped into his landlord.

"Goin' huntin'?" the man asked.

"Oh, yeah, huntin'," said Hoolie vaguely. "I'm gonna be gone three or four days. Look after things for me, will you, Lyle?"

"Sure, Hoolie, sure. Don't know what you'd be huntin' in springtime. That's too big a gun for squirrel," the landlord teased.

"Well, I might find something. See you in a few days."

Hoolie's landlord nodded a farewell, and Hoolie went to the street and cranked up the flivver. He drove to Sears' garage. He had to set the timing and get the spark right. Fixing J.D.'s Ford took longer than Hoolie had figured it would. It was mid-afternoon before he got on the road heading northwest out of Tulsa and into Osage County.

3

J.D.

After Hoolie left, J.D. got up and paced the floor for a few minutes. He was still working out a plan of action. At last, he went back behind his desk, sat, and took a deep breath. It had been an eventful morning. J.D. pulled his pocket watch out of his vest and looked at the time. Twelve-fifteen. Everybody would be out to lunch, so he could put off the several telephone calls he wanted to make until after he had eaten his usual Friday-afternoon bowl of chili. Besides, he needed to find another one of his "operatives." And there was little doubt in J.D.'s mind that this particular one would be at the lunch counter.

He put his coat back on and placed his new boater on his head, tilting it at a rakish angle over his right eye. Before he could get out the door, the telephone rang. It was Chichester.

"Yes, Mr. Chichester, what can I do for you?"

"You mentioned that you would like to meet with Mrs. Shelby and her daughter, Elizabeth."

"Yes."

"I'm calling to arrange a time that would be convenient for you both. Would tomorrow afternoon be all right? I realize it's a Saturday."

"Tomorrow afternoon would be fine. What time?"

"Two o'clock? The Shelbys would be pleased to meet with you then. Shall I send a car?"

J.D. knuckled his moustache with a self-satisfied grin. "Yes, by all means, send a car," he said.

"Very well, my man will be at your office at half-past one."

J.D. placed the earpiece back on the hook, turned, and left the office. It was twelve-twenty.

It was a short walk to Ed North's lunch counter. Ed's was a no-frills eatery. It had a counter, three small tables, and a big griddle. The pots on the stove always contained the same things: boiled cabbage, potato soup, and Ed's own special chili. Ed let J.D. keep a tab that he paid every Monday.

As soon as he saw J.D. enter the door, Ed ladled out a bowl of chili. J.D. raised his chin in greeting and to indicate that he'd be sitting at the counter, and Ed threw down a plate of saltine crackers. J.D. spotted a thin, blond youth with unruly hair carefully taking in a plate of soup; J.D. put a finger to his mouth, to signal to Ed that he was going to sneak up on the boy. Taking the pointer and middle finger of each hand, J.D. jabbed the blond youth in the ribs. The boy turned quickly, saw J.D., and laughed. Ed put J.D.'s bowl of chili down next to the kid.

"Hiya, Danny boy," said J.D.

Danny Ryan, who was widely known around town as a third-rate paperboy and a first-class pickpocket, shook his head heavily and said: "How's tricks, J.D.?"

"Well, boy-yo, pretty good. How's by you?"

"I'd be better if you'd spot me this plate of soup."

"Done. Ed, put this boy's meal on my bill."

"Gotcha, J.D.," replied Ed, who returned to grilling a large chunk of ham.

J.D. watched Danny spoon some soup into his mouth and took a spoonful of chili himself. J.D. had known Danny's family for over a year. They had been dirt farmers, driven out of Kansas by drought, debt, and ensuing poverty. Danny's father got to be one of the burly roustabouts in the oil fields, but he had helped the Wobblie organizers and was put out of work for it. John Ryan was a tough old bird who had fought J.D.'s flying squad of Great Western detectives as hard as he had fought the unyielding sod of the Kansas prairie—and with equal luck. He could rarely find work now, having been blackballed by most of the drilling companies around. J.D. found John likeable. Danny's mother and father reminded J.D. of his own parents and of his own rough and tumble upbringing in South Chicago. J.D. got John Ryan some work here and there, and occasionally, he slipped him some money. He would always tell John that the Irish had to stick together.

Danny knew the city well and could be counted on to ferret out information from a closemouthed citizenry.

"How's yer Da, Danny?"

Danny winced at J.D.'s use of the old Irish term for father. He narrowed his eyes and said:

"My pop's okay. Outta work."

"Well, how you doin'?"

"Long story."

"So spill it; I got awhile."

Danny launched into a story about being framed for stealing a young swell's wallet. The cops rounded up all the likely pickpockets under the age of fifteen, took them to the jail, and began interrogating them. The interrogators all wore leather gloves that covered thin layers of sheet metal on the backs of their hands. A backhanded slap punctuated each question, and the longer the suspect held out, the more of a beating he took. It was not enough to break bones, do any permanent damage, or kill; but it was good enough to extract reasonably clear confessions—to whatever crime the interrogators wanted to solve. Danny ended up confessing to the "dip," along with two other boys the coppers had hauled in. Danny, as the youngest, was let off with his bruises, a warning, and the knowledge that he would have to face his father. Sure enough, his father picked him up at the jail, took him home, and beat him more thoroughly than the police had done.

Danny wiped his mouth on a sleeve, "My pop wailed on me for about fifteen minutes. That ain't as long as I've had before. I think the old man thought the cops were workin' a frame-up, so he let me off easy." Danny paused, looked at his empty plate, "What's with you, J.D.?"

"Well, Danny, I got a job."

"For the old man?"

"Naw. I thought maybe you could do some nosing around for me. It's worth five dollars for some good information. I'll give you a couple of bucks now so you can pay off some of your contacts."

"Five bucks?" asked the boy excitedly. Five dollars was a healthy chunk of money.

"That's right, five. All you gotta do is find out what's it like workin' for the Shelby's. Not in the fields, but in the house. What kind of guy is Big Bill Shelby? His wife? His kids? You know, the dirt or whatever."

"I can do that standing on my head," said Danny. "When should I get back to you?"

"Come over to my office around four. I've got to catch up on some paper work and make some calls. Yeah, four's good."

"Right, J.D. I'll get on this right now."

Danny swung his body around and jumped down from the high counter stool. He waved to Ed and J.D. and went out the door.

Ed took up Danny's plate and let it slip into the standing wash water in the sink. He turned, put one hand on the counter near J.D., and said, "Boy's a pretty good kid. Wish I could get him off the damn streets. Don't have enough dishes or sweepin' for him to do, or I'd hire him here. Know of any real jobs for him to do?"

J.D. took a spoonful of chili and swallowed it quickly. "Maybe I could ask Hoolie Smith. You know Hoolie. Indian, one of my ops, took a bullet in the war. He's a mechanic. Maybe he could teach the boy something. I'll talk to old man Sears, down at the garage."

"That'd be good, J.D. That'd help the boy and his family out."

J.D. slowly rose and adjusted his hat. "Well, I'll see you around, Ed."

"All right, J.D."

J.D. went back to the Blackburn Building, took his "office bottle" out of his bottom desk drawer, and knocked back a stiff belt of rye. He called it his "lunch drink." He put the bottle back in his desk and stared at the telephone. He started to pick it up but pulled his hand back. Instead of making calls, he decided he'd go pay visits to the city police and the county sheriff's department.

He always let the cops know a little something about his cases. He had made a habit of it since his days with Great Western. It was a courtesy and served as a kind of backup. He never let the laws know exactly who his clients were or precisely what he was up to, but he always let them know generally what he was working on: missing person, theft, a philandering husband or wife. Besides, he was a former cop, and he just liked being around them and the station house.

Usually the police thought private investigators were pains in the neck. Detectives, they believed, were making big money on matters that any cop worth his salt could solve quicker, if only they had the time. The number of crimes in Tulsa had risen steadily since the end of the war, and small matters, like missing society dames, took a back seat to murder, grand larceny, and enforcing prohibition—not that many on the force were energetic about going after the speaks and bootleggers. Recently, the Klan was causing trouble. What the cops didn't like about groups like the Kluxers was that they undermined police authority, and the cops were always worried about maintaining authority. It was the only way to keep order. PI's undermined their authority, too. But J.D. was an exception to the cops' way of thinking.

Private investigators were normally a secretive lot who often dealt with crimes that rightfully should be left in the hands of the cops. The detective's independence was the very thing that galled the police. But J.D. always gave them their due. He reported his cases, and if "real" crimes were committed, he backed away and let the police do their job. Besides, J.D. was a pal who bought beer for them at the local speaks and came to the station house frequently to talk, tell jokes, and commiserate with them. Knowing J.D. the way they did, Tulsa city cops and county sheriff's deputies allowed him plenty of leeway. They were a new breed of law enforcement officers, in any case. To J.D., they combined big-city knowledge and cynicism with a wild-west willingness to shoot it out with the outlaws. Many of them still looked "wild west" and walked their beats with a chaw of tobacco in their cheeks and their hands on their police-issue revolvers. The only thing that distinguished them from the town marshals in the dime novels were their uniforms. Five or six years before, the cops had exchanged their high helmets for military-style caps. The new uniforms were easier to keep up. They struck a different chord with the citizens, too, who somehow felt more comfortable with the officers' new appearance. The sheriff's deputies, on the other hand, still tended to wear ten-gallon hats and suit coats to hide their big Colt revolvers.

The desk sergeant at police headquarters greeted J.D. with a near-toothless grin. He shook hands vigorously, even though J.D. and he had had a drink together only two nights before. The sergeant's name was Gottlieb, and his physical strength was both prodigious and legendary. He had lost his front teeth in clashes with criminals wielding baseball bats and crowbars. He had also spent twenty-odd years gripping billy clubs and blackjacks while he "interrogated" those miscreants unlucky enough to have been arrested by him. It was said that Gottlieb could turn young punks, pimps, and assorted thugs into choirboys in less time than it takes to make a telephone call.

"How are you, Sarge?" said J.D.

"Doin' pretty well, J.D., and you?"

"I've seen better days, but I'm on a case, so maybe I'll keep outta the poor house."

Gottlieb chuckled a bit and scratched his chin. "I think you're doin' all right. You look in the pink."

"Yeah, I'm feelin' pretty good."

J.D. paused and looked at his feet. "Sarge," he said, "I've gotta see Lieutenant Finch. He in?"

"Yeah, I think he's in the squad room upstairs, goin' over some paperwork. Go on up."

"Thanks, Sarge. Buy you a beer sometime?"

"Hey, J.D., any old time. See you around."

J.D. went up the stairs and found Lieutenant Finch, in uniform, sitting with his feet propped up on a large oak conference table. The lieutenant was an odd-looking gent. He was tall and heavily built but had a narrow face with deep lines in his forehead and also along his cheekbones, leading downward from the corners of his nose to the edges of his mouth. He looked as if someone had taken the head of a skinny, craggy-faced old codger and placed it on the body of a circus strong man. Finch glanced up at J.D. The lines in his face deepened.

"Howdy, J.D. You keepin' outta trouble?"

"I'm doin' all right, but I'm on a new case, and I wondered if you could help me out, Marv?"

"Be glad to, J.D. Getting tired of reading these reports. I swear that none of these jim-dandies in my squad ever went to school."

"I don't guess that the department pays enough to get the boys that went to college."

Finch looked even more craggy-faced than when J.D. had entered the squad room. "I don't ask for college," he said with a smirk. "Third grade would be good. Anyways, what can I help you out with?"

"What's routine lately? Kidnappings? Bodies in the morgue? Any young women locked up?"

"Aw, mostly petty theft, drifters, whores, and drunks stabbing each other. Quite a few Negroes beat up. The Legionnaires are after the Reds, and the Klan says that the Reds are tryin' to get the niggers riled up. So both of them are kinda helpin' one another. I don't want to have any more lynchin's goin' on. You know, we damn near lost the city last year. Ain't gonna happen again."

Finch's face had turned red. Despite that short diatribe, it was clear he secretly feared that the cops might not be able to maintain control if Tulsa was caught up in a lynching frenzy. Finch had been in the middle of the attempt to contain the mob that murdered the two boys last summer. He had had no success.

"This job is getting' to me," Finch said with an audible sigh. "There's more and more crazy sons o' bitches runnin' around town than ever before."

J.D. put on his most sympathetic face.

"Well, Marv," he began, "When a city gets any size at all, you got to hire more men on. Just ain't enough time to go picking and choosing. More men means more of a chance to end up with bad apples. So when something like last year happens, you can't depend on all the people you got working for you. It happened in Chicago. That's why I quit the cops there. Hell, that's why I quit Great Western."

"Yeah, I reckon," said Finch pensively. "Maybe we could get more money to get those college boys on the force, but I doubt it."

J.D. shook his head, commiserating with the big lieutenant. He paused just for a moment and then moved on to the next topic of conversation.

"Marv, I'm working a missing person's case. Young woman. Looks like she might've run off with an Osage boy. Her father's worked up. She comes from money."

"Anybody I know?"

"You know about them, but I can't mention names right now."

"That's okay. I don't want to get caught between big money and some kid running off. Too much aggravation. Besides, I gotta worry about paperwork and everyday two-bit crime."

"What's been up lately?" J.D. tried to get the conversation back to where he wanted it. "Any young women in the can who don't say who they are? Bodies on ice? White girls causing a ruckus? Some Indian hauled in with a white girl in tow? Anything like that?"

"Can't say as I've heard of anything." Finch pursed his lips and ran his hand over his slick, dark hair. "I'm pretty sure there's an Indian in the morgue. A white man, too, an oil-rig worker who got knifed over a whore down on First Street. We got the boy who did it. The Indian was found up north, just outside of town. That makes him the sheriff's problem."

"No young white girl?"

"Nope. Nothing like that at all, alive or dead."

J.D. put his hat back on and tilted it carefully. He held out his hand, and Finch stood to shake.

"Marv, thanks a lot. Don't let the paperwork get to you!"

"Okay, J.D., and don't take any wooden nickels."

"Don't worry. See you around, Finch-boy."

J.D. stepped into the hallway and stopped a few paces down from the lieutenant's doorway. He put his hand to his chin in deep thought. He stood there for a full minute before moving on.

Outside police headquarters, J.D. pulled out his watch. Time was money, he thought. His clients demanded swift solutions to their problems. He looked at his watch again. Not enough time to do what he wanted to do and still meet Danny at four. He hopped the next trolley and went back to his office.

J.D. unlocked the door and, without even removing his hat, walked to his desk and picked up the telephone. He clicked the hook three times, and a pleasant voice said, "How may I direct your call?"

"Sheriff's office, Deputy Joe Spiedel."

A moment later, a voice that J.D. recognized said, "Sheriff's Office."

"Hello, Tom, this is J.D. Daugherty. Is Spiedel in?"

"Yeah, J.D., I'll get him. How you doin'?"

"Good, Tom, good."

J.D. heard Tom put the telephone receiver down. After a minute's wait, a high-pitched man's voice answered, "Hiya, J.D., how's business?"

" 'Lo Joe. I'd like to ask you about a body you've got in the morgue. An Indian. I heard it was the Sheriff's case, so I called you."

"Hold on a minute, J.D., I'll see if anybody knows anything about it. Indian, you say?"

"Yeah, Joe. It's kinda important."

"I'll make it as fast as I can, J.D., no problem."

The delay was longer than J.D. had bargained for. He was able to take off his hat, loosen his tie, sit down behind his desk, and whistle several bars each of "Yankee Doodle," "Camptown Races," and "I've Been Working on the Railroad." Finally, Spiedel picked up.

J.D. could hear a long intake of breath.

"Listen, J.D., the Indian they got on ice was found two days ago, out by the road heading towards Pawhuska. Kids found him there. You know how kids always find stuff that nobody'd ever look for, let alone turn up. Looks to be around twenty, twenty-five, give or take a couple of years. Sometimes you can't tell about Indians. Had his throat cut."

"How long he'd been dead?" asked J.D.

"Truth is, we don't know when the boy was killed. The body wasn't stiff, but the doc says the rigor mortis wore off. Somebody tried to hide him under some dirt and leaves, but they didn't dig a hole or nothin'. When my men went out to get him, the body was pretty ripe, but one of the drivers said he noticed the smell of whiskey, over the way the body smelled in the first place." Spiedel paused and then snorted, "For all I know, that driver might've been smellin' his own breath!"

He went on, "There was quite a bit of blood on the boy's shirt, but none around the body. We figure that he got into a fight and got cut. The one who did the cuttin' moved the Indian from somewheres else, and he tried to make the body disappear, but he was probably drunk, too drunk to do the job right. The dead boy didn't have no identification and no money. The killer probably robbed him as well."

J.D. interrupted the flow of information. "Have you got anybody in from the Indian agencies to look at him?" he asked.

"No, not yet. We sent out word, but nobody's come in. The Indian Office people are pretty slow about these things. I seen it before. Nobody comes in. Nobody reports a missing Indian. I guess the county will end up buryin' him. I'd bet a dollar to a dime that the boy was killed in Osage County, too. Their responsibility. We can't do much. Got no suspects, no clues, nothing on him."

"That's a damn shame, Joe. I hate to see anybody end up like that. Well, anyway, I appreciate the information. If anything does come up on the boy, would you let me know right away?"

"You bet, J.D. I'll see you around."

J.D. replaced the earpiece, put his elbow on the desk, and rested his chin in the cup of his hand. Spiedel had no reason to complain that the killing was Osage County's responsibility: neither Tulsa County nor Osage County's laws would spend much time or effort on investigating the murder of an Indian. J.D. had to find out the dead boy's identity. From the moment that Marv Finch mentioned that a dead Indian youth was on ice, what J.D. called his "Irish intuition" had been yelling in his ear that it was Tommy Ruffle lying in the morgue. J.D. had a feeling that the Chichester operation was going to take a wrong turn. Something like a dead suspect clouded up a case like nothing else. The notion that Tommy Ruffle was dead made the hair rise on the back of his neck. Suddenly, the identification of the Indian boy in the morgue became all-important; J.D.'s insistence on being thorough demanded it. He had to get a full description of Tommy Ruffle; either that, or get somebody who had known the boy to go down to the morgue—somebody like one of the Shelbys.

J.D. once again lifted the telephone earpiece. It took several servants and about fifteen minutes, but he finally got E.L. Chichester on the line. The Shelby houseguest was seemingly annoyed. J.D. could not have cared less.

"Yes, Mr. Daugherty. I thought we would speak tomorrow. I was in the middle of something, so unless you have news for me about my daughter—"

"I've got a few questions, Mr. Chichester. Can you tell me exactly what Tommy Ruffle looks like?"

"Well, not really. I saw him once from a distance. Mrs. Shelby and Elizabeth know him very well. Why?"

"I'll talk to both of them tomorrow. I need a general idea of what Tommy looks like."

"He's an Indian," Chichester began, "black hair and eyes. He's over six feet tall. I can't add much to that."

"Okay. Now, who does your daughter go out with when she's in town? I want a list of her friends. Where she goes. That kind of information."

"Why would you want that, Mr. Daugherty?"

"I'll tell you straight. There's a chance that your daughter might not be with the Ruffle boy."

There was a long pause on the other end of the line. Chichester was letting the idea of his daughter slipping off with someone else sink in. Either that or he was readying himself for the possibility of a kidnapping or worse. His concern was evident in the tone of his voice:

"Mr. Daugherty, why don't you think she's with Ruffle? I can think of no one else with whom she might have gone. I know little about her acquaintances here in Tulsa, or what she does with her time away from the Shelbys. Mrs. Shelby has assured me that Rose and this Tommy were getting on quite well. And, well, my daughter is somewhat impetuous. She's found other boys attractive enough to become engaged impulsively."

J.D. tried to be tactful. "Sir, I am not saying for a fact that your daughter went with someone other than Tommy Ruffle. I just want to know if there's a possibility that she's with somebody else."

Chichester's answer was to the point. "No, Mr. Daugherty. Rose knows no one here except for the Shelbys and those of their circle. You must tell me why you asked the questions you asked."

"I assure you that I'm just being thorough. In my business you have to be. I'm just working on other possibilities. I'll meet with you and the Shelbys tomorrow. I'll know more then."

"Put that way, Mr. Daugherty, I can understand what you're trying to do. Be that as it may, I still can't think of anyone else with whom my daughter could be."

"Thank you, Mr. Chichester. You may as well know that I've sent my operative to Osage County and will hear from him soon. I'll talk to you tomorrow."

"Yes, that's right. A car will be there tomorrow. Goodbye, Mr. Daugherty."

The line went dead. J.D. took out his watch again. Not enough time to get to the morgue to see the "dead Indian" and be back at the office before Danny showed up. Besides, even if he saw the body, he still wouldn't be able to identify it. J.D. would have to get one of the Shelbys to come downtown tomorrow to see if it was the Ruffle boy, and he'd have to do it without Chichester having a breakdown.

A soft rapping on the office door interrupted his thoughts. "It's open," J.D. called out in an affable voice.

Danny Ryan opened the door, glanced around the room, and walked over to the client's chair. Without saying a word, he sat down, pulled a tobacco pouch and paper from his jacket pocket, rolled a cigarette, lit it, and exhaled a big puff of smoke.

J.D. put a lop-sided smile on his face and brushed his moustache with his thumb, "Those'll stunt your growth, kid." He paused, then dug into his own coat pocket, produced a factory-made Fatima, thumbed a match, and lit up. He inhaled deeply and asked, "Well, what have you got for me?"

Danny coolly exhaled another puff of smoke and wrinkled his brow. "Not much on Big Bill, but plenty on the two kids."

"Okay, spill it," J.D. commanded.

Danny straightened his cap and prepared himself for a relatively long speech.

"The Shelby girl is a real looker," he said with a grin. "Drinks like a fish and runs around all the time. She's kicked up her heels in every speakeasy in town and hung her bloomers on about every bedpost. She gets caught every once in a while; Big Bill spends plenty keepin' her capers quiet. I'll bet what he spends in payoffs would feed China for a year. When she ain't runnin' around, she's with her momma doin' society stuff. She likes to go out dancin' with the colored boys, too. I heard some talk about her livin' it up down on Greenwood. Likes that jazz music."

Danny's face took on a mysterious look, "I'd sure like to meet her."

J.D. gave a single, derisive laugh. "Danny, from what she sounds like, she'd chew you up and spit you out in ten minutes' time. You wouldn't want to run around with her, believe me."

"Speak for yourself, J.D. She's my kind of woman, even if she is a little old."

J.D. lowered his head and coughed once to keep himself from laughing out loud. "Tell me about the Shelby boy," he said, trying to get back to the point.

Danny looked at J.D. directly and pursed his lips as if contemplating his next sentence. "He used to be worse than his sister. Up 'til two years ago, he chased the skirts all over town." Danny paused for a moment. He looked like he was harboring a secret that would shock or dismay J.D. "Little Bill was a regular at Yang Foo's."

J.D. nodded his head in acknowledgment but did not look surprised. "Opium smoker, is he?"

"He *was*, for sure—he just don't smoke no more at Yang Foo's. He used to like the Chinese girls there, too. But they tell me that he don't come 'round no more. There's a rumor floatin' about that Little Bill goes with his sister to Little Africa. Not to the speakeasies on Greenwood though. They say he sees a girl up there. Don't know who she is. The guy I know at Yang Foo's wasn't around today. He'd probably know her."

J.D. mulled the information over, and finally, he asked a rhetorical question:

"Little Bill's got a colored girl, huh?"

"Yeah, and talk is she's a beauty."

J.D.'s mind was in high gear now. He needed time to think about these bits and pieces of information. He needed to work out the connections and stir the pot to let the spices on the bottom bubble to the surface. The trouble was that he couldn't work on the Shelbys until the next afternoon. He looked at Danny thoughtfully.

"You picked up quite a bit in just a short while, boy-yo. Anything at all on their folks?"

Danny cocked his head and looked at J.D. blankly. "Nothin' that you don't know already," he said. "People don't like workin' for Big Bill. Ain't nobody I know likes him. He's a regular sombitch. Most folks say they'd like to see him lyin' on the hot coals of hell with his back broke."

"That figures," J.D. said darkly. "How about the missus?"

"She's clean as a whistle, 'cept maybe for being too high and mighty 'bout makin' this burg look good."

"That figures, too."

"She don't do nothin' but charity work. Raisin' money. Buildin' things. High society stuff. Spends old Bill's money like it grows on trees. Only thing that I heard is that she can be real tough on people if things don't go her way."

"Like how?"

"I heard she stormed the courthouse on her own and took after the cops for arrestin' one of her servants. Madder than hell and ready for a fight. That's the only thing I heard bad about her. And that ain't *that* bad. Anybody who can push the cops around is okay in my book."

J.D. bobbed his head up and down twice, "Okay, she's clean. Has either one of the kids been thrown in the can?"

"Naw. The speaks pay the laws off. Yang Foo probably greases the cops' hands more than anybody else. Big Bill ain't gonna let his kids spend a night in the pokey. So he pays up. The places in Little Africa have to pay the coppers off, too, so the Shelby kids ain't gonna get caught up there either."

"And I thought those kids were Gibson Girl clean. Prep school and all that," said J.D. facetiously.

J.D. and Danny laughed together, Danny so much that he choked on cigarette smoke.

J.D. got up and pounded the boy on the back. Finally, Danny sputtered a few times like an old Ford coming to life and caught his breath.

"See," said J.D., pointing at the bent but still lit cigarette between Danny's fingers, "those things'll kill you."

J.D. reached into his coat pocket, extracted his wallet, and pulled out three crisp dollar bills.

"This what I owe you?"

"That looks good," said Danny, as he took the money. He looked at it fondly and said, "I think I'll go into the detective business."

J.D. shook his head and scowled. "You don't want the aggravation, kid. Tell you what, I'll take you down to the Sears garage. Get him to let you sweep up and learn how to be a mechanic. I know one of the best automobile mechanics in town. Name's Hoolie Smith. I'd bet he'd teach you how to work on cars."

"I'd like that kind of work."

J.D. nodded in approval. "Well, you already work with your hands. You'd probably make a good mechanic."

Danny smiled a knowing, sheepish smile.

After J.D. had showed Danny out, he returned to his desk. He took out his office bottle, poured his "after-five drink," and sat back. He sipped the liquor, savored the taste, and lit another cigarette.

He couldn't shake his apprehension about tomorrow. He would have to convince one of the Shelbys to view the body at the morgue. He drew out his watch and stared at its face for a full minute. Tomorrow morning was going to be a complete waste of time. Then he thought about his "operative and associate," Hoolie. J.D. conjured up an image of Hoolie driving through the countryside in J.D.'s flivver, happily watching the scenery going by, without a care in the world and without the slightest regard for the minutes ticking away.

4

Hoolie

J.D. was only partially right about Hoolie Smith. It was true that Hoolie's favorite part about being an "associate and operative" in J.D.'s business was driving around the countryside. He liked seeing the sights, camping out, and meeting people. If he got the chance, he would attend some Indian "doin's," like a dance or a horse race or a hand game. The Osages, Otoes, Poncas, and Pawnees were still holding men's dances for the boys returning from the trenches in France. He had gone to one of them near Pawhuska a year before, and it had really made him feel good. One of the Osage elders had found out that Hoolie had been wounded in the war, and the old man led him around the dance grounds, speaking Osage in a loud, high-pitched voice. One of Hoolie's friends told him later that the elder was making a speech about how honored they were to have great warriors; brave warriors were back among them once again. As Hoolie drove through Osage country, he began to think about the honor the Osage elder paid him. He felt good about it because it was an acknowledgment that he had experienced things the average person never would.

Hoolie's return to his own people had made him feel good, too, but in a different way. He remembered the trip home from France. On the crossing going to Europe, time on the troopship had been taken up with calisthenics and learning about who you were going to fight and who you could trust. On the voyage back home, the most interesting thing was that you stood in line for everything. You got up, stood in line for the "head," as the sailors called the latrine, and then you got in line for breakfast. As soon as you ate, you got up, rinsed your tray, and got back in line for dinner. You got back in line again for supper.

After landing in New York, Hoolie had ridden several trains to get to Tulsa, and from there, he took a rickety bus to Tahlequah. He rode a mule-drawn wagon, and then he walked the last few miles to get to his family's home in a hollow near Peavine. It was deep in the night when he halted before the old log cabin with the big washtub hanging on the outside wall, the dog run, and the tiny front porch. The dogs barked, and his father appeared at the door in the moonlight. He called out "Who's there?" in Cherokee twice before Hoolie could adjust to the sound of the language well enough to reply. After more than two years of speaking and thinking in English, he realized he would have to practice his first language just to get the sounds right again.

A few days passed before his family arranged for an Indian doctor to hold a ceremony to purify him of the taint of killing and death. His relatives sweated him, prayed for him, gave him medicines, and took him to water. A Cherokee who had been to war could not set foot on the ceremonial grounds, according to the doctors, without having the blood washed from his hands. All of this effort was made to bring him back into the family and place him on the White Path of peace.

After he was purged of the horrors of combat and the evil of war, his male relatives gathered around him to hear firsthand about the battles he had fought and the hardships he had experienced. His people hated war but loved to hear stories of courage in battle.

Hoolie felt somewhat guilty about being so honored by both the Osages and his own relatives. By his own lights, he got his wounds purely by accident. He had learned something about internal combustion engines working on a tractor at boarding school, and when he signed up for the army, they put him to work driving and repairing the lorries that moved supplies, troops, and ammunition from the rear areas to the front. On one occasion, Hoolie drove a wire-laying party up to the trenches and was helping them unload the big spools of concertina wire when the Germans opened up a barrage in preparation for an attack. Hoolie was diving for cover when the earth erupted before him in flame and metal. Luckily, the shell hit in front of him while he was moving in the same direction. That meant that when he dove and hit the ground, most of the shrapnel, which was pitched forward with the explosion, was directed away from him. He caught a little metal in his leg and torso. Hoolie's injuries were painful and he bled profusely. But he wasn't charging the enemy, as his grandfathers had done in the old days, and so he didn't consider his wounds evidence of heroism on his part.

The Osage County countryside through which he drove was not as hilly or rocky as his own home ground. It was more prairie-like, with rolling hills, draws, and low-lying bluffs. The few farmhouses looked solid and substantial and were set out in the middle of the rangelands. They had a few trees in the front and some outbuildings, like barns, privies, and smokehouses. One or two of the houses had brush arbors set next to them, and Hoolie guessed that these were Indian homes, for no other reason than he knew of very many Indian families who had them. Mostly, the homes in this part of the country looked lonely.

Hoolie decided to make camp before dark. It would have been a fairly easy ride into Hominy, and he probably could have found a place to sleep indoors, but he felt the need to be outside on this night. There were preparations to be made. Off to his right he spotted a likely place. He pulled off the main road and took a jostling ride overland to a copse of trees along a small, meandering creek. The creek bed was lined with smooth, oblong rocks. He found a spot close by the stream and built a good fire with several of the rocks from the creek in the middle. Using the big bowie knife he carried on hunting trips, Hoolie gathered a few saplings and set up a small sweat lodge. With his bare hands, he dug out a shallow hole in the center of the lodge, where he would place the rocks once they were hot. He layered some of his blankets over the structure, took off his shirt, wrapped himself up in his last blanket, and waited for the sun to go down.

Hoolie was all alone in the middle of a big, grassy field. He heard a crow cry and looked at the trees standing by the creek. Suddenly, some men emerged from the shadows. He knew they were Osages. Each one of them topped six-and-a-half feet in height. They weren't just tall either. They had the bulk to go with their height. Broad shoulders, heavy muscle.

The Osages didn't look angry, so Hoolie simply stood there. The men encircled him, but then they changed into tall fence posts strung with barbed wire. Hoolie was still surrounded, and now, sitting on top of each post, was a woodpecker. They began pecking at the posts. The drumming noise they made grew louder and louder until he couldn't take it any longer.

He woke with a start. The misty remnants of his dream were slowly melting away like a morning fog on a hot summer day. He shook his head and tried to clear his mind. The images of his dream remained. Almost instinctively, he realized that the sun would rise within a couple of hours. He had to get in and out of the sweat before it did so.

By the light of his kerosene lantern, he filled a collapsible bucket with water and hung it on a branch of a small tree by the lodge. Hoolie then spread the coals of the fire and eased out the glowing-hot rocks with a couple of long, stout sticks. He rolled the rocks into the hole, and he dipped a cup into the bucket. Then he pulled off the rest of his clothes and crawled into the lodge. As he poured the water on the rocks, steam enveloped him.

It was to the east that he directed his first prayer: "Red Man of the East come sit with me; Red Woman of the East come sit with me." He called upon the spirits from the cardinal directions and to Uhuyah Dagwalosti—the Great Thunder, who lives in the west. He also asked for the presence of the bat and the peregrine, his two personal helpers. These spirits had seen when hardships distorted Hoolie's thinking or threatened to do harm to him, his friends, or his family. They had talked to him in his dreams, and he was sure that they had picked him up after he had been wounded on the battlefield in France.

The German shell had blown up the lorry he had been driving and killed or wounded every man in the wiring party. The barrage had been heavy in their sector, but no one came to their aid. Within a span of thirty minutes, Hoolie watched four men breathe their last. One had suffered horribly. Hoolie feared that no one would come rescue him; only those wounded who had a good chance of survival were picked up and treated. Lying there, he prayed for help, and finally, he passed out. In his dream, the bat picked up one of his shoulders; the peregrine, the other.

He awoke at a dressing station. He kept asking who had brought him in, but no one claimed to have carried him the mile or so to the medics. He never learned how he got there.

Now, he intoned the proper prayers and spilled water on the hot rocks. He breathed in the heated water vapor and felt the heat draw the sweat and impurities out from his body. He asked that the spirits help him in his quest to find the lost daughter of the white man from Pennsylvania. He explained that the girl's father was distraught and did not know how to treat his daughter or how to get her back. Hoolie's appeal ended with him saying, "help me help him."

Then, Hoolie sat as still as possible, looking in the darkness for anything that would tell him that his prayers had been heard. He saw two glowing eyes in the rock pit. They blinked once, and Hoolie felt a bit of air against his chest, as if something were breathing on him. Hoolie knew that the peregrine—the far-seeing bird of Cherokee warfare—would be there to help him see at great distances. "The Great Thunder will cast his Blue side toward the enemy. Look to the water for help."

Hoolie then heard a fluttering sound, and he knew that the bat was close by. Its tiny voice came into his ears. "I will help. My time is the night, and you'll need to know the darkness to find the lost girl. Look to the water for help."

Hoolie sat in the lodge for a long time waiting, basking in the heat, and thinking about what he had understood from the spirits. The bat was the medicine animal of the ballplayers. Although small and hairy —which meant that he was in between the creatures coated in fur and those covered with feathers—he was nimble and quick. Most importantly, the bat could help him penetrate the dark night. To Hoolie, the appearance of the bat was a welcome omen; piercing the darkness meant that a mystery would be made clear and that harmony would be restored.

The presence of the peregrine unnerved Hoolie, however. In Cherokee tradition, the bird was associated with war, and indeed, it had helped Hoolie in France. But now, when he was looking for a runaway girl, the peregrine's presence was something different. Was the peregrine trying to warn him that violence and death and hard-ship and strife were a part of this case? Was the bird trying to steel him for terrible things to come?

Hoolie took a deep breath, crawled around the rock pit, and flung wide the blanket covering the door to the lodge. As he took the fresh, cooling air into his lungs, he tried to understand what all of his visions meant.

Still in the darkness, he waded into the creek and washed himself seven times. He reached the conclusion that war was upon him. He had the strong feeling that there was much more to this case than just finding Tommy Ruffle.

He took a big drink of water, spat it out, got out of the water, and began to dry himself with one of the blankets from the lodge. It was still pretty dark, so he felt that he had time to consider things some more before he would have to greet the sun as it came over the horizon.

For Cherokees, war medicine was not something to be used lightly or for one's own gain. Hoolie shook his head in dismay at the thought. Cherokee war medicine had been brought into this country over a hundred years earlier, specifically for use against the Osages. In order to get away from the whites, some Cherokees had moved into what would become the state of Arkansas. The story went that four scouts had been sent out to find a place to set up a ceremonial grounds and town. The scouts didn't return, and so more scouts were sent out. These eventually found the original scouts' heads hanging in a tree by their long scalp locks. It was an Osage message to keep out, but following Cherokee tradition, those deaths would have to be avenged to dry the tears of the scouts' grieving widows, mothers, and children. The Osage War erupted into a nightmare of fighting and bloody retaliation, as the Cherokees came from the east to raid the Osage settlements.

Later, Cherokees would use war medicine again, during the fighting that broke out between the members of the Treaty Party—those who signed the agreement to leave the Cherokee homelands in Georgia—and the Ross Party—those who did not. Even later, during the Civil

War, one of Hoolie's relatives had made the medicine that sent off the Cherokee warriors to fight against the federal troops. When a number of Cherokees went over to the Union side, they used medicine against their brothers who had stayed with the south. After the war, Cherokee sheriffs and light horsemen used war medicine to hunt down and capture outlaws. It was said that some of the Cherokee outlaws used this medicine to escape their pursuers. Perhaps the peregrine was telling Hoolie that war medicine would come to him because he was doing the work of a Cherokee lawman. But Hoolie couldn't shake the feeling of impending misfortune.

Both spirits had told him to look to the water. He cudgeled his brains, trying to guess why the water might be important. He could think of nothing.

He looked out across the field in the murky light that came just before sunup. He had other duties to perform. Hoolie stood, got his bearings, dug his corncob pipe and tobacco out, filled the bowl, and faced the east. When the sun rose, he said a prayer of greeting, lighted the pipe, and offered tobacco smoke to the great deity that gave life to all things. Hoolie then walked over to the creek and took another long drink. He stood at the water's edge waiting for another message, sign, or omen. It would come.

In his peripheral vision, Hoolie detected a slight movement on a rock a few feet to his left. He looked more closely. It was a snapping turtle, *saligugi*, finding a place to bask in the morning sun before he went hunting for his meal. The turtle turned his head toward Hoolie, and Hoolie quickly averted his eyes. He had grown up being told that staring was rude, but normally he wouldn't have thought that you could be rude to a turtle. This was different. Hoolie expected that this was the sign both the bat and the peregrine had anticipated.

The turtle turned, facing Hoolie. The spirit of the animal didn't speak, but Hoolie felt the message. "The Thunderers have heard you. I will tell the people of this place of your duty. Terrible times are here. It is war. As in the old times, I will be a shield. You have to be a warrior in the old way. You must remember all the stories and listen to others."

The last message frightened Hoolie. He knew that to be a warrior in the old way was more than being a soldier in the ranks of an army. He also knew that his task was to be much more difficult than he or J.D. could possibly have imagined.

He gathered up everything, piled it into the flivver, cranked over the engine, and got back on the road.

5

Hominy

Hominy was not unlike most other small towns in Oklahoma. It was laid out in an almost perfect rectangle, centered on a main street. Nothing much to it. The town had a mercantile store, a grocer, a bank, a telegrapher at the train depot, a pool hall, a lumberyard, and a feed store. Most of its streets were dirt, but near the bank, they were laying red brick on the road. Pretty soon they'd have concrete sidewalks to replace the old-time wooden ones. There was a new gas station and auto-repair garage standing next to a livery stable. The blacksmith was still operating, but now he concentrated on repairing tools and shoeing draft animals.

The town jail was located at the end of the main street. Hoolie took to heart J.D.'s admonishment to contact the local authorities when conducting a case in their jurisdictions. The jailhouse would be his first stop. Under his breath, Hoolie said, "The sheriff'll be there, unless he's over at the pool hall."

In his town clothes—bright white shirt with no collar, charcoal-colored suit coat, and dark blue trousers—Hoolie looked lean and serious. His hair was cut well above his ears, and in his small, roll-brimmed fedora, it looked as if his head were shaved. When Hoolie entered the jailhouse, the constable on duty eyed him with contempt. He quickly removed his hat, revealing a full head of healthy hair parted in the middle. As Hoolie was well aware, the pressure of the hat had formed two odd-looking black arches on each side of his head. Feeling self-conscious, he lowered his eyes. The constable read Hoolie's body language as showing fear. The man moved in to take advantage and assert his authority.

"What do you want?" the constable growled.

"Good morning," replied Hoolie trying to keep his voice pleasant despite the constable's obvious surliness. "Might you be the sheriff?" The lawman's voice soured even more. "No, I ain't. What business you got with Sheriff McKinley?"

"It's kind of a private matter, sir. I'd like to get some information about Tommy Ruffle. He's an Osage boy that I think lives up 'round here somewheres."

"You ain't from around here, huh?" It was more a contemptuous statement than a real question.

Hoolie shook his head slowly.

"Is this some kinda Indin business? Or you just lookin' around? Them Ruffles lives north o' here. The sheriff won't be back for a while. You could go off up north, or you could come back when the sheriff's here."

Shaking off the attempt to get rid of him, Hoolie said, "I have business with the sheriff. I work for a detective agency in Tulsa. My boss's name is J.D. Daugherty. He sent me to look for the Ruffle boy, and I want to tell the sheriff why I'm here. My boss wants to work with the laws and make sure the sheriff knows what I'm doin' around here."

"Well, you'll have to wait."

"That's fine with me. Should I wait here?" Hoolie said, motioning to a wooden bench next to the door.

"Naw. Come back in a couple o' hours," said the constable, waving Hoolie out the door.

As he turned to go, Hoolie looked around and noticed the locked gun rack next to a doorway that he guessed led to the cells. It struck him that the type and number of weapons was a bit much for a small, sleepy town like Hominy. On the rack were two sawed-off, pump 12-gauge Remington shotguns, a bolt-action '03 Springfield, three lever-action Winchesters, and surprisingly, a big Browning automatic rifle. There were places left for two more rifles or shotguns. Hanging on nails next to the gun rack were three billy clubs and a lighter blackjack. Hoolie gulped, shook his head once more, and quickly walked out of the jailhouse.

As he stepped out into the daylight, the thought that Hominy was not going to reveal its secrets easily made Hoolie mull over new approaches to finding Tommy Ruffle and the Chichester heiress. The white lawmen were obviously keeping everything under their own hats, even things about Indians, whom they didn't seem to like very much anyway. They weren't going to help out an Indian detective.

Hoolie decided that he would make a return visit to the sheriff, but he wouldn't offer information about his case. Hoolie could see that he'd have to get his information from other Indians. That's why J.D. had hired him in the first place. His boss was convinced that Indians were clannish, to such a degree that a white detective would be useless in conducting investigations among them. He also believed that Hoolie had the intelligence and the personality to pick up information from other Indians, no matter what their tribes. Hiring Hoolie was simply smart business.

Hoolie began a slow stroll down the main street toward what he guessed was the dry goods store. The whites he passed along the way paid no attention to him. Just another Indian. He kept his eyes on the wooden sidewalk.

Glancing up, he saw a middle-aged Indian couple emerge from the general store. The man loaded the paper-wrapped bundles he carried into a big, bright-green touring car with its top down. At around six feet, he was a shade over Hoolie's height. The man rested his elbow on the driver's door and put his foot on the running board. The woman, presumably the man's wife, folded her hands in front of her and stood, straight-backed, looking at the store's doorway. It was obvious that they were waiting for someone.

Hoolie decided to approach them, but as he accelerated his step, two young Indian girls coming out of the store cut him off in mid-stride. He nearly tripped trying not to bump into them. Both caught his awkward step in their peripheral vision and came to a stop themselves. They turned, and he lifted his hat clumsily. With charming smiles, the girls acknowledged his poor attempt at gallantry. The middle-aged couple were obviously their parents. Hoolie stood rooted for a moment, his ears burning in embarrassment, and then he walked over to the group, hat in hand.

The family was speaking what Hoolie recognized to be Osage. They were probably on a shopping trip into town and discussing what they had to do next.

One of the girls glanced shyly over her shoulder at Hoolie, who was now standing a few feet away, politely waiting for the right opportunity to speak. Both the girls were dressed in white high-collar dresses and black high-top shoes. Black shawls, hooked in the crooks of their arms, draped well below their shoulders. This dress was old-fashioned compared to what was being worn in Tulsa. The girl who was still looking at Hoolie out of the corner of her eye had her hair pulled back and tied in a big, white bow. The other girl, surely her sister, had her hair in two long braids entwined with red and blue ribbons. Both, Hoolie thought, were beautiful. After a short time, the girl in braids followed her sister's eyes toward Hoolie. She raised a piece of stick candy to her lips and appraised Hoolie with a slight smile.

Hoolie took her expression as a cue to approach the family. He looked at the father first.

"Hello. Pardon, folks. I wonder if I might have a word with you?"

The man looked up from under his big wide-brimmed cowboy hat. "Sure, sonny; no need to be shy."

"Thanks," said Hoolie. He turned to the man's wife and nodded to her. Those formalities over, he looked at the girls and said a quick "Hello."

Hoolie proceeded, "I wonder if you'ins know Tommy Ruffle and could tell me where he lives?"

As soon as the words came out of his mouth, Hoolie knew that he had made a bad mistake. Being too pushy was rude, especially around Cherokees; he imagined that it must be the same with Osages. The whole family tensed. The girls dropped their eyes to the boardwalk. The father's eyes narrowed, and the mother's lips were tight.

"I know the boy," said the man with a defiant edge to his voice. "Good family. What you want with him?" It was more of a challenge than an answer to Hoolie's question. Hoolie was a stranger, asking about one of their own. He could be a murderer, a thief, or a conjuror. He had to quickly explain himself to these two wary people with the beautiful daughters. He didn't want this family to think ill of him, and he especially wanted the girl with the bow in her hair to like him.

Hoolie extended his hand to the father, "Sir, I didn't mean to be so forward. My name is Hoolie Smith. I'm a Cherokee, from over near Stilwell. My name means 'Drum' in my language. I was born in the Wolf Clan." The father shook Hoolie's hand but said nothing.

"I work for a man in Tulsa," Hoolie continued. "He finds missing people for their families. He's a good man and tries to help out people who need a lot of help." Hoolie half smiled at the idea that the white people needed a lot of help. "Last week, a white girl was visiting here in Hominy, and she met up with Tommy Ruffle. Now her family thinks she's run off with him. I don't believe he's done anything wrong, but I need to find the girl, just so her people can talk to her."

It was clear that they knew that Hoolie was talking about an elopement, but they didn't quite understand the need to send him to find the girl. Children didn't run away from home unless it was filled with hatred and strife. In such cases, kindly kin with a stable home life would always step in to raise the child. Young people sometimes ran off with each other, but they always turned up somewhere—sometimes with a new baby—usually at a sympathetic relative's home. They were most always forgiven, especially if there was a new grandbaby to spoil.

Hoolie could sense the family's train of thought: In the white world, things were different. Children were always running away from home. It must be so if a man could make a living just finding them. And if there were great numbers of runaway children, then there must be much hatred and strife among the white people. And here's this Indian working for a white man whose sole job is to chase down runaways. It didn't make much sense. The girls shifted their eyes to their father, waiting for him to say something to this outsider.

The mother spoke first, breaking the uneasy silence. "You've come quite a ways to look for this girl. Tell me about her."

Hoolie held his Fedora down to his side and put his right hand out again to the mother. The mother had barely touched his hand before she pulled her own hand back. She rubbed her hands together.

"Thank you, ma'am. Her name is Rose, and she comes up here every now and agin with a wealthy white woman from Tulsa, who collects beadwork. Last week, they were here with a scientist from back east. They visited Chief Ruffle. Tommy interprets for his grandfather when these folks come to talk to the old man about the Osage ways. While she was here, Rose and Tommy spent a lot of time together, and he gave her presents. Rose and the woman went back to Tulsa, and about five days ago, the girl went missing. So, everyone figures the two might have made plans to run off."

The father put his hand to his mouth to hide a knowing smile. The mother spoke: "There was a big meeting up there, a week or so back. It was something to do with the oil money and our land. Lots of people came and camped. The Logans held a dance out at their place for one of their boys who went to fight Kaiser Bill. He killed a bunch of them Huns but he got wounded. Did these folks from Tulsa go to the doin's?"

"They probably did if the Ruffle outfit was there."

"Well, I know that the old grandpa was there," said the father. "He made a talk about the olden times, and the boys who went to the war. He hoped that this was the last war, like Mr. Wilson in Washington City said."

Hoolie looked down at the boards beneath his feet. Looking up at the mother, he said quietly, "I got wounded in France, so I hope it's the last war, too." Expelling the memories from his mind, he went on: "I'm pretty sure that if the old chief was there, then Tommy and the girl were there, too."

The mother contemplated Hoolie seriously, and then she offered, "You know, the girl might be around Tulsa. That's a big enough place to get lost in."

"That's true, ma'am," said Hoolie. "My boss stayed in Tulsa to look around for her."

Then it was the father's turn to speak. "Mr. Hoolie," he began, "I'm Ben Lookout."

Hoolie nodded politely, acknowledging Ben's willingness to introduce himself. Ben met Hoolie's eyes and continued: "This is my wife, Lizzie, and our daughters, Martha and Myrtle."

Hoolie didn't know Martha from Myrtle, but he smiled and nodded. "Good to meet you," he said.

In a bold move, the daughter with the bow in her hair stuck out her hand. Hoolie shook it once, lightly. She said, "I'm Myrtle. Pleased to make your acquaintance, Mr. Smith." She had done better than her father in catching Hoolie's last name. The girl in braids was obviously Martha. She limply held out her hand for a quick shake, withdrawing it with lightning speed when Hoolie's hand had barely touched hers. She said nothing.

Ben Lookout spoke up. "You look like a good man who's tryin' to help out. If you want to find the Ruffles you gotta go to their old place on Gray Horse Creek. But the old man's probably up near Pawhuska right now. One of Tommy's sisters has a new baby. The grandpa'll be there. Tommy moves around some, but you're right, he's been workin' with that white man from back east, helpin' him when he talks to the people about the old days."

Hoolie took the information in and asked, "Just how do I get up to the Ruffle place or the sister's house?"

Ben gave Hoolie a series of directions that amounted to taking dirt roads north and obliquely west. There were a few landmarks thrown in. It all seemed to make sense—like finding a stand of cottonwoods near a creek, where you turn due east for about a mile, before turning back west again.

When Ben stopped, Hoolie politely smiled as if he had the directions locked inside his head. He knew generally where he was supposed to go and that was enough. Once he got to Gray Horse or Pawhuska, he'd ask for directions again.

"Thanks, folks, for your help. I guess I'll be goin' along now. I have to see the sheriff before I head up there. My boss always says that I should get ahold of the local laws, just to let 'em know what I'm up to in their territory."

At the mention of the sheriff, the tension reappeared. The girls nervously fiddled with the fringe on their shawls. The mother shifted from foot to foot, frowning, as she said, "I'd be careful around that man. We don't want to go getting Tommy into any trouble. He's a good boy. Takes care of his family and helps out all the rest of the people. Wouldn't get involved in no wrong doin'."

"I'm sure you're right, ma'am," said Hoolie. "Tommy sounds like an upstanding man. I'm just hopin' that he might know where Rose is."

Myrtle spoke up, defusing the tension. "Well, Mr. Hoolie Smith, maybe if we see you again, you'll tell us what happened with the Ruffles."

This caught Hoolie off guard. He stammered, "Oh . . . oh . . . about the case? Ahh, ahh, sure." Struggling to regain his composure, he said, "I'd be happy to do that."

Lizzie Lookout cast a cagey eye on her daughter. Myrtle was obviously flirting, and the young man was acting just as tongue-tied and shy as a smitten young man should act in such a situation.

"My daughter," Lizzie began, raising her chin in Myrtle's direction, "was educated at Haskell. She's a little bit forward. Both of them are. Tell you what, Mr. Smith, why don't you come out to our place for supper?"

Hoolie didn't expect an invitation to supper. He was torn by his need to get the job done and his wish to be around Myrtle as long as possible.

Still stammering a bit, Hoolie explained that he needed to find the Ruffles. On the other hand, he stated, he could sure use a good meal.

"Well, then, Mr. Smith, you must join us," Myrtle's mother replied.

"Ahh . . . well, thanks. I'd like that!"

"Good," said Lizzie, "you can come out behind us after we get done shoppin'. After you see Sheriff McKinley, meet us down by the feed store. You shouldn't try to get up to Gray Horse in the dark, so you can sleep tonight in our barn. That way you'll get an early start tomorrow."

"Thanks much, ma'am. That would suit me just fine."

After shaking hands all around again, Hoolie took leave of the Lookout family. He walked back to the jail. It hadn't been an hour yet, but maybe he could catch the sheriff in. He was thinking of Myrtle and her glossy black hair when he entered the jailhouse door. The sheriff himself brought Hoolie back down to earth.

A tall, lean white man with narrow eyes, a shock of dead white hair on his head and an angry boil on the side of his neck, the sheriff shook Hoolie's hand roughly and ordered him to sit on the bench beside the doorway.

"All right, chief, I'm Sheriff Herschel McKinley. I think you've been lookin' for me. That right?"

"Yes, sir," Hoolie answered quickly. "I work for a detective in Tulsa by the name of Daugherty. J.D. Daugherty. He sent me here to look for a young man named Tommy Ruffle. You see, he might know something about a missing girl we've been hired to find. That's all. I just wanted you to know that I'd be asking a few questions here in your jurisdiction."

McKinley slowly brought his hand up to his face and rubbed his cheek. He looked down once, and then brought his eyes up to look directly into Hoolie's.

"I'm glad that you came to me first. Or did you? I saw you talkin' to the Lookouts down the street."

"Well, sir, I came here first and talked to your constable. Since you weren't around, I thought I'd walk around town. I saw the family, and we got to talkin'."

The sheriff stretched his mouth into a wolfish grin. Hoolie noticed that he had large, very white teeth. "I think you wanted to get a real good look at Ben's girls, didn't you, boy?" McKinley said, "You look like a young buck lookin' for sport."

McKinley saw the anger growing on Hoolie's face. The sheriff's eyes narrowed even more.

"You better watch out though. My own sister's boy is courtin' Ben's oldest." Hoolie prayed that Myrtle was not the older daughter. McKinley paused for a moment and then said slyly, "We need a good lookin' squaw in the family, 'specially when she's gonna come into some money when Old Ben goes to them happy huntin' grounds."

The sheriff's sneer and leering eyes angered Hoolie almost beyond reason. It took all of his will power to keep his self-control. At that moment, he hoped that Ben Lookout would be told that his daughter was marrying into a truly evil family.

The sheriff read Hoolie's thoughts and reveled in his discomfort.

"Well, no matter," said the sheriff. "Whatever you talked about to the Lookouts ain't a problem. Now, what is it that you want?"

Hoolie struggled to collect himself. After two or three breaths, he said clearly and with no trace of anger in his voice, "Sir, I heard that Tommy Ruffle has an old grandpa around here, and I'd like to talk to him. I'd like to talk to Tommy himself, but if he's with the girl, I don't think he'll talk to me."

"You're probably right. If the boy ran off with this girl, he won't want to be found . . . at least, for a while. Now, who's the girl?"

J.D. constantly preached to Hoolie about the need for client confidentiality. Next to "being thorough," it was J.D.'s most important rule of thumb; if you didn't do anything else, you had to keep the client's name out of the papers. Besides that, Hoolie carried with him a very deep-seated reluctance to let anybody know his business, and he was very much against giving this mean-spirited white man with the big teeth any information at all. "I'm afraid I can't tell you, sheriff. It's a private investigation and—"

In a sinister voice, the sheriff said slowly, "You'll tell me what I want to know or I'll throw you in the can after givin' you the beatin' of your sorry life."

Hoolie hadn't expected the threat or the intimidating manner from the sheriff. He was sure that the sheriff didn't really care about the law or his jurisdiction; he merely wanted to maintain control. He probably wanted to find out if there was any money linked to the case.

Hoolie tried to explain. "Sheriff, this matter has to do with a very prominent family in Tulsa. For the girl's sake, they want this matter kept outta the papers."

McKinley's reaction was unexpectedly violent. "You tell me who the girl is, boy, or I'll stove your head in."

Hoolie's anger welled up and nearly reached the breaking point. He balled his fists and his mouth tightened into a straight, thin line. The blood had drained from the surface of his skin into the depths of his muscles. He hadn't been this ready to fight since the war. Once again, he checked himself; he had been on the verge of attacking the sheriff. And where would that have put the investigation?

"Sheriff," Hoolie said in as calm a voice as he could muster, "the matter has to do with the Shelby Oil Company. The girl's almost a relative." He didn't know how else to put it without telling McKinley that the girl was Rose Chichester.

McKinley had deliberately provoked Hoolie. He knew that he had come very close to sending the young man over the edge. That Hoolie had settled down quickly and controlled his rush of adrenalin gave the sheriff a kind of victory. But McKinley was also thinking that Hoolie's remarkable patience made him a formidable opponent. The sheriff decided to ease up. McKinley showed his white teeth again, "All right, son. That's all you needed to say. If the Shelbys want it quiet, then it's quiet."

"One thing though, chief," the sheriff continued, "I want you to stay away from a few troublemakers around here. Don't want the town in an uproar. It's for your own good. Keep shy of the bootleggers and drunks. My boys don't always separate folks when it comes to enforcing Volstead. Just keep to the right folks."

Hoolie looked at the sheriff with a sly glint in his eye. "The Lookout family all right to be around?"

The sheriff knew exactly what Hoolie was up to, but he wouldn't let himself be drawn into the paradox of telling Hoolie that he didn't want him talking to them while at the same time owning up to the fact that his nephew was going to marry one of the Lookout daughters. McKinley's mouth wearily took a downward turn while he paused to run his fingers through his stiff, white hair. He looked at Hoolie and decided to dismiss the young man without further comment.

"You can go now," he said evenly.

Hoolie lowered his eyes, turned abruptly, and walked to the door. As he opened it, he called back over his shoulder, "Thanks, sheriff."

He didn't want McKinley to see the look of triumph on his face. Hoolie knew that the sheriff didn't want him to speak to the Lookouts for some reason or another, but McKinley also didn't want to place the Lookouts in the category of "bootleggers and troublemakers" that he wanted Hoolie to avoid. Hoolie was happy because he had been able to place McKinley on the horns of a dilemma. It wasn't a great victory, but it was a victory nonetheless.

Hoolie walked out of the door into bright sunshine. He looked up and down the street and saw a brand new Lincoln hardtop parked close to the jailhouse, with "Hominy Sheriff's Department" painted on the side. He considered pulling out his knife and puncturing the tires, but he shook the notion off. McKinley was Hoolie's image of a typical small-town lawman: corrupt, bigoted, and potentially deadly. In short, McKinley fit the description of the Cherokee word *sgini*, devil.

Hoolie got in J.D.'s flivver, pulled his hat low, and thought about supper with the Lookouts. He wished he could at least change his shirt and maybe dust off his coat before meeting them again. A hunger pang stabbed him suddenly, and he realized that he hadn't eaten anything since the day before. He got out of the car, walked up the street to the general store, and bought some crackers out of a barrel, a pickle also out of a barrel, and a bottle of soda pop. He was disappointed that the Lookouts' automobile was not out front, and he looked up and down the street but saw no trace of them. He hoped that they hadn't forgotten him. He returned to J.D.'s car to sit and eat.

The small meal was satisfying, and after finishing, Hoolie leaned back and closed his eyes for a short rest. He was more fatigued than he had realized, and he quickly fell into a deep sleep.

A tapping on the door of the flivver awakened him. He pushed his hat back on his head, rubbed his eyes, and looked into the face of Myrtle Lookout. She was smiling.

"We came back to the store," she said, "but when you didn't come, we thought you ran into trouble with the sheriff."

She giggled and covered her mouth with her hand. "I'm only teasing," she said, "Mama sent us off to look for you. I thought you'd be somewhere close, so I came here." She gestured toward the jail and laughed again. "Sure enough, you're right where I thought you'd be. You can't hide from a Lookout." She giggled once more, this time showing bright, perfect teeth. Hoolie couldn't help but smile back at her.

"I'm sorry. I came back here and must've dropped off. Did you and your folks wait long?"

"No, we went to the lumberyard. Mama thought the sheriff was talking to you. I thought that you just got lost," she teased.

He was enjoying her manner and her smile. "I wouldn't get lost and miss my supper, 'specially with you."

He squirmed at his own forward way of speaking. She noticed his discomfort, "Why, Mr. Hoolie Smith, are you flirting with me?"

"No . . . no . . . ahh," he stammered.

His pained expression stopped her from teasing him anymore. She looked away shyly, "Well, get this auto started and drive me over to the store. Then you can follow us home." She paused, then she said emphatically, "Let's go, we'll be late."

Hoolie set the spark and got out to crank over the engine.

6

Tommy Ruffle

J.D. was not one who could simply wait for an appointment or let business come to him. He rose early on Saturday morning, went to a small café near his rooming house, ate a big breakfast, and caught a trolley to his office. There he began to pull files, looking for those containing newspaper stories on any of the Shelbys or the Chichesters. Of course, anything mentioning the Chichesters also had to do with the Shelbys and sometimes vice versa. Because the Shelbys were Tulsa's most prominent family, they were literally all over the papers, whether bringing in another new big well or doing philanthropic work or getting sued over mineral rights by some local farmer in cahoots with a shyster lawyer.

He wasn't looking for anything in particular. Since J.D. prided himself on being thorough, he spent an inordinate amount of time preparing for interviews. He was a detailed, exacting, and well-organized interrogator, or so he thought. When interviewing someone connected with a case, he often threw all of his well-prepared and rehearsed questions out the window, and relied instead on gut instinct. The most important thing about his detailed preparations was that it kept him busy.

The newspaper clippings were not very revealing. About the worst thing the papers said about Mrs. Shelby was that she started up a philanthropic foundation that gave money to Negro colleges. The Tulsa newspapers did not exactly favor Negro progress.

Although J.D. certainly would have liked to ask personal questions to satisfy his own curiosity, he refused to do so out of a sense of propriety. It would be unseemly to ask about how she and Big Bill met or where she came from. It was also irrelevant to the investigation.

J.D. pushed the files and his list of questions to the side and pulled out his watch. He sat for a few seconds estimating the time it would take to do one simple task and still be back before Chichester's car arrived to take him to the Shelby residence. He shoved his watch back into his vest pocket, rose, grabbed his boater, and set out to find Danny Ryan.

J.D. found Danny loitering a few steps from North's lunch counter. It was obvious that with the money he earned from yesterday's errands, Danny had visited the haberdasher. He had a new cap, a new white shirt without a collar, and a brown vest with yellow embroidery. What topped it all off and made Danny look like one of the local young toughs was a pair of bright red sleeve garters. His black, ankle-high shoes were shined to brilliant perfection.

"Hiya, Danny-boy, how's business?" said J.D. as he sidled up to him.

The boy nonchalantly flicked a cigarette butt across the sidewalk into the gutter.

"Fine, J.D., couldn't be better."

"You doin' anything right now?"

"Just waitin' for a guy. He's got some money he owes me."

"Well, I'd like for you to run an errand for me. But I need quick results. You'll have to get back to my office before one."

"Depends on what you need done, J.D."

"This should be easy. You told me yesterday that you didn't get to talk to your pal down at Yang Foo's, right?"

"Right."

"Okay, here's what I want you to do. Go down and talk to the boy. Find out who Little Bill Shelby is seeing in Little Africa. Let me know before one and you'll get a bonus. Got it?"

"Hey, J.D., I can get there and back in five."

"How about half an hour? Get back to my office by one. And don't forget to get names."

"Gotcha, J.D. Do me a favor and leave word with Ed for my friend to meet me some other time."

"I'll tip old Ed. See you, kid."

J.D. stopped in to give Ed Danny's message, smoked a cigarette with him, and went back to his office.

He sat behind his desk but couldn't concentrate on his list of questions for the Shelbys. His mind was preoccupied with two thoughts. The first was how to get one of the Shelbys down to the morgue to take a look at the body of the Indian. Asking one of the most prominent socialites in Tulsa to visit the corpse cooler was like asking the king of England to clean out a barn. Maybe even worse. The king was used to being around horses. Mrs. Shelby, J.D. thought sardonically, probably hadn't spent much time with cadavers.

The second thought was about the information Danny might come up with. J.D. pondered what he would do if Little Bill was indeed a regular with one of the black girls uptown. The Shelby kids were out for the good times and could have pulled Rose into something shady or inadvertently introduced her to a criminal element.

J.D. knuckled his moustache for the fiftieth time since he sat down behind his desk. The possibility of the younger Shelbys introducing Rose Chichester to the underside of Tulsa was just one angle. Maybe the information that J.D. knew Danny would bring him would be useful; maybe not. But he had to cover all the bases.

Danny's soft knock signaled his arrival. "Come in," said J.D.

As usual Danny entered, sat in the client's chair, and lit a cigarette. This time it was a pre-rolled, packaged one.

"I've got some real news, J.D. The girl you wanted to know about lives on Greenwood. Right nice digs, too. Her name's Minerva Whitwell. She used to work for the Shelbys. Her mama was an old-time servant for 'em and lived in. She musta squirreled some money away, 'cause right after she passed on, Minerva quit. Or maybe she got fired by the Shelbys. Nobody knows where she got the dough to buy that house. She's just a few doors down from the undertaker, and you know he's in the money. She moved in about two years ago. Got a kid, too."

"Little Bill's seeing a girl with a kid?"

"Looks like it, yeah."

"Is this straight?"

"As a string, J.D. I got it from Teddy, the doorman at Yang Foo's."

"Is he the boy old Yang dresses up in the Arabian Nights costume?"

"That's him. He says he looks like a fool in that turban and them upturned, pointy-toed shoes. But he makes good dough and knows just about everybody in town. Knows everything that goes on around Greenwood. Says that Minnie—that's what he calls her—has got a kid. He don't know who the daddy is, but the kid is pretty light-skinned. She takes the baby out to stroll and to church, but don't go out much else. She don't work for nobody as far as Teddy knows. She ain't no whore either. Teddy's word is jake all the way, too."

"She's got money, huh?"

"Yep, Teddy says she don't hurt for nothin'. Says she dresses fine and keeps herself lookin' real good."

J.D. was silent. He rubbed the right side of his jaw as if he had a toothache. This operation could get more and more complicated. Another thought struck him, and he narrowed his eyes. Danny was somewhat taken aback; it looked like J.D. was getting angry.

"That's all I got, J.D.," said Danny timidly.

J.D. looked directly at the boy and made his voice sound reassuring. "I know, Danny, you did good. There's somethin' else . . ." J.D. drifted off for a moment in his own thoughts, and then he asked, "Danny, do you think that this Minerva's mama could've saved that much money?"

Danny breathed a relieved sigh, "Hard to say. Probably not. Maybe the Shelbys paid her better. But from what's said on the corner, old man Shelby is a tightwad. So's Mrs. Shelby 'cept when she's layin' out cash to her charities. Teddy says that Little Bill visits Minerva three or four times a week, sometimes every day. Teddy thinks that since Minnie's mama pretty much raised Little Bill, he feels close to Minnie. Kinda like brother and sister, 'cept one's white and one's black."

"You think Minerva's getting money from Little Bill?"

"Looks like it, doesn't it? Now that you say that, I did get a feelin' that Teddy thought so, too."

"Does this Teddy think that Little Bill and Minerva . . . ?"

"Naw, he thinks Little Bill's kinda funny. Know what I mean?"

J.D. leaned back in his chair, smiled, and pulled out his wallet. He counted out five ones and pushed them toward Danny. "Payday again, boy-o. Did you give something to this Teddy?"

"Sure did. Tipped him real good."

J.D. laughed. "You're learnin', boy-o, you're learnin.'"

The same big chauffeur who had brought Chichester the day before arrived precisely at one-thirty. This time he introduced himself as "Riley, the Shelbys' driver," as if the Shelby glory somehow rubbed off on him. J.D. came close to asking Riley from what county in Ireland he hailed, but he decided against it. They descended the staircase together, and Riley opened the automobile door for J.D.

The Shelbys lived near the Arkansas River, almost directly south of the center of the city. It seemed like all the rich folks lived out that way. They didn't live in houses either. They owned estates.

As soon as Riley pulled up to the front of the Shelby estate, an elderly black man in a short, red jacket jumped from a chair and swung open a huge iron gate. Riley motored through, drove up a long, looping driveway, and came to a stop in front of a columned "main house," which looked just like the southern mansions in the moving pictures.

Another black man, this time in a black coat, opened the massive front door before J.D. could touch the big, brass door knocker. The man took J.D.'s hat and immediately disappeared. Another man appeared, also wearing a black coat but with a white carnation boutonniere in its lapel. He explained to J.D. that the Shelbys and Mr. Chichester were awaiting him in the sitting room. The man turned quickly and walked away. J.D. followed.

The journey to the sitting room was short but impressive. The butler led J.D. through a large central hall that contained nothing but an enormous Ming vase and a few portraits of stern-looking Shelby men. J.D. guessed that most of the portraits were probably fakes. The Shelbys hadn't been rich long enough to have relatives wearing wigs with long curls. More paintings lined the corridor that brought them to the sitting room.

The butler opened the double doors, stood aside as J.D. entered, and said, "A Mr. Daugherty, sir." With a quick bow to the room, the butler turned and retired though the double doors, closing them as he went. J.D. felt like he was visiting royalty.

Big Bill Shelby was standing in the center of the room on a magnificent Persian carpet that looked like it was three inches thick. He was over six feet tall and had exceptionally large hands. He had one thumb hooked in a vest pocket. In the middle of his silk tie, he sported a diamond stickpin the size of a doorknob. Little Bill was standing next to his father in a white tennis outfit. The creases in Little Bill's trousers looked as if they could have sliced through a large steak. Chichester, sitting on a straight-backed chair that looked like a fifteenth-century torture device, rose and walked toward J.D., his right hand extended.

J.D. shook the hand, "Glad to see you again, sir."

Chichester nodded and turned to introduce the women first. Mrs. Shelby and her daughter were sitting on a large leather divan. Rose Shelby wore her hair in a slightly old-fashioned pile on top of her head. Her dress was a light blue silk affair that revealed about five inches of leg above the ankle. Her daughter's dress was also silk, but in a darker blue, and even shorter in length than her mother's. Elizabeth's hair was cut in the latest French style, which was, by J.D.'s estimation, much too short for a woman. Mrs. Shelby smiled brightly as she was introduced; Elizabeth simply looked bored.

Big Bill pumped J.D.'s hand several times and produced the fattest cigar J.D. had ever seen; it looked something like an elongated, dark brown beer keg. Big Bill motioned J.D. into an overstuffed leather chair that matched the divan. J.D. sat and clipped off the tip of the cigar with his penknife. Big Bill extracted a gold pocket lighter from his vest, leaned over, and lighted J.D.'s cigar. A costumed maid appeared and asked if anyone wanted coffee, lemonade, or iced tea. J.D. asked for coffee.

Because it was more or less his show, J.D. blew out a big puff of white smoke and said evenly, "As you all know, Mr. Chichester has contracted me to locate his daughter. Since you assume that she is with Tommy Ruffle, I've sent one of my operatives, Mr. Hoolie Smith, to

Osage County to see if he can find Miss Chichester or Tommy. I asked for this meeting so that I can ask you a few questions about the trip Rose and Mrs. Shelby made to Osage County before the girl disappeared."

J.D. paused and looked directly at Rose and Elizabeth Shelby. Rose lowered her eyes demurely; Elizabeth rolled hers upward in an obvious gesture of annoyance. J.D., undeterred, asked, "Mrs. Shelby, why didn't you suspect something at the time? Didn't Rose and Ruffle give any sign that they might be plotting an elopement?"

Looking somewhat perplexed, she answered, "I didn't suspect anything at the time. I suppose I was preoccupied with helping Mr. Potter, an ethnologist interested in the Osage tribe, who was trying to get to know some of the people better. My contacts among the Osages aid Mr. Potter in his researches."

"And why would you have contacts among the Osages?"

She pursed her lips in thought and replied, "I am dear friends with a mixed-blood Osage family, the Tinkers, who have encouraged my interest in building a museum here in Tulsa dedicated to preserving the arts and crafts of the Indians who first lived in our great state. I have also become close with Chief Ruffle. He treats me as a daughter, and I am deeply honored by this. It is through Chief Ruffle that the Osages have come to know me, and I am dedicated to preserving their history."

J.D. nodded and continued his interrogation. "And did you stay with Chief Ruffle's family during your recent visit?"

"When we travel to Osage County, we always stay at the boarding house of Mrs. Jedediah Henderson in Hominy. She is a widow, and her brother is the town sheriff. Her son, Peter, is engaged to be married to an Osage girl. The boy is studying law under Judge C. Edward Patterson. Judge Patterson is a widely respected jurist with a family connection to the Hendersons."

J.D. knuckled his moustache and casually regarded the cigar he held. This time he looked at Big Bill but continued to address Mrs. Shelby. "Ma'am," he said, "could you please run through your trip to Hominy with Rose and your daughter?"

"Certainly, Mr. Daugherty. We motored up on a Tuesday and went to Mrs. Henderson's to put our baggage in our room and then we—Rose and I . . . Elizabeth usually stays with Mrs. Henderson or does some horseback riding or visits the town—drove to visit Chief Ruffle. He's Tommy's grandfather, a very sweet old man despite his rather gruesome and savage past. Mr. Potter, Rose, and I talked with Chief Ruffle for a long time, and Tommy helped interpret as needed."

She stopped, cocked her head toward her husband, folded her hands, and continued: "Mr. Potter has learned a great deal from Chief Ruffle. The chief has learned to tell his stories into the mouthpiece of Mr. Potter's Edison recording machine. He tells them in Osage, and Tommy translates them into English for Mr. Potter. Sadly, the Osages are a vanishing race. These recordings will someday be all that's left of this proud and noble people."

Big Bill evidently couldn't stand being left out of the dialogue, "I might add that Mr. Potter's phonograph cost me a good bit of money, along with my wife's trips and all. Such is my wife's interest in preserving our American heritage."

"Oh, do be quiet, dear," Mrs. Shelby shot back. "Your money is being well spent, and it's not as if we can't afford it." Big Bill stretched his mouth into a benevolent and patronizing smile and said nothing further.

Rose continued, "Rose and Tommy took a walk. Perhaps I should have accompanied them as a chaperone, but I really didn't think of it at the time."

J.D. asked, "How did they act toward each other, Mrs. Shelby?"

"How do you mean, Mr. Daugherty?"

J.D. searched for the words. "Were they, er, flirtatious, or did they in any way act like lovers?"

"Well, they certainly weren't 'moony-eyed,' as the popular expression goes. And they didn't behave in any way improperly. They were simply quite friendly."

"Anything else?"

"There was an Osage celebration that afternoon and evening. Something to do with oil leases. The chief invited us to attend so that we could hear the traditional songs. We all decided that it would be a very good opportunity to enjoy a real Osage dance. There were several bonfires around the grounds, and Tommy and Rose sat together by one of them.

"Around nine that evening, we returned to the boarding house, but Mr. Potter stayed at the dance grounds to talk with several elderly Osages, and Tommy stayed with him to translate. As Rose and I were preparing for bed, she showed me a shawl Tommy had given her early that evening. It had some beautiful ribbon work appliqué on it. The Osage ladies are especially good at ribbon work. She asked me if I thought Tommy was a nice boy. I said that I thought he was extremely bright. After all, Tommy handles all of Chief Ruffle's money and has invested it very wisely. Mr. Potter and I testified at Tommy's competency hearing, and a judge ruled in his favor. Tommy is now fully qualified by law to handle his family's affairs. That may be upsetting to a few lawyers, but I'm afraid that's just too bad. I might add that he helps other Osage families handle their finances, too. Under his management his family has prospered. I dare say he is a true genius of his race."

"Where was Miss Shelby?" J.D. interjected.

"Oh, I was—" Elizabeth began.

Mrs. Shelby finished, "Elizabeth was visiting friends in Hominy. I think Peter Henderson drove her, isn't that right, dear?"

"Uh-huh," she replied, nodding in the affirmative.

"Please continue about Rose and Tommy," prompted J.D.

"She asked me about Tommy in a matter-of-fact manner. There was nothing to indicate she was considering him as a future husband. Since I've been so impressed with Tommy's business skill and intelligence, I suppose I went on a bit about him. Tommy has demonstrated that some Indians can handle their own affairs and, as a result, he is a constant thorn in the side of the Indian Office officials who—if you ask me—are out to cheat the Osage. He may become a thorn in my husband's side as well. Tommy negotiates the oil leases for his family in spite of the misgivings of the Indian Office. I think my husband is going to have a worthy negotiator in Tommy the next time they do business together."

Mr. Shelby commented, "I like to do business with someone as smart as Tommy. It's much better than dealing with those fools at the Indian agencies. Usually our lawyers deal with them. I'll sit down at the table myself to do business with Tommy."

"You are absolutely right, dear," said Rose Shelby. "We have added to the Indian's plight by giving him over to an uncaring government agency to be manipulated. We must remove this yoke from the Indian's neck. He must be set free so that he can become truly civilized and take his rightful place in our great country."

J.D. didn't want to hear a lecture about the plight of the Red Man. It was obvious that Mrs. Shelby was a passionate supporter of Indian causes. As she spoke, her husband moved beside her and rested his right hand on her shoulder. At least he acted the supportive husband. The others said nothing, and Chichester looked as bored as Elizabeth. Little Bill gazed off in quiet obliviousness. It was a litany they'd heard before.

"I'm sorry, Mr. Daugherty, I digress." She paused once more with her hand against her forehead in deep thought. "Oh, yes. There's not much else. I heard what sounded like hail against the windowpane in the middle of the night. I awoke, saw that there wasn't a storm going on and realized it's a bit early in the year for those kinds of storms. But I noticed that Rose was out of bed. Elizabeth was fast asleep, so I sat up waiting. In a bit, Rose came back and said that she had gone to use the lavatory. Mrs. Henderson does not have indoor plumbing."

J.D. thanked Mrs. Shelby. Looking around the room, he saw that everyone was looking at him, waiting for the next move. It was time to air the family's dirty linen.

J.D. directed his gaze at Elizabeth. "Miss Shelby," he began in a low voice, "when Rose is in town, do you frequent the speakeasies together? The dance hall in Little Africa?"

Big Bill left his wife's side and strode to the middle of the room. "Hold on there, Daugherty! I don't know where you're going with this, but you are impugning the character of my daughter. She doesn't go to those places. How dare you?"

Chichester chimed in, "Daugherty, you go too far. What right do you have—" He stopped in mid-sentence as J.D. raised his hand.

"To say these things?" J.D. finished Chichester's sentence. "I know that William Jr. here and his sister do like to live it up in the shadier parts of town. Mr. Chichester, if your daughter frequents those places with the Shelby children, I have to know about it. There might be a chance that Rose has been caught up in something, something dangerous."

J.D. turned back to the brother and sister. "Now, I'll ask you again. Does Rose go with either of you on your nights on the town?"

Both shook their heads. With a tone in his voice that indicated Rose was something of a "goody-two-shoes," Little Bill said, "She doesn't go anywhere we go. She sticks around here or maybe goes to the cinema or concerts with Mother."

"That's right," said Elizabeth in the same tone. "She's too prim and proper to go anywhere with us."

Chichester interrupted, "This is getting us nowhere, Daugherty. I want my daughter found."

"Mr. Chichester," said J.D., "you're right. We're not getting anywhere. So, I'd like to put a halt to this and speak to William Jr. and Mrs. Shelby privately."

"Is this necessary?" asked Big Bill.

"Yes, it is. I can't ask questions of anyone when somebody is always putting in their two cents' worth."

Rose Shelby's eyes narrowed, and she blushed a bit. Finally, she smiled slightly, "If Mr. Daugherty is adamant, I shan't object."

J.D. looked directly at Big Bill as if to challenge him, then he turned toward Little Bill, who shifted uncomfortably before nodding his consent.

"Thank you all very much," said J.D. confidently. "I'd like to begin with Mrs. Shelby." J.D. looked at Little Bill. "Mr. Shelby, please stay close, I'll talk to you next."

Everyone but Rose Shelby followed Big Bill out of the sitting room.

J.D., standing now as they exited, half-bowed to Mrs. Shelby before parking himself on the arm of the divan where she sat. He had long ago learned that having a bit of height during an interview established the interrogator's control. "Mrs. Shelby," he began, "you raised no objection when I asked your son and daughter about frequenting the speakeasies and dance halls in this town. Did you know about them running around like that?"

She shuddered visibly. "Yes, Mr. Daugherty, I'm aware of what my children do and where they go. My husband was not surprised either. However, by asking about their habits, he thought you were questioning the family honor."

"Does it cost a lot to cover up their shenanigans?"

Her downcast eyes told more than what she said, "A good amount, yes."

"I'm sorry to have to ask you these questions, but I'm looking for another connection to Miss Chichester's disappearance besides the possibility of Tommy Ruffle. That's why I asked to talk to you alone. I have a sad and disturbing request of you, but it's important."

"What is it, Mr. Daugherty?"

"Yesterday, I was told that a young Indian was lying dead in the county morgue. Often in the detective business we use our intuition—"

Looking somewhat distracted, Mrs. Shelby interrupted, "According to Conan-Doyle, Sherlock Holmes relies on cold calculation and logic rather than intuition."

J.D. nodded and replied quietly, "I'm not Sherlock Holmes, ma'am. And he's a product of the imagination. I take everything into consideration, even my intuition. And I have a strong Irish feeling about the body in the morgue." J.D. stopped and sucked in his lips; his moustache drooped to his chin.

"I want to ask if you, or someone else who knows Tommy Ruffle, would go to the morgue with me today."

Rose Shelby gasped audibly, "You think it's Tommy?"

"I can't say for sure, ma'am. If it is, then we'll have to go back and rethink the whole case. If it isn't, then we go on the same as we've been doing. Whatever the case, I have to know who's lying on that slab downtown."

Tears began to well up in her eyes, but J.D. also saw in them a steely hardness. "It just can't be," she said. "It can't be."

J.D. didn't expect this kind of reaction. Ruffle might have been a good friend, but Mrs. Shelby's reaction to the remote possibility of his death was as if the boy was a close relative. Not only that, but she looked as if she was already planning something, whether revenge, her part in the mourning, or her wardrobe and comportment J.D. couldn't guess.

"I hope that it's not, Mrs. Shelby," J.D. spoke softly.

"I pray it's not. He's such a beautiful and brilliant young man."

After a few more tears and minutes, Mrs. Shelby looked up, "I'll go, of course. I'll tell the butler to summon a car."

"I still have one more question, Mrs. Shelby."

"Yes."

"Did Rose run around with your son or daughter?"

"That again?"

"I'm afraid so. I have to know."

"Well, the answer is no. Rose spent most of her time here with me. I have always assumed that her quiet personality is due to her mother's early death. I knew her mother well and grieved for her for the longest time. She was very dear to me, and I promised myself that I would try to be a second mother to Rose. Unfortunately, we live across the country from each other. Still, Rose and I are very close, and I am a great deal more upset about her disappearance than I can afford to let on."

"Why is that, Mrs. Shelby?"

"To be frank, Mr. Daugherty, I am very angry with my own children's wild behavior. Your pardon, Mr. Daugherty, but I come from New England stock and believe in the virtues of hard work and benevolence. I also agree with Mr. Andrew Carnegie that we are the stewards of wealth—not its owners—and have an obligation through philanthropy to uplift the lives of our fellow human beings. Rose, unlike my son and daughter, feels genuine sympathy for the downtrodden and helpless. She is dedicated to bringing culture and learning to this unsophisticated boomtown.

"So, I hope you can understand this: I fear that I will only drive my children further from me if I show how distraught I am over Rose's disappearance. Perhaps through patience and example, I will be able to lead Elizabeth into doing her civic and moral duty, and that one day, my son will become a business and social leader in his own right."

J.D. didn't really want to hear about the Shelbys' civic duty or moral leadership. In his mind, Rose Shelby's charitable works and her digressions on the stewardship of wealth and the plight of the downtrodden were rationales for acquiring wealth at the expense of others. His father had worked himself into an early grave in Chicago's meat-packing industry. J.D., although he worked for the wealthy, never forgot his working-class origins or his parents' immigrant background. Nevertheless, he nodded his head in agreement, smiled admiringly, and shepherded Rose Shelby out the door of the sitting room. Thanking her profusely, he asked, "Would you please send in your son?"

Over her shoulder, Rose said, "I'll wait for you to finish, and then we'll go to the morgue."

Little Bill walked heavily into the room and fell into the divan. His face was drawn and sullen.

J.D. opened with, "All right, William—"

"It's Bill," interrupted the Shelby scion.

"Okay. Now, Bill, who's Minerva Whitwell?"

Half an hour later, J.D., Rose Shelby, and E.L. Chichester were motoring downtown in one of the Shelby cars. J.D. rode in silence. He was still trying to get a grip on what he had learned from Little Bill.

Little Bill was the father of Minnie Whitwell's child. Big Bill had reached an arrangement with her to stop working and care for the baby. Little Bill visited Minnie when he could get away from his full social schedule.

"You have to understand," Little Bill had told J.D., "I love Minnie, and she loves me; but we can't marry. It would not be accepted. I'll take care of my son. They'll never have to worry about a thing. It's the only thing we can do."

J.D. had asked him about the possibility of Minnie being involved in a kidnap ring or perhaps attempting blackmail.

"Do you always make these kinds of accusations?" said Little Bill in reply. "Is that the nature of your dirty little business?"

At that, J.D. had decided to let the boy off the hook, but he would still have to interview Minnie. That would clear up some things. Little Bill had hinted that his mother and E.L. were pressuring him to get involved with Rose Chichester. Little Bill's possible marriage to Rose Chichester could have motivated Minnie into doing something . . . perhaps arranging a kidnapping or even murder. Minnie would have a great deal to lose if Little Bill suddenly deserted her and the baby. J.D.'s thoughts were becoming so sordid that he sat in the Shelby limousine quietly shaking his head in disgust.

Rose Shelby was quiet, too. J.D. could see on her face that she was praying that the body in the morgue wasn't the Ruffle boy. Chichester acted as if they were on a leisurely drive to some bothersome but necessary social function.

"Is there something wrong, Mr. Daugherty?" inquired Chichester.

"No, just thinking over a few things." J.D. looked up. "Here we are."

Before they left the Shelby mansion, J.D. had called the assistant coroner, Irvin Chiles, to let him know that none other than Rose Shelby was coming to look at a body in Chiles' keeping. J.D. had known Chiles before the latter had been sacked from the city police force because he had something on a couple of captains and the police commissioner. Within three days of leaving the force, he had been appointed Assistant Coroner, thus staying on the city payroll and earning some credit with city officials for keeping his mouth shut.

The coroner's office had rolled out the red carpet for them. Chiles and the coroner himself, one Mr. Bennett McAfee, were waiting for the car in front of the morgue. As it rolled to a stop, Chiles opened the door with a flourish. McAfee greeted each of them with a handshake and a mortician's solemn frown. He looked directly into Rose Shelby's blue eyes. "Mrs. Shelby, we are sorry to put you to all this trouble, but an effort must be made to identify the unfortunate victims of crime in our city."

Mrs. Shelby put on a brief smile and looked with trepidation at the door of the building. Chichester removed his hat and took her elbow. J.D. followed, smirking behind the backs of McAfee and Chiles, knowing that they had made absolutely no effort to discover the identity of the dead Indian in their charge.

They followed the two men's brilliant white laboratory coats into a room about the size of a large closet. J.D. guessed that this was a special viewing room, designed to mask the face of death and spruce up the morgue to the level of a funeral home. The room had four chairs, a carpeted floor and subdued green wallpaper. A heavy curtain covered what J.D. supposed was a window.

Whenever J.D. went to see the morgue's charges, he was always taken back to the iceboxes. The place smelled badly, and the naked bodies were covered with nothing more than rubber sheets. The morgue was and would remain a gruesome place despite efforts to hide the horrors.

Before he parted the curtains, McAfee delivered a speech on the diligence with which his office conducted investigations and the dignity with which they treated every corpse that passed through the morgue. J.D. suspected that he was already running for office again and was attempting to woo the Shelbys' support. It was a relief that Chichester interrupted him and demanded that he show the body.

McAfee opened the curtains with a flourish equaling that of Chiles' door-opening gesture. Behind the window was a hospital gurney. Lying on the gurney with a sheet pulled up under the chin was the body of a young man with short, black hair. J.D. could barely make out the big, ugly stitches that closed the long slash mark across the man's neck. The face had a sort of grayish-yellow tinge that often made it difficult to identify even close relatives.

Rose Shelby stood and looked at the face for a full three minutes. It was as if she were mesmerized—she didn't want to look at the face, but she couldn't look away either. Tears spilled down her cheeks.

Like a vaudeville magician, Chichester instantly produced an un-soiled handkerchief, seemingly from out of nowhere. Rose began to shake her head in denial. At first, J.D. thought that she didn't recognize the body and that his intuition had failed him.

Then, she finally said, "That's Tommy Ruffle," and she began to sob uncontrollably. "Dear God, he was such a wonderful boy."

Almost as soon as she uttered these words, McAfee closed the curtains. The room was nearly dark now. Chichester ministered to the weeping Rose Shelby.

After a few moments, Chichester turned and whispered to J.D., "Daugherty, if that's Tommy Ruffle, where's my daughter?"

"We should talk about this outside," answered J.D. quietly.

After they put Mrs. Shelby in the car, Chichester led J.D. about ten feet away from the vehicle.

"What exactly does this development mean, Daugherty?"

Very slowly, J.D. brushed his moustache, and then he said, "I believe we should concentrate our investigation in the city and per-haps look into the idea that your daughter was kidnapped. We may need to consider bringing the police into the case."

"Oh, God," was all that Chichester could get out.

"Mr. Chichester, calm yourself. Kidnapping is only one possibility, since it is likely that the perpetrators would have contacted you for ransom by now. Rose may be with someone else, hiding somewhere here in Tulsa. Maybe she met someone through Elizabeth or Little Bill. I just don't know."

Chichester looked whipped. "Mr. Daugherty," he said, "I am des-perate." He took another, deeper breath, "Now there has been a kill-ing. I'm frightened. I can't come to this place again to look at—" Chichester's voice trailed off. He stood looking at the sidewalk, his arms folded.

"Mr. Chichester, I'll find your daughter . . . alive." J.D. led the shaken man back to the car and said his goodbyes. Mrs. Shelby offered to drive him to his flat or his office, but J.D. declined. As he watched the big automobile drive off, he began to rethink everything. He was becoming obsessed with interviewing Minnie Whitwell, just as he had become obsessed with finding the identity of the Indian in the morgue. Where the hell was Rose Chichester?

His thoughts turned to Hoolie. The Ruffle lead had played out. He needed Hoolie back in Tulsa now. But J.D. paused again to let a new thought take root. Why the hell was Tommy Ruffle dead in Tulsa County? Why not in Osage territory where he belonged? Maybe it was better to have Hoolie stay put. He couldn't get into much trouble in a backwater place like Hominy, Oklahoma.

7
Ben Lookout

Hoolie tasted the dust kicked up by the Lookouts' big Buick touring car as it bounced along the old wagon road in front of him. Watershed- and wheel-cut ruts made the going even more difficult. J.D.'s old Model T probably shouldn't have been driven over this type of road in the first place. The springs were just about sprung, and the tires looked like they could blow anytime. Not only that, but the flivver was beginning to overheat because they were going up some steep inclines.

Ahead he saw a large clapboard house built on a knoll. In the flat landscape of Osage County, that gentle slope rising out of the rolling prairie constituted a hill. He hoped that it was the Lookouts', so that he could finally let the Model T rest. For some reason he suspected that Indian homes were always built on hills. Hoolie reasoned that all Indians preferred high places because you were much nearer to the creator. Being on a hilltop also gave folks the advantage of seeing who's coming.

As they drew closer to the house, Hoolie began to realize just how substantial the Lookout place was and that they were wealthy beyond his understanding. The house was a big, two-story, white building with a roofed porch that ran across the front. A little ways down the slope stood an enormous white barn and several outbuildings, including a smokehouse, a brooder house, and three water troughs. Hoolie saw a corral with seven sleek ponies milling around. The barn, where he was supposed to spend the night, looked like it could hold a dozen mules or milk cows and enough hay for several winters.

The Lookouts pulled their Buick up close to the porch. Hoolie stopped behind them. Chickens, ducks, and guinea fowl populated the front yard. Two geese strutted around honking and trying to intimidate the rest of the feathered residents. There was a large arbor built near the side of the house. In its shade were some chairs, a big cast-iron cooking pot, and three sleeping dogs that didn't even bother to lift their heads when the two automobiles rumbled into the yard.

Another dog was standing next to a hand-pumped well, trying to catch a few drops of water leaking from the spout. Downslope, about two hundred yards off, was a tree-lined creek. Hoolie thought it was extravagant to have a well with a hand pump when a clear-water brook flowed so close by.

Hoolie went over to the Lookouts' Buick and began to help unload. He carried some flour past an elderly woman standing in the doorway. Since his hands were full, Hoolie dipped his head in acknowledgment of her age and presence. On Hoolie's third trip, Ben made him put down the sacks of sugar and beans. The tall Osage man looked at Hoolie thoughtfully, "My mother says you're here to help us . . . that you were sent. She said an ol' snappin' turtle told her." This confused Hoolie for a moment, but then he remembered the snapping turtle he had seen early that morning. He rubbed his chin, "I hope she don't think I'm a *sgili*."

"A what?" exclaimed Ben.

"A conjurer . . . a witch. An evil person with the power to do bad things."

"Oh, no! She says you're gonna help us out in some way. Says you're a warrior . . . in the old ways."

"I was in France."

"My mother says you carry wounds. But she means that you're gonna act like an old-time warrior. You'll protect us and make things right again."

The elderly woman and Myrtle had stopped on the porch steps and were staring at the two men in conversation. Ben turned and introduced Hoolie to his mother. Her name was Lily, but Hoolie knew she probably went by an Osage name, at least among the Osage people. After all, she had been born before the white people's names were introduced. She said something in Osage to her granddaughter. Myrtle responded by looking at Hoolie.

"Grandma speaks good English, but acts old-timey when company comes," said Myrtle.

She was teasing her grandmother. The old woman smiled and reached over to give her granddaughter a little slap on the rump for speaking out of turn. Myrtle giggled and ran away. The grandmother shook her head in mock disgust. Turning to her son, she made a long speech in Osage.

After listening carefully, Ben again looked at Hoolie and explained that his mother wanted him to tell Hoolie exactly what happened to her that morning. Lily Lookout had gone to the creek to say prayers and fetch some flowing water to drink. Ben's mother preferred the water from the creek because that was where she drank as a child and because she considered well water stagnant. A snapping turtle had foretold Hoolie's coming. Ben looked at Hoolie and said very seriously, "I don't know how your people take these kinds of signs, but Osages take 'em serious. Now, my mother says that you're a warrior, and we take that serious, too. So, you can stay here all you want, and we'll help you find Tommy and this girl you're lookin' for."

Hoolie nodded his thanks and dropped his eyes. His own upbringing had made him aware of the occurrence of mysteries and that he should treat medicine with reverence and awe. He had himself experienced a number of truly extraordinary and otherworldly events. Sometimes though, his penchant for mechanics and practical problem solving led to his questioning his own beliefs. He was torn now, because that very morning a snapping turtle had somehow communicated to Hoolie that he would act the warrior at some point during this case. That a snapping turtle would have talked to an old woman about the very same thing made him skeptical. Instead of one snapping turtle passing along a message, Hoolie pictured an intricate snapping turtle telegraph system that kept tabs on where he was at all times. The thought both amused and confused him.

Ben caught the look on Hoolie's face. "You don't believe in that sort of thing, do you?" he asked.

Hoolie looked up and said with sincerity, "Yes, sir, I do. But it scares me, too."

Ben was sympathetic. "Those things'll scare anybody 'cept maybe for the medicine men. And I've seen them get scared of what they see, too."

"Mr. Lookout," said Hoolie confidentially, "I saw and heard a snappin' turtle say the same thing to me this mornin'. I just hoped that somebody or something would tell me what was gonna happen to turn me into what the snappin' turtle said. I don't know what I'm supposed to do."

Ben shook his head thoughtfully. "Looks like nobody really knows what's gonna happen. I guess you gotta be ready though."

Hoolie took a deep breath. "I think you're right."

They finished putting away the goods from the day's shopping trip. The women began to bustle about preparing things for the evening meal. Ben went to take care of the livestock. That left Hoolie with nothing to do. He went to the Model T and took out a bag of tobacco. He stood and prayed, throwing some of the tobacco as an offering to the spirits of the place.

The day's portents made him uneasy. It was almost like going to the front again. He was excited at the prospect of fighting a good fight, yet fearful of what might happen to him. Like all soldiers, he thought that if fighting was inevitable, you might as well get it over with as soon as possible. He was walking back to the porch when a plume of dust caught his eye. He looked down the road and saw a big, yellow Packard motoring his way. A Packard was one of the best-built, heaviest automobiles around.

The Packard rolled into the Lookouts' front yard, scattering chickens and guinea hens in its wake. It came to a stop, and as the dust settled, Hoolie saw a young white man with sandy-colored hair step out of the automobile. He took off his driving goggles and cap and tossed them smartly into the back seat. He wore checkered trousers, and under his driving duster, a gleaming white shirt with a stiff celluloid collar. Under the collar was a red string tie. Leaning over the door, he retrieved another hat. It could have passed for a derby, except for the sharp crease down the middle.

At first Hoolie was impressed. He had seen few men dressed in such finery. But after a few moments, he began to see a dandified country boy, someone who would be laughed at in the big city.

The young man stood waiting for a few seconds while the entire Lookout family gathered on the porch. He was playing to an admiring audience, except for the old grandmother, whose look of disdain for the young man's clothing and car Hoolie clearly read in her eyes. While the grandmother stood her ground, the rest of the Lookout family moved in a group off the porch and toward the young dandy.

Martha almost broke into a run. Her look of joy at the boy's arrival told Hoolie several things. He was relieved that Myrtle was not the one the dandy had come to see. But as it dawned on Hoolie that this was the sheriff's nephew, his pleasure in knowing that Myrtle was not in love with the white boy shifted to anger. He glared at the young man, but he knew that in order to stay on the job, he would have to be civil to him.

At one point during the hubbub of his arrival, the dandy was introduced to Hoolie. His name was Peter Henderson. Hoolie was so obviously unimpressed that Myrtle sidled up beside him, "What's the matter, Mr. Hoolie Smith?"

"Nothin'. Ahh . . . just lookin' at the car. Real nice."

Hoolie puffed himself up and continued, "I'm a mechanic, you know. Fix these all the time. It's a Packard, good automobile. Self-starter, no need to crank it."

Myrtle smiled prettily. Intuitively, she understood that Hoolie was being boastful to impress her. She thought that Pete Henderson was all automobile and fancy clothes, and like her grandmother, she thought that Henderson was just a boy; Hoolie, on the other hand, was a man. Her grandmother thought that a man should be an old-time warrior. He should be brave and willing to sacrifice himself for the good of the people. He must also be generous and willing to give away the last thing he owned to aid the poor. It was only when a young man had proven himself able to be a true warrior that he could dress himself distinctively, dance in a dignified manner, and walk with straightened back.

Peter had not earned the right to put on any airs. His family kept him in money, clothes, and automobiles. Myrtle had a strong streak of Puritan morality, and in her view, it was unacceptable that Pete didn't work to earn even a portion of the McKinley-Henderson money. Worse yet, having heard gossip that Sheriff McKinley confiscated alcohol and sold it back to the bootleggers, she felt that the family's wealth was ill-gotten. The bootleggers were the scourge of the Osage people. Drunks were always on the streets of the towns in Osage County. They didn't act properly; they couldn't think straight. Myrtle knew some of them, and the girl felt nothing but pity for these people who had lost their land and their headrights. Meanwhile, Pete Henderson was sitting around supposedly learning the law from his relative, old Judge Patterson, a corrupt and powerful man who, she suspected, regularly robbed her people. Still, for her sister's sake, Myrtle tolerated Pete.

They all inched their way back to the house, Hoolie and Myrtle bringing up the rear. From the front door, Grandmother Lookout called out something in Osage. The girls and Lizzie Lookout filed in, leaving the men standing on the porch. Hoolie leaned against one of the ornate wood roof supports. Ben said, "Wait here; I'll be back."

Hoolie and Henderson stood in silence, taking surreptitious glances at each other from time to time. Ben stepped back onto the porch holding three cigars.

"Bought these in town. Let's smoke."

He handed them out, and each man in turn used Ben's knife to cut the tips off their cigars. Ben produced some matches. They all lit up and sat on the porch chairs.

The three men leaned back, puffing on the cigars and enjoying the smoke. Ben turned to Hoolie, "Mr. Henderson here is courtin' Martha. Looks like they might get married sometime soon."

Henderson smiled and said, "Well, I hope so, Mr. Lookout, but Martha hasn't said 'yes' yet."

He swiveled to look at Hoolie, "I didn't catch your name."

Hoolie sat silently for a moment and looked into Henderson's eyes.

He was thinking about how uncomfortable he felt being stared at. Hoolie wondered if Henderson felt the same way. If the young dandy did, he didn't let on.

"Name's Hoolie Smith," said Hoolie casually.

"Call me Pete. Where you from?"

"Over near Stilwell, in the hills. I live in Tulsa now."

"What you doin' up here, if it's all right to ask?"

Ben interjected, "Hoolie's a detective. He's lookin' for a girl that might'a eloped with Tommy Ruffle. He talked to your uncle in town today." He looked at Hoolie and asked, "How'd that go anyway?"

"Oh, the meeting with Sheriff McKinley went fine."

Pete said, "Tommy Ruffle, huh? He's a tough talker. Goes after the people at the agency and Indian Office. He's made some trouble, but I guess he's a good boy. He's got some powerful friends."

After a short pause, Pete said, "You connected with the Shelbys outta Tulsa? The Shelby woman comes up to Hominy often, and she knows Tommy Ruffle. My mama runs a boarding house, and Mrs. Shelby always stays there. I know her daughter Elizabeth, too. A professor from back east name of Arlen Potter works with Mrs. Shelby and Tommy collecting Osage history. Another girl, Rose Chichester, I believe, comes with 'em sometimes, too."

Hoolie was sure now that Peter Henderson had already talked to his uncle about Hoolie, Rose Chichester, and the case. "I knew they stayed at a boarding house in town," said Hoolie, "but I didn't know it was your mother's. You're right, Miss Chichester does come with them from time to time. In fact, that's who we think Tommy run off with."

Henderson put a shocked look on his face. "That doesn't seem right. Miss Chichester seems like a quiet girl. I don't think she'd take up with somebody like him. He's kinda wild. Right, Mr. Lookout?"

Ben chuckled and shook his head. "Yeah, that Tommy sure can stir up some trouble."

"Drinks whiskey, too," cut in Henderson.

Ben lost his empathetic smile and glared at Henderson. "I'll tell you, Pete, Tommy looks after his family. He's a smart boy, and people around here are getting pretty upset over the oil business. Tommy has been fightin' to save our land and get them Indian Office people to look after our rights. Seems like those oil companies just want to get control of everybody's leases and headrights. The Shelbys are part of that, too, I think. I hope that Tommy don't get too close to those people. He helps out Mrs. Shelby, and I met her. She seems like her heart's good, but when it comes down to this oil business, she'll stick with her own, and we'll end up with no land at all."

Ben's speech was heartfelt, but in reaction, Henderson tried to change the subject. He subtly tried to turn the older man against Hoolie by insinuating that the Cherokee had a close relationship with Big Bill Shelby. "Well, Mr. Smith," he asked, "are you working for Shelby Oil?"

"Nope," said Hoolie. "Me and my boss are workin' for Miss Chichester's father."

"I see," Henderson said, as he turned to Ben. "Mr. Lookout, besides Martha, you're the last person in the world I want mad at me. I know that Tommy Ruffle's been workin' hard for the Osages, and I suppose he's a good man in his way. I just don't want him to spoil what gains the Indians have made. Look at yourself. Your family lives very well. You and your daughters are educated. You've been able to have a hand in the lease negotiations. Believe me, if Martha will have me, when I become a lawyer, I'll personally handle all of these negotiations and make sure you are never cheated. I promise you this."

Ben leveled his eyes once more on the young dandy. "Well, Pete, you'll be goin' up against some of the smartest and meanest people I know of. Some of these folks want everything for themselves. But, thanks, we could sure use the help."

Henderson sat back with a self-satisfied grin on his face. He puffed on the cigar a few times before saying, "Well, Mr. Smith, I guess you'll go up to Pawhuska tomorrow to find Tommy?"

"I guess I will."

"Good luck. It'll be hard finding that boy; he moves around quite a bit."

Before anyone could say anything else, Lizzie Lookout stepped out on the porch and announced supper.

After a fine meal of roast beef, hominy, fresh-baked bread, and turnips, the Lookouts and their guests went out on the porch. A slight chill was in the air, and the women put on shawls. Ben went into the house and came back with a blanket wrapped around his waist. "Must be getting old," he said, "my legs and feet freeze up on me."

Hoolie and Henderson laughed. They sat for a while, then both went to their automobiles to retrieve their coats. Hoolie got his suit coat; Henderson, his driving duster.

When the men returned to the porch, Ben was hanging two coal-oil lanterns on hooks underneath the eaves, and he asked Pete to light them. Ben, Hoolie, and Grandma Lookout sat on kitchen chairs; Henderson and Martha, on the porch swing; and Lizzie and Myrtle, on two rocking chairs from the house.

The talk was mostly about town politics, the new brick street, and how much the dry-goods store had changed in the past year. Someone predicted that Hominy would soon have its own moving-picture house. The girls liked the idea, both having seen the "flickers" on visits to Tulsa. Hoolie wasn't much interested in the moving pictures. When the old people told stories, you pictured in your mind what was going on, but in the moving pictures, you saw everything. They didn't leave anything to think about. Hoolie began to feel that with the possible exception of Grandma Lookout, he was the most old-fashioned person sitting on the porch that night.

The small talk went on for nearly an hour. Finally, Henderson rose and announced, "Folks, I'd better go now. The judge is expecting me bright and early in the morning. Good night." He paused and smiled at Martha. "Martha, would you walk me to the car?"

Martha bowed her head and said with a shy smile, "Sure, I will." Martha rose and surprisingly so did the rest of the women. Lizzie made it known that it was time to clean up the supper table.

Ben and Hoolie sat in silence and watched Martha and Pete standing together, holding hands at the very edge of the light from the two lanterns. Pete got in the Packard, and they heard the motor of his automobile turn over. Martha reentered the porch light, walking slowly. Hoolie heard her murmur a weak "I'll help Mama" to no one in particular before she walked into the house.

As soon as she was out of earshot, Ben said, "She'll mope around here for the next few days 'til she sees him again."

Hoolie would have liked to know Mr. Lookout's innermost thoughts about Martha and Peter Henderson. He suspected that Ben would rather have seen his daughter courted by an Osage and in the traditional manner.

Ben had to have guessed Hoolie's thoughts. He swatted at some flying insect attracted by the lights and turned to Hoolie. "I reckon it's smart at times to bring in new blood. We used to arrange these things. The grandmas got together and figured out family lines so we didn't marry our kinfolks. Had to be careful about that. We're from what we call the 'Big Osages,' and we're supposed to marry with the 'Little Osages.' Lizzie comes from them.

"Now, it's all about love. The girls read them books at school and wait around for a boy that'll talk sweet things to them. Pete Henderson came along, and Martha ain't thought straight since."

Ben swatted at another bug and went on, "I was worried some about her marryin' a white man. They been stealin' us blind since allotment come. The oil money has been good for some of us, but we sure have lost a lot of land. We're changin' a lot, too. Some of the old ways are just about gone, and I miss 'em. The young people keep lookin' for somethin' to hang on to. My mother keeps the old ways as much as she can, but her and Lizzie and most all of my relatives are followin' the Peyote Road now. I got to be a Christian when they took me off to Carlisle nearly forty years ago, but I'm gonna start goin' to peyote meetin's. I guess when she marries Pete, Martha'll follow the Jesus Road."

Hoolie, sympathetic to Ben's religious and cultural dilemma, said, "Our people have been marryin' whites for a long time. Sometimes it works out, sometimes not. I suspect it just depends on who it is you marry."

Ben laughed a bit. "Speakin' of getting' married," he began, "the boy you're lookin' for—Tommy—once came around to court Myrtle. He did everything in the old way. Played a flute, brought his mama, handed out gifts, even brought some horses. Didn't take though. Myrtle said no. Said she didn't love him. Her mama and grandma said let her be. I know that Myrtle's been readin' them books about love, too."

Ben paused for a brief look at his hands. "I just hope Pete will be a good husband to Martha. Sometimes I worry because that uncle of his, the sheriff, can be real mean to the Indians."

"You all seemed to like Pete," said Hoolie, "I mean, you made him feel at home."

"That's our way, sonny. But you're right, I like the boy most times. He's real good to Martha. He acts like he wants to take care of her. My mama don't care for him much, but she's always careful around strangers. You're the only one I can remember that she took to right off. But that's because she saw you was comin'."

Hoolie's thoughts were on what the sheriff had said about needing a "squaw" in the family who would inherit her father's land, leases, and headright. He thought that if Ben knew about that, he'd run Pete Henderson off for good. Pete's whole family was trouble.

Hoolie tried to clear his mind. He had to stay focused on his job. Peter Henderson was just another greedy white man in a long line of greedy white men. Maybe he had Martha fooled for a while, but eventually, her people would lead her back to the right way. Meanwhile, Hoolie had to find Chief Ruffle.

Ben went inside and came back out holding two more cigars. Hoolie sighed wistfully as he put a match to the tobacco. The cigar tasted good. He settled into his chair and said nothing.

Minutes later the door opened and Myrtle and her grandmother stepped out. Myrtle spoke. "Mama and Martha are finishing cleaning up the dishes. They'll be out shortly."

Lizzie and Martha came onto the porch and took chairs flanking Ben. Myrtle said in a flirtatious tone, "What's the matter, Mr. Hoolie Smith? You look like somebody hit you in the face with a fish."

"I thought you all had gone to sleep."

"No, you didn't. You were thinking about something else, weren't you?"

"Well, I was wonderin' how you did the supper dishes. Didn't see nobody go to the well."

"I thought you lived in the city," she replied.

"I do."

"Well, don't they have running water indoors?"

"Yeah, and taps and commodes."

"Don't you think we can have a hand pump in the kitchen, Mr. Smith?"

"Sure . . . I was only . . . yeah, hand pump . . . I suppose so," he stammered.

Grandma Lookout said something in Osage to her granddaughter.

Ben and Lizzie laughed. The statement even brought a smile to Martha's face. Myrtle looked indignant. "I was only teasing," she said. "Can't I have any fun around here?"

Ben, Lizzie, and Grandma laughed even harder. Then Myrtle put her hand to her mouth, lowered her eyes, and smiled shyly.

Hoolie was in the dark. Ben explained, "My mother said that she shouldn't talk to you like that. That kind of talk is for a man's mother-in-law. Mama made a joke in Osage. She said that Myrtle was her own mother. If she keeps actin' like that she'll end up an old maid."

Hoolie understood at once and dropped his eyes in embarrassment. Finally, he said, "I was told that in the olden times, a husband didn't talk to his mother-in-law. Some folks believe that now, and you'll see a lot of Cherokee men who don't speak to their wife's mother, aunties, or grandmothers."

When Hoolie finished, he took a long pull on his cigar and leaned back and blew out a great puff of smoke. At that very moment, a rifle shot pierced the air with a loud crack. Ben crumpled in his chair.

Without thinking, Hoolie pulled Myrtle to the floor of the porch. "Down!" he yelled to everyone.

Hoolie pulled Ben's limp body out of the chair and felt for the man's heartbeat. He was still alive.

Hoolie's body seemed to act without any signal from his brain.

Leaping up, he grabbed the coal-oil lanterns and threw each one as far from the house as he could. Just as he released the second lantern, he felt a bullet strike a glancing blow to his right rib cage. He didn't feel any pain, but he knew that a rib was broken. He was breathing hard. Still, he didn't fall. He heard the lantern shatter out in the yard and saw it briefly flare up and settle into a soft glow. The small fires the lamps had set in the grass gave off light, but it was well away from the house.

Hoolie sprinted for the flivver. Another shot was fired. He thought he heard the bullet smack into the side of the house. And this time he had seen the muzzle flash down by the creek bed among the trees.

He jumped on the flivver's running board and reached over the door. Grabbing his Winchester, he threw the lever action forward and back, placing a round in the chamber. He pulled the trigger without aiming. He fired four or five rounds like that. He just wanted to put lead in the air and keep the shooter's head down. He pumped and shot blindly until the hammer of the Winchester fell with only a snap. He was out of ammunition. Thinking that he might find cover to reload if he could get to the house, he snatched the box of bullets out of the flivver, and rifle and ammo in hand, he turned to run. The moment he did, the pain from his broken rib filled his chest cavity. As he ran, he grunted with each breath.

All of a sudden shots came from the house. Someone was doing the same thing he had done, trying to pin down the attacker and preventing whomever it was from taking another aimed shot. A dim kerosene lamp was still on in the house, and the attacker could aim at anyone silhouetted in that light. Hoolie yelled, "Put the light out! Put the light out!"

The light went out almost instantly, as two more shots erupted from the house.

In his dash for the house, Hoolie tripped on the first step. He fell face first on the porch, cutting his upper lip and smashing his nose. He felt the blood trickling down his chin. He yelled once more, imitating his sergeant in France, "Cease fire. Wait 'til he fires. Fire at the muzzle flash."

Hoolie slid backward off the steps. He rolled over and aimed his empty rifle in the general direction of the creek. It was so dark now that he couldn't see anything over a few feet away. The pain in his ribs and his chin brought tears to his eyes.

There was absolute silence. No more shots came. There were no more muzzle flashes. As he reloaded his rifle, he heard a soft keening from inside the house. The women were crying but not wailing. Ben might still be alive.

He waited for a few more minutes. Finally, he couldn't wait any longer. He had to help with Ben. He put his hand on his rib cage and gasped for air. The intake of oxygen seemed to help, but his chest felt as if a two-ton rock had fallen on him. He rolled to his back and lay still, gathering as much strength as possible. He rolled back to his stomach, rose painfully to his hands and knees, and lurched to his feet. He staggered toward the porch and up the three steps. The person who had returned the fire of their attacker took Hoolie's arm and helped him inside the house. It was Grandma Lookout.

As she and Hoolie entered the doorway, she called out in Osage. A light came on, and Myrtle rushed toward them. She helped her grandmother ease Hoolie into an overstuffed chair. Lizzie and Martha were bent over Ben. Myrtle's kerosene lamp illuminated the scene and through his blurring vision, Hoolie could see that Ben was bleeding profusely from a wound in the chest.

Hoolie started to say something, but the pain and lack of breath made him take in air in short gasps. Words came between the breaths. "Cover it . . . air coming out . . . chest can't keep air in . . . cover it . . . hard, pressure . . . cover it."

Grandma Lookout got right in Hoolie's face. "You be still," she said in English. "You don't move."

She looked at Myrtle. "You girl, you put this over his ribs." She pointed at Hoolie with her lips and handed Myrtle a piece of her apron. She had seen that his injured face would be all right, but she didn't know whether or not the bullet had entered Hoolie's chest cavity. Perceiving that Hoolie was better off than her son, she turned Hoolie over to Myrtle and joined Lizzie and Martha on the floor with Ben.

Blood covered the floor under Ben Lookout. He was bleeding from his nose and mouth. Grandma Lookout found the bullet hole in his lower right chest. She sent Martha to get a butcher knife. When she returned with it, the old woman cut Ben's shirt from his body. She rolled him over and found a large exit wound on the upper part of his back on the left side. She lowered her head. She knew at once that her son would surely die. She had seen bullet wounds when she was a child, in the days when her people fought the Kiowas and Comanches. The bullet had probably entered her son's right chest, glanced off a rib or his backbone and ripped through his back, carrying fragments of bone and tissue with it.

She still fought hard for his life. She plugged both holes with material from her dress and apron. She called for water. Her son had not responded to anything she did. Then his shallow breathing stopped. He expelled what air was left in his lungs in one explosive breath. One eyelid popped open, and he was suddenly gone. Frantically, Grandma Lookout felt his heart. She pressed hard against his chest, trying to pump life back into her son. After a minute or two, she stopped, looked at his face, closed his open eye, and began to cry.

It was a cry of the most profound grief, "Eeeeeeee . . . Aieeeeee . . . Eeeeeeeee."

Hoolie heard it, and he knew Ben was dead. All the women were crying, "Aieeeeee . . . Eeeeeeeee." He felt his own great sadness, and then he blacked out.

8

Clients

Tulsa was a church-going city. On a Sunday, everything shut down but the churches, the speakeasies, the opium dens, and the whorehouses; only the oil rigs kept pumping, with skeleton crews.

J.D. sat in his room dressed in a pair of brown trousers, an undershirt, bedroom slippers, and a tan bathrobe covered with what passed for American Indian geometric designs. He had rented the second-floor, front apartment when he first came to Tulsa, and he had stayed on because it was close to his new office. Once he had gone into business for himself, he began acquiring furniture to replace what came with the place. His pride and joy was an easy chair of light green material. A yellow-green couch sat exactly across from it. On a side table was an old stereoscope with a box full of pictures. J.D.'s late mother had collected the stereoscope slides, mostly of landscapes out west and of rolling grassy knolls that reminded her of Ireland. His mother had never really gotten used to city life in Chicago. J.D.'s walls were bare, but an old tintype of his mother when she was in her twenties sat on another side table.

Every morning, J.D. smoothed the covers and put up his wall bed. And today, having done that, he sat back down in his easy chair. Staring at the wall bed's closed-up panel, he began thinking and re-thinking the Chichester operation. Nothing was making sense.

After watching Mrs. Shelby and Chichester motor away from the morgue, J.D. had reentered to talk to McAfee. A morgue was supposed to do serious work and aid the police in the investigation of murder. The dead themselves could divulge a great deal of information about how they had died, but only if autopsies were done thoughtfully and thoroughly. But McAfee and Chiles just filled out paperwork and, on occasion, ran an inquest at which the doctor who had performed the autopsy would give a brief report. "No," J.D. thought, "far from being investigators, McAfee and Chiles are just a couple of political hacks." Their jobs consisted of determining whether or not a death warranted a criminal investigation. They had no motivation to look for evidence beyond what was most obvious. J.D. hated the coroner system.

The examination of Tommy Ruffle's body, J.D. found out, had been about as superficial as it could get. "Pretty obvious what killed him, J.D.," said McAfee with a slight smile. "People don't usually live with their throats cut from ear to ear." The man actually chuckled.

J.D. persisted. "Look, Bennett," he said, using McAfee's first name to establish some semblance of a friendly relationship, "was there anything else the doc or you might have seen? Was there a lot of blood? How long ago would you guess he died?"

"I can't really say. Didn't get him in here in time. He wasn't all that stiff, so the rigor must've worn off. That could take a while. He stunk pretty bad, and the doc said he was bloated a bit. But that could be linked up with the weather, so he couldn't tell when the boy got cut. He had a good deal of dried blood on his shirt and britches though. After the doc cut the boy's clothes off, we burned them. I declared it a homicide and turned it over to the county sheriff to investigate as a possible murder or manslaughter."

McAfee paused for effect and then continued. "Anyways, sheriff's got it now, but they're so goddam backed up with grifters, whores, Volstead, and such that they're not gonna pay much attention to a dead Indian. Maybe if your friends the Shelbys got pushy, they'd do something. The Shelbys carry a bit of weight around this burg."

J.D. interrupted, "I'm on this case now."

"Yes, yes. I hope you can do something. Nobody should have to die like that."

"That's right," said J.D., as he glowered at McAfee, "nobody."

A long minute passed before he continued, "Did you notice any-thing else? Anything at all?"

McAfee bunched up his right fist and pounded it in his left palm. "I do remember somethin'. The doc told me to look at the cut. You could see bone. When I bent over to get a good look, I smelled a trace of whiskey. But, you know, it wasn't like it came from him. Or at least from his mouth. I think whoever dumped him poured it on him. Sad, ain't it? The boy got done in and then throw'd out like a sack of garbage."

J.D. was knuckling his moustache again in deep thought. "Yeah, sad . . . sad," he said dully.

"Now, this is something the doc just happened to mention," said McAfee with a hopeful look on his jowly face. "He said that the boy was probably cut from behind. The cut was real deep on the left side of the boy's neck. The doc said it trailed off toward the other side. There was just a bit of skin and the spinal cord holdin' the boy's head on. The doc said that if the boy had been cut from the front, the killer might've been left-handed and that he might've slashed backhanded across the neck, like this." McAfee made a slashing motion from right to left with his left hand.

"It would've been hard to cut him like this." McAfee then made a motion with his right hand from right to left. "The doc said that a slice from the front wouldn't have cut so deep on the boy's left side. The gash would've got deep toward the middle and right side of the throat. Me, I don't know from nothin'. All's I know is that the boy got cut bad, and he died real quick. Like I said, his head nearly come off."

"Yep," said J.D. absent mindedly, "like a hog in a slaughter house. The dirty, sniveling coward took him from behind." J.D. looked directly into McAfee's eyes. "Nobody deserves to die like that," J.D. repeated with a quiet resolve.

"You're right, J.D., the SOB needs huntin' down."

Their conversation ended half an hour later with McAfee observing that Tommy's hair was cut short and loaded with brilliantine. "I thought they wore their hair in braids," he said. When J.D. informed him that Indians were as style conscious as anyone else, McAfee said with a broad smile, "Well J.D., you sure know your Indians, don't ya?"

J.D. couldn't clear his mind of that conversation. He sat back in his chair, and despite the warmth in the late-May air, he couldn't help pulling up the collar of his bathrobe. He was unnerved and mystified.

Surely, Tommy had been somewhere up around Pawhuska or maybe Hominy. If so, why would his murderer want to ditch him close to Tulsa? It was ridiculous. Why not just dump him out in some field, or in a river, or, for that matter, in the woods. The animals would have gotten to him, and in a month or so, any trace would have been gone.

That thought put the dumping of Tommy's body in a whole 'nother light. Maybe his murderer wanted him to be found; but—and maybe the most important "but"—he wanted him to be discovered and identified at a later date. Obviously, the Tulsa authorities put the body of an Indian low on their list of crimes to be solved. If his body had been discovered in Osage territory, the Indian agency would have gotten somebody to identify him quickly. It was a message of some kind. Tommy was supposed to be "missing" for a while. J.D. wasn't sure why, but he was certain that he had figured out the reason behind Tommy's ignominious burial.

The most important thing was to find Rose Chichester. With Tommy dead in the Tulsa morgue, it was obvious that Rose was somewhere else. But where? If she had been with Tommy, then she might have witnessed his murder. She could've been killed, and her body might be as far away from Tommy's as an automobile could be driven from one point to the next in a day or so.

J.D. had to put such thoughts out of his head. He forced himself to concentrate on the problem at hand. The girl was still missing, and he had been hired to find her. Far better to think that she was alive. It was too easy to fall into doubt.

Three quick raps on the door broke J.D.'s train of thought. He rose and walked to the door. Only two or three people had ever been in his flat; he seriously doubted that anyone besides Sam Berg, Hoolie, or Hattie, the prostitute he hired every so often, knew his address.

Before he reached the doorknob, the visitor had tapped on the door three more times.

"I'm coming," said J.D.

To his great surprise, he found William Shelby Jr. standing in the doorway. It took J.D. a short, uncomfortable moment to say, "Come in, Mr. Shelby, come in."

Slim, pink cheeked, and with his light-colored hair slicked back with pomade, Little Bill almost glided over to J.D.'s couch. At J.D.'s gesture, he sat and put his hat in his lap.

J.D. spoke first. "What can I do for you, Mr. Shelby?" he said with his eyes narrowing.

It was clear that after their encounter at the Shelby mansion, Little Bill was nervous about talking to J.D. Now J.D. was on his own turf, and Little Bill hesitated. After pinching the crown of his hat several times, Little Bill said, "My mother has sent me to retain you to take care of a few things concerning the family."

"Oh, really? What might they be?"

"Well, Mr. Daugherty, she would like for you to make the arrangements to release Tommy Ruffle's body and see that it gets to a funeral home. Mother feels that your connections with the police and with the coroner's office will help get Tommy a proper burial in his own land. Mother would, of course, like to have it done as soon as possible. He's been missing for quite a while now and should be laid to rest. I concur, of course, and am willing to offer you twice your usual fee for however long it takes to arrange things. She . . . we . . . would like for you to find the murderer."

Little Bill stood and pulled a piece of paper from his inside coat pocket. He handed it to J.D., who immediately arched his eyebrows.

"This is my personal check for two hundred dollars. I hope that it will serve as your retainer."

J.D. stood in his bathrobe holding the check between both hands. He pursed his lips, "Mr. Shelby, if I accept this check it will constitute a conflict of interest. Mr. Chichester, your houseguest, is my client. Should I act on your behalf to the detriment of his own, I will have seriously breached a code of ethics that is essential to the maintenance of my business."

"Please, Mr. Daugherty. Neither my mother nor Mr. Chichester thinks that you handling arrangements of this nature would be a problem. Unfortunately both have left town so they aren't available to reassure you that taking Mother as a client will do anything to imperil your business relationship with Mr. Chichester."

"Where are they?"

"Mr. Chichester is accompanying mother to Osage County to inform Tommy's relatives of what happened."

"I see," said J.D. He thought for a moment then spoke. "Mr. Shelby, I can't accept your check, but I will see to all the arrangements and look into Tommy's murder. Let's just call this a gentlemen's agreement. If everything works out to Mrs. Shelby's . . . and your . . . satisfaction, then you can pay me my regular fees—and a bonus if you like—after the fact."

For the first time, Little Bill looked at J.D. with respect. "Thank you, Mr. Daugherty, thank you very much."

Fully dressed and sitting behind his office desk, J.D. was in deep thought about his next move. He was beginning to doubt the reasons he had gone into the detective business on his own. He believed he had left off helping the rich become richer when he quit Great Western; now he wasn't so sure. The memory of his experience at the 1896 Democratic National Convention in Chicago came back to him.

He was a young cop then and had been stationed inside the hall to prevent anarchist bombs or unionist demonstrations. That night, J.D. heard one of the most famous orations ever delivered at a political convention, and one that roused the crowd to a frenzy. William Jennings Bryan, the party's choice for president, talked about the working man, men like J.D.'s late father. He charged that the wage earners, the farmers, and the miners all across the nation were being crucified on a "cross of gold." The Republicans, in his eyes the party of the rich, wanted to keep the gold standard, which limited the amount of currency in circulation, to the benefit of the banks and capitalists. Bryan and the Democrats sought a conversion to the more abundant silver standard that would help the poor rise out of debt. The speech at its core was about the unfairness of having a rich elite controlling the vast wealth of the nation. At the moment that Bryan uttered the words "cross of gold," J.D. became a populist to his very core. As an Irish Catholic who had tasted prejudice himself, he began to detest all forms of discrimination.

When he first opened his agency, he thought he was taking advantage of his new wealthy clients. Now, he felt as if he was simply doing their bidding once again. The whole case was challenging J.D.'s understanding of the way things ought to be and the way things were. He even felt that his "gentlemen's agreement" with Shelby Jr. left him on shaky ethical ground.

His thoughts turned to Minerva Whitwell. She was a black girl who had been used by a rich white boy and was paid off to keep her mouth shut. Despite Little Bill's recent courtesy toward him, and the boy's admission that he loved Minerva, J.D. felt a growing antipathy for the Shelby scion. His folks aren't much better, J.D. thought. They had cast her out to avoid the shame of having a Negro grandchild. Along with J.D.'s anger at the Shelbys was a wish that he could right the wrong of Minerva Whitwell's ostracism and somehow protect her and her child from further misery. Even though he had never met the woman, J.D.'s notion about righting perceived wrongs and his stiff-necked formulation of justice clashed with his practical business sense.

9

Pete Henderson

Hoolie awakened to find both Myrtle and Martha Lookout hovering over him. This pleasant experience ended as he tried to sit up. A sharp burning pain seared through his rib cage, making it all come rushing back: the shooting, the fall, the blood, the death of Ben Lookout. He wanted to cry out in grief, frustration, and anger, and it took all his self-control not to do so. He closed his eyes and fell back on the thick down pillow.

"Please lay still, Mr. Smith," Martha said softly. Myrtle went to the door, saying, "I'll get Grandma."

In the attempt to comfort Hoolie and gradually bring him back from his long, restless sleep, Martha kept up a steady stream of talk. "You have to be still and gather yourself, Mr. Smith . . . Go slow . . . It's Martha . . . Don't move, please."

Hoolie opened his eyes again. He deliberately and slowly moved his elbows inward and lifted his head and neck up. Martha quickly moved the pillow to support him, and she said quietly, "Myrtle went to fetch our grandma. She wanted to say somethin' to you when you woke up."

"What . . . what day is it?" he croaked. He felt as if he had never moved his mouth before. As he spoke, his lips, sealed with dry saliva, pulled apart, and his jaw muscles burned. His throat was dry and scratchy.

"Remember? You were shot in the ribs. It's Monday, one whole day and a night since everything happened. Today's the funeral. People been comin' since yesterday. A lot of people. Most of 'em camped around the house."

Hoolie knew then that the terrible events of the ambush had not been a nightmare. "I want to get up," he whispered.

Just then the door opened and Grandma Lookout and Myrtle came in.

Myrtle stepped to the bed and carefully touched Hoolie's shoulder. Averting her eyes from his, she said, "Grandma's gonna talk Osage and I'll translate."

Hoolie nodded. He closed his eyes so that he would pay more attention to what was being said than to the beautiful girl. Grandma Lookout spoke crisply and in a high voice, almost as if she was making a speech to a large crowd. When she had finished, Myrtle began with what Hoolie knew would be just a summary: "Grandma says that you don't need a white-man doctor. She talked with a medicine man, and he says you'll be fine with our medicine. He can't do anymore than what we've already done. Grandma thinks you should eat soon. That would make you strong. If you get up, you gotta be real careful."

Hoolie opened his eyes and painfully raised himself up once again. "I have to get into town," he said in as strong a voice as he could muster. "I have to send a telegram to my boss."

"Go slow," Grandma Lookout commanded in English. "You move too fast." Expelling a loud breath, Hoolie slowly took air into his lungs, felt a pang in his ribs, and said, "It ain't a matter of me wantin' to get the telegram off, it's 'cause I have to."

The old woman pushed the girls aside and put a sinewy hand on Hoolie's shoulder. Glancing at her granddaughters, she let her gaze linger on Martha. Then, Grandma Lookout half-closed one eye and said directly to Hoolie, "Martha's man, this Pete, he'll help you . . . drive you around."

She continued, "You gonna be fine. You lose some blood. Now you gonna get the man who done this. Not gonna put him in no white man's jail."

Looking at Myrtle, she began speaking Osage again. The girl nodded and said to Hoolie, "Grandma says that you'll have to do most of the work at finding the man who did all this because Martha's man is a white man, and he's related to the sheriff. The sheriff don't help Indians, and Pete probably don't know enough about how to track a man down yet."

"Is that what she really said?" asked Hoolie.

Martha answered with a shy look in her eye, "Well, just about. She said that you'll go after the man who done this and kill him." The girl looked at the floor and said out of the corner of her mouth, "That's what she said anyway."

Myrtle spoke up, "Grandma don't want whoever did this to go to jail. She said that since Pete's white, he keeps their ways. He'll want to just put the man who did this in jail and then let him off when it's quiet again."

Hoolie looked at the Lookout women. Taking a gasping breath, he said through clenched teeth, "I'll get him, whoever he is."

Myrtle's and Martha's eyes narrowed, and they nodded their heads in unison. Grandma Lookout stared straight ahead. Hoolie pulled himself into a sitting position. He looked at Myrtle. "Could you get my clothes and a little food?"

She winced, "The clothes you had on got pretty bloody. Couldn't wash out the stain, so we burnt them. We'll get your satchel though."

The girls went, and when the door shut behind them, Grandma Lookout turned to Hoolie. "They good girls," she said. "When you get your clothes on, come downstairs, eat. Pete will drive you into town. You come back; you take a look down by the creek. That's where the shots came from."

"Yes, ma'am," said Hoolie, "I'll do just that."

"You're a good man. You'll find the one who shot you, and we'll take care of the one who was killed," she said, in the roundabout Indian way of referring to the dead.

Only the tension in the line of her jaw and the sadness in her eyes gave away her grief. Hoolie guessed that she was putting off mourning until everything was organized, including setting him on the trail of the murderer. Then she, her daughter-in-law, and her granddaughters would give in to the tears.

Hoolie moved and a sharp pain sliced through his right side to his backbone. Wincing, he moved his hand to the pain and discovered that someone had tied a bulky poultice around his lower rib cage. He looked at the old woman, who simply pointed to the bandage with her lips, "It hurts to move but that medicine will get you up and feelin' better real soon." She squinted as if she were trying to look through the poultice. "You a good healer," she said flatly, with a gesture that Hoolie thought might be sign language. "You get your clothes on and get outta bed . . . walkin' around will help. Gets rid of the stiffness."

Myrtle and Martha returned, carrying Hoolie's belongings. They had gathered up practically everything, including his old army blankets, his campaign hat, and the cartridges for his rifle. His Winchester had already been propped up in a corner of the room, freshly oiled.

Myrtle followed his eyes to the rifle. "Cleaned it last night," she said seriously.

"Thank you," replied Hoolie, gazing at her. Then he pulled himself back to business. "Where's the nearest telegraph office?"

"In Hominy. We'll get you there when you're ready."

"I think I can drive."

Grandma Lookout cast a doubtful look at him. "Pete'll do it . . . if not, then one of these two."

Hoolie looked up. "They can drive?" he said in a condescending tone.

"Probably better than you," Myrtle replied indignantly.

He looked at the women, and stretching his lips into a pitiful smile, he said, "I reckon I'd better get dressed. If you all would just step out of the room. . . . "

With that, the women walked out. Myrtle didn't exactly slam the door, but she did shut it with authority.

Hoolie closed his eyes and steadied himself for the ordeal of dressing. He tried to get out of bed without moving too fast, but he had to suppress the groans each time he flexed a muscle. He knew that the most difficult part of a wound in the ribs was breathing, so he tried taking shallow, short breaths. It didn't work. His ribs, at least two of which were cracked, had to flex outward with every intake of air. Instead of taking short breaths, Hoolie gasped each time he opened his mouth. The fall on the porch had left his nose so bloodied and bruised that breathing through it was nearly impossible.

Finally dressed, he carefully eased himself down the stairs and into the parlor. He found several Indian women sitting around Lizzie Lookout. He went to her, offered his hand, and gave her his heartfelt condolences. She held his hand for a moment, looked up at his face, and sobbed. There was no need for words. He saw the deep bloodstain on the wood floor.

Hoolie moved away and looked out the window. A large number of people were gathered in the front yard. They had spread blankets on the ground and were sitting there, smoking and talking. Most wore the white man's clothing, but a few were dressed in moccasins and leggings. Everyone wore large, bright-colored neck scarves, even the women, in their otherwise somber, store-bought dresses. Some of the men had fur turbans on their heads, in the old way; others wore unblocked, wide-brimmed hats with eagle feathers inserted in the hatbands. None of the women wore hats or veils, and their hair fell loosely over their shoulders and across the black shawls they carried. A few white faces were sprinkled in here and there, but this was primarily an Osage gathering.

After eating some cornmeal gruel, Hoolie went out and stood on the front porch. Off to his left, he could see two nearly perfect circles of burnt grass where he'd thrown the lanterns. Luckily, they didn't have much kerosene left in them and had landed in the short, tough sod. Had they been dropped on the painted-wood porch, they could've started a much bigger fire.

The flivver was sitting in the same place he'd left it. He looked at the car wistfully, but then he thought about starting it up: he dreaded leaning over the door, setting the spark, and turning the hand crank.

As he stepped off the porch toward the automobile, Myrtle, Martha, and Pete Henderson detached themselves from a group of elders and came over to him. All three looked anxious to tell him something. He shook Pete's hand, and Henderson began to speak, but Myrtle interrupted.

"Pete found out something yesterday. The one you're looking for is dead." She stopped and looked at the ground. Henderson came to Myrtle's aid, knowing that she, like most other Osages, avoided speaking of the deceased.

"Mr. Smith . . . Hoolie . . . The boy's been murdered," he began. "Mrs. Shelby came to my mother's place yesterday. A Mr. Daugherty— I take it that he is your boss—had asked Mrs. Shelby to view the body of an unknown Indian man in the Tulsa morgue. When she identified him, she came right up here to tell Chief Ruffle. They've gone to Tulsa to claim the body and will be bringing Tommy home tomorrow.

"I told Mrs. Shelby about you. She said that when Mr. Daugherty learned that she was coming to Hominy, he asked her that if she saw you, to tell you to come back to Tulsa."

Hoolie was having trouble taking it all in, but he managed to say, "I'd like to get to a telegraph operator."

"How about a telephone?" inquired Pete.

"I never had much luck with telephones, especially at this distance." Hoolie was thinking of the telephone communication problems in the trenches in France. Messages were always garbled; lines were always getting cut or tapped into. That's why the army used runners.

Henderson had that "Indians are backward" look on his face, but he quickly complied with Hoolie's wish. "I'll drive you into town right now if you want."

"I'd appreciate it. But first, I gotta go to the privy."

Myrtle and Martha dropped their eyes to the ground, and both moved toward Pete's automobile.

Hoolie stopped and said to them, "I think you two should stay with your momma. Me and Pete will do okay. I'm not hurtin' anymore."

The girls looked dubiously at each other. Hoolie was still in notice-able pain, and they obviously wanted to get away from the house for a while, but they nodded in agreement.

On the way into town, Hoolie told Pete that it was good of him to drive in, especially since Martha must need him during this trying time.

Hoolie's word of thanks prompted Pete to say offhandedly that Osages were clannish and didn't need him around the house. From that, he launched into a long-winded speech on Osage oil and the Lookouts' prospects without Ben. "You know, Ben was well liked by just about everyone. His cousin is the first chief around here and heads up the tribal council. Anyway, there'll be a lot of people at his funeral this afternoon.

"The Osages used to bury their folks sitting up, facing east. You know that? I reckon the old lady'll want Ben buried that way. I pretty much talked Lizzie and the girls into givin' Ben a Christian burial. I think it'd be a good idea, given their—the girls'—education and upbringing. Martha is practically a white girl anyhow."

He glanced at Hoolie, whose face had registered a deep frown at Pete's last remark.

Henderson quickly moved on. "Sorry, I almost forgot you're an Indian. No offense intended and nothin' personal. Of course, I'm speakin' realistically. I got nothin' against the race. After all, I plan to make an Indian girl my wife. But you have to admit that the old Indian customs are rapidly goin' the way of the buffalo. The Osages have to look to the future. Better to progress than wallow in the old ways? Right?"

Hoolie sat in silence. He would have liked to smack the white boy's face, but he felt helpless and frustrated. His father had told him to let the white man's arrogance go. Keep our ways hidden away from them.

Henderson continued talking, ignoring Hoolie's scowl and obvious discomfort.

"Some of the most prominent scientists—like Arlen Potter, who studies the Osages and likes them very much—feel that one day Indians will join our democracy and be just like us . . . it's inevitable.

"Take Ben's case. Even though the rest of his family started with that peyote stuff, Ben sent his daughters off to a good Christian school. His mother wants to go back to the days of the buffalo and the wild horse. Now Ben is . . . was . . . civilized, but he didn't know the potential lying right underneath his very feet. He kept arguing against drilling in certain areas. He gave away his money to poor Osages—goodfor-nothin's, you ask me—rather than invest in stocks and bonds. He could never see that investment promotes growth and that growth eventually will create more wealth for his people. But they have to give before they can get.

"Ben's failure to look into the future might have prevented his daughters and his grandchildren from benefiting from the money he's getting right now from the oil leases. I hate to say this . . . Ben was gonna be my father-in-law, and I love Martha . . . but Ben's death will help in the long run. Maybe now the Lookouts and many others will listen to reason. You're a Cherokee, a civilized Indian, you should know that."

Instead, Hoolie had had just about enough of Henderson's ideas.

"Pete," Hoolie began sternly, "I think you ought to know something about Indian people before you marry somebody of my race. We hate greed. It's the thing that busts up families, makes men do foul things, and even starts wars. Ben was a good man from what I saw. He took care of his people, his family. He even took me in, and I'm a stranger. He was murdered in cold blood. There ain't no good that I can think of that could come from that. And I don't think you better say anything like that in front of your future wife or the rest of her family . . . or *me*, ever again."

Henderson started to crawfish.

"You misunderstood me, Hoolie. Ben was a good man, but he was old-fashioned. That's all I'm sayin'. My uncle will find Ben's killer. Now, Martha and me will marry soon, and I can take care of all of them, by making them very wealthy through sound investment and management of their affairs."

"Well, Pete, I don't think you'd better say that to your wife, either," said Hoolie, shaking his head.

They drove the rest of the way to Hominy in complete silence. Hoolie was trying to find a way of preventing the Lookout-Henderson marriage. Ben might have been thinking the very same thing.

The telegrapher was a fat young man with stringy blond hair, bad teeth, and a red bow tie. He wrote Hoolie's message down and immediately began to tap out the code. Henderson again tried to talk Hoolie into telephoning, but Hoolie said that he doubted that J.D. would be in the office. After the discovery that Tommy Ruffle was dead, J.D. would be out running down leads.

Hoolie's telegram was short and to the point:

HEARD ABOUT TOMMY STOP SAW MURDER STOP
SHOT IN RIBS STOP MAN MURDERED STOP
WHAT DO I DO NOW STOP

The telegrapher asked Hoolie if he wanted to wait for a reply. It would take time for a messenger to find J.D., so Hoolie told the boy that he'd come back that afternoon. In a tone full of disdain for his Indian customer, the telegrapher said, "I'll hold any message for you 'til then."

Hoolie paid him and walked out, Henderson following. Stopping outside the doorway, Henderson said, "Hoolie, I'm going to go and talk to my uncle. I want to get him on the trail of Ben's killer right away. You rest in the car. I'll be back soon."

Hoolie earnestly wanted to listen in on the conversation between Henderson and the sheriff, but he let it go. He needed to get off his feet.

He got into the automobile, leaned his head back, and began to think about his next move. He had known Ben for only a day, but he had already begun to think of him as a friend. Now the man had been murdered while they sat next to each other. Hoolie felt that, as a detective, it was his duty to protect people from evil and danger. Detectives should be like the old-time scouts; they should be able to find the enemy before he finds the people.

He had to get back to the Lookout place and see what he could find down at the creek bed. The major stumbling block in his investigation was J.D., who wanted Hoolie back in Tulsa immediately. The Tommy Ruffle lead had obviously played out. Being dead, the Ruffle boy couldn't have been sheltering Rose Chichester. Still, Hoolie might make the case to J.D. that given the attack at the Lookouts, he ought to stay in Osage County and thoroughly investigate any leads.

Given the chance, Hoolie could follow up on the Chichester matter and find out who killed Ben. He also thought of Myrtle and how much he wanted to shield her from those who had killed her father and from people like Sheriff McKinley and her future brother-in-law, the dapper

Pete Henderson. He wanted more than anything to show that he was man enough to hunt down Ben's killer and earn Myrtle's appreciation and even admiration. That was really why he refused to wait for J.D.'s inevitable summons to return to Tulsa.

Hoolie's line of thought was interrupted when Henderson returned. He got behind the wheel of the big Packard, started it up, put it in gear, and drove them out of town.

On the way back to the Lookout place, Hoolie decided to pry some information out of Pete Henderson. It was easy to do. The young man was opinionated beyond reason and garrulous to a fault. While his mouth was working, he seemed oblivious to anything or anybody else.

Hoolie began with, "How long has your uncle been sheriff?"

As it turned out, that simple question was like dynamiting a dam on a big river. The information that streamed out was almost more than Hoolie could take in: The Sheriff's first name was Herschel. He was currently serving his third four-year term as town sheriff. McKinley's history as a lawman went back quite a ways. As a young man, he supposedly chased Geronimo. He then served as a deputy marshal for the court at Fort Smith. He had helped capture Cherokee Bill and had been in on running the outlaw cowboy Bill Doolin to ground.

"Yep, my uncle keeps pretty busy," Henderson continued. "He never took a wife. Always thinkin' about his job. He has to work with the county sheriff on Ben's murder. The county has jurisdiction, but the sheriff's office relies on local law enforcement because they just don't have enough men. Uncle Herschel has to investigate local crimes, help out the county, and enforce prohibition." Pete took a look at Hoolie and paused to get a breath.

"Once my uncle heard about Ben, he called up the sheriff and asked to take on the case himself. The high sheriff knows that if anybody can get the job done, it's my uncle."

Hoolie was finally allowed to ask another question. "How many people workin' for him?"

"I reckon five, if you count Jolene Belt who does the bookkeeping and paperwork. There's three constables: Tom Miller works nights, and Billy Wallace and Buford Fellows work days. Uncle Herschel puts Quincy Klutter and Jolene's husband, Fred, on when he's short-handed. With Fred and Quincy, that's seven. Fred works a lot."

"That's a lot of law for a small town like Hominy."

"You'd think, huh? But I'll tell you, we need it. I'm sorry to say that since there's a good number of Indians around, the bootleggers are thick as flies in a barnyard. When the oil payments come in, the drunks are all over the place. They're breakin' Volstead, gettin' into fights, and sometimes pullin' off a holdup or two. When these drunks fight, they'll go at each other with knives or whatever it takes to kill one another. We've had quite a few killin's around here lately . . . at least since the big wells came in."

"I wonder which officer I met?" asked Hoolie. "He was pretty young, long-faced, and was goin' bald."

"That was Billy. He was in the war. You was in the war too, wasn't you?"

"I was there," Hoolie said through tight lips. "I drove the supply lorries and hauled some of the big guns around. Didn't spend but a few weeks in the trenches. What'd Billy do?"

"I don't exactly know. Said he killed twenty-seven Huns though. Said he probably would have killed a whole bunch more if the armistice wasn't declared. Uncle Herschel put him on when he found out Billy had been a soldier."

"So Billy's only been a constable for maybe two years?"

"Not that long. Only about a year. He came into town about a year ago from Arkansas. Uncle Herschel said he needed good men like Billy."

"How'd he get on day shift that quick?"

Henderson laughed out loud, "That's because Tom Miller likes to work nights. He keeps a small farm . . . nothin' but a shack, a chicken house, a couple of cows, and a garden . . . but he's tryin' to build it up. Billy stays with him. It's usually pretty quiet at night, and Tom can get some sleep at the jail. It works out for them. They all have to do other things. A constable's pay ain't that great. Jolene's man, Fred, is a house painter. Buford Fellows is an old-time blacksmith. He still does some toolmaking and horseshoeing. They work staggered shifts, too, so they get off usually one day a week, maybe two or three, depending on what's goin' on at the time."

"Well, Pete, you sure know a good bit about the sheriff business. What do you do for a livin'? Sounds like you'd make a good sheriff your own self."

"That ain't for me. I'm readin' for the law with Judge Patterson over at Pawhuska. Gonna be a lawyer, maybe a judge someday. It'll be for the best when I marry Martha, 'cause then I can keep their affairs out of the competency hearings and deal with the banks and oil-leasing agents myself."

As they pulled up into the Lookout front yard, several people started moving toward the buckboard wagon that would carry Ben's body to the gravesite. The cemetery was located on a hill almost a mile from the house. Most of Ben's relatives were buried there, and the Osages had gathered to inter their brother in this most sacred place. Hoolie noticed that the Christians seemed to be running things. A white preacher made a speech and quoted from the Bible. Hoolie also saw that a few Osages sat apart, under the shade of a big oak. Myrtle, Martha, Lizzie, and Grandma Lookout were among them. One old man with his gray hair in braids waved an eagle feather fan over them and gave a lengthy speech. Hoolie guessed that he was a medicine man and was telling the women how they should comport themselves during the mourning period. Hoolie smiled in approval. Out of the corner of his eye, he saw Henderson watching the ceremony with an impatient and indignant scowl on his face.

The Lookout women followed the old man toward the buckboard. Henderson joined them and began an animated discussion with Martha. The way he was moving his arms and shaking his head told Hoolie that he was berating Martha for listening to a medicine man. Grandma Lookout turned and said something. Henderson immediately stopped his rant and docilely followed the women. Then Grandma Lookout squinted her eyes and looked out over the crowd. She spotted Hoolie and motioned him into a place between her and Lizzie.

He joined them behind the buckboard. He could see Ben clearly laid out in a good suit and a beautiful wool blanket in the bed of the wagon. Grandma Lookout touched his arm to take his attention away from the body.

"Boy," she said, "you don't need to walk to the cemetery. Maybe you start bleedin' again."

"I want to go. I'll take it slow. Don't worry," he whispered.

The woman nodded her head in approval. "You gotta strong heart. You walk with us."

As soon as they returned from the cemetery, Hoolie ate some stew and, with Myrtle's help, started up J.D.'s old Ford. He reluctantly had to get into town and pick up his boss's response to his telegram. He felt sure that J.D. was going to recall him and Hoolie, more than anything, wanted to begin the hunt for Ben's murderer.

It was intensely painful to shift the flivver's gears, deal with the play in the steering wheel, work the clutch, and drive over bad roads with a couple of broken ribs and a long gash covered with a poultice on your side. The Lookout women had fawned all over him, and Pete had offered to drive him to town once again. But Hoolie had to be alone; he could not have taken another drive with Henderson.

There were other reasons for going into town by himself. He was beginning to have deep feelings for Myrtle and for her family. It was a strange kind of feeling that made him draw away from them though. Here he was, a total stranger who had seemingly brought danger and death along with him. Ben had been killed while sitting on his front porch talking to him, and he was linked in a roundabout way with the murdered Tommy Ruffle. Hoolie even felt that maybe the Osages should have treated him like a sgili, a witch. He knew he wasn't the evil conjurer, but could he have been carrier of bad medicine? Could someone have witched him, and could he have inadvertently spread evil like some terrible disease? Yet, the family of the murdered man had taken him in as if he were a relative. They dressed his wounds, fed him, and guarded him while he slept.

Deep down he knew why Grandma Lookout cared for him like she would a favored child. He had been there when Ben was killed and had taken up a weapon to fight off the enemy. Despite being a stranger, he had acted like a warrior. His relationship with Grandma Lookout had altered in that exchange of gunfire. Once a recipient of Osage hospitality, Hoolie had been transformed into an honored defender of the Osage family. He had become a true warrior.

Grandma Lookout might have been looking at him as a future grandson as well. He caught the smile she gave him when he was staring at Myrtle like a lovesick puppy. Hoolie wanted to stay with the Lookouts. He wanted to enjoy Myrtle's slim, brown hands, the stately tilt of her head, her graceful neck, and her long, black hair. Grandma Lookout recognized his desire and apparently approved.

He snapped out of his reverie when someone screamed, "Crazy, goddamn Indian, watch where you're goin'!"

Hoolie had driven into Hominy thinking about Myrtle and had nearly run over an aged white man with a walking cane. He yelled "Sorry" and quickly parked the flivver in an alley between the dry-goods store and the pool hall.

Hoolie ran to the depot, picked up J.D.'s message, and was elated when he read:

NO ONE GETS AWAY WITH SHOOTING MY OPERATIVES
STOP BAD FOR BUSINESS STOP CONTINUE OP IN
OSAGE COUNTY STOP FIND HIM STOP REPORT
BACK THURSDAY STOP

Hoolie felt so good about being able to continue his work in Osage County that some of his pain subsided on the drive back to the Lookout place. The line about "report back Thursday" was open to interpretation—Hoolie could either send another telegram or drive to Tulsa, or so he thought. Thinking about the attack, however, his elation turned to anger. He agreed with J.D. Nobody was going to get away with murdering Ben Lookout. For Hoolie, it wasn't about bad business, it was about vengeance and ridding the Lookout family of a malicious presence. Whoever shot Ben was more than an assassin. He was a conjuror of malevolent medicine.

Sgili exist. Of that, Hoolie had no doubt. They persisted as a people on their own, with their own ways and ceremonies. They exist because evil exists. Still, one man's conjurer might be another man's doctor. A sgili could send back the evil to its original source or envelop you in a protective shield that would withstand evil's continued thrusts. But sometimes the sgili was out to get you, and then you had to kill it. The trouble was discovering who the sgili was. He once had heard of a conjurer that had disguised itself as a *kiyuga*, a chipmunk. It was hard to know just where that kind of wickedness lay.

When he returned to the Lookout house, he found that there were a number of families that had decided to stay over and camp out. The Lookout women immediately made him lie down and rest, so he was unable to inspect the area near the big oak by the creek. He was sure that the ambush had come from that position. Before he went to sleep, he told Myrtle that there was a family that was planning to camp at that spot, and he asked if her grandma would ask them to choose someplace else. It was getting dark, and he would have to wait until first light to look over the place. In the meantime, he wanted the area disturbed as little as possible. Myrtle agreed and went to her grandmother. When Hoolie awoke from his nap, he looked out the window at the creek. The family had indeed moved from the oak.

The family's concern with Hoolie's wounds and whether or not he was getting the proper amount of rest and food seemed to overshadow the day's events. It appeared that the Lookout women were not yet in mourning. In fact, they acted as if the need to preserve Osage hospitality was the most important part of the whole ritual of death.

When Myrtle discovered that Hoolie was awake, she insisted that he come outside by the fire and have something to eat. He complied without protest and sat down to a plate of beans and fry bread with several of the Lookout relatives. Henderson was there, but the Osages treated him with indifference—no out-and-out hatred, but no liking either. They probably distrusted his uncle, or knew that Grandma Lookout wasn't particularly happy about the proposed marriage between Pete and Martha. Maybe it was just because he was a white man. Hoolie quickly rejected the idea; he had seen a number of whites come and go who had been treated with warmth. Hating someone based on their race was not inherent in traditional Cherokee thought. In the old days, when the tribes took captives in war, they were often adopted and given full-status membership among the people. If these people, no matter what the color of their skin, took up the ways of their adoptive parents, they became kinfolk and, as such, were entitled to care, protection, and freedom.

Hoolie figured that the indifference toward Pete had another source. It crossed Hoolie's mind, too, that people might be comparing him to the dapper young man as a potential relative. Myrtle was sitting at his side and translating snippets of conversation. She translated everything that was said about Hoolie. And everything that was said was in praise of his actions during the ambush. He had acted the warrior. There was also mention that a snapping turtle had told Grandma Lookout that he was coming to help the people.

Henderson left early. He had seemed unaffected by the praise heaped on the Cherokee newcomer and by Hoolie's spending the night in the house with Martha and her family. Deep in his heart, Hoolie knew that, were the tables turned, he would have been jealous. He certainly wouldn't have been as deferential to Pete as Pete had been to him. Henderson had pulled chairs out for him, brought him a plate of food, and talked cordially with him. When Henderson rose to take his leave, Hoolie mustered up enough friendliness to shake hands and bid Pete a pleasant goodnight.

Concerned with his wound, the Lookout women commanded Hoolie to end his day and rest. He went up to his room, got into a nightshirt, lay down, and quickly went to sleep.

Hoolie was already down by the creek as the sun peeked over the horizon. He saw that there were several Osages doing the same thing that he was doing: They looked at the rising sun, spoke to it, and made offerings of some kind. Hoolie offered smoke and tobacco, which he tossed in the air, as he prayed for the safety of the Lookout family and for help in bringing peace to this land.

As soon as he had greeted the daybreak, he set to work combing the ground for signs. He realized that any clues were at least three days old and would probably have been disturbed. Any track left by the assailant could have been obscured or eliminated altogether. It was going to be a long and difficult search, especially with the wound in his side.

He felt that the shots had come from near the oak tree. Because the bullet had traveled upward through Ben's chest, Hoolie surmised that the line of fire had come from a lower level than that on which Ben had been sitting. Hoolie thought that the sniper was probably lying prone, on the house side of the creek bed, using the bank and undergrowth as cover. The shooter had to have been familiar with the lay of the land because he moved about relatively easily in the darkness. Hoolie found several places that a sharpshooter would have had a good line of sight to the house. As painful as it was, he even got down on his stomach a few times to gain the shooter's-eye view.

Near an old root, weathered out of the ground at the foot of the oak tree, Hoolie once more got into a firing position to see how the house looked from there. His ribs were aching, but he smiled grimly: he had found the place where the sniper had taken aim. Tree debris had been disturbed, and some old twigs were freshly broken. He tried to figure out where an ejected shell might be located, but it would depend on the type of weapon the rifleman used. The shooter had fired three times. Two of his shots were well aimed; the first killing Ben, the second striking Hoolie in the ribs. The third shot might have been fired in haste while the sniper was making his getaway. Hoolie had heard it hit the house, but he hadn't been able to find the bullet hole. The gunman might have retrieved his spent casings from the first two shots, but provided that he was, as Hoolie guessed, firing on the run, he probably would have been unable to pick up the last shell.

Hoolie pushed himself up to his knees, grunted as the pain shot through his chest, took several deep breaths, and got to his feet. Hunched over, he backed down the embankment of the creek bed, looking at the house all the way. Just before he got to the stream itself, he rose up to his full height and pretended to fire an offhand shot toward the house. He could just see the porch from there. Another step backward and the house would have disappeared from view. He groaned in pain again and began to scan the ground in a ten-foot circle around him. He concentrated on this area, scanning the circle again and again. Suddenly, the glint of metal caught his eye.

Hoolie went to the spot, bent over, gasped for air, and picked a new cartridge case from the rocks just under the water. Having been in the water, the shell wouldn't retain the distinct smell of burnt, smokeless powder. Hoolie was familiar with all manner of firearms and the bullets they used. This one was especially familiar. It was a round from a 1903 model Springfield rifle—the kind of weapon he and his comrades carried in France.

He put the shell in his trouser pocket, turned, and waded to the other side of the creek. He scanned that side of the bank for any sign of human imprint. Sure enough, he found a trail coming out of the water and straight into an old, unplowed cornfield. The boot prints were a few days old, because the ridges around the tracks had been worn smooth by the rise and fall of the stream. Had they been fresh they would have been sharp and distinct. Some of the smooth rocks on the edge of the stream had been dislodged, too. The tracks vanished as the ground became harder. Hoolie walked on, still concentrating on the ground, searching for anything.

To his satisfaction, he came upon some automobile tire marks almost half a mile from the creek. He followed the tire tracks to the road that led to town. As a mechanic, he could recognize the make of some automobile tires and match them with the automobile companies that used them. The car had sure taken a beating from whoever drove it that night. It had been driven over jostling ruts and bounced through deep holes. The driver had steered it over tangled roots, hard ground, and sharp rocks. What all this said to Hoolie was that the car the sniper had driven was well built and kept in good condition.

He pulled the shell out of his pocket and stared at it for a time. He began to walk back to the house, re-tracing his—and the sharpshooter's—steps to the creek bed. As he walked, he thought about the army-issue Springfield. Hoolie had grown up around firearms. He and his maternal uncle—in a Cherokee family, his father—went hunting on almost a daily basis during the fall and most of the winter. He was a good shot and knew how different weapons worked. The army taught Hoolie another way of shooting. Before being sent to France, the drill sergeants had Hoolie firing his Springfield at targets up to 500 yards distant. The rifle had a flip-up rear sight that could be adjusted for different distances. It also fired a jacketed bullet that could shred a man's flesh or pierce bone with ease. The Springfield was easily the most powerful and destructive rifle he'd ever handled.

Hoolie recalled that one time, he had to go up to the front on a resupply trip. As he was carrying boxes to the trench, he noticed a man armed with a Springfield with a scope mounted on it. The man was a sniper. Hoolie started talking to the sharpshooter's helper or spotter, who told him that the sniper might lie in one position for a very long time, waiting for a perfect shot. Hoolie asked if the sniper could shoot at night. The spotter immediately replied, "Night's the best. Any Hun that lights a pipe, starts a fire to cook a meal, or turns on his electric torch, even just for a second, is a dead man." The spotter also bragged that the Springfield was copied from the German Mauser Gewehr 98, and so the German and American snipers were equally matched. The spotter had a chalkboard set up, and it had tally marks for six kills. "That's two days' work. We're only on the line for a week."

Hoolie kept rubbing the shell casing between his thumb and index finger. Everything that had happened since the shooting kept going through his mind. As he climbed up the bank and passed the big oak tree once again, it hit him who Ben's killer might have been. Now, he had to find out why Ben was killed.

10

Arrangements

Thanks to the Shelbys, J.D. had had a busy Sunday, and he was just about to pack it in and go for some supper. While Rose Shelby had been in Osage County telling Chief Ruffle about his grandson's death and bringing the old man back to claim the body, J.D. had been making the arrangements for the mortuary to embalm and encoffin Tommy Ruffle according to the state statutes for transporting dead bodies. In order to comply with the law and to smooth the way for his clients, J.D. had had to clear everything with the county sheriff. Tommy's death was still an unsolved homicide, and in spite of the fact that few in the sheriff's office really cared about finding the murderer of a young Indian male, a certain amount of investigative paperwork had to be done.

The idea that Rose Shelby depended on him to make the arrangements both irritated and flattered J.D. Apparently no one else could be bothered. Big Bill was involved in yet another business deal of some sort. The daughter had gone to Osage County with her mother, as had Chichester. Little Bill was useless, J.D. thought, except for writing checks or handing out cash. At some point, J.D. would have to question Minerva Whitwell, but dealing with the coppers and other dubious city officials was about all he could handle.

The phone on J.D.'s desk rang. Picking up the earpiece, he held the speaker to his mouth, "James Daugherty."

"Hello, Mr. Daugherty, this is Rose Shelby," she announced, "may I speak to you for a moment?"

"Certainly, Mrs. Shelby," J.D. answered.

"We've just now returned with Chief Ruffle. I'd like to know what arrangements you've made."

"Well, ma'am, things are nearly ready. I have to go to the sheriff's office in the morning to sign a few papers. I'm afraid that Indians don't count too much with the coppers in this town, so the sheriff isn't all that concerned about finding Tommy's murderer. All the same, the body is still evidence in a crime, and as such, it's not supposed to be released or buried. I had to do some fast talking and throw your name around to get things as far along as I did. I'm sorry about that."

"Go ahead and use our name all you want, just so things get done," Rose responded.

"I do need to ask that you and Chief Ruffle go tomorrow to Johnson Brothers' Funeral Home. The law requires that the boy's next of kin or a family representative sign for the release of the remains."

"Yes, of course, that won't be a problem. Thank you for your help, Mr. Daugherty."

"Mrs. Shelby, I know that you were pretty busy up there, but did you hear anything about my operative, Mr. Smith?"

"We were very busy while we were there, yes. Mrs. Henderson, the lady in whose boarding house we stay while in Hominy, mentioned that her son's fiancé, who is an Indian girl, by the way, lost her father in a cowardly attack by an unknown gunman. Peter, her son, was kept just as busy with that unfortunate affair. In any case, there was an Indian man staying with the family. Peter said he was working for a detective in Tulsa. I took it that he was your man."

There was a long silence. "It was so sad, Mr. Daugherty. So many terrible things. I tried to find out exactly what happened, but Peter did not have a minute to spare. I think he said that your operative was injured in the attack but wasn't badly hurt. No one could tell me anything about Rose, either."

"Thank you, Mrs. Shelby. If you hear anything else, would you let me know?"

"Of course. I have to go now. Will I see you tomorrow?"

"Perhaps at the funeral home. I'll call you when all the arrangements are final."

"Thank you. Goodbye."

J.D. replaced the earpiece and sat back in his chair. He was thinking about Hoolie. He hoped that nothing had gone wrong. He was confident that Hoolie could take care of himself, but if he had been hurt, J.D. would have to go to Osage County. Having an operative hurt on the job was bad for business. And J.D. realized that it was more than just business, he was worried about his friend. Although J.D. had trouble admitting it, even to himself, Hoolie was more to him than just one of his ops.

"Time to go home," he said quietly to himself.

J.D. locked up the office and rode the trolley to one of his favorite haunts, where he had a bite to eat and his "Sunday evening" shot of whiskey. When he got back to his flat, J.D. felt fatigued to his very bones. He couldn't seem to keep his eyes open. He took off his hat and coat, loosened his tie, unhooked his celluloid collar, sat down in his easy chair, and promptly fell asleep.

J.D. woke up on Monday morning still fully clothed and in his chair. His neck was cramped and his back ached. He awoke, in short, in one of the foulest moods he could have possibly been in.

Everything went from bad to worse. He got to the office late and found a few bills in the early mail. He would have to pay those as soon as possible. Then around 10 a.m., a messenger arrived with a telegram from Hoolie. J.D. was deeply relieved to get word of his operative and have confirmation that he was not seriously hurt. It was too close a shave. J.D. was going to have to give some thought to what their next move would be.

He placed a few telephone calls, and fortunately, he got the answers he was looking for. Leaning back in his chair, he put his feet on the desk and burned a cigarette.

The Chichester case had been completely sidetracked. Tommy was dead. Rose was still missing. Hoolie had been shot. It looked like three separate occurrences that just happened to coincide. The attack that Hoolie had been caught up in was the result of being in the wrong place at the wrong time. Or was something much deeper going on in Osage County? J.D. didn't believe much in coincidence. Hoolie always told him that in Cherokee beliefs all things were interconnected. So, J.D.'s chief operative and man on the scene thought that *everything* was linked together. J.D. just couldn't figure out how the two murders could be related and how Rose Chichester's disappearance was at all connected with Osage County—at least now that certain facts had been made clear.

J.D. had to reorganize the case. First, he would deal with getting the Ruffle boy back to Osage County; then he would concentrate on the Chichester case. Since it seemed like Hoolie's search for Rose Chichester was at a dead end, he would let Hoolie recuperate up in Hominy for a couple of days. If he could wrap up things in Tulsa, J.D. would go to Osage County and work not just on finding Rose but on finding the man who shot Hoolie and murdered the other man. One thing was clear: J.D. would eventually find the assailant who had ambushed his operative.

He was hoping that he could take care of the Ruffle business in a few hours and then go to Greenwood to talk to Minerva Whitwell. He believed that she would be able to give him some background information and set a few things straight. Maids, especially a maid who had borne a child fathered by the scion of the mansion, might know and reveal a good deal more about the Shelbys and Chichesters than he could get out of a member of the immediate family. And there was the possibility that Minerva had had something to do with Rose Chichester's disappearance. Maybe Rose had set her sights on Little Bill, and Minerva could not chance losing the Shelby payoff. J.D. still had no idea when he would be able to look for her. Even though Little Bill had promised his full cooperation, J.D. knew that the young man would not cross over certain lines. The only solid lead was Danny Ryan's five-dollar information.

J.D. went to Western Union and sent a wire to Hoolie. Returning to the office, he placed telephone calls to the sheriff's office, the morgue, the Johnson Brothers' Funeral Home, and the police records clerk—another drinking acquaintance. Finally, he called Rose Shelby.

After several rings, a servant answered and said that he would "summon Mrs. Shelby."

"Good morning, Mrs. Shelby," J.D. said after waiting an inordinate amount of time for her to come to the telephone. J.D. was in a hurry.

"Oh, hello, Mr. Daugherty. Have things been arranged?"

"Yes, ma'am. I called you to set up a time to meet you and Chief Ruffle at the funeral home. I just received word that my operative, Mr. Smith, *was* wounded in the attack you mentioned yesterday. I've telegraphed instructions to him and—"

"Is he all right?" she interrupted.

"He was hit in the ribs, but he was able to send me a wire this morning. I have to take care of a few things and go to the sheriff's office to conclude the arrangements concerning Tommy Ruffle's body. I'd like to wrap up a few things regarding Mr. Chichester's operation and get to Hominy to see about Mr. Smith."

"I understand that completely," she said with a note of concern in her voice.

"I should have everything taken care of by one or one-thirty. Could you meet me at the Johnson Brothers' Funeral Home at two?"

"Yes, two will be fine. Chief Ruffle, Professor Potter, and I will be there. Have the arrangements been made for a hearse? I'd rather have Tommy driven back than to ship his remains on the train."

"No, Mrs. Shelby, I didn't think of it at the time. I'm sure that it can be managed. It might be very expensive."

"Cost doesn't matter. I'll have my husband arrange the hearse, Mr. Daugherty. Thank you. I'll see you at two."

J.D. barely got out a " 'bye" before the telephone went dead. He stared pensively at the earpiece for a short time, looked out the window, and decided that he would walk over to Sam Berg's office for a bit of advice.

After some small talk with Sam's secretary, J.D. was ushered into his lawyer's small, cluttered office. Sam quickly obliged J.D. by explaining that if Chichester didn't mind if J.D. did some work for the Shelbys, it probably wouldn't constitute a conflict of interest. "If Chichester doesn't complain, how's anybody going to accuse you of having a conflict?" Sam concluded. J.D. gave Sam a cordial tip of his hat, smiled at Sam's secretary, and left the office, saying with irony in his gruff voice that he was on his way to the sheriff's office.

The stroll to the courthouse was actually very pleasant. The month of May in Oklahoma was usually mild and sunny, but May would be gone in two days. It would start getting hot in June, and the humidity would shoot up. During the summer, nearly everybody in Tulsa slept on a screened-in back porch in the hope of catching a breeze off the river. Those without screened porches often slept outside, but then they had to contend with the mosquitoes from the river bottom and the violent thunderstorms. Summer also brought the tornado season and the very real possibility of having whole towns blown away.

Some years back, a twister completely destroyed the town of David, located just about fifty miles northeast of Tulsa. The residents rebuilt just over the hills from the old site of David on the chance that when another tornado struck it would jump the hill and miss the town. They also renamed it "Chelsea," because some thought "David" was a bad-luck name.

Tulsa had never been hit by a tornado, or at least, there was no record of one touching down. Some old-timers maintained that because the town was located at the bend of the river, it was sheltered. Tulsa had been a Creek town back when Oklahoma was Indian Territory. J.D. thought that the Creeks probably knew more about where tornadoes would strike than white people did, so he figured that Tulsa wouldn't be blown away.

As he walked into the courthouse, J.D. caught a glimpse of Sheriff McCollough talking with Chief of Police John Gustafson. Generally, those two didn't confer unless a problem over jurisdiction or political matters required their mutual attention. J.D. thought that both were no more and no less corrupt than other law enforcement officials in a relatively large city. J.D. liked McCollough better. The tall, lanky official with the big moustache was good humored and, for the most part, even-handed. Police Chief Gustafson hated and feared the fact that the city's black population had grown by several thousand over the past ten years. Rumor had it that Gustafson was the Grand Dragon or some high muckety-muck in the local Ku Klux Klan. Of course, there were very many members of the secret society, including, or so J.D. had heard, Oklahoma's governor.

J.D. suspected that Sam Berg had a hand in spreading the rumor of

Gustafson's ties to the Klan. While he admired Sam for keeping tabs on these officials, J.D. doubted that Gustafson would let the Klan undermine his authority. If the Klan got out of line like they had the year before, J.D. was sure that Gustafson would be in the forefront of kicking them back into line once again. To a copper, authority and jurisdiction were everything.

J.D. saw a deputy he knew and walked casually over toward him. The man's name was Franklin, and he was standing near where Gustafson and McCollough were talking. By the time J.D. was close enough to speak to Franklin, the sheriff and the police chief were saying their goodbyes. The police chief walked out the door, and McCollough, his head hung low and his shoulders drooping, started climbing the stairs to his office on the second floor.

J.D. started up a conversation with Franklin. " 'Lo, Franklin, how's everything?"

Franklin managed a scowl, "Hiya, J.D. Don't have much time."

"What's the rumpus? McCollough and Gustafson getting together for a little tea?"

"Ha! Nothin' like that, you can bet."

J.D. kept smiling, trying to stimulate Franklin into letting him in on whatever was going on. "Well, they don't get to talk much, I guess," said J.D. "They just keeping in touch?"

Franklin paused and looked furtively around the building. "Listen, J.D.," he said, "can you keep something under your hat?"

"Sure, sure. What's going on?"

"Don't say nothin'. But stay in for a couple of days and keep your house and office locked up. We might have another lynchin' here in a day or two."

J.D.'s smile vanished. "By God," he exclaimed, "what happened? This town can't handle somethin' like that again."

"Keep it down," whispered Franklin. "I'll tell you." He pushed his hat back on his head and continued: "Some Negro boy went after a white girl in an elevator. He ran off, and she's screaming bloody murder. McCollough and Gustafson got to work things out."

"Damn," J.D. swore again. "Wha'd they work out?"

"City police are goin' after the boy. They've got two, three Negro coppers who'll pick him up. After that, we get him here at the county jail. They was workin' out details."

"I hate to see this happen again," said J.D. "That lynching last year was bad news for the whole town. People'll go crazy. The Negroes won't put up with it again. There's gonna be hell to pay. And that don't make your job easier."

"Ain't that the lowdown," said Franklin. "I'd better get back upstairs, J.D. See you around."

J.D. just nodded his head and stood there for a minute or so. He drew a thumbnail across the bottom of his moustache and walked over to the stairs. He climbed to the second floor and entered the meeting room. There were three deputies deep in discussion, and J.D. didn't really want to bother them. He turned to leave, but a man coming in from the opposite door called out to him. "Ho, J.D., don't leave just yet."

It was Joe Spiedel. J.D. walked to the middle of the room and shook hands with him. The other officers looked up and acknowledged J.D. He nodded a greeting to the men, looked directly at Spiedel, and said, " 'Lo, Joe, I came to get some papers signed on the body in the morgue I talked to you about. Got him identified, and I need to get him moved to the Johnson Brother's mortuary down the street. He's evidence, so you guys have to give me permission to get the body out."

Spiedel's eyes narrowed slightly, then a glimmer of remembrance edged across his face. "Yep, heard about it. Mrs. Big Bill Shelby came down herself, eh? You must have some pull with the bigwigs, J.D. I got the papers in the other room. I'll get 'em for you. Just dangle for a minute or two."

J.D. sat down and dangled. A few minutes later, he had signed a ream of paper that allowed Tommy's body to be delivered to the Johnson Brothers' Funeral Home.

"Thanks, Joe," said J.D. "I appreciate your help. I don't think anybody's gonna get worked up over the killing of this boy, particularly if what I heard downstairs is gonna happen. He needs to get buried proper like." The officers at the table looked up once and dropped their eyes to the floor.

Spiedel's eyes narrowed once again. "Wha'd you hear downstairs?"

"Just about the colored boy the city boys are gonna arrest."

Spiedel shook his head. "Damn, none of those guys can keep their tongues from waggin'. Listen, J.D., you gotta keep mum on this," he whispered hoarsely.

"Sure, Joe, just fill me in."

"I reckon that won't hurt. You don't want no lynchin' any more than we do."

"That's right. Hell, no. Hurts business everywhere."

"Okay. You know that shoeshine joint over on Main across from the Drexel Building where Renberg's is, next to the Boston Shoe Store?"

"What happened? Bootblacks get outta hand?"

Spiedel produced a frown. "Sort of. Renberg's lets the shoeshine boys use the bathroom when they need to. A white man owns the shine parlor, and he worked things out with the folks who own the Drexel building. Renberg's lets the boys use the can on the fourth floor. I tell you, if the boys in the Klan heard that the colored boys was usin' the same crapper as the whites, the roof would come off. 'Course the boys in the Klan don't go there anyways, Renberg hisself bein' a Jew.

"Now this mornin', a boy from the shine parlor—don't know which one yet—goes over to use the facilities. He goes into the elevator. A girl—somebody told me she's seventeen or eighteen—is runnin' the thing. Don't nobody know her name. Anyway, the boy gets into the elevator, and the next you know, the girl's screamin' that the nigger tried to rape her.

"The boy runs outta Renberg's like a devil's on his tail. Nobody tried to stop him. That's funny, 'cause to most of the clerks, a colored boy runnin' outta the store like that means he stole somethin'. The elevator girl runs over to this one clerk, Bob Millstone, and throws herself down in front of him. She's screamin' and holdin' on to him. He calls a cop and tells the story. Now, he says that her clothes was tore, and she had scratches on her hands from fightin' off the black boy."

J.D. was following the story intently. When Spiedel finished, J.D. said, "That's a helluva tale. But I don't get it. Nobody's that goddam dumb to try and rape a girl in the daytime with customers and clerks all over the place. It doesn't make sense."

"You're right there, J.D. Nobody's seen any evidence that the boy attacked her. We got just what Millstone said. I'd bet money that the boy only bumped up against her, and she flew into a fit."

"Sounds like there might be something else," said J.D. thoughtfully.

"What might that be?" said Spiedel with a sardonic smile.

"Well, it sounds like she made a beeline to this Millstone. Maybe she's after him and made up the rape just to get his attention."

"Damn, J.D., you got a suspicious mind."

"That I do, Joe . . . that I do. I just don't think anybody's that dumb to go after a girl in Renberg's."

"Since we're only supposin'," said Spiedel, "maybe she was just tryin' to start somethin' with the blacks. You know, there's been a couple of lynchin's in the state lately. Maybe she's startin' somethin' just to get things flared up and get her name in the papers. There's some people in town that want to burn out niggertown and move 'em 'cross the river."

J.D. pulled on his moustache pensively, "I suppose it could be just about anything, and I sure wouldn't want to be in your shoes once you all bring the boy in. We got a bunch of thugs in this town that would just love to storm the jail and lynch somebody. But most of all they'd like to roam the streets stealing anything they could get their grubby paws on.

"It scares me to think what could happen. I've seen miners lynch claim jumpers out west just to get the chance to run through the streets raising hell. Mobs get away with too much—rape, murder, you name it.

"Some of these boys are crazy enough to start a war in Little Africa.

And those boys over there aren't gonna take it lying down. Some of them just got back from France, and they know how to take care of themselves. They're gonna shoot back, and I can't say I blame them much if they do. But you and the city coppers are gonna end up in the middle if the shooting starts."

Spiedel sighed deeply, "I hope you're wrong, old man. Maybe we can get the boy outta town. But I know what you mean, stoppin' a mob is like stoppin' a runaway train goin' down a steep grade."

"I'm damn sorry, Joe," said J.D., with heartfelt heaviness in his voice. "I hope that nothing goes wrong."

"Me, too. Well, gotta get back to work. See you later, J.D."

"Right," said J.D. as he turned and left the office.

J.D. exited the courthouse and caught the trolley to Ed North's diner. As he was enjoying a plate of corned beef and cabbage before going to the coroner's office, he began hearing exaggerated stories about the rape at the Drexel building coming from the other customers.

Two seats down at the counter, a bearded man in a black derby said, "Now, I heard that two niggers grabbed that little girl and held her down while a third one had his way with her. It was sheer luck that one of Renberg's clerks heard somethin' and scared the niggers away."

Another man, sitting at a nearby table, listened intently. His puffy face grew redder with each of the Derby-hat's words. Finally, he said loudly, "Why ain't the laws in this town out roundin' up them niggers? By God, bring 'em all in, and let the girl pick 'em out. Then we take 'em out and string 'em up. Make an example of 'em. The rest of the spooks would catch on that they can't go messin' around with no white girl."

The man looked around cautiously, saw that no women were in the establishment, and added, "While we're at it, we oughta cut their peckers off, too."

Everyone in Ed's, except for J.D. and the proprietor himself, laughed uproariously.

When the laugher died down, J.D. said quietly, "Well, I remember the lynching last year. Wasn't pretty. And I've seen these things happen before. A lynch mob can wreck a whole city. People could get killed. Anybody here ever been in a riot?"

When no one spoke up, J.D. continued, "I didn't think so. There isn't anything good about them. Looting, windows broke, shooting, fires. Wanting to get something like that started is crazy."

The puffy-faced man bristled. "You callin' me crazy, mister?"

J.D. spun angrily on him, "I said that any man is crazy to want to bring that down on his town. That's right, you want to start something like that, you are nuts."

The man rose, and J.D. slid off the counter stool. Ed quickly came from behind the counter. He got between the men, "Let's simmer down, gents."

Ed looked sternly at the puffy-faced man and spoke to him softly, "Believe me, mister, you don't want to tangle with J.D. here. He's a cop."

"Sorry, mister, didn't know," the man said. "You ought to know that I was mighty riled up hearin' about a young white girl gettin' raped by a pack of niggers. Nothing personal to you."

J.D. was angry. "Just get outta here," he said in his most threatening voice.

The man hurried out the door. Too late, Ed called out, "Hey, pay up!"

When it was clear that the man would not return, J.D. said, "Sorry, Ed, I lost you a customer. Put that guy's meal on my bill. I'm really sorry about all this. Lynching talk and riots get me plenty scared. If the coppers and the firemen aren't ready, a town can get wrecked real fast."

"You're right, J.D.," said Ed softly, "I've got my business to look out for. Let's hope this talk stops soon."

J.D. leaned over close to Ed's ear and whispered, "I'll tell you something, Ed, the talk around the courthouse isn't much different from here. The coppers are getting ready. This could boil over. Lock up tight the next few days . . . and board up the windows."

"I'll do it, J.D. But let's hope it don't. I got a business to run. Go ahead and finish your corned beef."

J.D. sat down once again and began to take small bites of his meal;

the corned beef and cabbage was delicious. Old Ed was one damn good cook.

When he finally polished off the last of the cabbage, J.D. stood and told Ed to put the meal on his tab. He left a shiny quarter on the counter. A tip for Ed.

His first trip was to the coroner's office. He had to take the papers from the sheriff's office to McAfee and spend some time talking to the coroner and Chiles. He needed those two birds on his list of confidants.

As J.D. might have predicted, both McAfee and Chiles were all genteel smiles and hand-patting sympathy. When J.D. told them about his suspicions prior to talking Mrs. Shelby into identifying Tommy Ruffle, McAfee kept repeating, "Tch . . . tch . . . tch . . . it must be difficult." Chiles, not so repetitious, finally said that J.D. sure had his work cut out for him and that his association with the Shelbys could only help business. "Maybe I should have gotten into the private dick business after I left the cops," he said.

J.D. smiled as he thought that the chances of that were slim since few people would trust Chiles with anything more than a dead body or two.

After he left the morgue, he caught a trolley and rode the four blocks to the funeral home. J.D. waited ten minutes or so outside the building before the Shelby limousine and a long black hearse pulled up to the curb. He slowly walked to the automobile as it rolled quietly to a halt. As he was reaching for the rear door handle, the limousine's front passenger-side door swung open. A deep voice intoned, "I'll get that, sir." It was more a warning than a courtesy. J.D. took a step back from the curb and the footman, or whatever he was, sprang out of the car and flung wide the rear door.

Three people were in the rear of the limousine. A slender, balding man with pince-nez glasses balanced on the bridge of his nose exited the car first, and J.D. guessed he was the professor, Arlen Potter. Potter held a hand out for Mrs. Shelby. An elderly Indian man with braids, whose right eye didn't quite synchronize with the left, followed Mrs. Shelby out of the vehicle.

Rose Shelby was dressed entirely in black. She had a new-fangled veil on, one that didn't cover her whole face. She carried one of her prize-winning roses—the new Osage Rose—in her right hand. As if to reassure herself of the rose's velvety softness, Mrs. Shelby would from time to time gently touch the blossom to her small chin. The first time she did it, J.D. was taken aback with the thought that Mrs. Shelby was probably the loveliest woman he'd ever seen in spite of her veil and mourning clothes.

She looked up at J.D. "I'm glad to see you again, Mr. Daugherty, even on this sad occasion."

Her sad, sweet smile made J.D. pause for a moment. "I'm sorry to see you under such circumstances, Mrs. Shelby."

Mrs. Shelby's sense of decorum brought her momentarily out of her melancholy state. "Mr. Daugherty, please allow me to introduce you to Chief Ruffle and Professor Arlen Potter."

Potter removed his pince-nez and held them in his right hand. He gestured with the glasses as if they were a pointer in a classroom. "Pleased to meet you, Mr. Daugherty," said Potter, "Mrs. Shelby has told us that you discovered Chief Ruffle's grandson and had her identify him. May I say on behalf of Chief Ruffle that he certainly appreciates what you've done. I'm personally indebted to you, too. Tommy was a fine young man who will be mourned by hundreds of people . . ."

Chief Ruffle spoke in Osage. Potter listened carefully until the Chief had finished. Then he said, "The chief adds his thanks to mine and wishes to say that in the old days, a warrior who had brought back the body of a comrade killed in battle was highly honored. He wants to say that you have done the work of a warrior and will no doubt be honored in your old age."

J.D. smiled a rather puzzled grin. He really didn't know what to make of the old chief's comments.

Potter noticed J.D.'s perplexed look. "The chief likes to put things according to his own notions and Indian traditions. Warriors are especially respected among the Osages for many reasons. When they acted as scouts, warriors had to be truthful at all times because the whole village depended on them to find game and to warn everyone of the enemy's approach. Like a warrior, you went into enemy country to recover the body of his grandson so that the young man's spirit could be returned to his home country. Doing something like that was considered courageous, but most importantly, it was viewed as a religious act. The chief was saying that your concern for his grandson's spirit and proper burial was an unselfish act that will be recognized by the people. The spirits will no doubt help you and make you happy in your old age."

J.D. felt genuinely proud, if still somewhat confused. Hoolie would probably understand what all that meant; J.D. thought that he was just doing a job.

"Tell the chief that I thank him for what he said, but that I was simply doing my job. Tell him I'm deeply sorry that his grandson was killed."

Potter answered, "Chief Ruffle knows what you've said, he . . ."

The old man interrupted. Potter listened, then translated, "The Chief thanks you again, but says that we're talking too much. He wants to bring his grandson home."

J.D. dropped his eyes to the ground, "He's right; let's go in."

Potter held the door for Mrs. Shelby, Chief Ruffle, and J.D. The chauffeur and hearse driver followed Potter into the foyer. There, a very fat man in a black mourning coat, gray vest, striped tie, gray pants, and spats stood solemnly beside a fake marble column that supported a big, green, drooping fern in a fake Greek vase. J.D. knew that he was one of the Johnson brothers, easily the two most experienced morticians in the state. The brothers were portly, soft-spoken, and grand masters of the rituals of death. In a gesture that appeared like a priest's benediction, Johnson raised his right hand and swiveled his entire body toward a curtained doorway. Everyone except the driver followed the Johnson brother into the next room.

Tommy's casket sat on a raised catafalque. He looked almost serene in his black coat and tie; the high, white collar hid his wound. Rose Shelby walked forward and laid her rose on Tommy's chest. She took two steps back and began to cry softly. Chief Ruffle's face was grim as he gestured to the Johnson brother, who quietly closed the coffin. Mrs.

Shelby turned to J.D. "Mr. Daugherty, please," her eyes turned steely once again, "will you take care of this for me?"

"I'll take care of everything." He turned to Potter. "Professor, if you would escort Mrs. Shelby and the chief to the car, I'll look after things here."

Potter nodded and led the woman and old man from the room.

"Mr. Johnson," J.D. continued, "I'm sure you know the Shelbys. Please allow me to sign the receipt and take care of this. Your fees are assured." J.D. smiled briefly and added, "Besides, we all know where they live."

Johnson returned J.D.'s knowing grin, produced a paper from an inner pocket of the mourning coat, and asked J.D. to put his signature on the bottom line. J.D. did so, and then he joined the rest of the party outside as they waited for two porters to load the hearse.

Potter and Chief Ruffle talked for a few moments in Osage. The professor then said quietly to Mrs. Shelby that once back in Osage country, Tommy's body would have to be removed from the coffin and his clothing changed in order to bury the boy, according to Potter, "in the old way." J.D. guessed that there would be an Osage ritual, but he refrained from asking questions about it.

Before she took her seat in the limousine, Mrs. Shelby turned to J.D., "Mr. Daugherty, I know that you have E.L.'s case to attend to, and I've prevented you from putting your full time into it. E.L. agrees that not much can be done at the moment because of Tommy's death. He understands. I also want you to know that Rose means a great deal to me. Once she's found, I will add something to your bonus. You've done the Ruffle family and me a great service that will not be forgotten."

"Thank you, ma'am. I haven't lost much time on finding Rose. I'm going to do some searching today, and my operative is still following leads in Osage County. He'll report back soon. Judging from her previous conduct, it looks as though Rose has simply disappeared for a short time and will no doubt show up again soon. I'm sure she's not in any danger."

"How is your man doing?" inquired Rose Shelby.

"He's apparently doing all right. Mr. Smith knows how to take care of himself. He was in the war and is as tough as boot leather. He'll get back with me shortly."

"So, you have a lead in town?"

"Yes, ma'am, I do. But we'll have to see how it pans out. Right now, I have to go to the telegraph office to see if Mr. Smith has returned my message."

"I am sorry, Mr. Daugherty. These last few days have been terrible. You have been a godsend."

"Thank you. Please reassure Mr. Chichester that he'll soon have his daughter back."

Rose Shelby turned to the waiting car. "We should go now. We have to be in Hominy before nightfall. The Hendersons are expecting us, and the Ruffle family is waiting as well. My husband, children, and Mr. Chichester are motoring up there early in the morning to attend Tommy's funeral. I wish you could be there. Good-bye."

J.D. shook her hand and gave her a slight bow as she slid into the limousine. He looked after the cortege as it started up, gathered speed, and began the journey to bury Tommy Ruffle.

J.D. stuffed his hands in his pockets and started to walk back to the office. He took out his watch, and discovering that it was only two-thirty-eight, he decided that he might try to talk to Minerva Whitwell. He crossed the street, and after waiting a few minutes, he hopped aboard a northbound streetcar. After two transfers, he found himself on north Greenwood Avenue, in the heart of the segregated black neighborhood.

J.D. found Minerva's address, but she wasn't at home. He tapped on the doors of three of the neighboring houses. No one answered.

When J.D. finally found his way back to the office, he wearily sat down and thought over the day's events. He had taken care of the Ruffle boy, but he had accomplished nothing on the Chichester case. He resolved to interview Minerva Whitwell the next day.

11

Jailhouse John

Hoolie stood holding the Springfield's shell in his hand and watched as three elderly Osage men finished their morning prayers. Then, he walked slowly back to the house and sat on the front-porch step. A single casing from a Springfield was not enough to bring a murderer to justice in the white man's courts.

He sat and watched as the families began to pick up and leave. Myrtle came out and sat down on the step behind him. He turned, looked at her, and uttered a soft greeting. He dropped his eyes to the ground to conceal his astonishment and sadness at her appearance.

Myrtle had cut her long hair very short. In the back it didn't reach the collar of her high-necked dress. Not only that, but she had streaked it with ash.

Her downcast eyes were melancholy and contemplative. She wanted to share something with Hoolie but was hesitant to speak. Her eyes filled with tears. She was moved by his concern for her and her family, and it made her very happy when he paid her special attention, but Myrtle was reluctant to explain her customs to him. No matter how much she liked him and honored his bravery, Hoolie was still a stranger. She was torn between her desire to include him and her feeling that she didn't need to explain her actions to anyone.

Finally, forehead wrinkled in determination, Myrtle looked off into the distance and spoke gently, almost in a whisper. "We cut our hair when somebody dies. And put ash in it. It's the old way and the good way. My mother and grandmother were gonna cut their legs with a knife, but Grandma decided that it might upset you."

Hoolie felt as if he'd been included in something very important and intimate. When Myrtle finished, he dropped his eyes, and then said just as softly, "I understand. We have certain things we have to do when our people pass on. You don't have to explain anything to me if you don't want to."

She tilted her head to one side, "I'm glad you know about these things."

Abruptly she stood up. As she opened the screen door, she said under her breath, "You're a good man, Hoolie Smith."

Not looking back or acknowledging that he had heard her, Hoolie smiled to himself.

That afternoon, Hoolie drove into Hominy. Herding the flivver—as he put it—was getting easier. His side was still very sore, but the rest he had been forced to take had helped his breathing. Every time he inhaled, the pain was a little bit less.

He pulled up to the depot, walked in, and greeted the same blond telegrapher with a nod. Hoolie picked up the message form and began to write. He worried that the strange-looking telegrapher would tell someone about the contents of his message, so he had to be subtle. Hoolie knew that he couldn't be too careful, especially in Hominy. The message that went out to J.D. read:

HEALING STOP HAVE AN IDEA WHO STOP HAVE TO
FIND WHY STOP CONTINUING OP STOP

From the depot, Hoolie sauntered down to the general store to buy a bit of candy and possibly strike up a conversation with anyone who wanted to talk to him. He figured that he might discover something by talking to the locals—that is, if any of the locals would talk.

He entered the store and tipped his hat to the man with the clean apron behind the counter. He made his way through the barrels and tables piled high with goods to the big glass jars holding the hard candy he loved. He lifted the lid on one and pulled out a cinnamon stick. He laid a penny on the counter, tipped his hat once again to the clerk, and walked out on the street.

He stood in the sun for a while, getting his bearings and looking over the buildings that made up the town of Hominy. He spotted an Indian man squatting with his back against a building in an alley across the street. Hoolie thought that the man was probably one of the local good-for-nothings that hung around town. He had always liked those men even though his own inclination and upbringing leaned toward hard work and keeping busy. It seemed like the ne'er-do-wells were always good people. He headed across the road toward the squatting man.

Hoolie's shadow came over the man just as he brought a small jar of clear liquid to his lips and took a sip. Putting the jar down, he raised his head and said bluntly, "Who the hell are you?"

Hoolie reached for his hat to tip it in a friendly manner, "Name's Hoolie Smith. I'm a Cherokee from over near Stilwell. I'm staying out at the Lookout place. New in town. Don't look like the white people want to talk to me much. I saw you and thought I'd speak to you."

The man was dressed in a pair of faded blue jeans, a bright red, collarless shirt, thin black suspenders, and black high-heeled cowboy boots. He wore leather cuffs with shiny silver studs in the pattern of a circle and a blue neck scarf with a silver slide. The man pushed back a black ten-gallon cowboy hat with a large eagle feather tied to a silver hatband. Skinny and long-legged, he looked to be about thirty years old.

Hoolie turned slightly and felt a stab of pain from the wound in his side. The man caught sight of the way Hoolie flinched, "You hurt?"

Hoolie simply nodded and offered his hand in greeting. The man gave it a quick pump from his sitting position, tilted his head as if to get a better view of Hoolie, and then took a quick pull from his liquor jar. The jar was filled with a local moonshine, distilled illegally back in the hills and very likely sold out of the back of a wagon on the streets of the town itself.

After his drink, the man scrunched up his face and looked into Hoolie's eyes. He squinted one eye, "You there when the man was shot?"

"I was there." Hoolie's head bobbed once.

"You shoot back?"

"Yeah."

"That's good. Kill him?"

"No."

"Goin' after him?"

"Yes. Want to help?"

"I do. What you want to know?"

"You got a name?"

The man, still squatting with his back against the clapboard wall, nodded. He took another drink, "Name's John Tall Soldier. The man who was killed was a relative of mine. Not a good idea to mention his name for a while. I heard about you. People say you're a good man."

Hoolie looked around cautiously. "You probably know that I was looking for Tommy Ruffle and a runaway girl, and the laws around here ain't very helpful. Now, what I'd like to ask you is what do you know about the sheriff and his deputies?"

John Tall Soldier laughed derisively, "That's a bad bunch. They been in cahoots with a couple of judges 'round here to take our land."

Hoolie rubbed his cheek. "One of the judges named Patterson?"

"That's one of 'em."

"How about Pete Henderson?"

John offered Hoolie the moonshine jar. When Hoolie refused, John pointed with his lips to a place on the ground next to him. Hoolie complied and sat down beside John with his back against the building. Both men looked straight ahead. Finally, John began to speak. "I know 'em all. They're all bad, and Pete's the worstest. He's mean." John paused, collecting his thoughts. "Listen," he said in a low voice, "I was sleepin' out near Homer Eagle's place one time when the sheriff, Deputy Wallace, and Pete come out. They was tryin' to get old Homer to sign up with a new lease-man. Homer didn't like the man, and he hated the judge who appointed the lawyer to look out for his land and headright. The lawyer was greedy and stole from him. Homer wanted the judge to make it right. Well, the judge listened to him and didn't say nothin'. Next day, those three showed up at Homer's place. I was sick out under a bush. They took Homer out to a tree, tied him up, and that boy, Pete, beat Homer with a buggy whip. They left him out there, too. When they went away, I woke up and found him like that. He told me what had gone on. I cut him down and doctored him up. He was a sight. That Pete . . . he's a mean sombitch."

"What about this Deputy Wallace? He as mean as Pete?"

"I ain't for sure about him. I think maybe he's just trying to keep his job. Mostly he's just one of those hillbillies come from Arkansas. Billy's kind of crazy. I think the war's still givin' him trouble."

Out of the corner of his eye, Hoolie spied two young white men in big hats and cowboy boots walk by. Both of them narrowed their eyes at the sight of John and Hoolie sitting together in the alley. Hoolie's spine tingled. He hoped that the two cowboys would just walk on.

Just as he was about to say something to John, the two cowboys stopped. They walked into the alley and planted themselves directly in front of John and Hoolie, balancing on their toes, readying themselves for a fight. The freckle-faced redhead spoke, "I thought that the sheriff was gonna clean up these piles of red nigger shit from off the street." The dark-haired one with the crooked nose stood with his fists clenched, glowering at Hoolie.

Hoolie started to rise from a sitting position. He pushed his back up against the wall and used his good leg to push himself up. It strained his side, but he slowly rose, ready to take on Dark-hair.

John kept his back to the wall, waved one hand as if he could shoo the two cowboys away like flies, and took another drink from his jar. He remained in a squat, legs under him. Hoolie stood to his full height. Hoolie thought that if he kicked Dark-hair in the gut, he would quickly give up, giving Hoolie enough time to turn on Freckle-face. John didn't look as if he was going to do anything but sit on his haunches and wave his hand.

Freckle-face glanced at Hoolie. "Just keep gettin' up, Indin. You're gonna be layin' back in the dirt with your head busted in real quick."

Hoolie clenched his fist, and the two cowboys seemed to back off a bit. Maybe he looked more formidable standing than he did sitting down. Freckle-face tried to bluff his way through the confrontation. "Just get off the street. Go on, git. Git, I said."

It was like he was trying to chase off a dog. Hoolie thought that he had the advantage now. Dark-hair's eyes had the look of fear in them, and Hoolie wasn't backing down. "Why don't you boys go on about your own business," said Hoolie with a warning edge to his voice. "We ain't bothering you."

Hoolie had seriously misjudged Dark-hair. He drew back his fist and launched a blow aimed at Hoolie's head. Hoolie tried to twist away, but he felt a searing pain flash across his rib cage. Still, he was able to avoid the full force of the punch. The cowboy's fist glanced off Hoolie's cheekbone without causing much damage. Freckle-face, not expecting the attack, jumped back a step and turned to look at Dark-hair's assault on Hoolie. His movement allowed John to react. From his squatting position, John pushed with the full power of his legs away from the wall and upward toward Freckle-face's stomach. John drove his head squarely into the cowboy's sternum, driving the breath from his lungs and crushing John's unblocked hat. Somehow, John held onto his moonshine jar without spilling a drop of the clear liquid.

Freckle-face was driven clear across the alley into the opposite clapboard building. He smashed his own cowboy hat against the wall and collapsed in a heap. John turned his attention to Hoolie and Dark-hair.

The glancing blow to his cheek hadn't really hurt, but Hoolie's knees nearly buckled from the pain in his side. He was thinking that his gunshot wound had been torn open again just as Dark-hair aimed another punch to Hoolie's forehead. This time Hoolie took the blow full on. Tears burst from his eyes. He felt as if his brain had been driven backward and had bounced off the back of his skull. Little lights floated around the periphery of his vision like so many lightning bugs. His legs gave out this time, and he seemed to cave in on himself. He dropped to one knee and had to steady himself with his left hand on the ground.

Hoolie was vulnerable in that position, and Dark-hair was just about to finish him with a kick to the jaw. At the very moment the cowboy was about to strike, John drove his fist into the man's right ear. He went down immediately, allowing Hoolie to recover enough strength to stand, put up his fists, and ready himself for Dark-hair to get up. But John's blow had poleaxed the man. He was out cold.

Freckle-face was on his hands and knees, taking deep breaths and trying hard to recuperate from John's head butt. With no warning, John gave Freckle-face a merciless kick in the ribs with his own pointed-toe cowboy boot. Hoolie actually heard the breath leave the redhead's lungs as he collapsed, belly first, in the dusty alley.

Now, Dark-hair was inching upward. Hoolie stood over the cowboy as he rose on his shaky legs. Hoolie struck Dark-hair squarely on the nose with his right fist. Blood erupted from the cowboy's nostrils, and he staggered forward. Hoolie side-stepped the oncoming man and hit him again with a left hook on the temple. Dark-hair went face first into the wall of the building opposite to where his friend, the now prone Freckle-face, lay. The fight was over almost as soon as it had begun.

Carefully placing his liquor jar on the ground, John reached into the pocket of his jeans. He extracted a large jackknife, pulled the blade open, and bent over Freckle-face. He rolled the cowboy onto his back. Freckle-face's sky-blue eyes fluttered open. John bent low, showed the man the blade, and rasped, "I think I'll cut out your goddamn yellow eyes and make you eat 'em. You'd better give me one good reason why I shouldn't scalp you and leave you out in the street for the buzzards to clean up."

John was about to say something else when a voice from behind them yelled, "Stop right there, Indian. Don't make another move. It's the law. Now, hands up, move over to the other wall, and put your faces agin' it."

John dropped the knife and raised his hands. He turned, walked to the wall, and leaned against it with his forehead. Hoolie followed John's lead, but when he put his forehead against the wall, he quickly pulled his head back. Dark-hair's blow had raised a knot that throbbed with every one of Hoolie's heartbeats.

"Okay, boys, turn around real slow."

Hoolie and John turned as ordered and faced deputies Billy Wallace and Buford Fellows, who were staring at them over the sights of two sawed-off, 12-gauge Browning shotguns. Three or four towns-people stood behind them, mumbling to each other. Billy Wallace laughed, "Well, if it ain't Jailhouse John. I just let you go this mornin'. Now you're goin' back to the can. This time you'll have another Injun boy with you."

"What charges, Billy-boy?" asked John with a smile.

Wallace strode forward and shoved the shotgun under John's nose. "How 'bout assault and attempted murder? Sound right, Buford?"

"Sounds good to me," answered Fellows.

"Yep," said Billy, looking menacingly into John's eyes, "for a change, Jailhouse John is goin' to the hoosegow for a long stretch. Witness came and got us. Said you all started a fight with these boys. And I saw you with a knife to the throat of young Bobby here."

The two cowboys were coming to life now, rising from the dust, picking up their hats. Dark-hair was trying to stop his nosebleed. Freckle-face, now known as Bobby, was still taking deep breaths.

Billy Wallace turned from John and placed his shotgun's muzzle against Hoolie's crotch. "I remember you," he said. "You came into town and asked about runaway girls a few days ago. Then I heard you was involved in a shooting out at Ben Lookout's place. You been around a good deal of trouble. Might help to lock you up for a spell, too. No matter what, I got Jailhouse John locked up for a long time. I swear it's gonna be the last time you make trouble in this here town."

Hoolie could see a gleam of secret triumph in John's eyes. Fellows picked up John's liquor jar, smelled it, and threw it against the wall. "Got 'em on Volstead, too, Billy," he said flatly.

"Now, we really got you," said Wallace triumphantly. John said nothing. Hoolie opened his mouth. "Hold on, deputy—"

Hoolie's protest was cut off. Wallace made a clean upward butt stroke with his shotgun under Hoolie's chin. His head snapped back, and he fell to the ground unconscious.

Hoolie heard himself groan. He woke up feeling as if he had been through this before. But this time, he was in jail on a hard, steel-spring cot. And instead of waking up in the care of two beautiful girls, he opened his eyes to the smiling, angular face of John Tall Soldier.

Hoolie tried to raise his head, but a wave of nausea forced him to lie still. John spoke to him in a whisper. "I'm glad you're not dead, brother. You only been out for a little while. Billy-boy hit you pretty good with his gun. That's all right though, we'll get 'em back someday. I ain't never been in jail with a Cherokee Indin before. You from Stilwell, you say?"

"Uh-huh, right around there," Hoolie answered groggily. "What happened to the cowboys?"

"Nothin'. They let 'em go right away. I shoulda cut Bobby a little; let him know he was in a fight."

Hoolie was too tired and sore to say much.

John continued in his whisper, "So, what was you gonna ask me about the sheriff and the rest of the deputies?"

At that moment, Hoolie felt like he knew all he needed to know about the Hominy town constables. "What's gonna happen to us?" he asked.

John was slow to reply. He looked around the cell, felt the cold bars, and rubbed his hands together. He didn't answer the question. Instead he evasively told Hoolie that he had fought well, especially for a fellow who had a recent gunshot wound.

Then, Hoolie asked the important question. "Do the white folks around here act like that all the time? We didn't do nothin' to them."

John pondered the question for a short time and then said, "The whites—some of the old men call 'em yellow eyes—like to push us off the sidewalks, and some would kill us if they had half the chance. The smart ones just want to steal our land. A lot of the younger white boys like to start fights. The boys we whipped today were Bobby Hopkins and Joey Pendergast. Most times, Bobby and Joey like to start somethin' just to try and beat up one of my brothers. I figure this fight was for what I did to Joey's brother, Wiley, last week."

"Wha'd you do?"

"I bit off part of his cheek. Spat it right back at him. The whole family's out to get me."

"Damn!" said Hoolie in awe.

"Wiley don't come after me—too scared—but I think he's taken a few shots at me with a rifle. He ain't a very good shot though. Joey's a pretty tough boy, but I keep a few steps ahead of him."

Hoolie turned slightly and a rush of nausea shot up from his gut. Right now, his head was aching so badly he thought that it might explode. His cut mouth hadn't really had time to heal, and the fight in the alley made it hurt worse. His knee, chin, and right hand all throbbed in pain. His rib cage burned as if it was on fire. His shrapnel scars hurt. Hoolie doubted that he had ever felt worse in his entire life. His wounds from the war hadn't caused him this much sheer agony since they were fresh.

John looked at Hoolie's face, "You got beat up pretty bad."

"It sure feels like it," said Hoolie. "How about you? You hurt?"

"Nope. Didn't even take a punch. My hat got beat up. Billy and Buford wanted to work me over some, but they're both pretty weak-hearted. They just hauled us over and threw us in here."

"I hurt all over," said Hoolie in a low voice. "You got to answer me now. When will we get outta here?"

John put on a pained expression. "Brother, I'm sorry to say that we'll be in here for maybe three, four days. The sheriff'll wait 'til we promise not to fight no more. Then, he'll let us go as soon as my relatives come up with a touch of money. There won't be any charges. Word will get back to my mama, and she'll get somebody to come to town and get me. I'll see if they can get you some medicine. You lie around jail for a spell, and you get healed up. Then you can go after the one who shot you. I'll even help."

Hoolie tried to get up again, lifted his head a few inches, and sank slowly back down on the cot. He mulled over what John had told him. No charges. It looked like the sheriff ran a petty extortion racket aimed primarily at Indians. That might be fairly profitable in Osage County given the oil money floating around. The deputies threw Indians in jail and their families were forced to come up with some cash. The sheriff would let the alleged criminal go without actually filing charges, appearing before a judge, and staging a jury trial. The Osages probably didn't want to force the issue either; it was faster to get a relative out of jail this way.

"John," Hoolie began, "I can't wait around even a few days. I gotta find the man who killed your relative."

John didn't know how to handle his newfound friend and fighting partner. "Well, maybe one of my relatives heard about the fight and is goin' after my mama," said John without conviction. He knew more about the sheriff's procedures than just about anyone else in town. The whites called him "Jailhouse John" because he was put behind bars so often.

"I hope so. I gotta get outta here," groaned Hoolie. His breathing became quiet. The cell became utterly silent. John stared intently at Hoolie.

Finally, Hoolie whispered, "You said Billy Wallace was in the war, right?"

"Sure was. But he was one of those men who shot people from a mile off."

"A sniper?"

"That's it."

"Pete Henderson told me that Billy killed twenty-seven Germans. The only ones I heard about over there who knew exactly how many Germans they killed were snipers. They kept score, like in a game."

Hoolie paused to let John put two-and-two together. "You reckon Billy shot you and killed my relative?" John asked.

Hoolie had an idea who the murderer was but didn't really want to tell John everything. "I don't know for sure," he said, "but the more I think about it, Billy seems likely. The thing that puzzles me is who the sniper was shooting at. It could've been me. I was looking for somebody who was connected to Tommy Ruffle. And he had been murdered a few days before."

John winced. It was clear that he, along with many other Indian people, didn't like to speak the names of the dead. Hoolie felt the same way. Somehow it was disrespectful. But he'd sort of gotten used to it between having been to war and now being in the detective business. Now, he struggled to avoid saying the name, "The Osage boy's body was left down near Tulsa. I come to town askin' around about him. Somebody gets wind of me lookin' for him. The killer doesn't want me to find out something, so he goes gunnin' for me."

John's brain was working hard. "I thought you were lookin' for a girl, too?"

"Yep." Hoolie told John the whole story about Rose Chichester and also about the ambush at the Lookouts' place.

"And my relative was shot first the other night?"

"That's right."

John rubbed his hands together. He searched for words. He probably could have articulated it better in Osage, but his cellmate didn't speak the language. John looked down at the floor, "It sure looks like he was gunnin' for my relative. If not, why didn't he shoot you first? Is there two different things goin' on at oncest?"

"Could be," said Hoolie. "You're right about me gettin' shot. I was second in line."

"Let me figure out some more things," said John. He sat on his cot and rested his chin in his right hand.

After a short time, he said, "This whole thing has to do with the oil, and it's all tied together. Look, the girl's daddy is an oilman. She's with the Shelbys, and they know the Ruffles. My relative was all the time talkin' against the way the leases and headrights were bein' handled. The Shelbys are always cheatin' us. The one who got killed in Tulsa stood with my relative, and he helped his old grandpa who sure carries a lot of weight in these parts. People still listen to the old chief. And he listens to his grandson. See?"

Hoolie waited a short time to see if John was going to continue. When he didn't, Hoolie said,, "All right, so what?"

John became more animated. He rose and held up his right hand as if to grasp something out of the air. "It seems to me," he said, "that the first thing you gotta do is find that girl."

Hoolie couldn't lie still anymore. With great effort, he spun his legs over the edge of the cot and placed his feet on the floor. Making it that far took a major effort, and he sat and breathed for a while to fight back the agony. When the pain subsided somewhat, he said, "Damn, you're right. Every one of them's got something to do with the oil people. There's somethin' else. Martha Lookout is bein' courted by that Pete Henderson. The Shelbys stay with his mama when they come here. I gotta think more about this."

John smiled wistfully, "I guess you got time. We'll be locked up until old Sheriff McKinley gets his money."

Hoolie sat still. His breathing was getting better, but it seemed that every time he moved, another part of his body ached. John yawned, lay down on his cot, threw his arm over his eyes, and tried to sleep.

Hoolie didn't want John to sleep. He wanted to use his new, violent friend as a sounding board for more ideas. "John," said Hoolie, "don't go to sleep yet. I've got some more questions that I gotta ask you."

John Tall Soldier's eyes popped open. He rolled to one side and faced Hoolie across their small cell. "Well," he said, "what?"

"I have to find out how these things are all tied together. I know they are . . . but how?"

John rubbed his cheek and took a deep breath. "The old people," he began, "used to tell me that things always fit together. The women would plant our corn at the right time, and everybody would pitch in and get it ready to grow. You cleared and weeded, and when it cut through the ground and was startin' to tassel out, we'd pack up and hunt buffalo. The calves was already born and the winter wool was loose. It was the time to get hides for makin' the clothes and such. When we'd taken enough buffalo and when a certain kind of flower had bloomed, it was time to head back to the villages. And you know what? The corn would be ready to harvest. Everything was connected —the corn, the buffalo, the ground, the flowers, and us."

Hoolie nodded. The Cherokees went through the cycle almost in the same manner . . . or used to.

"When the white people came things changed. They work things different, but they still fit everything together. That's where you kinda get lost, ain't it?"

"I see how we fit things together. But white people . . . I don't know."

After a long pause, John continued, "All right. The way I figure it, they gotta have steel, timber, oil, and coal to run the railroads. They need the railroad to get the wheat and corn back east, so people can eat, so they can cut timber, make steel, dig coal, and pump oil. Some of that comes from right around here. They have to get more and more land, so they can get more oil, timber, coal, and steel. They get all of the land from us. See, it all fits together just like in the old days, even when the white man does it. The white people don't even know what they do is all connected up.

"To keep the oil comin' to run the railroads and make the steel, the sheriff and his deputies have to keep me in jail, and the two who got killed silenced, because we hollered about the cheatin' goin' on with our headrights and oil leases. Shuttin' us up helps the Indian Office deal with the lawyers who deal with the oil men. Some judge says that an Indian man can't handle his own affairs and appoints a lawyer to handle things for him. Indians who are too smart have to be gotten out of the way or beat up until they keep their mouths shut. Then the lawyer can take over and make a whole lot of money. See how it works? The judge works with the Indian Office, and it works with the lawyers and the oil men. The oil men and lawyers get them a sheriff or two to keep Indians from complainin'. The white man gets all the land. It all fits again."

Hoolie sat in silence. It was coming together. He began to see the reasons for killing Tommy and Ben. The white men would benefit. The oil men, lawyers, sheriffs, and the Indian Office people didn't care if a few Indians got killed. They were all together in wanting Indians either moved off or buried under the land that produced the oil, coal, steel, wheat, cattle, corn, and timber.

Hoolie shook his head at the thought. This wasn't some localized disappearance and murder. It was like a big rope that broke down into cords and strands and threads. Put them all together and the rope spun out for yard after yard. The murders were part of the whole scheme to loot Indians and the land.

Everything came together in Hoolie's brain. He clapped his fist into his hand and said in a voice that sounded like a gust of wind, "John, we gotta get outta here."

John leaned back on his cot once more. "I know. Sorry, brother, we ain't gettin' out for a while. At least not until somebody makes the trip out to see my folks. Might as well sit back and make your plans."

Hoolie sat for a few minutes and finally gave in to despair. He lay back down on his cot and quickly fell asleep.

12

Minnie

J.D.'s plan to interview Minerva Whitwell that morning went awry almost as soon as he reached his office. As he closed the office door behind him, the telephone rang. He picked up the earpiece and said sharply, "Daugherty."

The person on the other end of the line was Martin Haskins of the Tulsa county sheriff's office, who immediately informed J.D. that the paperwork he had signed the day before had been filled out incorrectly. McAfee and Chiles at the coroner's office had given him the wrong papers altogether.

"How about the sheriff's letter?" asked J.D. derisively. "Did he misspell his name?"

Although Haskins laughed at J.D.'s sarcasm, he insisted that J.D. go back to the morgue, get the right paperwork, and return it to the sheriff. "That Indian boy shouldn't have been released like that, J.D. Everybody shoulda known better."

"Marty," said J.D., "what if I didn't do a goddam thing? The boy's body is gone and about to be buried. He could already be in the ground. So what?"

J.D. heard Haskins sigh over the line. "J.D., that body's evidence. You can't just bury evidence. Not only that but we gotta know where the boy's planted."

"What?" cried J.D. "Why?"

"We gotta know where the cemetery is."

"God almighty, how should I know?"

"Damn, J.D., you gotta find out. We need to know just in case something's turned up on the case. We might have to exhume the body."

"That's crazy. The boy might be buried out in the hills somewhere."

Haskins bristled even over the telephone. "Listen," he said with authority, "we just got to keep everything in order. Besides, McAfee and Chiles might've botched the autopsy report. That body's evidence, dammit."

"All right, all right," said J.D., "I'll find out where they buried the boy and get back to you today."

"That's good, J.D.," Haskins said in a mollified tone of voice. "I'll be here."

J.D. changed the subject to further soothe Haskins' humor. "Say, Marty," J.D. began, "is anything happening on that rape case I heard about yesterday?"

"You mean the nigger?"

J.D. shook his head in dismay at Haskin's unthinking bigotry. "Yeah, Marty," he said with a note of disappointment in his voice, "that's the one."

"Somebody's pickin' up the boy right now. We don't expect no trouble."

"That's good. Well, Marty, I'll see you later."

J.D. put the earpiece on the hook and sat for the first time in his chair. He had no sooner begun to think of a way to find out where Tommy Ruffle was being buried when someone knocked on his door. The visitor was a Western Union messenger.

"Telegram, sir," the boy said in a soft voice.

J.D. took the envelope, fished in his pocket, withdrew a shiny nickel, and handed it to the kid.

"Thanks, mister," said the boy as he walked out the door.

J.D. mumbled something, stopped in the middle of the room, and tore open the envelope. It was Hoolie's message saying that he was healing and continuing the investigation. "Thank God for a piece of decent news!" J.D. said out loud.

He resumed his seat and began placing telephone calls to try and find out where Tommy Ruffle's last resting place was. No one at the Shelby mansion knew where the Shelbys or Chichester had gone. A call to the Johnson Brothers yielded nothing. The hearse had been dispatched to Hominy—no cemetery was mentioned. Knowing that in a small town the local telegraph operator usually knew every bit of business in the town, J.D. placed a long-distance call to the Hominy telegraph office. The telegrapher knew about the funeral and that all the Ruffles were interred in what he called the "Indian cemetery."

Since he had the man on the telephone, J.D. asked about Hoolie.

"That Indian who sent a couple of wires to Tulsa? They go to you? They get there okay?"

"Yeah, they sure did, and that's the man. How's he look?"

"Looked fine to me. I think he got himself in trouble though. There was a fight down the street just a little while ago. Him and Jailhouse John Tall Soldier got hauled in."

"You sure?"

"Yeah, pretty sure."

"Was he fighting with this Jailhouse guy?"

"No. What I hear, they was fighting two other boys."

Another problem. Hoolie in jail. J.D. placed another long-distance telephone call to the Henderson boarding house and had the dubious luck to get Elizabeth Shelby on the line. Tommy had been buried, and the Shelbys were about to return to Tulsa. After being told where Hoolie had been staying, Elizabeth said that she would get Peter Henderson to tell the Lookout family that their houseguest was locked up in the Hominy jail. Elizabeth ended the conversation with the supercilious question: "Do all of your operatives operate from jails, Mr. Daugherty?"

J.D. just replaced the earpiece without further conversation. More trouble. He had been on the telephone nearly the whole morning. J.D. hung his head for a short time; then he rose, put on his boater, adjusted its tilt, and, armed with a bit of information on Tommy Ruffle's last resting place, caught a trolley to the morgue.

McAfee was out, and J.D. had to deal with Chiles. He talked to the assistant coroner for about as long as he could stand it, signed the papers, and walked out on the sidewalk. He burned a cigarette and decided he'd eat on his way to the courthouse.

He walked over to a lunch stand on Boston Avenue. The place was abuzz with gossip about the so-called rape at Renberg's. The suspect in the case had been arrested. The rumors were still flying that it had been a gang of blacks that had attacked the girl. He found out that the man who had been arrested for the crime was a teenaged boy named Dick Rowland and that he had been arrested without trouble.

It looked like the police and the sheriff's deputies had handled everything with expertise and professional competence. J.D. finished his lunch, went down the street to a tobacco store, and bought a big Cuban cigar. He smoked with relish and decided to hail a taxicab to police headquarters.

The same old faces littered the station. Gottlieb was behind the main desk and three or four other officers J.D. knew came and went upstairs or through the various doors lining the main entrance hall. J.D. asked Gottlieb if Marv Finch was in, found that Finch was in the squad room, and walked up the stairs. The craggy-faced lieutenant was hunched over a stack of papers laid on a table in the middle of the room.

" 'Lo, Marv," said J.D. Finch was only too happy to push aside the paperwork and talk to J.D. The conversation was kept light, and J.D. found out very little else about the arrest of the alleged rapist Dick Rowland. He did hear a great deal about the competency or lack of same of the men under Lieutenant Finch.

"Who made the arrest?" J.D. asked.

"Haven't got the written report yet. They sent out Barney Cleaver, he's one of our Negro coppers, and Ike Doolittle. They sent out Will Pack, too; he's another Negro officer. Rowland was at his mama's place, just waitin' for us. The boy came along real peaceful. Knows he's in trouble."

"Scared?"

"What colored boy in a jam like that wouldn't be?" Finch looked around conspiratorially. "You know, I don't think he did anything to that girl."

"Why?"

"Nobody's that goddam, plug-ugly dumb to try and rape a girl in a store like Renberg's. It's nuts."

The door opened, and Gottlieb walked in with more papers. "Lieutenant, I got the report from Will Pack on the Rowland arrest. He finally got it done."

Finch rolled his eyes, "Took him long enough. I'd bet money that I'll have to rewrite the whole goddamn thing." He sent Gottlieb back to the front desk and squinted at the report. He clucked his tongue a few times and expressed the idea that the requirements for becoming a police officer should be raised. "I swear, J.D.," said Finch, "these boys never even seen a school much less been inside one." He paused and continued, "We're a city now; time of wearin' spurs and six-shooters is over."

J.D. asked if they had collected any more witness statements about the alleged rape. "Yeah, and they make this rape business bunkum," sniffed Finch.

"Oh yeah, how so?"

"The girl said the boy scratched her and tried to rip her clothes off. It's all bunk. There's no rips, and the scratches look like she did them herself."

"What about the clerk?" J.D. paused thoughtfully, "What's his name? Millstone?"

Finch rolled his eyes at the mention of the store clerk's name.

"That boy has quite a story to tell. He's making it look like he jumped in and pulled five or six colored boys off the girl. That's more bunk. The customers say he didn't do anything except look stupid when the girl came running up to him.

"I think he's got a sweetheart, and the elevator girl was trying to get his attention. He acts like he don't want to be around her, but all the same, he wants to look like a knight in shining armor. He's nuts."

Finch stopped speaking, reached in his pocket, and pulled out a pack of cigarettes. He offered one to J.D. and put one between his lips. J.D. produced a lighter and touched the flame to Finch's cigarette, then to his own. The lieutenant took a long pull, coughed once, and continued. "The girl's pretty loony herself. Don't know where she's from, and she ain't saying. She's young but not all that innocent, if you know what I mean. She's playing everything up, so folks'll feel sorry for her."

"Has Rowland been questioned yet?"

"I haven't seen that report yet either. I'm sure that I'll get it late, and it won't be written up worth a damn. They shoulda questioned the boy before they made out the arrest report. If they didn't, I'll tack their hides up on a wall."

J.D. chuckled. "I have to go now, Marv. You take care."

"I'll try. Where you headed?"

"That's something I oughta ask you." J.D. paused briefly. "Hear anything about what the reaction is to all this up on Greenwood?"

"Why?"

"I gotta question a girl lives up there."

"As far as I know, everything's quiet up on Greenwood."

J.D. said goodbye and went downstairs. On his way out of the building, he saw Barney Cleaver, the city's first black police officer. J.D. had met the man on several occasions.

"'Lo, Barney," said J.D.

"Oh, hiya, J.D. What you doin' down here?"

"On a case. You bring in the Rowland boy?"

"No. That was Will Pack. Will's talkin' to him right as we speak."

"Think he done it?"

"No. He's a good kid. Got through the ninth grade at Washington School, but started workin' to help out the family. He's nineteen years old. Never been in any trouble."

"You know," said J.D., "I think you're right. From what I hear, the girl and the clerk are just playing up the whole thing to get attention. Too bad it has to involve somebody who didn't do anything wrong."

"Ain't it the truth!"

J.D. thumbed his moustache. "Say, Barney," he said, "I have to go up on Greenwood today. Gotta question a girl up there. Everything quiet?"

"Shouldn't be any trouble. The lynchin' talk made folks pretty worried. There was some talk about gettin' a bunch of men together and coming to the courthouse to stand guard, but it might just be talk."

"Thanks, Barney, I'll see you around."

"Bye, J.D."

J.D. caught a trolley to the courthouse, brought the paperwork to Haskins, and signed the correct forms. He told Haskins that Tommy Ruffle was buried in the "Indian Cemetery" in Hominy.

Haskins was in a talkative mood. He told J.D. that Dick Rowland had been spirited out of town immediately after he had been booked. The sheriff had taken no chances. No matter who came to the jail, Rowland would not be lynched.

"You think the good citizens of Tulsa will get mad about getting Rowland out of their reach?" asked J.D.

"Who cares? Just so he ain't lynched in Tulsa."

J.D. returned to his office. He wanted to rest for a while and collect his thoughts before he made the trip north to Minerva Whitwell's place. He was taking a short sip of whiskey when he heard the paper-boy shouting outside. J.D. looked at his watch: three-thirty. The paper had put out an extra, afternoon edition. He craned his neck to hear the paperboy, who was saying something about an exclusive story concerning the rape of an orphan white girl by a Negro. Then the boy called at the top of his lungs:

"Read all about it! Lynching tonight! Nigger to die for crime! Read all about it!"

J.D. bolted out of his office, went to the paperboy, and thrust two bits into his hand. The paperboy gave J.D. a paper, looked at the quarter—an unbelievably generous tip—and yelled "thanks mister" at J.D.'s back. J.D. was returning to his office absorbed in the newspaper's headline:

TO LYNCH NEGRO TONIGHT

J.D. walked slowly into his office, his eyes locked on the article underneath the banner headline. It said that the elevator operator was a seventeen-year-old orphan girl, who was working at the Drexel Building to pay her way through business school. It also stated that her clothing had been ripped off and that her face, hands, and arms were covered with scratches and bruises caused by her assailant. A Renberg's clerk was said to have come to her assistance and had caused the attacker to flee. In summation, the article reported that both the victim and the clerk identified the culprit as "Diamond Dick" Rowland.

J.D. whispered a curse. The inflammatory article was clearly designed to stir up trouble. He would not put it past the local American Legion or the Klan to use this as an excuse to run riot through Little Africa hunting for blacks and Reds, burning as they went. J.D. at once decided that he had to find Minerva Whitwell, get her and her baby out of the neighborhood, and question her in a safe place. It was unlikely that the Shelbys were back from Osage County, so he could not turn to Little Bill for help.

He hurried over to Main, hailed a taxi, and told the driver to take him to North Greenwood. Overcoming the driver's protests with a big tip, J.D. ordered, "Frisco Railroad Station!" After being deposited there, between First and Archer, J.D. walked eastward to Detroit Avenue, and then turned left and headed up Brady Street. He followed Brady east to Greenwood.

Back in the segregated part of Tulsa he began to feel something that he had not experienced there the day before. The people who passed him on the street looked at him out of the corners of their eyes. They were suspicious, fearful. He had been in this part of town on several occasions and had always been treated kindly. Perhaps their demeanor was just a face they put on for the white man; but J.D. had never felt this uneasy before. Maybe he was suspicious himself after reading the newspaper story. At any rate, he walked all the way to Minerva Whitwell's house with a deep sense of foreboding.

Minerva wasn't at home, so J.D. sat down on the front steps of the house determined to wait until she returned. He stared down the street. It was getting late. "Come on, Minerva," he whispered to himself, "come on." Summoning her through sheer will power didn't work.

People's faces darted in and out of his mind. He thought about the Shelbys and about those their power and wealth had affected. J.D. worried about mob violence. He'd seen it in Colorado and Arizona mining towns. A mob could easily get out of hand, especially if their quarry had been taken from them. Once a mob discovered that Dick

Rowland wasn't at the courthouse or even in Tulsa, it would vent its frustration on others. The mob would come to Greenwood and seek vengeance on anyone it could throw its coils around.

J.D. was contemplating the irony and danger of sitting on a black woman's porch just when the city around him might erupt in a race riot. As he was mulling this over, he spotted one of the loveliest girls he had ever seen. The young woman was pushing a baby carriage down the other side of the street, and as she approached the corner, she looked back and forth several times before crossing. J.D. knew it was Minerva. It had to be. She was dressed in a powder-blue dress that struck her at mid-calf and a white hat and gloves. When she wheeled the carriage through the front gate and saw J.D. on her porch steps, she stopped abruptly, stared at him for a moment, and said, "Is there something I can do for you, mister?"

"Are you Minerva Whitwell?" J.D. asked in reply.

She looked at him warily, "I don't know you. What do you want?"

J.D. strode toward her, right hand extended. Minerva turned the buggy toward the street and stood protectively between it and the approaching J.D. He stopped directly in front of her and said quietly, "I'm J.D. Daugherty, Miss Whitwell. William Shelby Jr. has probably told you about me. I'm a detective and working a case for Mr. E.L. Chichester. I didn't intend to frighten you. Please, could I have a word or two?"

Her eyes narrowed, and she wouldn't shake J.D.'s hand. She took a deep breath, put both hands on her hips, and said finally, "All right, Mr. Daugherty, William did indeed mention you. We'd better go in the house, there's some bad news on the street."

J.D. bowed slightly and gestured for her to go first.

When they entered her large front room, Minerva smiled sweetly at J.D. She told the detective to make himself comfortable in an over-stuffed chair. All of a sudden, she seemed to be everywhere and doing everything at once. She took J.D.'s hat, changed the baby's diaper, and put him down for a rest in an expensive, handcrafted walnut cradle, rocked him for a while, and began preparing coffee for herself and J.D. The baby turned over in his cradle, sat up, and smiled at J.D.

J.D. asked her to forgo the coffee and answer a few questions concerning Rose Chichester.

"Mr. Daugherty, I'll be happy to answer your questions, but coffee first. I need the coffee to keep me goin'. Thomas is growin' like a weed; he keeps me jumpin' all the time."

J.D. smiled despite his nervousness and growing aggravation with her untiring domesticity. His first question was directed toward her back as she bustled into the kitchen. "Miss Whitwell," he said, "would you be willing to come downtown with me? I'll get a taxicab."

She walked back into the parlor, laughed, and said, "I don't think you could get a taxi right now. But why on earth would I want to go downtown, Mr. Daugherty?"

"Miss Whitwell, I don't want to frighten you, but the newspaper is stirring up a lynch mob. This neighborhood could be a mob's target. I'd like to get you and your baby to a safe place."

Minerva wrinkled her brow and sat down on the divan across from J.D. She looked pensively at the baby sitting up in his cradle, "I remember last year when they lynched those two boys. It was terrible. But the mob didn't get up here. I think we'd be in more danger travelin' around town."

She paused once more, looked thoughtfully at the baby, smiled brightly, and said, "I'll tell you what. I'm gonna fix us some supper. Then we can talk all you want. I can't leave my home. It might upset my baby." Her voice became very serious as she added, "And I can't have that."

Like many other black people in Tulsa, Minerva was convinced that a degree of prosperity would make her neighborhood immune from mob violence. The *New York Daily News* had referred to the Greenwood community specifically as the "Black Wall Street" and praised Tulsa as a "Magic City" in which even Negroes could prosper. The houses along Greenwood were well-appointed brick dwellings with beautifully manicured lawns and gardens. Hatred and bigotry were certainly a part of life in Tulsa. But many black people believed that their quiet acceptance of segregation, property ownership, and demonstration that they were industrious would force the Tulsa authorities to defend the Greenwood community as a matter of civic pride. White Tulsans, Minerva deeply believed, would not stand for the destruction of any part of their beautiful city.

She abruptly stood and went into the kitchen, leaving J.D. to ponder his next move. He knew he was in a losing chess game with her; but he still wanted to get the two of them out of Greenwood. J.D. had no confidence in the white citizenry of Tulsa.

Minerva returned with a coffee pot and two porcelain cups on a lacquered tray. She set the tray down and poured two cups and handed one to J.D. "Have some coffee, Mr. Daugherty," she said with authority. "You might as well, 'cause I don't plan on leavin'." She paused and sighed deeply. "Let me explain a few things to you. This is my home. My baby lives here, and my baby's father comes here. I have a shotgun in the other room. Nobody is gonna do anything to me and mine without gettin' three, four ounces of buckshot in their behinds. I'm not scared of them, Mr. Daugherty. I don't run from nobody."

J.D. smiled in spite of himself. He admired her grit. "Miss Whitwell . . . may I call you Minerva? And would you please call me J.D.?"

"Of course, J.D. But most of my friends call me Minnie. You can, too."

"Thanks. I'd—"

A knock on the door interrupted what J.D. was going to say. Minnie rose to see who the caller was. J.D. tensed as she threw wide the door, without even so much as a "Who is it?"

The caller was a tall man in a striped suit coat, brown trousers, and a white shirt. His stiff celluloid collar was wrapped tightly around his thick neck. His gray fedora sat cradled in the crook of his right arm. A little behind him stood a skinny girl of about twelve or thirteen, her hair in braids tied with blue ribbons.

Minnie smiled and said "Hello." The man shifted his weight from one foot to another and spoke nervously, "Miss Minerva, I live a few doors down. I'm Theodore Welbourne."

"Yes, Mr. Welbourne," said Minnie, "I know who you and your daughter are." She looked at the girl, "Your name is Louisa, isn't it, hon?"

The girl dipped her head quickly in the affirmative. Minnie looked at Mr. Welbourne, "What can I do for you?"

Welbourne couldn't hide his nervousness but he forged ahead. "A number of our men are going to the courthouse downtown to protect the jail and to see that the young man who was arrested this morning has his day in court. I'm goin' down to join them." Motioning his head toward his daughter, he continued, "If you remember, my wife passed on with the flu. Could you watch my daughter for the time that I'm away? She won't be no trouble."

Minnie moved easily outside the door, put her arm around the girl's shoulders, and said, "Louisa is always welcome, Mr. Welbourne." She paused and looked into the girl's eyes. "Maybe you'd like to see the baby?" Louisa nodded and smiled brightly. Minnie took her in and led her to the baby's cradle. J.D. stood as Minnie came in from the foyer. Welbourne stepped forward through the door and stopped short when he caught sight of J.D. He did not expect to see a man in the front room, let alone a stout, middle-aged, mustached white man with a suspicious look in his eye. Minnie saw Welbourne's discomfort and J.D.'s glowering countenance. "I'm sorry, Mr. Welbourne," she said, "I've been rude." She gracefully swept her left hand in J.D.'s direction and continued, "This is Mr. Daugherty. He works for the same folks I used to work for. We're old friends." Although she lied, her eyes told Welbourne that J.D. could be trusted.

Welbourne acknowledged J.D. with a quick nod of his head, "Pleased to meet you."

"Likewise," answered J.D. He brushed his moustache with a thumb and went on. "Mr. Welbourne, I overheard what you told Miss Whitwell. I know a lot of people connected with the law in this city. I am very concerned that a terrible crime might be committed by a mob. The men I know on the police force, including a Negro officer, told me that everything is under control. I know I'm butting in, but I'd like to discourage you from going to the courthouse this evening."

Welbourne was angered but tried his best to remain polite in front of his daughter and Minnie. "Well, Mr. Daugherty," he said, "that ain't exactly what I hear. I heard a crowd of white men"—he paused long enough to silently remind everyone in the room that J.D. was a white man—"has gathered at the courthouse to lynch the Rowland boy. I've been told that the sheriff ordered them to leave but they wouldn't go. We're goin' down there now. Nobody wants trouble, but we gotta protect our own."

"I understand," said J.D. "But take my advice and don't go there with guns in your hands. From what I hear, the sheriff took Rowland out of town. Some of those white men would just as soon shoot a colored man as look at him. Don't give them the chance."

"Well, sir, if he ain't there, then nobody's gonna have a problem with us makin' sure he's all right. Nobody's gonna be armed, but we have to do what's right," said Welbourne firmly. With that, he thanked Minnie, gave J.D. a military salute, put on his hat, and walked out.

A look of despair appeared on J.D.'s face. Minnie tried to explain. "J.D., Mr. Welbourne, like so many of our boys, was in the war. He saw terrible things in France, but because he did his duty—and saw what he saw and did what he did—he became a free man. He can't stop bein' free. That means he has a right to go to that courthouse. If he don't go, he's no longer free. I hope you see what I mean."

J.D. looked down and shook his head. "I understand you . . . and him. I'm just worried that somebody's gonna start shooting."

"They might, J.D., they just might. But he still has to go down there."

She smiled once more, went to Louisa, picked up the baby, and placed him in the girls' arms. "Louisa, bring Thomas back to the bedroom. We're gonna change him, and you can play with him for a while. Then we'll eat something and pretty soon you both are gonna have to go to sleep." She looked at J.D. and commanded "You sit down. I have to rustle up some food for all of us. I'll be a few minutes, and then we'll talk."

J.D. returned to his chair and gloomily sat sipping his lukewarm coffee. After about half an hour, Minnie called him for a warmed-over supper of chicken and dumplings. The baby sat in a handmade high chair, and Louisa sat next to him, beaming at the baby and Minnie in turn. Once in a while, she cast a shy glance at J.D. After supper, there was more coffee and a nice piece of apple pie. The food was excellent. His concerns returned from time to time during the meal, but Minnie kept up a flow of pleasant conversation.

While Louisa played with the baby, J.D. helped Minnie clean up. She made him smoke in the kitchen, evidently thinking that the cigarette smell would blend in with the odor from the woodstove. J.D. sat, figuring out how to begin his long awaited interview with Minerva Whitwell.

Louisa and Thomas were playing with his toys in the back room, and Minnie finally sat down for their talk. J.D. began, "Minnie, Mr. Shelby—William Jr.—told me that your beautiful child is his. I realize that Bill Jr.'s father and the state of Oklahoma won't let him do the right thing by you and your boy. I'm also aware of the fact that the family was pressuring him into a relationship with Rose Chichester . . . you know her, don't you?"

Minnie nodded.

"Good," J.D. said. "Now, do you have any grievance against Miss Chichester?"

Looking straight into J.D.'s eyes, Minnie grinned, "Miss Chichester ain't locked up in one of my back rooms or down in the cellar. You can look."

It was J.D.'s turn to be amused. He laughed, "No, Minnie, I don't believe she's around here. What I really wanted to know about was why the Shelbys let you go. My suspicion is that it was over the baby, but perhaps it was something else. Perhaps it was to get you away from William Jr. and to clear the way for him to court the Chichester girl."

Minnie pensively cast her eyes upward and answered, "William loves me. I know that. He loves our son. I know that, too. Rose Chichester and William couldn't get married, no matter what Mrs. Shelby and Mr. Chichester want."

J.D. furrowed his brow. Minnie had apparently deluded herself into thinking that Little Bill loved her enough to eventually defy his family, society, the state's miscegenation law, and Jim Crow, in general, and make her his lawful wife. Somehow he had to get it through to her that Little Bill was trying to have his cake and eat it, too.

"Minnie, I know you're in love. The baby's beautiful, and you can be proud, and maybe William Jr. will help you take care of him . . . but . . . but . . . there are things that will . . . " J.D. had run out of words. He was becoming agitated at the unfairness of the way their world worked. She was such a beautiful young woman, why shouldn't she marry whomever she pleased?

J.D. blurted out, "Minnie, you know you can't marry Bill. And what's more, you know that eventually he'll have to find another woman to marry. A white woman."

She looked back at J.D. with a sad expression in her eyes. What she was feeling didn't come from a sudden realization that she could never marry her lover. The sadness was more out of sympathy with J.D.'s frustration. It was as if J.D. had just discovered what Minerva Whitwell had always known.

"J.D., look at me," she said earnestly. "I know the rules. Me and William broke them. But look at the treasure we found when we did. Our baby is the most beautiful baby in the world."

Her eyes brightened, and she put her fingers to her lower lip. "I know we can't get married. But I know that William will always be here for me and our baby. We may even have more children." She paused again. "He's my man. I know him. He won't marry anybody else. Maybe we won't get married by law, but we'll be together until we die. I know that."

J.D. sat very still, drinking in every word. Maybe she was right. J.D. was smitten with her, and, at that moment, he couldn't believe that there was a man in the world who could or would leave Minnie Whitwell.

"Now," she continued, "since William said that I should tell you all I know, I'll tell you that William can't marry Rose Chichester. He couldn't do it even if he wanted it. His daddy won't ever let it happen. Rose is William's sister."

J.D. was stunned. He sat bolt upright in his chair. "What?" he said, as if he hadn't heard her. "I don't understand. How could . . . ?"

"Drink your coffee," she said calmly, "or it'll get cold. I'll tell you the whole story. This has been kept from William. He don't even know. I know about it because my mama was the Shelby maid for years and years. I grew up in that house, right beside William and Elizabeth."

J.D. was trying to absorb the information and fit it into an explanation for Rose's disappearance. On the surface, it seemed to be obvious. The girl had learned who her real father was, and she simply ran away. That sounded reasonable to J.D.

Minnie brought him back from his speculative musings. "Now, this comes straight from my mama," she said. "She worked for the Shelbys and got to know the Chichesters. The families were always visitin' each other, and Mrs. Shelby would bring Mama along, so she knew all the Chichesters' help, too.

"Mr. Shelby was dallyin' with Mrs. Chichester. My mama even caught them once in a clothes closet. Mama heard from their maid that Mr. and Mrs. Chichester didn't have nothin' to do with each other in the bedroom, if you know what I mean."

J.D. nodded and Minnie resumed. "So, when Mrs. Chichester got with child, she had some quick explainin' to do. She convinced her husband that she had gotten pregnant by him one night when he was drinkin' heavy. Now, he don't have no trouble believin' that story 'cause that man does put away the liquor. He was drinking so much because he was runnin' through his oil money real fast . . . "

"Hold on a minute, Minnie," interrupted J.D., "Chichester was losing money?"

"Oh my, yes. See, Mr. Chichester backed Mr. Shelby when he first began investing in Oklahoma oil. When Shelby Oil did well, Big Bill paid Mr. Chichester back. But by then, Pennsylvania oil—what had made the Chichester fortune—had begun to play out. So, Mrs. Chichester goes to Mr. Shelby and asks him to help her husband out . . . to keep them up in high society, I guess. That's when her and Mr. Shelby took up with each other. Mama thought that that was the price Mrs. Chichester had to pay to keep up appearances. She was a beautiful woman, and Mr. Shelby likes women. It galled Mr. Chichester that he had to turn to Big Bill for help. But after his wife died, E.L. turned things 'round financially, as anyone can see from the way that man dresses."

Minnie paused briefly. The baby gave a short cry. She jumped up and hustled into the other room. She emerged carrying the crying child, with Louisa walking behind saying, "I didn't do nothin'."

Minnie took Thomas to his cradle and changed his diaper. He quickly quieted down. Minnie looked at Louisa, "See, honey, all he needed was a clean diaper; you didn't do nothin' wrong. Babies cry like that if they get wet or hungry or just want their mamas. You see?"

The girl nodded, wide-eyed, and still a little scared. Minnie put the baby on the floor, and Louisa sat down with him. Soon the girl had the baby playing happily with a hand-carved, wooden pull toy.

Minnie looked at J.D. "I've got to get these children to bed. It's after nine."

J.D. pulled out his watch. The time had gone by quickly, and he still hadn't got the full story. Minnie picked up the baby and, with Louisa in tow, went to the back of the house.

Minnie came back to the parlor a short time later. "I put Louisa on a pallet on the floor, next to the baby's crib. She loves to be close to that baby. Seems like her daddy should be back by now."

J.D. was anxious for her to resume the story of the Chichester-Shelby clans, but for politeness' sake, he waited until Minnie was seated once again. The mention of Louisa's father caused J.D. some concern, but he focused back on Minnie's story. "I'm having a hard time following everything. Could you tell me the bare bones of what happened to Mrs. Chichester?"

She paused to straighten a fold in her skirt, "Mrs. Chichester told Mr. Shelby that she was havin' a baby. He wanted her to go to a doctor he knew to get shed of it. For her part, she figured he'd leave Mrs. Shelby and marry her once she divorced Mr. Chichester. Mr. Shelby musta told her that he was stickin' with Mrs. Shelby, 'cause Mrs. Chichester pitched a fit. After that, she was confined to her bedroom until she had the baby. She didn't tell on Mr. Shelby to her husband 'cause he woulda left her. They all treated her like she was a lunatic.

"White folks seem to think that women are supposed to go off their rockers or else have to lay in bed all the time when they're with child. Everybody but the household staff thought that Mrs. Chichester was havin' problems. They took everything away from her, like she was a prisoner. The poor woman was locked up and waitin' for the baby. After Rose gets born, Mrs. Chichester names her. . . "

"I thought she was named after Mrs. Shelby?" interrupted J.D.

"She was named after her, all right. But it was pure meanness that got her that name. Mrs. Chichester give that baby her rival's name. She wanted Mr. Shelby to be reminded of their affair every time he looked at that girl. Nobody knew, except for the household servants and Mr. Shelby. About two weeks after the baby got born, Mrs. Chichester took a bed sheet and hung herself. The doctor wrote it up like she died of an infection from birthing, but she killed herself, sure as I'm sittin' here."

J.D. sat and reflected on all the twists and turns Minnie's story had taken. Her ability to tell it and her mannerisms while doing so had held him spellbound. J.D. had to physically shake himself to get his mind back on track.

"Minnie," he asked, "how many other people know about this?"

"Mama did, but she's gone. Maybe some of the Chichester help. That's about all. There was gossip."

"Did Chichester find out?"

"No, I don't believe so. He's been treatin' that girl like a princess ever since she was born. I believe he thinks that she's his all right, 'cause he's the one that's been tryin' to get my William and her together since we were all children."

"You were brought up with them?"

"Yes, we all played together. My mama watched us. William was the oldest, then came Rose, Elizabeth, and me. My daddy was a kitchen boy. He left us to work on the railroad. Ain't seen him in years. Mama passed on two years ago of the Spanish flu."

"You were with the Shelbys for so long. I suppose they fired you because of the baby."

"Yes and no. William didn't want me to work no more, and his daddy agreed. But I don't think that the Shelbys woulda let us stay, what with Thomas's daddy right there in the house."

"And William knows nothing about his real relationship to Rose Chichester?"

"No, no. Until she told me, only Mama knew. Mama had promised the Chichesters' maid that she'd never tell. And she kept her word. You know, I still got a few kinfolks workin' for the Shelbys."

"You do?"

"My cousin, Bernard, works in the house. If I went and told, he'd be let go just like that." She snapped her fingers. "Besides that, I know William; if it got out, he'd hate his daddy. And those are two tempers I don't want to get between."

"Minnie, how long has it been since Mrs. Shelby and Mr. Chichester started talking about a match between William and Rose?"

"Long time. Since we were children."

"Do you know anything about Rose's attraction to Tommy Ruffle?"

"I really can't say. Rose is a quiet girl. To tell you the truth, I think she ran off with him because she just couldn't take it no more."

"Couldn't take what?"

"The lyin' and cheatin' of bein' one of the rich snobs. Her daddy would do anything to ride around in fancy cars and wear fancy clothes. The rest of them are just the same, except for us."

"Us? What do you mean *us*?"

"Young people, J.D., young people. William, me, Elizabeth, Rose. We're gonna change everything. William doesn't like his daddy's business deals. Folks my age are gonna win the right to vote for all black people. Rose hates the city and wants to go back to the natural life. Elizabeth is interested in the arts, not just in the symphony and collectin' old paintings. She wants to get new styles of music and writing and painting out, so that everybody can enjoy them. Thirty or forty years down the road everybody's gonna be listenin' to jazz music, lookin' at modern art, enjoyin' the mountains and the streams, doin' business in the right way, and marryin' who they wanna marry. Just you watch, J.D., we're gonna change the world."

J.D. smiled and laughed quietly. "You know, Minnie, I believe you will."

An automobile's racing engine and two gunshots punctuated J.D.'s sentence. There was the noise of another automobile, and the shout, "Come out, nigger!" The reason for Mr. Wellbourne's failure to return earlier was apparent. A race riot had come to deep Greenwood.

J.D. would later learn that while he was talking with Minnie, a street battle had broken out between whites with Klan and American Legion ties and a few armed blacks, like Mr. Welbourne, whose daughter was sleeping in Minnie's back bedroom. Barney Cleaver had tried to get Welbourne and the rest of his group to go home since Dick Rowland wasn't at the courthouse, much less in Tulsa. No lynching would occur for the simple fact that a lynch mob had no victim to string up. However, the leaders of the Klan had heard that there were armed black men at the courthouse and decided that the organization should lead the charge against "uppity" Negroes. Somehow, the leadership was able to link together Dick Rowland, all black males, the Reds, the Industrial Workers of the World, and the rape of an "innocent, orphan white girl." A group from the American Legion—veterans all—joined the white march on the courthouse. It was their intention to disarm the blacks and send them packing back north of Archer, maybe busting a few heads in the bargain. When the whites arrived, the white police backed off, leaving Barney Cleaver as fodder for the Klan's accusations that blacks had taken over the city. The members of the Klan, minus their bedsheets, began ordering the black men to lay down their arms. Several scuffles broke out on the courthouse steps.

A number of white groups began to fan out across the city. One contingent of mixed Legion and Klan members surrounded the National Guard Armory. Fortunately, the commanding officer was able to disperse the group.

A number of white police officers joined Klansmen and legionnaires in looting local hardware stores to secure weapons. Later, these officers would say that they had been confiscating rifles and shotguns to prevent criminal elements from getting hold of them. The criminal elements were, in their view, two black groups, armed only with hymnals. They had come to the courthouse to stand between the Klan and their own angry and armed men.

As was bound to happen, it seemed in retrospect, a shot was fired, and one of the men carrying a hymnal dropped to the ground. That set the riot off. Whites and blacks began to pour gunfire into each other from as little as ten feet away. Casualties mounted rapidly. More whites began to show up with the weapons looted from the hardware stores. The black fighters, though seemingly a better organized force—most having served in the war—lacked ammunition and were relatively few in number. They began a slow retreat northward toward the railroad tracks, firing as they went.

Taking advantage of the back streets and skirting around the armed black fighters, a number of whites used their automobiles to mount raids into the black neighborhoods. They sped down the streets of north Tulsa throwing bottles, bricks, epithets, and more than a few bullets into black homes, churches, and places of business. Minnie and J.D. experienced one such raid.

When they heard the gunshots, the mother and the detective both reacted quickly and ran to the baby's room. Both children were asleep, but Minnie decided that they should be taken to the cellar. J.D. agreed and picked up the sleepy Louisa. Minnie pulled some blankets together and cradled the baby in her left arm. They carried the children through the kitchen and down the stairs to the basement. Minnie spread the blankets out on the hard-packed earthen floor and laid the baby down. Louisa whimpered in fear because a strange white man was carrying her around like she was a baby herself. Minnie soothed the girl, and she finally lay down beside the baby. Minnie pulled a chair out of a corner and sat down, breathless after the exertion. J.D. was enraged that the Rowland affair had gotten out of hand and that he had failed to get Minnie and the baby to a place of safety.

Silently, J.D. went back up the steps. He pulled a chair to a front window, fished a small .32 caliber pistol from the pocket of his suit coat, and sat down. He was ready to fight, should it come to that. He sat for perhaps ten minutes when he heard a small creak in the floor behind him. He jumped up, whirled, and brought his pistol to bear on Minnie, who had come up from the cellar.

J.D. growled, "I'm as jumpy as a cat. I wish you would've warned me. I could've shot you." He put the .32 back in his coat pocket.

She tried to ease his tension. "I'm sure you wouldn't shoot unless you knew who it was."

He chuckled nervously. "Seems like I'm scared of my own shadow these days. Getting old, I guess." J.D. put his hand to his chin in deep thought. "Minnie," he said finally, "I don't want to compromise you or anything, but I think I should stay in your parlor tonight. Those boys in that automobile might return. I know you can take care of yourself, but I'd like to stay just in case." He chuckled again, this time from embarrassment, as he said, "And I'm kinda scared to go out right now, being a white man, after those fools in the car have been shooting up the place. I have the feeling that a riot's on the way. Right now those babies downstairs need you. Maybe we'll talk more in the morning."

"All right, J.D.," she said. "I'll just get a few things and go back down. You need a quilt or somethin'?"

"No, I'll be fine. Thanks."

J.D. sat down on the chair near the window and pulled out the pistol. He could hear Minnie gathering up things from the back rooms. He finally heard her footsteps go into the kitchen and down the stairs to the cellar. J.D. was tired. He tried to make himself as uncomfortable as possible in the hope of staying awake and alert the rest of the night.

Within thirty minutes, he was fighting desperately to stay awake, stretching, whistling to himself, crackling his knuckles, and humming a few bars of the Tin Pan Alley tune *Pocahontas, Her Wooing*. J.D. saw one a.m. go by, and sleep was winning the battle.

A gigantic black dog was chasing him. J.D. could see that the dog was baying and howling but no sound came from it. J.D. decided to end the chase. He turned on the dog, staring into the animal's fiery red eyes. The dog growled but still no sound came from its mouth. Its muzzle was covered with foam, and it was jumping at J.D., yet never coming close to him. Finally, J.D. began to hear the dog's mouth snapping shut, over and over again.

J.D. still heard the snapping sound as he began to wake up. The snapping was coming from behind him. He looked over his shoulder. It was just barely daybreak, and the light was playing tricks on him. It was moving, jumping, dancing, growing, and dying all at the same time. Then he smelled the acrid scent of smoke, and he suddenly realized that what he was seeing, hearing, and smelling was fire. The house was burning.

J.D. sprang from the chair and ran toward the kitchen. The fire, burning in the dining room, was still small. Someone must have set it right outside the window. He could smell kerosene. Dodging the flames, he headed toward the door to the basement. Just as he reached the kitchen, he heard a window break behind him. A large rock had sailed through the glass near the chair he had just vacated. J.D. threw open the basement door and scrambled down the stairs.

He found Minnie holding the baby with her back against one wall. Louisa was pressing against Minnie's right arm. They were frightened but calm. J.D. had the terrible thought that the floors would start caving in. If they came out without some warning, the ones who set the fire would simply shoot them down. He pulled Minnie by one arm and took Louisa by her hand and led them close to the cellar door that led to the backyard. "You wait here," he said, "I'm going up to see what's going on."

J.D. quickly climbed up the steps and pushed open the door. He peeked outside first, then crawled out into the morning air. Someone close by shouted, "Hey, there's somebody comin' out." The voice said nothing for two or three beats then, "It's a white man, by God."

Four white men ran over to J.D. as he stepped up onto the grass. He raised hands in a sign of submission. The men, armed with rifles and shotguns, surrounded him. One of the older men asked, "What you doin' in nigger town, mister?"

At that moment, Minnie stepped out of the cellar door, baby in her arms, leading the terrified Louisa. "Hey, there's a gal comin' up, too," was the new cry.

More white men began to show up. Soon, Minnie, the baby, Louisa, and J.D. were being herded to the front yard, away from the house, which was now completely on fire. They did nothing to Minnie and the children except move them along with their guns. Minnie's eyes narrowed in rage over the fire, but she cooperated out of the fear that they would hurt her child if she dared resist. When they got to the front yard, they began to prod and provoke J.D. with gun barrels as well as with their insults.

"Well, well, I think we got one of them nigger lovers here," a tall man said to the rest of the mob. Then he addressed J.D. directly, "You up here gettin' a little or are you helpin' them get away? Either way, let me tell you, we're gonna burn the niggers out."

Suddenly, Minnie screamed. One of the men had lifted up her skirt and shoved a shotgun at her privates. J.D. whirled and shouted, "You touch her again, boy, and I'll make you eat that shotgun, stock and all."

The tall man grabbed J.D. by the lapels and said, "You ain't doin nothin', nigger lover."

J.D. stomped on the man's foot as hard as he could and felt a bone give way. The man let go of J.D. and collapsed in pain on the grass, holding his injured foot. As two others moved toward him, J.D. dodged and smashed his right fist into the first one's nose. J.D. sprang toward the man holding Minnie. With his open hand, J.D. landed a blow on the attacker's left ear that must have broken his ear drum. He let Minnie go and started screaming in pain. J.D. then placed a kick in the man's groin, and he dropped.

J.D. held out his arms and swept Minnie, the baby, and the girl along with him in a dash for the street. The mob was momentarily stunned into inactivity. J.D. had Minnie and the children outside the picket fence and heading north before one of the mob reacted. The man raised his rifle and fired a shot at the retreating four. Minnie was hit. She faltered and fell, trying her best to hold the baby to her breast and go down on her back to cushion the child as she hit the ground. J.D. stopped, thought about pulling his own revolver but didn't, bent over Minnie, and picked up the baby. No one else fired. The white men were still not spurred into movement. They milled about, undecided and without a leader. A couple of them were bending over their wounded comrades.

J.D. thrust the baby into Louisa's arms. Looking at her with wild eyes, he gasped, "Take the baby. Run. Don't stop for anything. The whites are out to kill you. Run, goddammit! Run!" The girl ran, carrying Thomas close to her chest.

J.D. looked down at Minnie and realized that she'd taken a bullet in the back. There was no life in her eyes; she was either dead or so badly wounded she would be dead in a few minutes. Tears jumped into J.D.'s eyes, and the anger welled up to the bursting point.

He turned toward the mob. The men were still milling around. He screamed, "I'll kill you sons of bitches!" and charged into their midst. J.D. grabbed a shotgun away from a short man in bib overalls and, gripping the barrel, swung it hard into the man's chest. He changed his grip and speared another man in the face with the gun butt. Then a fat man in a brown fedora stepped forward and said in a calm voice, "Shoot the bastard, but don't kill him."

J.D. heard the crack of the rifle and felt the blow to his right leg at the very same instant. He dropped to the ground.

The mob flowed over him. Two of the men went to retrieve Minnie's body. No one tried to run down Louisa.

The men quickly trussed up J.D. and dragged him over to a large oak in Minnie's front yard. He thought that they were going to hang him.

Instead they tied a long rope around his wrists and threw the opposite end over a tree branch. Someone hauled on the rope until J.D. was half standing; behind his back his arms were being pulled upward until the pain in his shoulders was unbearable. He roared at his tormentors, "I'll kill you! I swear—" His cries were pinched off with another tug on the rope. The fat man in the fedora ordered J.D. lowered to a sitting position. They took the rope down and wound it around J.D. and the tree trunk. Then they began to kick and punch him in the face and ribs. His eyes became swollen and saliva and blood dripped from his mouth. He retched once and the attackers backed off for a second. Then someone said, "Hold on, let's bring the nigger bitch over and fetch some coal oil."

J.D. conjured up an image of being burned alive. Thankfully, Minnie was beyond further pain. He couldn't get his pistol out. He would have taken a few of them with him. He heard one of the men say, "Turn her over."

J.D. blurted out, "Leave her alone, you gutless bastards! I'll kill you! I'll—"

The fat man kicked him in the face. He looked as if he was going to land another kick when someone near Minnie's body said, "Hey, Cunningham, what'll we do now?" The man turned, took off his fedora, and wiped his brow. "Pour the coal oil on her."

J.D. started to protest again. The fat man turned and placed a kick on J.D.'s right cheek bone.

After the blow, J.D. could see only a blurred outline of a human figure before him. Then another blow was landed on his forehead. A blazing, white light seared through his brain. His head dropped, but somehow he remained conscious of what was going on. He tried to make his mouth work, but all he could do was blow bubbles of blood through his nostrils. He heard everything that went on.

"Pull her over closer to the house."

"Strip her off."

"She's dead. I don't wanna see no dead nigger naked."

J.D. heard the coal oil being splashed about. Then he heard a distinct *whoosh* and felt the heat of a fire. At first, he could smell only the coal oil, and then he saw the flames and caught the odor of burning flesh. He vomited and began to sob uncontrollably. One of the men turned to him and said, "How do you like the bonfire, nigger lover?" Then he kicked J.D.'s wounded leg.

J.D. was beyond feeling the pain. Through the sobbing, he managed to spit out in a flat, deadly whisper, "I'll get you if it's the last thing I do."

He was the warrior-prince Cuchulain. When he went into battle his eyes grew out on stalks and his mouth became a long slash that stretched from one ear to the other. His hair became a bright red flame. Before the battle, Cuchulain had a vision that foretold his death the next day. Having sworn an oath that he would never fall before his enemies, when he came to the battlefield in the morning, he had his men tie him to a great rock that stood in the middle of the grassy plain. When the enemy charged, Cuchulain fought as never before, and his enemies lay in heaps about his feet. In the end, a spear pierced his breast, and war clubs beat against his face. His eyes receded into their sockets, and his mouth resumed its normal shape. He hung, tethered to the rock, while his life ebbed away.

When he had become the fair prince once again, Cuchulain closed his eyes for the last time.

J.D. heard something in the midst of his dream. It was a voice. He tried to open his eyes, but they were swollen shut and hurting badly. He forced himself to see through the mist and saw a knot of men in National Guard uniforms standing around a charred body. One of the men was looking at him. He bent and looked more closely, then said, "I think this one's still alive. He's coming to."

Three of the men turned toward J.D. Then someone shouted, "Get the damn ropes off him, private. See where he's injured. You people quit standing around."

The sergeant's voice spurred the guardsmen into motion. J.D.'s bonds were loosened, and he was laid out flat on the grass of Minerva Whitwell's front yard. A guardsman knelt beside him, saying, "You're gonna be all right, pal. Somebody caught you down in nigger town and beat you up. We'll get you to a hospital."

The guardsman splashed water from his canteen onto a hand-kerchief and began to bathe J.D.'s face. The cool water felt good. J.D. tried to speak but the words came out with difficulty. "Shot . . . shot in leg . . . bastards . . . didn't have a chance . . . find the baby."

"Easy, mister, easy. An ambulance is on the way. Rest easy."

J.D. began to rave: "I'll get them . . . by God . . . get them."

"Easy, mister, easy."

He heard the clang of the ambulance bell, and J.D. passed out again.

13

Rose Chichester

Somebody was clanging on the bars of the cell with a hardwood nightstick. Deputy Fellows did more barking than talking. "Get up, you two! You got company!"

John poked Hoolie's arm several times lightly, not wanting to overstep the boundaries of polite behavior, even in a place like the Hominy jail. But he didn't want his new friend, who'd been asleep on the cell's steel cot for almost eighteen hours, to miss whoever it was coming to see them. Hoolie slowly opened his eyes, "What's goin' on?"

"We're gonna get out, brother. Somebody's here."

Hoolie sat up on the edge of the bunk. He still had all the aches and pains, but the hours of sleep had helped. Hearing the outer door open, he stood up. Everything spun around, but he grabbed the bars of the cell door and steadied himself. Fellows led Myrtle, Martha, and Pete Henderson to the cell. Both women had cut their hair in mourning, but to Hoolie, they seemed to be wearing the latest Paris hairstyles.

Before Hoolie could speak, a barrage of Osage emanated from John Tall Soldier. Hoolie kept trying to get into the conversation, but then he realized that John was doing this for a reason. He was speaking Osage to keep his conversation personal and secret from Henderson. Hoolie noticed that even as Myrtle talked with John, she was staring at Hoolie's battered face with an expression of mixed sympathy and anger. There he stood—dirty, smelly, in a jail cell, beat up to boot, and looking like a bum—and she still cautiously cast him a quick smile.

Henderson also was trying to interrupt John and Myrtle's conversation, but Martha put her index finger to her lips, and the white man fell silent. John continued, and Myrtle answered a few questions.

It was Martha who said, "We'll get you out, Hoolie. The sheriff said that you were probably forced into the fight and didn't have much of a chance to walk away. But he also says that Mr. Tall Soldier here started the whole thing. The only way we'll get John out is to go and get his folks." John said something else in Osage. Myrtle shot back in English, "Be still now, I'll bring in your mama myself. You know I will."

John lowered his head in frustration, and Myrtle turned to Martha and Pete. "Why don't you two go get things cleared up with the sheriff?"

Once her sister, Henderson, and Buford Fellows had gone into the main office with the deputy, Myrtle said in a whisper, "This has got to be quick. John was talking Osage 'cause he doesn't trust the deputy or Pete Henderson. Martha didn't like it, but she went along for my sake. John needs to get out of here, too. He's figured out where Rose is, and he thinks somebody's gonna try and shoot you again. I'm frightened."

"I'll be fine," said Hoolie. "But, you're right, we gotta get John outta here today. As soon as you spring me, we'll go see John's folks. Is that all right?" John and Myrtle nodded their heads in unison.

The outer door opened, and Fellows, Martha, and Pete returned. The deputy opened the cell door. As he walked through it, Hoolie looked over his shoulder at John and said, "Sit tight. We'll get you out real quick."

In a few minutes, Myrtle, Martha, Pete, and Hoolie were on the boardwalk in front of the sheriff's office. They stopped to debate what Hoolie should do first: get John out or go straight to the Lookout place to recuperate. Henderson insisted on Hoolie going back with the girls to be cared for by Grandma Lookout.

Hoolie wasn't about to tell Pete the real reason he was so eager to bail John out, so he said, "Tall Soldier took care of me. He did his best to doctor me up when the deputies wouldn't lift a finger. They threw me in jail when it was the two cowboys that started the fight. One of them was gonna beat me up good, but John stopped him. I gotta get him out; you always gotta take care of the people who helped you."

Now, Hoolie needed John's help again, but he wasn't about to let Pete in on his plans. John had worked out where Rose Chichester was, and Hoolie knew who'd done the killings. John had provided the key when he'd said, "It's all tied together; one thing is connected to another."

Henderson went on arguing, saying that Hoolie's injuries were interfering with his logic. "Rest first," he said. "We'll get Mr. Tall Soldier out. You got beat up, and your ribs must be hurtin'. You're not thinkin' right. Let's go home. Mr. Tall Soldier spends most of his time in the jailhouse anyway. I can't see what's so important about gettin' him out so fast. He'll be okay."

Hoolie rubbed his temples with hands, making his hat go askew. He wanted to clear his head. He looked directly at Myrtle, "Just let me talk to John's mama. I gotta find a place to wash up. How far is it to the Tall Soldiers' house?"

Martha answered, "Not but about four miles outside of town."

"Let's go," said Hoolie in his most commanding voice. "It ain't that far."

Myrtle and Martha nodded their heads. Henderson had been out-voted.

Hoolie saw a large woman looking through the screen door as they pulled up in front of the house. She opened it in an effort to see her unexpected visitors better. They all got out of the car and stood still for a few seconds, letting Mrs. Tall Soldier get a good look at them. What she saw made her take a step back. The two girls were relatives, distant but nevertheless part of the family. The Indian man was a complete stranger; but from his looks and his obvious injuries, she guessed that he was the man who was trying to find out who had killed the girls' father. The white man in the group was the nephew of the loathsome town sheriff. Although she knew that the nephew was courting Martha, it didn't lessen Mrs. Tall Soldier's aversion to him. She would welcome them into her home solely because of her relationship to the girls.

Mrs. Tall Soldier walked down the steps and embraced the girls in turn. Then she led the party into the cool darkness of her parlor. Myrtle explained things to her in Osage and introduced Hoolie and

Pete to her. Everyone could tell that Mrs. Tall Soldier disliked Henderson; her eyes said it clearly. She looked curiously at Hoolie, but he said nothing but "hello."

"So," began Mrs. Tall Soldier, "my son's in jail again. Well, that's the way things are. He fights. He fights against the people tryin' to steal our land," she looked pointedly at Henderson. "I'll get my husband to get our lawyer so we can get him out. I need the lawyer to talk for me. I've got the money here. Always keep money around to get John out."

Hoolie spoke up as soon as she finished her last sentence. "Mrs. Tall Soldier, Mr. Henderson here can act as your lawyer." Both Henderson and Mrs. Tall Soldier looked at Hoolie as if he had asked them to commit adultery. Henderson began to protest, but Martha again put her finger to her lips, and he fell silent.

"Ma'am," Hoolie continued, "Pete here is studyin' to be a lawyer and, besides, he's the sheriff's kin. He can get John out faster than anybody."

Hoolie wanted John out quickly, and he also wanted to trap Henderson on a fence rail to see which way he'd fall. Pete's direct interest in not alienating Martha in the end outweighed his inclination to let John stay behind bars and rot.

"All right," assented Mrs. Tall Soldier. "Now, we'll get something together to eat." She led the two girls back into the kitchen, leaving Hoolie and Pete to sit in uncomfortable silence in the parlor.

Within ten minutes or so, an enormous man blocked the sunlight streaming through the screen door. He walked in, and the screen slammed behind him. He stood still and looked the two strangers over carefully. He knew Henderson and could tell that Hoolie wasn't an Osage. The white man, as usual, was dressed in fancy town clothes; the Indian was dirty and beat up. Both of them had stood as he entered the room, hats in their hands. After a lengthy pause, Mr. Tall Soldier asked, "What do you two want?"

As Hoolie was about to open his mouth, Mrs. Tall Soldier's voice came from the kitchen. She spoke in rapid Osage while walking into the room.

Mr. Tall Soldier nodded his head several times and stretched his mouth once or twice into a grimace that for him passed as a smile. He wore blue jeans, cowboy boots, and a blue chambray shirt. He still had on his giant, black felt hat. The man easily topped six-foot-four and must have weighed close to three hundred pounds. He was one of the biggest men Hoolie had ever seen. After he was introduced as Henry Tall Soldier, they were all called to eat.

They took a quick lunch of fry bread and warmed-over beef stew. While they ate, Myrtle and Martha explained things in Osage to Mr. Tall Soldier. He nodded approval several times but otherwise did not acknowledge that anyone else was at the table. He finished, wiped his mouth with a napkin, and left the room. He returned, holding a wad of money, and barked, "Let's go." Even though none of them had actually finished their meal, they rose, gathered their things, and followed Mr. Tall Soldier outside. They all jammed themselves into Henderson's automobile since the Tall Soldiers' only form of transportation was by horseback or buckboard. Pete wasn't particularly happy about it.

The six of them walked into the sheriff's office together. Much to his liking, Pete Henderson became the center of attention. The Tall Soldiers had given him one hundred dollars to negotiate the release of their son, plus another hundred to grease the palms of his jailers. It was the way of things in Osage County.

Henderson first asked Wallace and Fellows under exactly what charges John Tall Soldier was being held. The deputies were struck dumb. Henderson pursed his lips, "You mean he hasn't been charged yet?"

"Well, no," said Fellows, "but it don't work like that around here. You know that, Pete."

"Just what do you mean by that?"

Fellows and Wallace looked at Henderson incredulously. Pete knew exactly how things worked; he was just trying to prove to his intended and her sister that he was a friend to their people. The deputies' skepticism showed and, to Hoolie at least, so did Henderson's hypocrisy. The haggling went on for a time, until Henderson said with finality, "Now Deputy Wallace, if John Tall Soldier is not charged with anything, then why hasn't he been released?"

"All right, Pete, I'll tell you. See, when John ties one on . . . when he get real drunk, he gets picked up and thrown in the can. He sleeps it off. After a few days, when he's all sobered up, his folks come get him. We keep it simple. No charges, and his folks pay for the damages he done and for his keep for a few days. That John can sure eat." Fellows ended his speech with a self-satisfied smile.

"It don't sound to me like John did any damages this time." Henderson looked at Hoolie who, in turn, shook his head. "Since there aren't damages, how about releasing him?"

"Huh? Why don't you talk to your . . . uh . . . the sheriff? He'll fill you in on how we work it out with John and his folks. I'll get him."

"I'll go with you," said Pete sharply.

Five minutes later, they emerged from the main office. Pete was beaming. He said to Hoolie, "He's free."

Pete turned to Fellows, "Is there anything to sign?"

"Ain't no papers," said Wallace. "I'll just bring him out. He can go on home."

When John emerged, he immediately began a long speech in Osage to his mother and father. They said nothing but joined Myrtle and Martha in nodding their heads as John finished speaking. Once the party was outside, John took Hoolie by the arm and pulled him some forty feet away from the rest.

"We have to do somethin', brother," said John. "You know I know where that girl is, don't you? Let's you and me go out to my place, and let the rest of 'em go home. We got to get away from that Pete."

"Why don't we just go get her now?"

"We gotta get some things done for us first. If we don't, we might be in trouble."

Hoolie was beginning to understand. "John," he said in a whisper, "you think there's gonna be a fight, don't you?"

John dropped his eyes to the ground and said out of the side of his mouth, "Could be. We got to sweat and get ready. Sharpen your knife, brother."

"Okay, John. I've got a car here. Drove it in just before we got thrown in jail. Me, you, and your folks will go to your house. Myrtle, Martha, and Pete can go on. You tell Myrtle so that she understands."

J.D.'s flivver was still parked by the depot. Hoolie changed the plans somewhat. John and Mr. and Mrs. Tall Soldier would ride with Hoolie back to their home. Myrtle and Martha would go with Henderson. But Hoolie insisted on taking both cars to the Tall Soldier place, dropping off John and his parents, and then following Henderson and the two girls out to the Lookout place.

"I have to pick some things up there," he said quietly to John, "and besides, I want to make sure the girls get home all right."

"I see," said John, "but Pete won't."

"I'll tell him I have to get back to Tulsa today. He won't know any different."

After saying their goodbyes to the Tall Soldiers, Hoolie followed Henderson's automobile as he drove to the girls' house. Once there, Hoolie gathered up his belongings and piled them into the Ford. He was getting ready to start it up when Myrtle called to him. He turned and saw her walking alone toward him.

She strode up to him and looked at his swollen face. As she was about to speak, Hoolie raised his hand to stop her. Leaning forward, he said quietly, "I don't want anybody else to know, but I ain't goin' back to Tulsa."

She pursed her lips and reached up with one hand to touch his cheek. "Poor man," she said, "I wish you could just rest. I know what you've gotta do. Pete and Martha think you're goin' back to Tulsa. But our mama thinks you're gonna go after somebody for beatin' you up, and Grandma thinks you're goin' after the killer."

She paused and dropped her arm to her side. "Please, Mr. Hoolie Smith," she whispered with sincerity in her lowered voice, "come back to me. Don't get hurt no more."

A chill moved up and down his spine. He looked at her. She brushed back a bit of hair that the breeze had moved over one eye. "Don't worry, Myrtle Lookout," he said, "I'll be back. It'll take a while, but I'll be back."

Fighting back the pain, he turned to set the spark and crank up the engine. He was gone without saying another word.

Hoolie got to the Tall Soldiers' place just in time to see the sun go down. John was waiting in the front yard to greet him. "Ho, brother," said John, "glad you're back. We got a lot of things to do."

Hoolie started to pile his gear on the ground next to the flivver. He pulled out his rifle and worked the lever to eject the unspent cartridges. He picked them up, put them into his pocket, and laid the rifle down on the Ford's front fender. He was about to break it down to clean it again when John said, "No time for that. We got to move firewood down to the creek. Help me hitch up the wagon."

As Hoolie and John were strapping the team's harnesses to the wagon tongue, Hoolie saw an old man come out of the house. He was in the six-foot-seven range, taller by about three inches than John's father, but by no means as heavily muscled. He was carrying a large bundle wrapped in what looked like an old deer hide, and he was heading toward a big clump of trees close to a creek on the east side of the building. Hoolie asked John, "Is that your grandpa?"

"Yep, he stays with us. Well, mostly he stays in a tipi out past the barn." John stopped and considered his next words carefully. "My grandpa is an old-time medicine man. That ain't the right word, but that's what we say in English. Anyways, he knows the songs and the ways that go with them. He don't really heal people, but he knows how to find out what's wrong with 'em. You know what I mean?"

Hoolie nodded his head slightly. He pointed with his chin toward where John's grandfather had walked, "My mama's brother is an Indian doctor. Cures folks. I got another relative who's a dance leader, singer, and a little captain in the *gadugi* back home. That's a kind of men's outfit that helps with buildin' barns and brooder houses and such. I know quite a bit about medicine but not nearly enough."

Hoolie tightened a strap on the right-side mare's harness, gathered the reins, and lifted them back to the buckboard seat. He looked at John and joked, "I wonder why we got beat up and thrown in jail if we both come from such powerful people."

John snorted and said, "I didn't get beat up. Or shot. I reckon you need to try some Osage medicine."

Hoolie nodded in approval "I reckon so. Hope this thing you got planned for tomorrow won't get us killed."

John turned serious. "We're gonna do somethin' that people will talk about for a long time to come. If we get killed, we'll be talked about forever."

Hoolie was smiling at his new friend. "Well, let's get this thing loaded up," he said with finality.

John ordered Hoolie into the seat and jumped up beside him. John took the reins and gave them a quick shake. "Giddup," he said, and the wagon rolled. They pulled up beside a woodpile near the barn. John got down and started throwing billets of wood into the wagon. Hoolie started to climb down as well. "You stay and hold the horses," said John. Hoolie complied with relief; his side and face were aching again. "I'll get the wood; we need you strong for tonight and tomorrow," said John. Hoolie winced, anticipating the violence. He had observed John in action, and if anyone could bring on a quick resolution—violent or otherwise—to a problem, it was John.

They drove the wagon to a clearing near the running stream. John's father was preparing a dirt altar before the uncovered saplings of a sweat-lodge frame. John unloaded the firewood, and he and his father began gathering some large rocks from a nearby pile. They built a big fire in a well-used pit. Hoolie had been told to sit on a log and be patient.

John sat down beside Hoolie when the fire heating the rocks was going well. "I gotta tell you what's goin' on." He paused, searching for the right words. "All this," he began, "is Heyluska stuff. *Heyluska* stands for warrior, war dance, war medicine, and warrior ways. It takes in a lot of things. We're gonna sweat, and my grandpa is gonna call on the spirits to help us in the battle we're gonna fight. He's gonna sing some songs for our safe journey, too."

"You reckon it'll come to that?" said Hoolie. "I mean shootin'?"

"Listen," said John in a low voice, "I know where the girl is. I think you know who's doin' the killin's. But it might be part of a bigger bunch of people. You think Billy Wallace did it, don't you?"

"That's what I was thinkin'. I couldn't say nothin'. Not while he was right there."

"Well, I think you're right," said John in a low voice. "It all comes together. The oil people, the judges, the Indian Office, the railroads, the sheriff, and the farmers are all mixed up in it—one leads to another. Billy Wallace was a soldier who killed people from far off. My relative was shot from far away. Billy's tied to the sheriff, who's tied with the judges. Now, Tom Miller and Billy Wallace really want to be farmers, but they can't 'cause they don't have the money to get a real operation goin'. That girl's there. I'm betting on it."

John paused again to collect his thoughts. He was letting his logic run away with itself. He had to slow down.

"All right," he continued, "when we was in jail, and you went to sleep, I prayed a lot. Asked for help. Now, for a long time, I been helped out by a boy and an old man who come into my dreams. I saw in a dream them two pointin' to a flower standin' right outside an old shack in the country. There was a small cornfield close by. I recognized the place. It was Billy Wallace's and Tom Miller's. I saw that, and I knew that they was all in it together. Billy was in the war, and I know he's skittish. That's why I think there'll be a fight."

Hoolie spoke up, "Maybe we should just go to the county sheriff. My boss always told me to avoid a fight. Fightin' hurts business, he says."

"Brother," said John, "I think that this is what I gotta do. Let me tell you, when I was small, my grandpa over there saw that I would be a warrior, maybe one of the last ones. I did all kinds of things that were pretty reckless just to prove myself. I went out one time in an ice storm to get back one of our horses. I found him but lost two of my toes to frostbite. Funny thing, my grandpa told me that no Osages ever got frostbite in the old days. I don't know why. Well, I tried to get into the war, but the army wouldn't take me 'cause of my toes. Now, I get drunk and get into fights with the white people.

"I still thought I could be a warrior, but the time never came 'round. I asked my grandpa if I could be a warrior if I talked against the white man for takin' our land. He said that facing real warriors in battle was the only way. So, for years, I've been lookin' for signs on what to do. I think this is it. We're gonna go after the enemy and revenge a wrong. We're gonna go and return a woman who has been captured by the enemy. It's gonna be a great thing."

Hoolie grimaced and whispered, "You know, I had somethin' come to me in a sweat I did right before I went into Hominy. I saw a snappin' turtle. Then when I went out to the Lookouts, Grandma Lookout said that a snappin' turtle told her I was comin'."

"Brother," said John, "I saw bullets bouncin' off a turtle shell. We're gonna be all right."

"I still hate the shootin' part. Ain't there no other way?"

"Nope, can't see it," said John with a grin.

Hoolie shook his head. He was having a hard time with John's apparent zest for fighting, especially when it came to shooting. John's passion for combat seemingly put it on the level of a spiritual responsibility. He needed it like other men need shrines and talismans. To be convinced that he knew Rose Chichester's whereabouts, Hoolie needed more than logic and John's dream. "John, I gotta ask you, is there any other reason for thinkin' that the girl is at Miller's place?"

"Sure is. Do you know how Chief Ruffle's grandson died?"

"No."

"Wilford Logan told me that his throat got cut. I think somebody killed him when that girl was around, but they couldn't kill her."

Hoolie took up the trail of reason. ". . . they couldn't kill her because she's linked to the oil people, who don't want her killed. Or the killers are lookin' to get some ransom money out of her rich kinfolks."

"Right. Billy Wallace coulda done it all. He might be workin' for the sheriff, who works for the oil people, or he might be holdin' the girl so the oil people will pay up or give more Indian business to the sheriff.

"I sit in that alley across from the general store a lot. Lately, I seen Wallace and Miller buy more canned goods than they can use by themselves. I saw Billy buy a dress out of the dry goods store. Now, I know that no woman would stay around Billy Wallace long 'nuf for him to want to buy her a dress, so it was easy to put together after you told me about the girl."

Hoolie nodded, "That's all I need to be sure. But now I don't know if Billy's got it in him to do all that killin'. He killed people from as much as a mile away in the war; he just don't figure to be the one who'd cut somebody's throat. I know somethin' else."

"What's that?"

"Tell you tomorrow."

"No good. Tell me now."

"Can't."

"All right. I'll let it go. We got to get ready for the songs and the sweat. We need the strong hearts for what's gonna happen."

John's father walked over to them and spoke in Osage to his son. In turn, John simply nodded and turned to Hoolie. "My dad says that it'll be a while. So rest."

Hoolie didn't need too much coaxing. He lay down on the ground, closed his eyes, and began to think and re-think his end of the Chichester operation. He had to talk to Billy Wallace, and to do that he needed Billy under his control. That would probably take a fight. Billy was going to talk because the good hearts of Hoolie Smith and John Tall Soldier would prevail.

His mind wandered. He thought about what J.D. was doing at that moment. Hoolie pictured J.D. sitting behind his desk, a cigarette burning under his drooping moustache, going through the newspapers in the never-ending endeavor to be "thorough." J.D. would be angry about Hoolie even contemplating a shoot-out with someone who—criminal or not—was connected with the law. J.D. always tried to maintain very good relations with the various sheriffs, cops, constables,

marshals, and deputies he met. Hoolie believed that his boss over-
looked their shortcomings and bad behavior in order to keep them out
of J.D.'s business. Fighting, getting shot, carrying out vendettas, and
making enemies of the local lawmen were, as J.D. reiterated time and
again, bad for the detective business. Somehow on this operation,
Hoolie had managed to break all four taboos.

Hoolie heard a noise in the underbrush and rolled over to see the
two elder Tall Soldiers coming into the clearing. In their wake walked
John and a young man in his teens, both carrying rifles—one was
Hoolie's 44.40 taken from the flivver. They set the rifles against a
tree stump. John reached down, helped Hoolie up, and asked, "How
you feelin'?"

"I'll be fine," said Hoolie, "a little stiff."

"Grandpa and Dad will take care of that." John paused and pointed
with his lips at the young man. "That's my little brother. He's learnin'
medicine, and he'll put the rocks in the sweat bath for us. Reckon we'd
better get stripped down."

Everyone started to get undressed, except for John's little brother.
Hoolie looked over at John's grandpa and was startled to see that the
elderly man's chest and shoulders were completely covered with geo-
metrical shaped tattoos. Hoolie remembered that Cherokee warriors
used to get tattooed with various medicine symbols in commemora-
tion of their acts of valor. Maybe Osages did the same. John's grandpa
had been around in the buffalo days.

John's father called them all together. Hoolie was put at something
of a disadvantage because he didn't speak Osage. He recognized the
word *Wahkondah*. It was the word, John had explained in jail, for God
or the Great Spirit, or the Creator, or the Great Mysteries.

Hoolie felt the power of the pipe, the blessings, the prayers, the
songs in the sweat lodge, and even of the word *Wahkondah*. The
strength that flowed into him was immeasurable. Hoolie's pain from
the bullet wound, his fall against the Lookout porch steps, and the
aches from the fight with the cowboys had vanished. He was no longer
sore. His joints were in working order and his muscles felt strong and

supple. Even his old shrapnel wounds had stopped aching. Hoolie was as ready as he had ever been to become a warrior.

He was in a state of controlled euphoria. He opened and closed his eyes. Right before him appeared Saligugi, the snapping turtle of his dreams; it would be his shield. The old man said prayers over their weapons. Even they would be in perfect working condition. Then he sang a few more songs.

The ceremony lasted most of the night. Several hours before sunup, Hoolie and John went back to the house and packed up the flivver. Hoolie wanted to thank the two older men for preparing them, but Henry Tall Soldier had gone inside and the grandfather had gone to his tipi next to the barn.

Hoolie set the spark, and John jerked the crank. John jumped into the Ford, and off they rattled, probably the strangest Indian war party ever. A Cherokee and an Osage—ancient enemies—riding in a tin lizzie and carrying the white man's weapons, off to stage a raid on a couple of white lawmen to reclaim a rich white woman for her family.

The two men discussed the plan of action as they drove. "Miller works nights," said John, "so he won't be there. Billy might not want a fight without backup, and we'll get the girl."

"I hope that'll happen," said Hoolie, "but what'll we do after we get her out?"

"I figure we drive to Pawhuska, leave her with my relatives up there. My sister Marie'll take care of her while we go in with Billy to the high sheriff in Pawhuska. We just have to get Billy so's he'll talk about what's been goin' on."

"We might have to wait and take Miller, too. I worry about the Lookouts."

"That seems right," said John. "I think that Pete's somehow all mixed up in this. Acts real docile 'round Martha Lookout, but I told you, he can be mean as hell."

"As soon as we get those people to Pawhuska, we go straight to the Lookout place. That okay by you?"

John nodded in agreement, and Hoolie continued, "John, you

gotta stay with them 'cause I gotta get back to Tulsa. Rose Chichester is going to have to stay up here until I know it's safe for her to go to Tulsa. I don't want to get ambushed takin' her back."

"That's a good idea. Don't worry. I'll watch over the Lookouts. Right now, we got a fight comin' up. Pull over."

The flivver rolled to a stop, and Hoolie shut off the engine. By John's reckoning, they were about a mile away from Tom Miller's cabin. A three-quarter moon cast a dim light. In an hour or so it would be sunup, and the moon would fade from view. John rolled and then lit a cigarette to test the wind. The smoke drifted slowly off to John's right. He looked at the dissipating smoke, coughed softly, and said, "We'll come in so's the dogs won't smell us out right off. Now, let's take off some of these clothes."

John took off his shirt and lifted a canvas water container from the back seat. He walked to where Hoolie was crouched by the dirt road and said, "Let's make us some mud pies."

John squatted and poured water onto the ground. He mixed dirt and water together, and began smearing the mud on his face, chest, and belly. Hoolie took off his shirt and did the same. John, his eyes shining out of the dark mud, smiled, showing white teeth, "This'll get dry in a little while. It'll feel like you're wearin' a clay pot, and before we're there, a lot of it will flake off. That's all right 'cause it'll leave some color behind and take the shine away from our skin."

Hoolie nodded, "That's camouflage. We learned it in the army. The mud'll leave streaks and help break up our outline."

"It might hide our smell a little, too," said John. "Keep it from the dogs for a time. Let's hope that the dogs are lazy and don't care if people come and go a lot."

John looked at Hoolie directly and held out his right hand. Hoolie took it and gave it one quick pump. "Let's go," said Hoolie and John almost in unison.

They went to the car and got their weapons. John had a Winchester 30.30 and Hoolie his 44.40. They both had hunting knives in sheaths attached to their belts, and John pulled out a small hatchet and shoved the handle into the back of his belt. Hoolie noticed for the first time that John wore moccasins, and he wished that he had a pair of his own.

As they walked across a recently turned field, Hoolie thought about an incident that occurred when he was a teenager. Near Panther Creek was the site of an Osage village that a Cherokee war party had massacred and burned a hundred years before. His parents had warned him to stay clear of it. Since it was a place of blood and hatred, it was likely that a sgili or group of them gathered there to make bad medicine.

Warning a Cherokee boy away from any place effectively issued a challenge to his sense of manhood. Hoolie had to see it, and he recruited two of his cousins to go with him. They managed to sneak away from a dance one night, borrow two horses from another cousin, and ride the few miles to see what went on at this unholy spot. They had to crawl up a rise to look down on the hollow where the old village had been. As they were quietly sneaking toward it, a blue light suddenly appeared ahead of them. It danced for a while at the top of the rise, before shooting straight up in the air. The boys were stunned. The color blue had deep meaning for them. Blue was the color of the north. It meant tragedy and terror and sickness. They didn't know whether they should lie still or get up and run for their lives.

Despite their fear, a power kept drawing them toward the top of the hill. When they got there and peered down into the hollow, they saw blue lights bouncing, dancing, darting this way and that, shooting straight up into the night sky, and hovering over a large blue fire in the center of the old village. The boys were awestruck, but they knew they were being conjured. The sgili was making them his own. Either that or they were being given some kind of illness to take back to their families. Then an owl hooted. At that moment, their fear of owls overcame their rapt fascination with the dancing blue lights. The boys jumped up and ran as fast as they could to the horses. They rode away without so much as taking one look back.

Hoolie grimaced when he thought about that experience. The old owl had really saved them. Maybe it had been a messenger rather than something to fear. He'd have to think about it some more. That is, he'd think about some more if he lived through the night. Fear began to inch up his spine.

Hoolie and John carried their rifles as if they were setting out on a hunting trip. As they neared a small cornfield, they both shouldered their weapons. Hoolie saw the dim outline of a cabin just beyond the field. The corn was pretty short, but it would provide some cover as they crawled on their bellies through the rows.

Hoolie and John got down and lay prone. Hoolie spoke in a whisper, "You go to the right, and I'll go straight ahead toward the door. I'll yell out for Billy to give up. If he starts somethin', you start shooting, and I'll find cover."

"Sounds good," said John. He looked off in the direction he was to go and whispered, "At least the dogs ain't caught wind of us yet. There's a corral up near the house, and the horses'll raise billy-hell if they smell us."

"I know. Let's get it done quick—before Wallace has time to get ready. When you get so you can see the door and got cover, give me a crow call."

"All right."

"I hope," said Hoolie with a sigh, "she's there."

John's teeth flashed in the dim light. Then he was gone.

Hoolie crawled forward as quietly as possible through the corn rows. He heard a dog bark from somewhere near the cabin. He froze. The dog began barking more insistently. It knew something was wrong, but whether the animal was barking at John or himself, Hoolie couldn't tell.

The cabin door creaked open, and a man bellowed, "Goddammit, shut up, you mangy sombitch."

Something was thrown, striking the dog. It yelped once and was silent.

Hoolie waited until the door slammed shut before he began making his way through the corn again. He was just at the edge of the field when he heard John's crow call.

He lay breathing deeply, gathering himself to approach the cabin.

He exhaled very slowly, rose to his feet, and stepped out of the corn. He was less than thirty feet away from the cabin door. The dog had slunk away. A tiny bit of light shone through a crack in the door. The windows were shuttered tight.

Shouldering his rifle, Hoolie walked forward a few cautious steps. He stopped, "You, in the cabin! Billy Wallace! Come on out. We gotta talk! I don't mean you no harm."

The sun had yet to crest the horizon, but the darkness was giving way to a shadowy gray light that hid more than it illuminated. Hoolie caught a movement to his left. It was the dog. The animal approached him slowly, head low, growling. Nothing seemed to stir inside the cabin. Hoolie shifted his rifle from the dog to the cabin door and back again. The dog stopped his advance but continued to growl deeply.

The cabin door suddenly swung open and a shotgun blast ripped through the predawn shadows. Instead of trying to run, Hoolie dropped to the earth, prone, and squeezed off a shot in the general direction of the cabin door. He cocked the rifle again but didn't fire. No more shots were fired. Hoolie could hear low voices coming from inside, but he couldn't tell if either of them was female.

John called from his position. Hoolie realized that John was pretty close to the cabin, too. "Billy Wallace," called John, "you better come on out! We know you got the girl. This is John Tall Soldier. You know I'll burn you out and put a bullet through your head if you don't do what I say. This detective out here is holdin' me back from pourin' coal oil all over the side of your cabin. Get out here, now!"

In the gathering light, Hoolie could make out movement within the cabin. Shadows seemed to cross between cracks in the log walls and the lights within. Suddenly, the window shutters to the right of the door were thrown open, and two more shotgun blasts were fired in John's direction. John returned the fire, and Hoolie got off three shots in rapid succession. The shotgun answered again. Billy was loading quickly, or he had more than one shotgun.

The sun was now peeking over the cornfield directly behind Hoolie. It cast a brilliant light against the front of the cabin. He realized that the cabin's defender would be blinded.

John threw two quick shots at the cabin window. His Winchester 30.30 made chips fly off the log wall.

Hoolie saw a shape begin to form in the window. The shape became Billy Wallace. The sun was in his eyes, and he raised his left hand to his forehead in the effort to block the rays. John's rifle cracked, and Billy dropped from view. Billy screamed, "I'm shot, I'm shot! Help me, I don't wanna die! Please, help me!"

Then, a woman screamed, "He's shot! Help! There's blood all over!"

John shouted from his position, "Keep me covered. I'm goin' up." He immediately sprinted to the door, slammed his back against the wall, pointed his rifle skyward, and called once again. "Come on out!"

The woman's voice answered, "He's hurt badly. He can't move."

Hoolie ran to join John. "Drag him out," called Hoolie.

There were some grunts and a few groans from inside the cabin. John heard slow, shuffling footsteps. "Don't shoot. We're comin' out."

Hoolie backed away from the cabin and positioned himself directly in front of the door, rifle cocked, shouldered, and ready. The door pushed open. A young girl, dressed in a dirty gingham shift, emerged first. The door swung shut behind her. John started to reach for the door handle when two more shotgun blasts fairly ripped the door from its leather hinges. The girl fell face forward, hit by some of the pellets and splinters from the shattered wood.

John roared and kicked in what remained of the door. He raised his rifle and shot Billy Wallace in the middle of the forehead. The bullet blew out the back of Billy's skull and plastered the cabin's rear wall with blood, brains, and bits of bone.

Hoolie was on his knees beside the girl. She was alive. There were several pellet wounds in her back, but she wasn't bleeding badly; the door had absorbed most of the blast and had slowed the shot that had hit her. She was sobbing when Hoolie rolled her on her side. Hoolie recognized her, dirty and skinny as she was. It was the socialite Rose Chichester of Pittsburgh, Pennsylvania. She had a small greenish bruise on her cheek, probably from a slapping that she must have taken a couple of days before. Her hair was in tangles, and the rims around her eyes were bright red. Hoolie spoke to her in a low voice, "It's goin' to be all right now, Miss Chichester. We're here to take you home. We'll get you to a doctor and get you fixed up."

Sobbing, she said, "Why did he shoot me? I did what he told me. He pointed the gun at me and told me to scream that he'd been shot. He said we were coming out. Why did he do this to me?"

Hoolie tried to soothe her. "Don't talk now, miss, just lie still. You're gonna be fine. He was a bad man. We'll take you home."

She buried her face in the crook of her arm and wailed, "I can't . . . my father . . . he'll never want . . . to see me again."

John walked over, looked down at Hoolie and the girl, and said in a flat voice, "Billy's a goner. I just now saw a trail of dust comin' up the road. It's Miller comin' home. We got to lay a trap for him. Take him with us."

Hoolie felt a twinge of anger at John for shooting Wallace without hesitation. But thinking it over, he realized that John couldn't have done anything else. Billy had obviously gone crazy; he would have shot anybody and anything. Hoolie had to question somebody; it might as well be Tom Miller.

Hoolie gave the orders. "Quick, take her inside and put her to bed. I'll drag Billy out here. You hide in the cabin, and I'll go back in the corn. When Miller drives up, he'll get out of the automobile to check on Billy. We'll take him then. Don't shoot him."

John nodded in assent. Rose Chichester groaned when John picked her up. He carried her into the cabin laid her on a rickety bed. Hoolie followed and took Billy by the heels and dragged him out in the yard. Billy's corpse lay in the dirt, sightless eyes staring up into the sky. The hole in Billy's forehead was small and looked like a black dot. The back of his head was gone, but that was relatively well hidden because Billy lay on his back. Miller wouldn't know that Billy was dead until he looked at him from fairly close range. By then Hoolie and John would have him in a crossfire. He would have to surrender.

As Miller slowed to a stop, Hoolie could see that he was confused. Billy was lying out in front with the door of the cabin dangling from a hinge. The car stopped, and Miller jumped out. He went straight to the cabin instead of checking to see what was the matter with Billy

Wallace. He stopped about ten feet from the door and yelled, "Rosie, Rosie. Where are you? Somethin's happened. Where are you now, gal? You better get out here quick. Else you're in for another beatin'. Dammit, Rose, get out here."

Hoolie stood, leveled his rifle at Miller's chest, and said, "You ain't gonna do nothin' to Miss Chichester ever again, Miller. Now lie down right there with your face in the dirt. Don't move; don't even breathe hard."

John was standing in the door. He took aim with his rifle "Do what he says, boy. You know that I'll shoot you down without thinkin' twice. Face down, quick!"

Miller eased himself down in the dirt.

John got a length of rope from the cabin and roughly tied Miller's hands in back of him. Then he hog-tied the man's ankles and looped the rope around Miller's neck. Miller had to arch himself backward to ease the pressure against his throat. Hoolie looked down at the gasping deputy and spoke in a harsh whisper, "Now, you better tell me what's been goin' on around here. I want to know why that girl's here, and I want to know why you've been keepin' her. I want to know just how the sheriff's wrapped up in this. Start talkin' or I'm gonna take a half-hitch on that rope you got 'round your neck."

Miller coughed and yelled between gasps, "I ain't sayin' nothin' to you goddam prairie niggers," he screamed. "The sheriff'll eat your gizzards for what you done. Murder, too! You killed Billy!"

John was somewhat confused. He didn't expect someone with a rope around his neck to be defiant.

Hoolie's mouth was a slash and his eyes narrowed into slits. He took his knife from its sheath, bent over, and cut the rope leading from Miller's ankles to his neck. When the rope relaxed, Miller screamed again, "About time you got wise, you red nigger. I'll—" Hoolie kicked Miller in the ribs and rolled the man over on his back. Hoolie reached down, grabbed Miller by the shirt collar, and dragged the deputy from the cabin to the corral. Hoolie spotted another length of rope on the gate and took it down. He stood Miller up, pinned him against the corral gate, and looped the new rope around the man's neck again. He took the free end of the rope, dropped it over the top rail of the gate and pulled it out from under the bottom rail. John was watching Hoolie curiously. He said to Hoolie, "Brother, we ain't got time for this now. We got to get the girl some medicine."

Hoolie looked over his shoulder and said, "Just a minute." He continued to wrap the rope elaborately around Miller's ankles, and over and through one of the middle rails. Then, he took ahold of the rope, gave John a quick look, put his right foot against the gate, and pulled the free end of the rope as hard as he could.

Miller's feet were jerked off the ground and at the same time his head was pulled back sharply. He started to scream but the rope cut off any sound. All he could do was gag. Hoolie let go and Miller pitched forward. He landed in a heap at Hoolie's feet.

John looked in utter amazement at Hoolie, "I don't guess you like bein' called names, eh?"

Hoolie said, "Nope," and bent over the gasping deputy. "Now you listen," he said to Miller, "that's a little bitty sample of what I can do to you. We're gonna put you in the car now and drive to Pawhuska. You're not gonna make a sound. Then, we're gonna have a long talk. You better tell me everything I want to know or you're goin' back up on the gate again. Shake your head 'yes' if you understand me."

Miller, his eyes wide with fear, nodded once.

"That's good," said John, "Miss Rose ain't shot too bad, but what there is, is plenty painful. Let's get her to my relatives. We'll talk to Mr. Miller at my sister's house."

Hoolie agreed. When Billy failed to report to work, someone would be sent to investigate.

They wrapped Miller's legs with the rope and pinioned his arms to his body, then they gagged him and threw him into the back of his own automobile. While John went to get J.D.'s flivver, Hoolie made a poultice of tobacco and bacon grease he found in the cabin, applied it to Rose's back, and bandaged her with a long strip of calico. Only a few of the pellets were under the skin, a good sign that nothing penetrated to her organs. She objected to the poultice, but he assured her that it was an old-time Indian remedy and the combination of tobacco and bacon grease would draw out the poisons from the wounds. Hoolie wished that he had some clean material for a bandage, but it was the best he could do for now.

When John returned, Hoolie helped Rose into J.D.'s overworked Model T. They pulled Billy's body inside the cabin and closed the wrecked front door. Hoolie got in the flivver with Rose. John got behind the wheel of Miller's car, reached back and slapped the deputy's head, laughed out loud, then put the car in gear and roared away, Hoolie and Rose in his wake.

At John's relatives' farm, they put Rose in the care of his sister Marie and carried the trussed-up Miller to an immature post oak tree. They loosened some of his bonds and tied him to the tree in a sitting position. John's cousin, Ned, followed them and squatted out of the way so he could watch the general proceedings. Hoolie and John took positions sitting comfortably cross-legged in front of Miller. Miller had been badly frightened when Hoolie nearly hanged him on the corral gate. He was wary, but he was also mad.

"Miller," Hoolie began, "I want you to tell me about how the girl got into your dirty hands. And don't leave nothin' out."

"You ain't gonna kill me, are you?" whined Miller.

"Don't know yet," answered John, "but you'd better not lie to us. If you do, you'll get worse than that rope trick my brother here pulled on you back at the cabin."

A racist to the marrow of his bones, Miller was chafing with the knowledge that he had been manhandled, badly frightened, and trussed up by Indians. Now they were questioning him. He tried to put fear into their hearts. "You all know," he said in a deadly serious tone, "that I'm part of the invisible empire, 'The Brotherhood.'"

"What's that?" asked a truly interested Hoolie.

"I'm a proud knight of the Klan."

"The Ku Klux Klan?" Hoolie asked.

"That's right. That means that you red niggers better leave me alone, or we'll burn out your families and hang you from the highest tree."

Hoolie and John knew exactly what Miller was thinking. Two Indians trying to bring charges against a white man was going to be difficult enough. Miller could call on others, including Sheriff McKinley, who carried a great deal of weight in Osage County. Maybe Rose's wealth and connections would balance out McKinley's influence. They had to make Miller talk in front of white officials in Pawhuska. Making him talk now might loosen his tongue later.

John grinned and leaned toward Miller conspiratorially. "They'll have to find you first, white man," he said with finality.

Hoolie stood and kicked Miller's foot. "Answer my questions, boy, or you'll be hangin' from a tree your own self. I want to know about how you got hold of that girl."

Hoolie took out his knife, leaned over, and stabbed the tree not two inches from Miller's head.

Miller quaked and began, "Sheriff McKinley brought her to my place. Told me she was just a crazy gal and didn't have no folks. He said that she'd tell me that she's rich and that her daddy'd pay me to bring her back and all that. Told me not to pay attention to that stuff and just keep her around to do chores. We didn't touch her in the carnal way; me and Billy don't do that. But I had to smack her around sometimes, or she'd get uppity. I don't take no uppity women. My daddy taught me that."

"I bet daddy's real proud of you," said John sarcastically.

"Go on," ordered Hoolie, "I want the full story or that rope goes back around your neck."

"All right, all right. Billy told me the whole story. That gal is crazy as a loon. What sent her over the edge was a killin'. Billy was in the war. He was a sniper and killed close to thirty Huns. He gets real jumpy sometimes, but he don't like to hurt people no more. He's been teachin' all of us how to use the new army guns that's getting' out to lawmen nowadays. Billy knows more about guns than anybody I ever knew. He taught us how to handle a Springfield and the Browning automatic rifle. Shootin' army style is a lot different than I learned to shoot."

"Okay, Miller, that's enough," said Hoolie, "Why was the girl out at your place?"

"Well." He trembled. "There's a lot of money in Indian oil, see, and the sheriff tries to make everything run right. Sometimes the redskins don't want to cooperate with their lawyers, so the sheriff, Billy, and the sheriff's nephew roughs 'em up a bit."

"Pete Henderson beats people up for his uncle?" asked Hoolie.

"I reckon Pete seems to like it."

"Go on," said John.

"Billy went with Sheriff McKinley and Pete to rough up Tommy Ruffle. Tommy was givin' fits to Judge Patterson. Tommy's grandpa, Old Cockeye, got oil and the judge was his legal guardian. Tommy don't like the way they been handlin' his grandpa's leases and said so.

"They went out to Tommy's place. He's got a little house pretty close to his grandpa's spread. Tommy wasn't there, but then him and this Rose gal shows up. Pete knew who she was, so he had Billy take her over to the car. Pete told Tommy that he was gonna take her back to her folks. Pete said somethin' like he knew that her daddy wouldn't want her livin' with no Indian.

"Anyway, Tommy starts fightin', tryin' to get the girl. He got Sheriff McKinley by the shirt. That was when Pete ran up and pulled a knife. He grabs Tommy by the hair of the head and cuts his throat."

Everything went silent. Hoolie dropped his eyes; John leaned toward Miller menacingly.

"After that, Rosie faints dead away," Miller continued. "Pete starts sayin' that they'll have to kill her, too, and Billy stands up against him. They argued for a while, and the sheriff finally tells 'em what they have to do. The sheriff knows her people, I guess, and don't want her killed. He sends Pete and Billy off to get rid of Tommy, and he takes the girl over to my place. He told me to keep her or else I won't have no job anymore."

Hoolie and John looked at each other. They had been astonished by what they had heard. Pete Henderson was Tommy Ruffle's killer.

Hoolie leaned toward John and whispered, "We better talk to Rose."

"Right," John answered. He then looked at Miller. "Miller, we're gonna let you alone for a while. You think about what you done wrong. You're gonna have to tell the county sheriff all what you told us. Comin' clean might keep you outta jail."

Miller nodded silently.

Hoolie and John rose, asked Ned to keep an eye on Miller, and walked to a nearby tree stump. Hoolie folded his arms across his chest. "I think he's tellin' the truth, at least as much of it as he knows. He works nights and probably wouldn't know Rose Chichester from a jack pine. We gotta talk to her."

"What puzzles me," John began, "is why she didn't run off after Miller starts beatin' on her."

"She might not've known where to go. We just have to ask her."

Hoolie dropped his hands to his side and looked around. It was late afternoon. It had been a long day—the gunfight, the long drive to John's sister's place, questioning Miller. Now they had to talk to Rose.

They went back to Miller and made sure his bonds were snug and well tied. They left Ned with a rifle to stand watch. As they were walking back to the house, John asked Hoolie, "Are you gonna tell me what you wouldn't tell me yesterday? Just exactly what else do you know?"

Hoolie scratched his cheek. There was some dried mud that still clung to his face and chest. He needed a bath. So did John, for that matter.

"I'll tell you now. You and me both thought that Billy was the sniper. Now, it looks like he didn't kill anybody.

"The day after the funeral I looked for signs the killer might of left in the creek bed near the Lookout house and in the field beyond. I found a Springfield shell casing and tire tracks. When I was in the sheriff's office the first time last Saturday, I saw a couple of Springfields, one with a scope, on the wall. I saw the sheriff's new automobile, too. Bein' a mechanic, I recognized that those tire tracks in that field behind the creek were made by the sheriff's car. I followed them to the road into town. The sheriff's car was parked along the road before it went into the field. But a car had stopped next to it, a car that had been heading into town from the Lookout place. There were footprints between the two cars. I knew that automobile, too. It was Pete Henderson's Packard."

John had to put his hand over his mouth to hide his surprise.

Hoolie continued. "Pete Henderson set us up that night and drove off. He met up with his uncle. They both got into the sheriff's car and drove into the field. One of them snuck up with that rifle and the other stayed with the car. After the shots that night, I heard an automobile start up. When I got to look over the field and found the tracks, I thought the car started up too quick after the last shot. The car had been parked quite a ways from the creek. Nobody could've run that fast over that field. Somebody was waitin' with the car. The tire tracks and the sound of the car startin' up told me that it was that new Lincoln police car the sheriff drives. Either the sheriff did the shootin' and Pete stayed with the car, or it was the other way around. Those two killed a man in cold blood. A man I liked, your relative, was shot by them, and I'm gonna find a way to get them. I worry about Myrtle, Lizzie, Martha, and Grandma Lookout. I just couldn't do anything about it. The Lookout women might not have believed me. Pete is out there, schemin' to get all of the Lookouts' land, money, and oil rights. He as much as told me so.

"Both men were killed for the same reason. They wanted to have a say in what happened to their land. They killed Ben so that Pete would get control of the family once he married Martha. Who knows, they might've killed her too after the weddin'."

They reached the front porch of the house. John put one foot on the first step and turned. "Grandma Lookout can take care of herself. I don't know how we get to Pete and the sheriff."

"That's why I been playin' along with Pete," said Hoolie. "They're gonna be lookin' for us now. That fight's comin'. I just don't want it to happen at the Lookout place."

John's sister Marie came to the door and announced supper.

They had some corn soup and fry bread. Marie said that she had dressed Rose's wounds and put her up in the second bedroom down the hall. She also sent her son down with soup and bread for Ned and the tied-up white man. She said that she would go down with a lantern and take care of some of the man's scrapes, bruises, and cuts. "You don't want him to look like you beat him up," she said. "He's gotta talk to the sheriff."

Knowing that she was right, Hoolie and John finished eating and accompanied her while she went to fix up Tom Miller. Hoolie was happy to find out that he really hadn't caused much damage to the man as a result of what John called "the rope trick." Marie's husband, who had been sent to town to purchase a few necessities, was back by the time they returned to the house.

Standing outside on the porch, John and Hoolie could hear Rose protest and moan as Marie wrapped new bandages around the girl. John said, "We shouldn't try to get either one of them to town tonight. She's still in bad shape, and Miller needs a bit more coolin' down."

"I think so, too," said Hoolie. "There's too many bad things goin' on in the dark. We'll talk to Rose now, and take them in first thing in the morning."

"Marie's taking good care of her. She says that Miss Chichester is just happy to be around somebody who treats her good."

Marie came to the door and said quietly, "Rose is awake. She's in some pain, but she can talk to you'uns. So, go in, but I don't want you to get her excited or movin' around. She's got to lie still."

Both men stood and assured Marie that they would do as she said. They walked to the bedroom and opened the door.

Because her wounds were in her back, Rose Chichester lay on her right side, facing a blank wall. A kerosene lamp burned low on a table on the opposite side of the bed.

John walked over and turned the wick up in the lamp, then he stood with his arms folded, his back against the wall. Hoolie pulled up a chair and sat down facing Rose. She gazed at him with a sickly expression.

Hoolie spoke first. "Miss, I'm Hoolie Smith. This is John Tall Soldier. His sister Marie has been caring for you."

Hoolie stopped for a moment and rubbed his hands nervously on his pants. He looked at John standing on the other side of the bed and said, consciously avoiding eye contact with Rose, "Your father sent me here to find you, and me and John took you away from Miller and Wallace. Now if you're able, I'd like for you to tell us about what has happened since you left Tulsa."

"I want to thank you," she said softly. After a long pause, she continued, "I don't know how to tell you what happened or where to start."

She turned her head slightly, and a tear rolled down onto her small nose. She brushed it away with her left hand. She moaned a bit at the movement, but she turned her head a little and stared straight at Hoolie. Hoolie's eyes were on the floor.

"Can you tell me about Tommy?" said Hoolie out of the corner of his mouth.

Rose sobbed four or five times. John winced at hearing Hoolie speak the name of the dead man, but Hoolie knew he had to talk like a white person to a white person. He would have to violate that particular taboo over and over again before this case was wrapped up.

"I had to get away from the Shelbys. Mrs. Shelby is wonderful. She treats me like I was a daughter. I love her. But there was something wrong between me and Mr. Shelby. I didn't know what it was, but it wasn't healthy. I know why now.

"Tommy and I became very good friends. We talked a lot, and he gave me things from his heart. I loved him, but not like a lover—do you know what I mean?"

"I don't really know," said Hoolie. "But go on, please."

"I talked Tommy into helping me get away from Tulsa. We snuck out of a place in the wall around the Shelby estate and took his car. We drove out to his house. He lives alone now that his mother died."

Hoolie looked to John for confirmation. John nodded his head but said nothing.

"The sheriff, Pete Henderson, and Billy were there," she continued.

"I knew Mr. Henderson from our stays at his mother's boarding house. He stared at me with a terrible look in his eyes.

"The sheriff and Billy took out their guns and told Tommy to go over to the horse trough. Mr. Henderson took my arm and twisted it. The sheriff and Billy started to beat up on Tommy and hold his head under the water. They told him not to interfere with any of Judge Patterson's decisions about his grandfather's money, land, or oil leases. They told him they'd kill him if he said another word about land or headrights again.

"Then Peter Henderson spoke up, saying that they should go ahead and kill Tommy anyway as a warning to all the rest. He called Tommy frightful names. Names I wouldn't say to anybody."

"We think we know what them names are, miss," said John.

"He called me a whore. That's when Tommy broke away and pushed the sheriff down. Tommy was heading for me and Henderson. Billy Wallace caught him and turned him around. They were wrestling near the trough, and Peter let go of me. He took a knife from his pocket and opened it. He ran toward where Tommy and Billy were fighting. Then he took Tommy by the hair and . . . and . . . cut Tommy's throat. I know I screamed and fell down."

Hoolie gave a quick nod to John. It sounded almost exactly like the story Miller told. Rose broke into sobs. Hoolie said, "Miss, if you want us to leave, we will."

"No, Mr. Smith. I have to tell it. Just give me a moment."

Rose composed herself and continued. "Billy drew his pistol again and pointed it at Henderson. They started yelling at each other. Finally, the sheriff told Billy to put the gun away, and for them both to settle down. The sheriff gave the orders. He told Billy and Pete to put Tommy into his automobile and drive it to Tulsa. They were to leave the body in a ditch somewhere, then drive back to Miller's farm. The sheriff would take me there and wait for them. Sometime in there I fainted. Blood was everywhere, and the sheriff was yelling. I woke up in the car. The sheriff was driving. He took me to the farm and told Tom Miller that he had to keep me there."

John interrupted. "The sheriff brought you there?"

"Yes." She stopped her narrative abruptly, put her face into the pillow, and cried. Hoolie wanted to pat her on the back or something, but thought the gesture might be too forward. Her shoulders shook from the sobbing and the pain in her back.

Eventually, Rose ceased her shaking. With a little choking noise, she said, "I became a prisoner. And that's about it."

"Excuse me, Miss Chichester," said Hoolie, "but why didn't you just run away?"

"I didn't know where I was . . . I wanted to." She stopped and sobbed once again. "What's the use?" she asked nobody in particular. "I didn't run away because there's nothing in Tulsa or Pittsburgh for me anymore. I learned a terrible secret about myself and the Shelbys. I know why I felt uneasy around Mr. Shelby."

As she became more distressed, Hoolie said, "Do you want to stop, now, miss?"

"No. "I'll get it all out."

John had drawn up a chair and was now sitting by her, and he said, "You tell us in your own way, and in your own time."

"I wanted to leave, but I had nowhere to go. Mr. Smith, the man who hired you is not my real father."

Hoolie shook his head. It was as if Rose had started speaking Japanese to him.

"What! Why would you say that?"

"Because my real father is William Shelby. That's the secret. That's why they didn't just kill me. Can't you see? All of them work for Shelby Oil. None of them thought that I'd be with Tommy when they confronted him. They made a mistake beating up Tommy instead of just going away. There must be something about the oil leases coming up soon; otherwise, it wouldn't have been so important to hurt Tommy."

John quietly interrupted: "You're right, miss. There's a meetin' comin' up on Monday about the leases. The council is gonna ask the Indian Office people to look into the judges, the oilmen, and the leases."

Rose closed her eyes and went on. "My real father wouldn't let them kill me, but he needed me out of the way, hidden away, so that

I wouldn't marry my half-brother, which is what Mrs. Shelby and my . . . adopted . . . father wish. It's got to be true. Otherwise I'd be dead."

"Now, Miss Chichester, you don't know that," said Hoolie. "Who told you all this?"

"Sheriff McKinley."

John half rose from his chair. "Miss, that sheriff's a liar. You can't believe anything he says."

Rose cried harder and clutched her pillow until her knuckles turned dead white. "He's telling the truth," she sobbed. "I'm William Shelby's illegitimate child. McKinley learned about it from Judge Patterson, who drew up Mr. Shelby's will. That judge has known the family for years. He got a letter from my mother before she died telling him the truth about me. She gave the information to the judge so that he could force Mr. Shelby into putting me in his will. She was blackmailing him from the grave.

"The judge, the sheriff, Mrs. Henderson, and Pete Henderson have been using the knowledge about me to guarantee Shelby Oil's cooperation in defrauding the Osage people. One hand washes the other. The judge and the sheriff force the Indians into bad deals; Shelby Oil makes money and pays off the judge and sheriff. I don't think Mr. Shelby would have had anything to do with these petty criminals if they didn't have my mother's letter forcing him to cooperate in the fraud."

John and Hoolie both stared straight ahead. They didn't know where to go next. Rose Chichester had stunned them.

Hoolie shook his head and took a deep breath. "Miss Chichester, you're thinkin' wrong. Your real father is E.L. Chichester. He raised you and cares about you. He hired me and my boss to look for you. I think that it wouldn't make any difference to him if Shelby was your blood daddy. He'd want you back."

John kept opening and shutting his mouth. When Hoolie's speech started to fade into the last few words, John began, "Listen, miss, Shelby's got to come up with some answers about what's goin' on around here. He's got to come up with some answers for you, for your daddy—the one who counts—and for Mrs. Shelby. Most of all, he's got to account for why there's been these killin's. Two of my people have been killed, and Shelby has somethin' to do with it. I don't care if he's bein' blackmailed. Sometimes you have to stand up for what's right, no matter what happens. And you, miss, you gotta help us. You gotta tell this story to the laws in Pawhuska. We're Indians. They won't believe us. Will you do that?"

John could see at once that his speech deeply affected her. She raised her head, "You're right, Mr. Tall Soldier. I have to do what's right, no matter what. We'll go tomorrow. I'll be better then."

Hoolie said, "After we get done in Pawhuska tomorrow, I'll have to head back to Tulsa."

Rose lowered her head down into the goose-down pillow, "Mr. Smith, when you report to your employer, tell him I want to remain here until I'm fully recovered and ready to talk to my father." She stared at John and added, "The one who counts." She paused again. "I'll pay your sister for my keep, Mr. Tall Soldier. Meanwhile, we'll do what's right."

John shook his head again, "You don't need to pay anybody. We take care of our own. And you're one of us."

Hoolie looked at the girl, "I'll handle things just like you want, miss. My boss will get it straightened up with your daddy. I have some visitin' to do, and then I have to come back and finish up around here."

"Mr. Smith has to see a sweetheart, I think," said John.

Hoolie scowled at John, and a faint smile crossed Rose's face.

14

The Panther

Hoolie's journey back to Tulsa was long and circuitous. After spending the night splitting the responsibility of watching over Tom Miller between them, John and Hoolie piled the deputy in his own automobile and asked Marie if Rose was ready to travel.

Rose greeted them in Marie's parlor, wearing a borrowed dress, and with her hair washed and combed. Though still thin, she was beginning to look more like a socialite than the rag doll they'd rescued the day before. Even though she still felt a good deal of pain, she was cheerful. For their part, John and Hoolie had taken hurried baths in the creek, washing the rest of the dried mud from their bodies, and dressing in what they could put together from what Hoolie had packed and what Marie's husband, Silas, could spare. Rose giggled at John's too-short trousers and Hoolie's bright red hunting shirt and pair of threadbare blue jeans.

They headed into Pawhuska, John driving the flivver with Rose in the front seat, and Hoolie with a trussed-up Tom Miller moaning in the rear. Coming into town, they spotted a shingle hanging from a two-story clapboard building next to the lumber yard: "Owen Parker, M.D." The stairs were in an alley outside the building.

They walked Rose up the wooden steps and into Dr. Parker's office, and then they returned to the flivver to retrieve Tom Miller and carry him, still bound, up the stairs. They laid him in a heap on the office floor. Dr. Parker had been tending to Rose's wounds in an inner room. When he came out and saw the bound man on his floor, he growled, "What's going on here, you two?"

Hoolie started to speak, but John made the ill-timed mistake of pulling the gag out of Miller's mouth. As soon as he took a breath,

Miller screamed, "These red niggers tied me up and beat me. Call the law, goddammit."

Rose hastily garbed herself in a sheet and appeared in the examining-room doorway, "Doctor, you must listen to me." She pointed at Miller. "This man abducted me, and his partner in the crime shot me in the back. These two men rescued me," she said indicating John and Hoolie.

Miller roared, "She's a crazy bitch! Don't pay her no mind. Get the law."

Every bit the socialite, Rose looked at Dr. Parker, "I, too, insist that you call the county sheriff. Have someone come over here, and I will explain everything."

Hoolie added his plea. "Doctor, this is Miss Rose Chichester from Pennsylvania. Her father, E.L. Chichester, hired me to find her. When we did, the man who was holding her put up a fight and was killed. This man," he pointed to Miller, "was in on the kidnapping."

Dr. Parker looked from Hoolie to John to Rose and back to Hoolie. He pondered what had been said for a few seconds and decided that Rose and Hoolie were telling the truth. He looked deep into her eyes, touched her shoulder, and walked over to the telephone. John replaced the gag. After calling the county sheriff, Dr. Parker took Rose into the examination room and continued treating her wounds. Hoolie and John sat in the outer room, with Miller tied up at their feet.

By the time a deputy showed up, Dr. Parker had removed four shotgun pellets and a few wood splinters from Rose's back. Rose didn't make a sound while the doctor did his work, and only when he bathed the wounds in iodine did John and Hoolie hear Rose gasp.

Dr. Parker came out to greet the deputy, and looking at Hoolie and John, he said, "Rose is a brave and strong woman. In a few weeks, she'll be fine."

Rose explained everything to the young deputy, who was so taken with her good looks that he forgot to write anything down. He put in another call to his office. The county sheriff himself made an appearance, and once again, Rose had to patiently explain all that had happened to her. After hearing the tale, the sheriff called his office and requested the presence of yet another deputy. Then he told Hoolie and John to wait downstairs in the alley.

The two men sat on the wooden stairs and waited. It was clear that the Osage County sheriff was having some trouble with the idea of arresting one of his brethren from Hominy. The weight of a Chichester was not to be ignored, however, and so, after a long spell of sitting, Hoolie and John rose to let the deputies carry the still trussed-up Miller off to jail. The sheriff stopped long enough to commend Hoolie and John as "heroes." Finally, Dr. Parker escorted Rose down to the alley and into the Ford's backseat. Hoolie tried to offer him some money, but he waved it off. He looked at John, "I understand that your sister is going to look after Rose here?"

John nodded in the affirmative. Parker then asked, "Does she have the supplies?"

John was irritated, "My sister knows Indian medicine and will take good care of her."

The doctor's face showed his contempt for Osage practices. Rose caught the look, "Dr. Parker, Marie has helped me recover. I trust her. Please, do so as well."

The doctor was beguiled, "You know what's best, Miss Chichester. Your general health is very sound. Those wounds will heal, even on their own accord."

They started up the flivver and were soon on their way out of Pawhuska. After placing Rose back in the care of Marie, Hoolie and John made the long trip to the Lookout place. Once there, they learned— not much to their surprise—that Pete Henderson had not been seen since he'd dropped off Myrtle and Martha two days before. Pete and his uncle had undoubtedly found Billy Wallace's body and knew that Rose and Tom were missing. They would need to plan a cover-up, perhaps one that would require yet another murder. The thought frightened Hoolie, and he asked John to stay with the Lookout women while he reported back to Tulsa.

Everyone objected to Hoolie's immediate departure. "It's kinda late to go now," said John. "You can't get there before nightfall. Nobody'd be around for you to report to."

"Yeah," replied Hoolie, looking at Myrtle rather than John. "I suppose you're right. I'll go in the morning."

Myrtle put on her prettiest smile.

Hoolie drove into the outskirts of Tulsa exactly one week and one day after he had left. Something strange was in the air. He could sense that evil was roaming the streets and that something terrible had occurred. There was a burnt-out smell, and an odor of destruction and death. He hadn't felt anything like it since he had been in the trenches.

At a roadblock on the north side of town, he was flagged down. A soldier put one foot on the flivver's running board.

"Where you goin', boy?"

"Just gettin' in from Hominy," said Hoolie. "I live downtown. What's goin' on?"

"You an Indin, ain't you?"

"Yes, sir. A Cherokee."

"I reckon you didn't hear. We had us a riot. A nigger was gonna get lynched, and they fought back. The whites burnt out nigger town and killed a bunch of 'em. The governor called us out and declared martial law."

The soldier paused to roll and light a cigarette, "They'll be a few more checkpoints on your way downtown. Just tell them that Sergeant Holmes said you could pass."

"Thanks, Sergeant. I'll do just that."

Hoolie was stopped three more times. At one barricade, a private thought Hoolie was black and tried to arrest him.

"All right," the soldier said, "stop the motor and get out. You're goin' to a detention area."

"Private, I live here. I've been outta town. I have to get back to my job. Sergeant Holmes said it was all right for me to go through."

"Listen, boy, I don't care—"

A booming voice interrupted, "What's goin' on, Morrison?"

The private turned, recognized his company first sergeant, and said, "Sorry, sir, but this here nigger won't cooperate. Says he's got a job and was outta town durin' the riot."

The first sergeant spoke out angrily, "Morrison, did somebody steal your goddam brains? This man isn't a Negro; he's an Indian. Now, leave him be."

The soldier looked stupidly at the sergeant, "He coulda been a light-colored one."

The first sergeant told the private to shut his trap and waved Hoolie through, shaking his head in frustrated disbelief.

Hoolie drove to J.D.'s office and parked the flivver next to the curb. No one was there, so Hoolie began a systematic search of J.D.'s nearby haunts. He started out for North's diner to ask Ed about J.D., but when he got there, he saw a boy who fit J.D.'s description of Danny Ryan. Hoolie knew J.D. gave the kid small jobs to do. He walked up to him, "You're Danny, ain't you?"

The boy responded warily, "Do I know you?"

"I work for J.D. Daugherty. Name's Hoolie Smith."

"Oh," said Danny, "you're the mechanic."

"That's right. You know where J.D. is? I just now got back in town."

"You ain't heard?"

"Heard what?"

"J.D.'s in the hospital," said Danny, shaking his head. "He was in Little Africa when the shootin' started. Some white men took him and tied him to a tree and shot him in the leg and beat him up real bad. I hear that ol' J.D. nearly cashed in his chips. I guess he's a tough ol' bird though. He's at City Hospital. If you're goin' up there, tell him I said hey."

He thought that he'd find J.D. in a general ward, but when Hoolie got to City Hospital, he was told that Mr. Daugherty was in the care of one of Tulsa's most prominent physicians. No one was allowed to visit Mr. Daugherty unless Dr. Jeremiah Blackthorne gave his approval.

Hoolie was made to wait an agonizing thirty minutes before permission was given for him to go to Room 302. As he ascended the stairs, he couldn't stop himself from breaking into a slight run. By the time he opened the door to Room 302, he was out of breath and the pain had returned to his side.

The light was dim, but Hoolie recognized his boss. J.D.'s bulk gave him away. Not much else could be easily seen. Sitting quietly in the shadows on the far side of J.D.'s bed were two other people. One was a pretty, middle-aged woman dressed in black lace and a narrow-brimmed hat. The other was a well-dressed man of short stature. Almost in a whisper, the woman addressed Hoolie, "You are Mr. Smith, are you not?"

"Yes, ma'am." But Hoolie couldn't focus on her. All he saw was J.D. He seemed to be sleeping. The closer Hoolie looked, the worse off J.D. appeared. His head was bandaged. His leg, held in the air by a system of braces and wires, was in a plaster cast. Half of his luxuriant moustache had been shaved off so that a line of stitches could be sewed from J.D.'s lip to his left nostril. One eye was swollen shut. Another set of stitches closed a long cut along the right cheekbone. It was only the sound of J.D.'s shallow breathing that told Hoolie that his employer was still alive.

The woman spoke again. "Mr. Smith, I'm Rose Shelby and this is Mr. E.L. Chichester."

Hoolie, hat in hand, bowed slightly in acknowledgment. He shook hands with Chichester. Mrs. Shelby continued, "Mr. Daugherty was badly beaten by a band of thugs who were rampaging through the Greenwood neighborhood. We were able to speak briefly yesterday, and he told me that if anyone could solve our case, you could."

"Mrs. Shelby . . . Mr. Chichester, I think I already have. I found Rose."

Chichester nearly crumpled with relief. "Oh, thank God! Where is she? Is she all right?"

"Mr. Chichester, Rose is gonna be fine. But you need to understand somethin'. She was kidnapped. One of the men who did it is dead and another is behind bars, but some who were involved are still at large."

"Kidnapped!" gasped Mrs. Shelby.

"I demand to know where my daughter is!"

"She's in a safe place near Pawhuska, Mr. Chichester. She's been shot with some pellets, but she's recoverin'. My friend's sister is takin' good care of her, and a doctor was called in. He ordered that Rose rest a bit more before she travels."

Chichester stepped closer. "I want my daughter, Smith. Are you daring to refuse to let me see her? I won't let you get away with this!"

"No need to make threats. She asked that you not come up until she's ready to see you. She's gonna send a wire. I'm sorry, but she was hurt in more ways than one."

"What exactly do you mean by that!" blustered Chichester.

"She don't want to talk to anybody just yet. And you've got to understand, with those men loose, there's still some dangers around. We gotta be careful."

Chichester was red in the face. But when he began to threaten again, Mrs. Shelby broke in. Her face had hardened into the tight-lipped expression of someone in absolute command of all those about her. "Let's be calm, E.L.," she said evenly. Hoolie heard the authority in her voice.

"We're in a hospital room," she continued, chiding him. "Mr. Smith says Rose is fine. Your daughter has been through an ordeal, and we must respect her reasons for not wishing to see anyone at present. So, please, let's not threaten anyone anymore. There's been so much damage done. Let's trust Mr. Smith."

Chichester wilted, and she turned her attention to Hoolie. Her face had softened, but the authority in her voice remained. "Mr. Daugherty has been unable to talk today. He needs rest. However, Dr. Blackthorne told the nurses that you are free to come and go. Stay if you like or return later. If there is anything you would like to talk about with Mr. Chichester or me, please do not hesitate to telephone."

She handed Hoolie a calling card. Chichester, not looking too happy, opened the door and followed Mrs. Shelby as she turned and swept out of the room.

Hoolie stood looking after them, wondering what to do next. He decided that since J.D. was asleep, he would get his things together for a needed trip to his parents' place outside Stilwell. He could come back to the hospital after he had gotten J.D.'s flivver gassed up. He was about to step out into the hall when a weak, lisping voice addressed his back.

"Hool, don't leave. I was faking. I'm awake. I need to talk to you before I see those two again." J.D.'s hand came up to his mouth, and he coughed once harshly. "Goddammit, every time I do that it hurts." Through the bandages, he looked at Hoolie. "How're you doing?"

"I'll be all right, Jimmy." Hoolie was grinning now. "But what about you?"

"I'll be better when you quit callin' me 'Jimmy.' But I'm sure relieved to see you standing on your feet. Now, tell me everything!"

Hoolie walked over to the chair next to the bed and sat himself down as he proceeded to tell his boss every detail of what had gone on in Osage County. J.D. took it all in: the death of Ben Lookout, Hoolie's time in jail, John Tall Soldier's help, the shoot-out, Rose Chichester's cooperation in Pawhuska, and, most of all, Hoolie's obvious concern for the safety of the Lookout women, especially Myrtle. When Hoolie told J.D. about Rose Chichester's paternity, J.D. was astonished to learn that many more people than just the servants of Chichester and Shelby families knew the story.

Then, it was J.D.'s turn to talk about his findings in the case. And when it came time to speak of Minerva Whitwell's murder, J.D.'s face grew red with anger and frustration. Hoolie could tell that her death had affected his friend much more than J.D. would ever openly admit.

Finally, Hoolie said, "Somethin's got to be done in Osage County. They're killin' people off for their headrights. They're shootin' everybody who makes trouble about leases. And it's gonna keep on until somebody steps in. I'm real scared about the Lookouts and the Tall Soldiers. That sheriff and his nephew don't give a damn about killin' people. They gotta be stopped."

J.D. answered. "Yes. And we have to look out for Rose Chichester. She's still in the middle of it." J.D. looked seriously at his "operative," and said, "You better get back up there as soon as possible. I'll tell Chichester everything. We'll see if he's any kind of man. I have to find Minnie's boy. I'll send Little Bill out. He'll have the money to bribe city officials into finding the child. The little girl, Louisa Welbourne, ran for her life, and I'm praying she got to somewhere safe. They've got most of the Negro population locked up in detention areas."

Hoolie sensed that there was something else that J.D. was hiding. "I've got to find her baby," said J.D. firmly. "And if the Shelbys don't help him out, by God, I will."

"J.D., here's what we're gonna do," Hoolie said with finality. "You get healed up. Rest. I'm goin' back to Hominy after I go to see my grandpa back home. I'm goin' to get some medicine."

"Medicine?" asked J.D.

"Never mind. I'll be gone a few days. You tell Chichester and Mrs. Shelby about his daughter. When Rose is ready to talk, she'll get John or Myrtle or Marie to wire you. I just hope that these white folks can work things out among themselves. Big Bill's gonna have a lot to answer for, but they'll probably let him be, 'cause he's rich."

"You'd be surprised by what they can do."

"Maybe so, but I'll have to see it first. I'll get things done, you know I will. When I get back, we'll clear up things with whoever did this to you."

J.D. almost sat up. He looked piercingly at Hoolie and said quietly and evenly, "Don't worry about it. I'll find Minnie's son, and I'll take care of the bastards that made him an orphan. Don't think for a minute that I can't do it."

"I didn't mean anything like that, J.D. I want to get them, too."

"Hoolie. You're a great partner. I'm going to sleep now." J.D. closed his eyes.

Hoolie smiled. "You do that, boss, and I'll see you later."

He returned to his rooming house to get some clean clothing and restock his meager supplies. He had nothing left in his old footlocker except for one pair of trousers and a union suit. He didn't need the union suit, but he would have buy some clothes. Lyle, his landlord, saw him and informed him that his rent was due, and so Hoolie had to take care of the mundane business of going to the bank and buying canned goods and two new shirts.

An hour later Hoolie had paid his rent, done his shopping, and loaded up J.D.'s tin lizzie. Soon, he was heading east out of town once again. He knew he badly needed the guidance and the healing that came from simply being around his relatives and elders. He yearned to renew his sense of belonging by speaking his own language, standing on his own land, hearing his own stories, and taking part in his own rituals.

It always surprised Hoolie that every time he came home, he was greeted as if he had only been gone for a walk in the woods. At some point, his mother would ask him if he was going to stay for good, but most of the family assumed that he would return to Tulsa. They still viewed Hoolie as young, though at twenty-six, he felt like an old man. His family believed that when he grew older and wiser, he would see that he was needed to lead the community and help with the ceremonies. Then he would return for good.

His grandfather on his mother's side once explained that in the old days, young men tested themselves in war so that they would be ready to understand the ways of peace. That's what he was doing back in his home settlement—preparing himself to be tested.

Hoolie told his father and his mother's brothers about working for J.D. They were concerned about his injuries, but he assured them that he was healing. They listened carefully, talked it over among themselves, and finally advised Hoolie to go see his *edudu*, his grandfather, who lived in a nameless hollow about three miles distant.

Hoolie and his father rode in the flivver as far as they could until the track ran out. Then, they walked the last mile or so. The old man lived in a one-room cabin perched on the top of a small hill above the hollow. They found Grandpa sitting in an old rocking chair out front. The cabin had no windows and no porch. The door was an old army blanket, and a tree stump served as a step-up into the cabin. Grandpa was smoking a clay pipe and rocking gently back and forth. "I saw you were coming," he said in Cherokee. "I've got something for you."

Hoolie's edudu was not prepared to give any advice about hunting down the killers or protecting the women who looked to Hoolie for help. All he did was pray, smoke, and sing a couple of songs. He told Hoolie to sleep in the yard under the arbor that night. "Let's see what you dream about. It might help. I should take you to water. Maybe I should scratch you like ballplayers; it's like a little war you're going on anyway. I don't think we have time though. You want to leave in the morning, don't you?"

Hoolie said that he did want to leave at daybreak. The three sat and talked for a long time that evening until Hoolie's father finally said he was going to sleep. Grandpa did the same. Hoolie got a blanket and rolled himself up under the arbor as he had been told to do.

Hoolie knew that his grandpa put great faith in dreams, and Hoolie knew that a dream would no doubt come to him that very night. He only hoped that he could remember it, so his grandpa could interpret its meaning.

He was just getting settled comfortably when he heard his grandfather or his father stirring around inside the cabin. Hoolie opened his eyes. It was very dark, either late at night or early, early in the morning. He realized that he had been on the disorienting and timeless edge of sleep. It was probably closer to midnight than it was to dawn. He closed his eyes again.

As soon as he had done so, he began to hear the noise that woke him in the first place. It sounded like someone walking softly around the yard, pausing at times either to move something on the ground or to sniff the air. Hoolie was suddenly frightened. It might be a bear. He wished that he had built a fire.

He listened closely. There were no grunting sounds, heavy breathing, or heavy footfalls. He convinced himself that it wasn't a bear. Perhaps it was a man—a man like Sheriff McKinley, someone trying to kill Hoolie.

The soft footfalls came to a stop about three feet from the top of Hoolie's head. Unless he rolled over onto his stomach, he wouldn't be able to see who it was. Whatever it was expelled air from its lungs and said in a deep voice, "Don't be afraid. Look at me now."

Hoolie rolled to a prone position and stared directly into two glowing, yellow eyes of large, sleek panther.

"You see me in a dream," it said. "You're hunting two men. They will come to you where you found the woman. They're hunting you, so you have to hunt. Hunt as I do, alone. Bringing another along would be dangerous."

Hoolie woke with a start. Thoughts poured into his brain. Once the sheriff found out that Billy was dead and that Miller had been arrested, he and Henderson would have figured out that Hoolie, along with John and Rose Chichester, were the key witnesses against them. Pete and McKinley wouldn't have a clue where to find Rose or John. It was Hoolie the wily old man hunter was looking for. He and his nephew would be there, at the cabin, waiting for their prey.

When his grandfather and father awoke before dawn, they led Hoolie to a secluded place behind the cabin. There, Grandpa sang a few songs and scratched his arms and calves to draw blood, just as if he was going to play ball as in the old times. Grandpa apologized for not knowing enough of the old medicine. There was not enough time for him to consult with the other old men of the local gadugi or with the chiefs and medicine men at the stomp grounds.

When Hoolie told them about the panther in his dream, his grandfather questioned him for a while and simply reaffirmed what the spirit had told his grandson. Hoolie had to hunt the two men alone, as the big cat would. The grandfather also admonished Hoolie that the old stories held all the answers. "Just remember the stories," he said to Hoolie. "They'll tell you what to do. When these men are dead, take their scalps to the women."

"Grandpa, I can't do that. It's illegal. I'll get in trouble."

"You'll get in big trouble anyway if you get caught killing them, isn't that so?"

"Yes."

"Then don't tell anybody about it. Let them hear about it later."

"The women are Osages. I don't know if they did the same things our people did." The talk about the old-time practice of scalping upset Hoolie.

"They took scalps, all right," said Grandpa. "The older ones will understand what you're doing. The old woman will know."

He said goodbye to his grandfather and father and made his way down the hill to the flivver. His father would stay and help grandpa for a few days and then make his own way home.

The long drive to Hominy took Hoolie around the outskirts of Tulsa. He didn't really want to go back through the city again and so took as many back roads and byways as possible. He hoped that J.D. had recovered sufficiently to speak to Mr. Chichester. He wasn't certain what Chichester would do after finding out that his oldest friend had committed adultery with his wife and that his daughter wasn't actually his. Hoolie wondered, too, what Mrs. Shelby would do once she found out.

Hoolie remembered the roads and knew exactly where he was going. He pulled off two or three times to think and also to kill time because he wanted to get to the Miller cabin after dark. As he crossed over into Osage County, he fought the urge to see Myrtle. If he went to the Lookout place, John would insist on helping him go after the sheriff and Henderson. Worse yet, the sheriff might have an ally or two watching the farm. Hoolie wouldn't risk a shoot-out there. He would go straight to the Miller place.

When he came to the same spot where he and John had left the car before the shoot-out, he pulled over again and shut off the engine. He had to formulate some kind of plan.

He sat with his elbows on the steering wheel, trying to think of an old story that would outline how one man could locate and kill two other men who were no doubt armed to the teeth and lying in wait for him. Although Henderson and McKinley might have absconded somewhere outside the state of Oklahoma, Hoolie doubted that they had gone very far. They had family here; they had power and money. Through their connection with Judge Patterson, McKinley and Henderson would have been forewarned that Rose Chichester had reported them to the county sheriff in Pawhuska. They knew they were being hunted—although Hoolie guessed that the county sheriff's boys weren't trying very hard to find them. All the same, sooner or later, they would have to prove they were innocent of the charges—or they would have to eliminate all of the witnesses. Hoolie felt sure that they were very near.

The hunter's stories filled his mind. There was the story of the lazy Cherokee who kept bringing the same dead deer back through the town every day in order to prove that he could provide for a girl he wanted to marry. Her father discovered the deceit, demonstrated that the deer's carcass was rotten, and showed the suitor to be nothing more than a lazybones.

Hoolie's favorite story was about what the different animals did when the human beings came with bows and arrows. The bears tried making bows themselves. One of them even sacrificed himself to provide gut for making the bowstring. Finally, they discovered that their long claws prevented them from using the bows. So, they decided they would defend themselves with those claws and their sharp teeth. The deer took a different path. Their leader, Kawi Usdi, Little Deer, decided to give rheumatism to the hunter who did not ask permission to take a deer's life. If the hunter failed to do things correctly, Kawi Usdi would follow the trail of blood to the hunter's house and strike him with the disease that would make him humpbacked and crippled.

From that tale, Hoolie understood that a hunter had to be both physically and spiritually prepared to make a kill. Otherwise, he would become the hunted. Hoolie kept turning the words "do things right" over and over in his mind. He knew he had to be cautious, especially since he was back in enemy territory. The story of Kawi Usdi also told him something else. He would have to plan the hunt with care and make sure he covered up the trail of blood once the hunt was over.

Hoolie sat down on the running board of the old Ford. He wished that he had the old-time power to make himself appear in one place while he was really in another. His grandfather had told him that the power to do so was old Cherokee war medicine. There had been some who used it during the Civil War, but since the Cherokees were committed to the White Path of peace now, many felt that the war medicine should be put away for good. Hoolie didn't agree, but because he didn't know the sacred incantations for that particular power, there was nothing he could do. If he had known the words, he would have used them to beat McKinley and Henderson at their own game.

Now he kept turning "appear in a different place" over in his mind. He thought of his mother's story about how the terrapin beat the rabbit in a foot race. He fondly remembered listening to his mother's stories during the winter. The terrapin story was very old: Rabbit once challenged the whole world to a foot race. He had beaten all comers and was prone to bragging about his deeds. Little Terrapin took up the challenge because he had grown tired of Rabbit's conceit and his big mouth. Rabbit laughed at Terrapin and said that he wouldn't consider racing such a slow-moving and slow-witted animal. Terrapin persisted, and the rest of the animals began to accuse Rabbit of being scared of losing. Terrapin's cousin, Snapping Turtle, called Rabbit a coward to his face. Rabbit couldn't get near Snapping Turtle for fear of getting bit. So Rabbit finally said that he would race Terrapin, and a date for the contest was set.

The signal was given, and Rabbit and Terrapin took off. Rabbit was way out in front and running like never before because he wanted to win in a grand manner so that no one would ever dispute his speed again. But as he ran up a rise, he saw on the trail ahead of him Little Terrapin walking very slowly along. Rabbit couldn't believe that he had fallen behind in the race. He summoned up more speed and overtook Terrapin. Soon he came to another rise, topped it, and once again saw Terrapin in the lead. Rabbit passed him again. But no matter how many times he overtook Terrapin, Rabbit would top a hill and find himself losing the race. In the end Rabbit could not overtake Terrapin, who won the race handily. What Rabbit didn't know was that all of Terrapin's brothers had stationed themselves along the road, and each one of them walked along until Rabbit raced past them. The last brother walked across the finish line well ahead of the Rabbit. Little Terrapin and his relatives had tricked old Rabbit and stopped him from bragging so much.

Hoolie had once told this story to J.D. who, in turn, told the "real" story of the tortoise and the hare: Tortoise won the race by maintaining a slow and steady pace while Hare ran in fits and starts. After telling his version, J.D. teased Hoolie. "How do you Indians make a moral lesson about hard work, perseverance, and self-reliance into a story about trickery and deceit?"

With a laugh, Hoolie shot back, "How do you white people take a story about helping one another and turn it into a story that don't make sense? No terrapin could beat a rabbit in a race unless he had help!"

Right at that moment, parked on the far side of the cornfield, the story started making tactical sense to Hoolie. A plan for bringing McKinley and Henderson to justice was beginning to form. Recalling the race between the terrapin and the rabbit had given Hoolie an idea. He would play a trick on McKinley and his nephew, using the notion that, like Rabbit, they would not want to venture too close to Snapping Turtle—Hoolie being the dangerous snapping turtle. Hoolie's sighting of Saligugi on that first morning was a meaningful omen.

He rose and began to rummage in the pile of things he had stowed in J.D.'s automobile. He collected several items and set to work in the dark. First, he pulled out the lead slugs from a few Winchester 44.40 bullets. He poured the black powder into a bowl, added some dirt and water, and mixed it all up. Then, he began to build a dummy of himself, constructed from some sticks of wood, rolled up blankets, and bits of cloth. He put one of the new shirts he'd bought in Tulsa on the dummy, topping it off with his campaign hat. He used some cord and some wire to hold everything together. When he was satisfied with its appearance, he put the dummy in the backseat of the flivver.

Then he stripped himself, keeping only his dark trousers on. He painted himself with the gunpowder and mud mixture, picked up his rifle, and walked quietly to the cabin. In the dark, he painstakingly searched the entire area. The dogs and the horses had been taken away. He found some matted grass that could have been tire tracks, but it was too dark to tell. As he expanded the search to the edge of the cornfield, he heard a curious sound. Hoolie stopped immediately and dropped to one knee. He closed his eyes, opened his mouth slightly, and stared in the direction of the muffled noise. He heard it again and smiled to himself. Someone out there was breaking wind under a blanket. Hoolie put his hand to his mouth to keep from laughing out loud. He couldn't help but whisper in the direction of the sound, "Found you boys. Shouldn't have et 'em beans."

Hoolie took his time walking back to the car. Once there, he took stock of his supplies and reviewed his plan. He threw a blanket over the dummy, started up the tin lizzie and boldly drove to the cabin. He parked very close to the shack, took the dummy out of the car, and propped it up just inside the shattered door. He got his rifle and carefully made his way to the cornfield. Hoolie was counting that driving up so boldly would wake his quarry out of a deep sleep. They would be disoriented for a few moments and get up to investigate. Then, he hoped, they wouldn't see much; there was a good cloud cover and the moon wasn't full. About all that they would be able to make out would be the profile of the car and maybe the dummy's white shirt. That would give him time to hide. They'd know it was either Hoolie or John, or both, and they'd set up an ambush in a place with the rising sun to their backs. Hoolie would set up his own ambush.

Hoolie was almost invisible in his gunpowder-and-mud paint. He took a position lying in the corn row immediately opposite the door to the cabin. He thought that McKinley and his nephew would take a shot at the dummy with the sniper rifle, and when they came to make sure of their kill, he would trigger an ambush from the cornfield. If he was patient, he was sure they would swallow the bait. It was like being in two places at once—like having the old-time war medicine.

The hours passed in silence. Nothing stirred until the sun began its leisurely rise over the eastern horizon. Birds began to sing and insects hummed. The wind picked up and blew the clouds away. The corn leaves rustled and brushed against Hoolie's back. Ants foraged. Hoolie began to feel vulnerable. He couldn't place why. Something he forgot? Something he didn't think of? Would his enemies see him in the sunlight?

It began to get warmer. Hoolie was shielded by the corn, but the crust of mud covering his face, arms, and body made him want to scratch and peel it away. His right leg began to cramp. The scar tissue from his shrapnel wounds throbbed.

He was thinking about giving up and going to the pump to douse himself with water when he heard a metallic click and a human cough. It came from a small knoll near the creek bed exactly due east of the cabin door. Hoolie froze. McKinley and Henderson were directly behind the cornfield on higher ground. Maybe they could see him. He knew that they were about to make their play.

Hoolie inched his way to the edge of the cornfield to get a better view of the cabin door. He expected the report of the Springfield at any moment.

After a minute or two that appeared to stretch into an hour, a sudden explosion tore through Hoolie's brain. It sounded like a burst from a machine gun. The gunfire dropped the dummy and splintered the already shattered door. Another burst sent wood chips flying from the cabin's log wall. The ambushers weren't merely sniping with a Springfield; they were tearing the place apart with a Browning automatic rifle. Only a few army units had received BARs during the war, and Hoolie had not seen any of them in action, but he had heard that one man with a BAR could do the damage of five marksmen armed with bolt-action Springfields. The BAR was as devastating as a machine gun, but it could be carried and operated by a single man.

The firing stopped for a moment, and Hoolie heard another metallic click. The shooter was changing magazines. Hoolie heard the noise of the bolt going home, followed by another burst tearing into the log wall. A few shots hit the Ford, but the target was clearly the cabin. Hoolie suspected that the ambusher would want to move the automobile somewhere to hide it and so left it alone; it would be easier to drive it to a pond than push it. After they had killed Hoolie, they would get rid of all the evidence that he had even been in Osage County. The shooter put two more magazines into the cabin and stopped firing. The ensuing silence was almost as frightening as the loud din of the automatic rifle.

The logs of the cabin had absorbed nearly eighty rounds. It looked bad in places—some of the chinking between the logs was shot away, and the door couldn't be called a door anymore—but some of it held up surprisingly well.

Surely McKinley and Henderson would come down to examine the damage. They would be planning to make sure that Hoolie was dead, then bury the body and get rid of the tin lizzie. He figured that both men would come down from their ambush position to back each other up. Hoolie was a good shot; he would pick them off.

Off to his right, Hoolie heard someone moving through the corn. He watched the man emerge from the field and run to the cabin. He had the Springfield sniper rifle, and he leaned with his back against the wall next to the door. It was Henderson, and he'd fallen for the decoy trick. Hoolie thought that the man's next move would be to step quickly inside the cabin. Then, as Pete came back out, but before he could warn McKinley that all they'd done was blow apart a dummy, Hoolie would pick Pete off. When Hoolie killed Henderson, however, it would give away his position to McKinley.

Pete took his time looking over everything in the front yard. Then, suddenly, he turned and jumped through the doorway, rifle at the ready. He looked down at the dummy. Hoolie saw him spin around. Pete knew he was in Hoolie's sights. As Henderson opened his mouth to shout a warning to McKinley, Hoolie squeezed the trigger. The bullet took him square in the sternum, a mid-line shot that Hoolie was certain pierced the man's heart. Henderson crumpled, dead on the spot.

The moment Hoolie fired, he knew he had to move. Hoolie's heart was pounding, and his hands had begun to shake. He saw his mistake in still using black-powder cartridges in the old 44.40. The large puff of white smoke that came with each discharge would surely draw the sheriff's attention. McKinley would not panic, even though his nephew had just been shot down. Not that sgini, the old devil.

The burst from McKinley's BAR kicked up dirt clods three feet from Hoolie's face. He rolled to his right. But rolling only served to flatten the corn almost like a mower. Bullets followed him. He got into the middle of a row and crawled forward with his face in the dark earth. At least he wasn't crushing the corn stalks down and exposing himself to McKinley's fire. The only thing he could do was keep moving so McKinley would not have a clear shot at him.

It came into his mind suddenly that the only chance he had against the BAR was to get inside the cabin. He kept edging his way toward the patch of grass that bordered the cornfield. The sheriff continued firing bursts, but they were placed randomly. He had lost Hoolie's track in the field and was probing with gunfire. If Hoolie made a break for the cabin, there was the possibility that McKinley would be aiming at a different part of the field and wouldn't be ready for Hoolie's sprint to the doorway.

A loud metallic click told Hoolie that McKinley was changing magazines again. He wondered how many of them the sheriff was carrying around. At some point, the sheriff would have to reload the magazines with bullets.

Another burst made Hoolie flatten himself into the dirt. He couldn't see the dirt fly from the impact, but he sensed that the burst had hit somewhere to his left and slightly behind him. McKinley was now shooting at any movement in the corn. He was probably firing at a wind-blown leaf. Another burst was fired to Hoolie's right. McKinley must have been close to changing magazines again. A gunner had to turn the gun to the side in order to fit the magazine in. Hoolie would take a chance. Crawling slowly to the edge of the cornfield, he picked up a large dirt clod. He readied himself and threw the dirt clod over to his left. It landed and must have moved a cornstalk. A burst ripped from the BAR. Hoolie lurched to his feet and sprinted, zigzagging his way to the door. No shots followed; McKinley was changing magazines.

Hoolie dove over Henderson's body and into the doorway. Once through, he rolled to the right, just in time to avoid another burst from the BAR. McKinley had changed magazines quickly. The old sgini had learned to operate the weapon very well indeed. Billy Wallace had served his purpose.

Behind the log wall, Hoolie felt relatively safe. The sheriff had stopped firing. He was either waiting for an open shot at Hoolie or he was reloading his spent magazines. Whatever the sheriff was doing, it gave Hoolie respite to think over his position and to plan another move.

Seeing that Pete was dead, the sheriff might just up and leave. If so, Hoolie could hunt him later, or maybe the county lawmen would catch up with him. But Hoolie's instincts told him the sheriff wouldn't go; he'd wait until hell froze over to kill Hoolie. And it was Hoolie who was trapped inside an old, dilapidated log cabin. The gunpowder-streaked, mud crust on Hoolie's face and torso itched. He was getting both hungry and thirsty. Maybe taking refuge in the cabin hadn't been such a good idea. McKinley could just lay siege and kill him at his leisure.

Hoolie looked at Henderson's body in the doorway. It would start to smell pretty soon; the day was going to be warm. The flies were already zooming every which way. Surely McKinley wouldn't want to sit out there and watch his own nephew putrefy in the sun. Hoolie decided on another ploy.

"Sheriff McKinley," he called, "I know it's you. I think Pete here is still breathin'. Give yourself up to me, and we'll get him to a doc."

Silence. Hoolie heard the wind blowing through the cracks in the chinking between the logs.

"You dirty red nigger!" McKinley yelled. "I know a dead man when I see one. And you're gonna be layin' with flies buzzin' around you in a few minutes." He fired a three-round burst from the BAR that tore up part of the door frame.

But now, for the first time, Hoolie saw where the sheriff lay with his automatic rifle. He was on the down slope of the small hill, between some large rocks. Hoolie could see the muzzle and the bipod of the BAR. He caught a glimpse of the sheriff's shock of gray hair sticking up above the BAR's barrel.

The sheriff called down to Hoolie, "I got you now, you sombitch. You're the dumbest dummy I ever saw. You're in a trap. Like shootin' fish in a barrel. You're dead."

He paused for a moment then called down again, "Why don't you come on out, and I'll kill you clean. That's better than you give Pete. You cur-dog, you ambushed him like the sneaky prairie nigger you are. Come on out and fight. Don't hide."

Hoolie was getting thirstier. His saliva was thick and pasty. He knew that the thirst came from his fear and that his entrapment was the result of making the wrong move at the wrong time. He considered the possibility of simply charging McKinley. He could end it all in a quick action; either he or the old sgini would be dead. Discarding that rash action, it dawned on Hoolie that he needed to provoke the sheriff into a similar reckless move. That might just be the solution to Hoolie's problem.

"Sheriff!" Hoolie called. "You're an old white devil! You couldn't hit me even if I painted a target on my chest and stood up ten foot away from you. You're gonna run out of ammunition. Then, I'm gonna walk up on you and club you down just to save my bullets. Won't have to fire a shot."

"Damn your dirty red hide! Come on out here!"

"I will, Sheriff . . . I will."

Hoolie busied himself with the dummy. He wadded up the old shirt that he used for the head, and put his old campaign hat back on it. He noticed a clean bullet hole in the brim. He knew that coated in mud, he looked a lot different than the dummy, but he hoped that it would distract McKinley, if only for a moment.

Cherokee cabins were often raised off the ground with wood plank floors. This white man's shack was built directly on the ground with about six or seven inches of sod dug out, so that the dirt floor lay below the level of the ground outside the cabin. If he laid down flat on the floor, the sheriff could have fifty BARs out there riddling the walls, and Hoolie would never be hit. That is, he'd never be hit if his enemy wasn't sitting on a higher level. The white sgini had wisely set himself up on the high ground.

Hoolie reattached the fake head and hat to the dummy's body. He then eased it into the door opening. On the movement, the sheriff reacted and fired. The long burst blew off more chunks from the logs that surrounded the door frame. Hoolie jumped from one side of the door to the other. He took the knife from the sheath on his belt.

"You go on and shoot up the cabin!" Hoolie yelled at the sheriff. "You might give me a few splinters!" he taunted.

Another burst came from the BAR. Hoolie's plan to keep the sheriff firing was working.

Hoolie noticed that, like all cabins, the logs were never perfectly even. A log laid one on top of the other will always leave gaps between the two, some big, some small. The chinking was thin in some spots and thick in others. Some of it had been blown out as a result of the rifle fire. McKinley could see movement inside the cabin but could not get a clear shot. Not only that but when a bullet struck a log it ricocheted off into another log or buried itself. The logs were actually very good protection against gunfire.

Hoolie looked for and found several places where the chinking was heavy so as to fill large gaps between the logs. He went to work with his knife poking out the chinking to make firing ports in the cabin wall. All the time, he gave the sheriff brief glimpses of himself and continued to taunt the lawman about his poor marksmanship, his age, how easy it had been for Hoolie to kill Henderson, and that the best McKinley could hope for was a quick death.

"You better give up now, old man," called Hoolie. "Maybe your judge friend'll feel sorry for you."

McKinley's anger boiled over. He fired the BAR almost continuously.

"You're gonna burn out the barrel, you old fool!" yelled Hoolie.

McKinley kept firing. It seemed like he was going through magazine after magazine. Hoolie was unhurt and had not fired a shot since he killed Henderson.

He knew that the sheriff, although angry, was not going to be stupid enough to jump up and charge the cabin. Hoolie had to take a shot. He found a perfectly situated gunport in the logs. He poked his rifle barrel through the hole, sighted carefully, and squeezed the trigger. Dust kicked up about five feet short of the BAR muzzle. McKinley fired several more bursts that chipped the logs but didn't penetrate them. Hoolie poked out another large piece of chinking and rested the Winchester in between the logs.

He knew he had fired short, but he had been on the center line of his target. The two rocks on either side of McKinley were a hindrance, but at the same time, they served to bracket Hoolie's aim. He realized that the sheriff, firing from a prone position with a bipod, would be lying at an angle. The man's shoulder and part of his back would be directly behind the BAR's muzzle. Hoolie adjusted himself for that possibility, purposely aiming higher, and pulled off another round hoping that he would put a bullet into McKinley's head. Luck or the spirits would decide the outcome of this fight, but Hoolie had done his best to influence it with a perfect shot.

It turned out not to be a perfect shot, but it scored. Hoolie knew instantly that McKinley had been hit; his body slumped, and the muzzle of the BAR flew upwards, meaning that the butt had dropped from the sheriff's shoulder. A few seconds later, Hoolie heard a bellowing scream of pain. The sheriff wasn't dead, but he was badly wounded. What mattered was whether or not McKinley was still dangerous.

Hoolie walked to the other side of the cabin and picked up his dummy. No shots were fired at him. He put the dummy in the doorway and still no shots were fired.

The sheriff cried out instead, "Goddam your soul! I can't move."

Hoolie dropped the dummy, levered another round into the Winchester's chamber, and slowly went outside. He eased himself over to the flivver and crouched down by the left fender. Nothing happened. He came out from behind the automobile and began walking through the cornfield. Still nothing happened; no shots; no yells; no threats. He eased the hammer down on his rifle and walked straight up to the sheriff's firing position.

McKinley saw him and said through clenched teeth, "I see you, you sombitch. I'll see you in hell."

Hoolie kept walking. When he got within ten feet of the sheriff, Hoolie could see what had happened. His shot had passed slightly over the sheriff's left shoulder, which had been lowered in order to sight the BAR. The bullet had plowed into McKinley's backbone, paralyzing him instantly. If the sheriff had had his left shoulder raised half an inch or so, or if his right shoulder had been lowered, the bullet wouldn't have struck him in the spine. When the bullet hit, the man had fallen on his left side, his head resting on his useless arm. All the sheriff could do was lie there, screaming and cursing.

"You goddam, filthy, blanket-ass nigger! You're goin' to roast in hell for this!"

Hoolie came forward and bent over the paralyzed man. He must have been in terrible pain, and Hoolie thought about nothing else but putting him out of his misery. Unable to move, the sheriff stared at Hoolie's feet, "You'll . . . fry . . . I swear . . . you're goin' to hell!"

Hoolie had never before seen such hatred imprinted on a man's face. It frightened and sickened him. "Sheriff," said Hoolie quietly, "when we die we go to the west and do the same things we did in life. We ain't got a hell like you're goin' to."

Hoolie thumbed the hammer back on the old Winchester.

15
Rose Shelby

J.D. heard the soft knock on the door and answered in a low voice, "Come in."

Rose Shelby put her head inside the room, looked over at the patient, and walked through the door. "You're looking better, Mr. Daugherty," she said with a bright smile. "Dr. Blackthorne says you're improving daily. I've brought Mr. Chichester with me."

Although Chichester was J.D.'s client, he would have preferred that Mrs. Shelby had come alone. From his bed, J.D. raised a bandaged hand and motioned them into the hospital room. He had dreaded this meeting. It was time to tell them how they had both been deceived and betrayed by husband and friend Big Bill Shelby.

Mrs. Shelby entered; Chichester following with a frown on his face. He had his hand in one coat pocket. E.L. had not seen his daughter yet, and he was angry. He pulled out a gold cigarette case, opened it, took out and lit a gold-tipped cigarette, and sat down.

Rose Shelby opened the meeting. "It's been six days since your man said he found Rose, and we've not been able to see her. E.L. and I are very worried."

J.D. offered a quick wave of a bandaged hand, indicating that there was no need to worry, and then said politely, "I've got good news for you, Mr. Chichester. I received a wire from Mr. Smith. I've also been in contact with Miss Myrtle Lookout, a fine young woman from Osage County."

Rose Shelby interjected, "I know of the Lookout family. Miss Lookout's father was the one who was killed the night Mr. Smith was wounded."

J.D. nodded and proceeded. "Yes, Miss Lookout has been in contact with Rose, and she assures me that your daughter is doing well."

J.D. looked right at Chichester. Then turning slightly to Mrs. Shelby, he continued, "You probably know more about Osage Indian families than I do, Mrs. Shelby, but it seems like everyone up there knows what's going on with who, who's who, and so on. Rose is staying with Marie Logan and her husband. Marie is John Tall Soldier's sister. Mr. Tall Soldier helped Mr. Smith rescue Rose."

J.D. caught his breath and heaved a large sigh. "That said," he began, "I have some important news and some very distressing information that I have to pass along. You might not want to hear it. Be assured that what I'm about to tell you is all true. I will also guarantee that this information will not be made public."

J.D. turned his gaze on Chichester first and said quietly: "I have to say this for your Rose's sake. She will not see you right now because she's been through some terrible times." J.D. took a deep breath, "She has been told that you are not her real father. Rose fears that, as an illegitimate child, you will no longer accept her as your daughter."

Chichester jumped up. "Who put that idiotic notion in her head? I *am* her father. I've taken care of her since I lost my wife a few days after Rose's birth." He sat and popped out of the chair once again. "By God, man, this is an outrage! Who put that idea in her head?"

"Chichester, I'm not recovering as fast as I'd like, despite what the good doctor says. I can't tolerate your jumpin' up and down like some goddam jack-in-the-box! Excuse my language, ma'am."

Rose Shelby spoke for the first time since J.D. announced the news. "Yes, E.L., calm down." She turned to J.D. "Please explain everything, Mr. Daugherty."

J.D. laid out the entire story with all its intricacies and intimacies. He had to fight back the tears when he got to the part about Minnie. His contempt for Big Bill Shelby's actions over the past twenty-odd years was imprinted on his mostly hidden face.

J.D. did not mention Hoolie's gunfight with the sheriff. As far as everyone else knew, McKinley and Henderson were now simply wanted criminals on the lam. However, Tom Miller was spilling his guts in order to keep his own jail time to a minimum. So J.D. related the news about Judge Patterson's suicide in Pawhuska two days before.

It had come out that the judge was the legal guardian for several Osages, and the public assumed that the judge knew he'd be linked to the conspiracy that had led to the deaths of Tommy Ruffle and Ben Lookout.

When J.D. told his visitors the truth about Rose Chichester's paternity, Rose Shelby looked shocked, and then she began to weep silently. Chichester lost all his bluster. He simply looked back and forth between Mrs. Shelby and J.D. with his mouth open and a dazed expression on his face.

J.D. looked at Mrs. Shelby, "Did you know? Or suspect?"

She raised her head and gently wiped away some tears with her gloved hand. "I had no idea," she said in a tiny voice, "no idea at all."

She pulled a frilly handkerchief from her sleeve and dabbed at her eyes once more. Then, her steely gaze returned, and her face became edged with hard, straight lines. She took a deep breath and continued, "I know that my husband has been a philanderer. I have stayed with him for the sake of our children. I never suspected that he seduced Rose's mother, may she rest in peace."

J.D. spoke first. "I'm truly sorry to have to tell you these things. As Hoolie told me, everything's tied together. There was a conspiracy to rob several Osages of their land, mineral rights, and homes. Mr. Shelby might not be involved directly, although Shelby Oil would have profited from the conspiracy. Your husband might very well have been blackmailed into complying with their schemes. Apparently, Mrs. Chichester wrote to Judge Patterson telling him about Rose's paternity so that she would eventually benefit from Mr. Shelby's will. McKinley, Patterson, Henderson, and the rest kept Rose alive either because Mr. Shelby would not tolerate having his daughter harmed or because those men wanted to collect a large ransom from Shelby Oil. I really don't know how far your husband's guilt extends."

J.D. passed his eyes up and down the well-groomed and sharply dressed Chichester. "Mr. Chichester," he said, "do you still consider Rose to be your daughter?"

"What kind of question is that? Of course, I do! I love my child."

"That's something that I wanted to hear and something that Rose needs to hear," said J.D. bluntly. "She's a very brave girl and deserves every bit of your love. I'll get word to her. She's able to travel now and soon you'll be reunited. Please be patient for just a bit longer."

E.L. nodded wearily.

Rose Shelby wanted something more from J.D. She practically pleaded with him to tell her more about her husband. "I beg of you, Mr. Daugherty, tell me everything."

"Mrs. Shelby, I have, honestly. Your husband thinks in business terms. I don't know if he's directly committed a crime. I'll be frank and tell you that I personally don't think very highly of him, but it's not my place to say that. This case is pretty well wrapped up. Credit my operative, Mr. Smith, and an Osage man named John Tall Soldier, for rescuing Rose. They put themselves at great risk to save her."

"Where is Mr. Smith now?" asked Chichester.

"He's at the Lookouts' home."

"Has he fully recuperated?" asked Mrs. Shelby.

"Yes, pretty much."

Rose sighed heavily. "I can't believe my husband's business has led to so much tragedy. I'm at a loss as to what to do."

J.D. tried to ease the strain in his neck. He looked at Mrs. Shelby, "I have an idea about what you can do, Mrs. Shelby." She looked at him, as he continued, "You knew about Minerva Whitwell and your son. Minnie was a wonderful mother to their boy. Thomas Whitwell is your grandson. Please . . . please . . . look after him. I want to add that during the riot, a girl named Louisa Welbourne saved your grandson from certain death. She's a little girl and all by herself got Thomas to a place of safety at the ballpark. She, Thomas, and her father are at the detention center to this day. You could personally secure their release. Your son found them, but the authorities have not let him bring them home."

"She was a good mother?"

"The best."

Rose dropped her head and with the handkerchief blotted the tears. "I'd like to ask you a few things about the night of the riot if I could?"

"Ask me about Minnie and the boy. I'd prefer not to think about the riot right now."

"I understand." She gathered herself and went on, "Was Minnie given a decent burial?"

"I can't say. I don't know what happened to her body. I was unconscious. You found me in the ward."

"She grew up with my children . . . in my own home. I want to give her a proper funeral. Would you please find out what happened to her?"

"I will try. I'll put an associate on the case as soon as I can. You have to remember that some of the victims of the riot were simply thrown in the river."

Rose Shelby opened her mouth for a moment in amazement, then the steely gaze returned to her eyes. "I should put you on permanent retainer," she said.

"I don't think I could survive that, Mrs. Shelby."

She lowered her eyes and a wry smile crossed her face.

While J.D. and Rose talked, Chichester had begun seething in silence. He rose and faced Mrs. Shelby. "I can't stand this anymore, Rose. You're asking questions and taking care of things as if everything was perfect once again. Your husband has betrayed both of us. Doesn't that make you angry? Everything's falling apart. My daughter isn't mine."

Chichester sunk back into his chair and sobbed.

Somehow Rose Shelby drew strength from his diatribe. "E.L.," she said with disciplinary snap to her voice, "straighten up. Yes, this is all quite terrible. But we must deal with it. The people who have done wrong will be punished, my husband included. Justice will be served. This belief has sustained me through many, many hard times.

"Now, *you* must think of nothing else but Rose. I must think of nothing else but taking care of my grandson and those who saved him. I will deal with my husband, and you will carry on as if you know nothing about his infidelities and his profiteering. Most especially, you must give Rose your love and do everything in your power to make her happy."

Chastened and contrite, Chichester slowly raised his head and silently nodded his assent to everything Rose had said. She turned to J.D. in the bed. "Mr. Daugherty, I appreciate everything you've done. E.L. will, of course, pay your fees, and I'm sure add a healthy bonus. I do want to hire your firm to take care of a few matters of importance for me. May I ask who your attorney is?"

"Certainly, it's Sam Berg."

"I know Mr. Berg. He helped a Creek friend of mine, and he's been a thorn in my husband's side for quite a while." Another smile flickered across her face. "I've used his services on several occasions. I'd like to talk to Mr. Berg as soon as possible. Can you do that for me?"

"I'll arrange a meeting."

"Now?"

J.D. was taken aback. "Now?" he repeated.

"Yes, please. If you'd telephone him from here, I'd appreciate it."

She handed J.D. the telephone. He asked the operator for Sam's office. Although surprised, Sam agreed to meet with Mrs. Shelby in twenty minutes.

Before Rose Shelby and Chichester left, she rose, went to J.D.'s side and gently kissed him on the bandaged forehead. J.D. lowered his eyes in embarrassment. "Thank you . . . thank you so much," she whispered.

After she went out the door, the scent of rosewater she wore remained in his nostrils. It made him recall a story his mother told him about Ireland: There was once a woman who had lost everything in the Great Famine. Hunger and grief had changed her from a handsome, robust woman into an emaciated, toothless hag. She was on the verge of taking her own life even though it was against her beliefs and Church law. She was about to slit her own throat when an angel appeared and ordered her to stop. The old woman began to weep. And when she wiped away her tears, she noticed that they had an oily texture and a wonderful scent. God had forgiven her for her suicide attempt and from that day forward, wherever she went, people could smell the scent of the wild rose. Even during the darkest days of the famine, the woman carried with her that glorious bouquet. The peo-

ple began to see her as a gift from God. It made them happy to think
that there was still beauty in the world and that blights could come
and go, but God's grace still caressed Ireland.

Driving along the dusty road to the Lookout place, Hoolie was feeling
as good as he had since before the war. He had spent several days with
his grandfather, father, two uncles, and a *didahnuhwisgi*, a medicine
man, who purified him in an ancient Cherokee ceremony reserved for
those who had done battle against the enemy. It was his second such
ceremony, and it had been better than the first. He was bringing
gifts, which had also been purified, to Grandma Lookout and John
Tall Soldier. Whatever Indian medicine or combination of medicines,
whether corn smut, tobacco, or sundry other herbs, that the Osage
medicine man used on his wound had completely healed him. But
most of all, he felt happy because he was going to see Myrtle again.

Myrtle, Lizzie, and John Tall Soldier were sitting on the porch when
they saw the dust raised behind an automobile coming up the road.
Myrtle brushed her cropped black hair away from her face, her expression softening. She knew it was Hoolie. She stood and slowly walked
down the steps and into the yard as J.D.'s flivver rolled to a stop.
Grandma Lookout and Martha emerged from the house. The screen
door shut with a loud bang that startled John. He got up and walked
into the yard to greet Hoolie, too. Chickens and guinea hens scattered
as they walked up to him. Myrtle and Hoolie looked shyly at each
other; a wordless greeting that was given with a slight movement of
the head or a quick batting of an eye. His bruises and cuts were
starting to heal and he wore fresh clothes. Myrtle put out her hand,
and Hoolie shook it quickly. In turn, he shook hands with John. Then,
Hoolie walked to the porch and shook hands with Martha, Lizzie, and
Grandma Lookout.

John and Myrtle remained behind, gaping at the flivver. It had four
bullet holes in the front right fender and one on the passenger side
door. Rumors had been circulating of a gunfight, but no details were
to be come by. Myrtle doubted that Hoolie would explain.

When they had all gathered on the front porch, Hoolie said that he'd like to talk to Grandma Lookout and John alone down by the creek. Myrtle was somewhat hurt by being excluded, but she also knew that Hoolie had been in his home settlement being healed. She knew that he had done something very holy. She also had not a doubt that she would soon become the center of his attention.

Myrtle thought about her sister. Martha had been in love with Pete Henderson. Now that he had disappeared, Martha understood that he had been in on the evil doings that had occurred in the last few weeks. With her mother and grandmother's gentle guidance, Martha had also realized that Pete was, in fact, courting her to gain control of her family's headrights. She had reasoned out that Pete was really out for her oil money. She felt betrayed but she also felt a deep sense of loss. There was just too much grief.

Grandma Lookout was gazing at Hoolie with pride. Both he and John Tall Soldier had become "old-time" warriors. She said something in Osage, which Lizzie quickly translated as "the warriors have come back to us. We should get up and dance." Then the old woman said in English, "You healing all right, boy? Wounds gone?"

"Yes, ma'am," said Hoolie while twisting his body to show that his ribs hurt no longer. Myrtle leaned over and touched his arm. "Why don't you and John and Grandma get your business done?"

Stopping just to pull a white pillowcase with something inside out of the flivver, Hoolie led the way down to the big oak tree. He told John and Grandma Lookout to sit on the ground by the tree roots. John sat cross-legged; Grandma Lookout knelt. Hoolie asked John to interpret for him so that Grandma Lookout would understand. The elder looked puzzled for a moment and then said, "I understand. Better in Osage."

Hoolie unpacked two items from the pillowcase, each one wrapped in red cloth. He carefully spread the pillowcase out and laid the small red bundles on the white material. He sat for a moment collecting his thoughts; Grandma Lookout and John patiently remained silent.

Then, Hoolie began to talk in a low voice. His speech came in short spurts, which gave John time to interpret. Hoolie looked at the two bundles intently.

"Uh, this is hard for me to say. . . . I'm givin' you somethin'." Hoolie paused. "We tell stories about all kinds of things. One was about how the Sun grieved so much for her daughter that her tears caused a big flood. When people grieve, we believe that it causes misery and hard times all around. . . . So, the warriors used to go out and take captives and scalps to show that they fought the enemies. The captives and the scalps were given away to the women to stop them from grievin' and to get everything back to normal. . . Now, we've put away takin' scalps. These things here," Hoolie pointed with his lips to the red bundles, "are for Grandma Lookout."

She didn't move to pick the bundles up, but her eyes narrowed into slits as she stared at them.

Hoolie continued, "I talked things over with my relatives and a medicine man. They told me I did the right thing." He took a deep breath, expelled it, and said, "I hunted those two down. I killed Pete and the sheriff. I don't care what the white man says. It was justice." He looked directly at Grandma Lookout. "They killed your son."

The woman nearly buckled under the weight of her grief. Then, she gathered herself and sat up straight, back stiff, her hands primly folded in her lap. Hoolie leaned over, picked up both small bundles and placed them closer to her. She nodded, picked one up, and opened it carefully. It contained a sheriff's badge; the second bundle held a gold watch with chain and fob.

Grandma Lookout prepared for a speech. She looked up at the sky and lowered her eyes to the ground. She nervously wiped her hands on her apron and spoke. John interpreted.

"I know what you did was right. We can't tell people about it. Lizzie should know. But maybe Myrtle and Martha shouldn't. These two men killed others. John will go to Eagle Ruffling His Feathers On A Cold Day and tell him of the deaths of his grandson's killers. Tell him about this young man, and tell him not to tell the white people he knows. He'll understand right away. The white people don't like killin' other white people; that's as it should be. Osages can't kill other Osages. If the white people know they'll come after Hoolie. We don't want that.

"Hoolie Smith, you've done a good thing. Hopefully, we'll settle down now and go about livin' our lives. My granddaughter will stop mournin' after a year, four seasons. You visit, but don't get too close until that time's over.

"Hoolie Smith, you took the badge and the watch because you didn't want to take scalps. When I was a girl, the warriors only took the scalps of brave enemies. The men you fought were cowards who shot from far away. It was right not to take their hair.

"You're a brave man. If you married my granddaughter, I'd be happy."

Hoolie covered his mouth to hide his emotion.

Grandma Lookout wrapped up the badge and watch again and put them back in the pillowcase. The three of them rose. They walked slowly back to the house, and Hoolie saw no one else but Myrtle standing on the front porch, waiting for him.

Epilogue

Pulling off his glasses, Hoolie leaned back in his metal porch chair. He folded the newspaper he was reading so that a particular article was in plain view. Then, he stared across the green grass toward the distant stand of cottonwoods. The article had put his thoughts back thirty-five years, to what his old boss always called "The Chichester Operation."

Hoolie put his glasses back on and reread the article. He shook his head, took his glasses off again, and put them carefully into his shirt-front pocket. He got up and wandered into the house, folded paper in one hand. He called for Myrtle.

"Myrtle, Myrt . . . where are you?"

He moved through the house until he got to the kitchen. "Myrtle, you around?"

She answered from the backyard, where she and her mother, Lizzie, were feeding the chickens. "What is it? What's come over you?" She stepped up onto the porch and into the kitchen with him. "What is it? I thought you were readin' the paper."

"I was," he said. "That's what I came in for. I need to go to Tulsa."

"What for?"

Lizzie had come to the top of the steps and was gazing through the screen door at them. Hoolie glanced at his mother-in-law for a moment and proceeded. "Well," he began, "it looks like J.D. is in trouble again."

"That man's always in trouble," said Myrtle. "He doesn't need you anymore. Both of you are gettin' way too old to do the kinds of things you used to do. For near-on forty years, you've been a-helpin' him out every time he calls on you. You don't have to go anywhere."

As he handed her the newspaper and pointed to the article, all Hoolie could say was, "He's my friend." The story read:

FORMER PRIVATE EYE
CONFESSES TO MURDERS

Tulsa, June 8, 1956—An 83-year-old man today confessed to a string of murders dating back to the 1920s. James Daniel Daugherty walked into the downtown office of the Tulsa County Sheriff's Department and told deputies that two weeks ago he had shot and killed Roger Ray Elam, 64, of nearby Jenks. Since finding the body on a north Tulsa street corner, County Sheriff's deputies have been baffled by Elam's murder. There were no witnesses, and no clues have been found.

Daugherty has also confessed to five other killings. He has given details about each one of the crimes that, according to the authorities, only the killer would know.

Daugherty said that he killed Bryant Paul Cunningham in 1923, Philbert John Sooles in 1928, Terry Peter Moody in 1936, Jesse James Poindexter in 1943, and Ralph James Cunningham in 1949. The Cunninghams were brothers. All of those murder investigations are still considered open, but no information had been found to link them to anyone, let alone to a single killer.

Each of the victims was killed in a different way. Bryant Cunningham was killed with a pickaxe. Sooles had been burned to death; Moody was hanged; Poindexter was stabbed; and, after being knocked unconscious, Ralph Cunningham had been laid on the Frisco tracks to be crushed under a locomotive.

"All of the murders," remarked Tulsa Police Chief Inspector William Bowles, "were exceptionally brutal. It was as if the killer was paying back each one of these men in a particular way."

"Frankly," Bowles continued, "I'm surprised that it was a single killer. Mr. Daugherty, being close to law enforcement, knew how to cover his tracks."

Daugherty gave no other motive except to say that he killed

each man for a crime they had committed in 1921. Investigators are searching their records for unsolved crimes committed in that year.

In 1920, Daugherty established the first independent private detective agency in Tulsa. When he retired in 1938 at the age of 65, he sold the agency to a national corporation. Tulsa authorities say that Daugherty operated one of the best, most exclusive, and efficient private investigative services in the city. The Tulsa Chamber of Commerce honored Daugherty as "Businessman of the Year" in 1927.

Daugherty had a long career in law enforcement. Before opening his own detective agency, he had served on the Chicago Police Force and with Great Western Investigations, Inc. Daugherty came to Tulsa in 1917 as an operative with Great Western when the agency was principally concerned with rooting out Communism and anarchy in the railroad and oil industries.

Sheriff's deputies and police investigators are convinced that Daugherty is the perpetrator of this series of ghastly crimes. His arraignment is set for June 10.

Berg, Berg, Chandler, Whitwell, and Shotz, one of the oldest and most prestigious law firms in Tulsa, will handle Daugherty's defense.

ABOUT THE AUTHOR

Tom Holm has been a professor of American Indian Studies at the University of Arizona in Tucson since 1980. During that time, he has won several prestigious teaching and mentoring awards. His latest monograph, *The Great Confusion in Indian Affairs: Natives and Whites in the Progressive Era*, was published by the University of Texas Press in 2005. In 1996, his book, *Strong Hearts, Wounded Souls* was a finalist for the Victor Turner Prize in Ethnology.

Holm is Muscogee Creek and Cherokee, enrolled in the Cherokee Nation, and is very active in Native community affairs. Born in northeastern Oklahoma, he attended Northeastern State College in Tahlequah and later received three degrees from the University of Oklahoma at Norman. Since 2004, he has served the Cherokee Nation as a member of the Sequoyah Commission, a group of Cherokee scholars, and he has been named as a member of the American Indian Graduate Center's Council of 100, a group of elders, scholars, and leaders.

A Vietnam veteran who served with Bravo Company, 1st Battalion, 3rd Marines, from 1967 to 1968, Holm has a deep interest in veterans' affairs. He was a member of the first Native American advisory committee to the Veterans Administration, and he is a former president of the Arizona Territory Gourd Society and the Southwest Gourd Society (Native American veterans' societies). He sings with the Panther Creek Singers, a traditional Southern Drum group. Professor Holm and Ina, his wife of thirty-eight years, have two sons and four grandchildren.

Library of Congress Cataloging-in-Publication Data

Holm, Tom, 1946–
The osage rose / Tom Holm.
p. cm.
ISBN 978-0-8165-2650-5 (pbk. : alk. paper)
1. Detectives—Fiction. 2. Osage Indians—Fiction.
3. Oklahoma—History—20th century—Fiction. I. Title.
PS3608.O494325O83 2008
813'.6—dc22   2007025509